THE LADY'S TUTOR

"Beau," she whispered. "Beau, I had no notion . . . of this."

"So. 'Tis done," he answered, his mouth against her ear, his arms about her as he rolled her above him.

"Is it?" she asked with poignant, innocent disappointment. "Why?"

"Why?" he roared, this time with a bark of laughter. "Because you've been deflowered, that's why. Isn't that what you asked of me?"

"Isn't there more?"

"Well, there could be, if you'd like another, more advanced love lesson. Shall I illustrate further? Would you like me to?"

"I *would* like. Go on. Do that again and show me what more there is. Show me all of it . . . everything."

"Not just yet." He grinned, raking back her long, silky hair with both his hands. "I'll demonstrate again. I'll soon teach you some more, show whatever you want to see, do . . . whatever, but all and everything? That would take time. How many nights do we have to practice?"

"We have nearly a fortnight. Is that enough time?" She tossed back her hair and peered into the hot green glow of his smiling eyes.

"It will take all night, every night, but you'll likely get it right."

"Then what are we waiting for?" She sighed, kissing his mouth.

Books by Jane Howard

FOR MY LADY'S HONOR
FOR MY LADY'S HEART

Published by Zebra Books

FOR MY LADY'S HEART

Jane Howard

Zebra Books
Kensington Publishing Corp.
http://www.zebrabooks.com

ZEBRA BOOKS are published by

Kensington Publishing Corp.
850 Third Avenue
New York, NY 10022

First Printing: April, 2000
10 9 8 7 6 5 4 3 2 1

Printed in the United States of America

Prologue

London
January 25, 1543

"We've got a boy!" Katesby Beaumarais proclaimed, holding up a slippery, brawny baby as her husband lunged into the room for what seemed his hundredth visit in the past few hours.

Baldwin Beaumarais had been too restless, as his wife's labor progressed, to do more than hover over her for a few minutes at a time before he sprinted away again to report on her progress to the festive, noisy group of friends gathered below in the taproom of the inn. Between contractions, when Baldwin was beside her, Katesby had insisted he not worry. "Win, *I'm* laboring to birth this baby, not you, and *I'm* doing fine . . . .better than fine. Ask anyone," she had insisted, glancing about the room. The midwife and the doctor in attendance both nodded their agreement

"That's so, Baldwin, absolutely," concurred Adelaide,

Lady Seton, long a mentor and confidante of the endearing young couple. Despite her matter-of-fact tone, tall, elegant Lady Addy was pacing the room, her hands clasped behind her.

"This lady was created to bear you babies, Beaumarais," insisted Gwyn Stark, a pretty, petite fifteen-year-old cook and barmaid at the inn, who had been given the evening off by her employer to be with her dearest friend, Katesby. "She's a natural breeder, our Kat, been chatting and laughing all through this labor. There's hardly been a peep of complaint out'n 'er, eh, Bessy?" Gwyn asked an old woman who was seated at a table near the window and calmly shuffling and dealing cards.

Bessy Mortlock, preoccupied, mumbled her agreement. The bent, aged man peering over Bessy's shoulder, Dorsey Dibdin, also concentrating intently on the cards, responded to Gwyn with a touch of annoyance.

"Don't interrupt, girl, when a Wise Woman is reading a child's future in the Tarot."

"His future?" queried Baldwin.

"Or *her* future," interjected Katesby.

"His," said Bessy. "The cards tell it's going to be a boy child."

"What else do the cards tell?" Baldwin asked with interest. He wasn't a man to put unguarded faith in every cartomancer and soothsayer who crossed his path, but his practical curiosity, combined with an awe for some of life's finer mysteries—love for one—made it impossible for Baldwin to resist hearing out a fortune teller, especially Bessy Mortlock, who was more often right than wrong.

Before Bessy could answer, Kat yelped at the onset of another contraction. Baldwin gripped her hand, whispered encouragement in her ear, loudly proclaimed his love several times, then smiled with relief when Kat relaxed again somewhat.

"That wasn't so bad, was it, Win? You were wonderful!" she bantered between shallow, huffing breaths.

"No, *you* were wonderful." He grinned sheepishly, appreciating the respite. It was a short one. The next contraction came almost at once.

"It shouldn't be long now," pronounced the doctor with aloof confidence.

"Push now, bear down—there's a good girl," the midwife told Kat.

"I shall give the orders here," the doctor said curtly.

"Am I *not* to push, sir?" gasped Kat.

"Indeed, you are, but on *my* order. Indeed, do so now. Push." The doctor glared self-importantly at the midwife. The midwife, vindicated, looked self-righteous.

Kat pushed. Her low moan was followed by a great yell. Baldwin roared more loudly than Kat that someone must do something right quick to give his wife ease. He was unceremoniously ejected from the room by Gwyn. A few moments later, as he paced the hallway, he heard Kat's piercing cry that was more triumph than pain, and then she called his name. Hurtling, almost tumbling, into the chamber, Win stared at Kat and the wriggling infant now on her stomach, not in it, mother and child still joined. Baldwin bolted away again at once.

"Kat, I said to you no man but a physician belongs in the birthing room, and even he" —Addy Seton glanced at the doctor—"is a modern divergence from accepted custom, his attendance here frowned upon by many, midwives most especially." Now Lady Seton's gaze went briefly to the midwife, who nodded vehemently.

"No male person, not even one such as *him,* should be in this place, and here is Miss Kat permitting three no less: doctor, husband, and wizard," said the midwife.

"Katesby dear, I imparted to you the wisdom that a newborn creature is beautiful to his mother but not necessarily to anyone else. I *said* let the babe be washed and swaddled before his father gets sight of him. Now Baldwin is no doubt bilious, distressed, and startled off," scolded Addy Seton indulgently. The midwife, Hetty Quine, a middle-aged woman neat in a starched, spotless white apron and cap, deftly cut the umbilical cord.

"Begging your pardon, *sir,* if I've overstepped my bounds," Hetty said to the doctor, who had made no move to perform the task. "But there was no need for you to soil your hands, eh, sir?

"Indeed not, Mistress Quine," he answered coldly as Hetty carried the gurgling infant in her own large, strong hands, extended before her, to a basin of warmed water near the fire.

"It don't sound to me as if the father's gone queasy," said Bessy Mortlock, who was still shuffling and dealing out Tarot cards just as she had been doing since Kat's labor began a few hours earlier.

"Nor do it sound so to me neither," agreed Bessy's consort, Dibdin, himself a Cunning Man—an aeromancer who read omens in clouds, and also a tiromancer who made divinations with cheeses, though he was most renowned as an astrologer. He began charting the baby's stars at the precise moment of birth. "The twenty-fifth day of the month of January at four of the clock in the afternoon," Dibdin noted. "A lot of 'em—the most of 'em, it seems—comes in the small morning hours, but your son, Mistress Katesby, has joined us for vespers."

"And in good time for eventide merrymaking, for which his sire and mum both have great talent!" Gwyn noted, laughing. "I've known Kat and Win since we three misbegotten, castoff waifs were living by our wits on the streets of London. Baldwin's no man to get all wambly at the sight of a little creature covered with a bit of grease and grime, 'specially if the little creature's his own firstborn son. There's naught in the world could make him happier than a bonny big baby. Win has always craved a family and at last he's got one," said Gwyn. She was hovering at the side of the bed, where the new mother was radiant with pride at her amazing achievement.

"Hurry, please, Hetty, with what you're about. I have the most powerful longing to hold my son now." Kat sighed as Baldwin, just outside the door on the stair landing, was heard to roar with joy to the odd assortment of humanity carousing below in the tavern, "The bloke's a boy!"

Cheers exploded like cannon fire from the crowd of clerks, artisans, merchants, sailors, fine gentlemen, ladies, and other, less savory folk—London street people of uncertain occupation. The shouts of jubilation were followed by a thundering on the stairs as the celebrants pounded up to grapple affectionately with the father, laud the mother, and gaze upon the child of two such fine, handsome, well-loved young people.

"No, *no*. This will not do! This nasty rabble is a danger to mother and son with all the noise and foul reeks they bring," the doctor protested with distaste.

"I do beg your pardon, sir," mocked one of the men trying to crowd into the room behind Baldwin, "but don't categorize me with these others. They are indeed a rabble, but I am not one of them, not *me*."

"Andrew! I'm so very pleased you've arrived in time for our child's birth," Kat exclaimed happily.

"I was in the north of England doing work of some importance. Tell this . . . .this doctor, please, that I have been a mummer, a player upon the stage, a thespian in service to great lords. Now I am a playmaker destined for fame and great good fortune."

"Close your mouth, Master Danter, or I'll close it for you," warned a tall, amiable-appearing young man in naval officer's dress. "You babble insufferably, man. And as for you—" The seaman, abruptly unsmiling, turned to the doctor, who took a step back.

"By heaven, I won't have a fracas at *my* inn. No brawling

allowed under The Sign of the Kat, 'specially not on my son's birthday!" Katesby protested. Her frequently heard directive made, as always, in a spirited, good-natured way, in conjunction with the small, upraised hand of Lady Seton, stopped the surging throng.

"You clamorous buffoons, show respect for a distinguished personage," Addy said. "This is the renowned Dr. Turner. He is always in attendance at my confinements *and* he is a member of the King's College of Physicians. He orders you out, and out it is. In truth, we will *all* leave now except the good doctor and Hetty. Go on. Go on, the lot of you," Addy insisted, gracing the subdued crowd with her cool, patrician smile. "You pair of blessers and sorcerers, quit this place too," she insisted, clapping her hands at Bessy and Dorsey. "Even you, Baldwin. Begone until you're sent for—*after* order is made of this room. Your son needs tending to, and your wife needs rest. When she's bathed and brushed and serene and beautiful, she may call for her handsome husband. In a proper household, Kat's confinement would last a month. She'd rest peacefully in bed in a quiet room with the shutters closed, and she would be waited upon, tended to while the milk mother saw to the infant and—"

"We're just *ordinary* working folk here, not highborn, Addy, and my own milk will be best for my boy. Besides, I'm too stirred up and gladdened to rest now," Kat insisted.

"Working folk sure, but *ordinary* mightn't apply," Andrew Danter pronounced in his deep, projecting actor's voice. "Once the particulars I've ferreted out in South Essex are confirmed, ordinary would not be the word to describe you, Kat."

"Out, out, damned Danter," Gwyn ordered. "This is neither the time nor the place for your melodramatics."

"Speak civilly to your elders and betters, chit," he rumbled.

"Hetty, I don't mean to meddle, but please bring my baby to me, *please*, just for a moment or two!" implored Kat.

"Make Kat beautiful? Kat is always beautiful, especially *now.* So why must I go?" Baldwin grinned over his shoulder, shaking his hair from his eyes as Lady Seton tried to urge him along. He sidestepped and evaded her to get to Kat's side. "Kitten, you're beautiful! So's this boy beautiful. I love you, wife!" He smiled down. His bronze hair and clear green eyes reflected glints of candlelight, while the hollows beneath stark cheekbones and the cleft of his chin were exaggerated by shadows. Kat raised her eyes from the baby's tiny, perfect face to look adoringly up at Win. The chaos, movement, and noise about them stilled.

"Amn't they a perfect, beautiful family?" Gwyn sighed. "Them two are so loving, so happy. Their son will be like 'em, I predict, with a winning smile like his father's and a sweet nature like his mother's." Lady Seton, also affected by the lovely tableau, nodded. A sentimental smile, a rare thing for her, touched her lips.

"Yes, and all the tribulations and troubles of the past will be behind them," she said, nodding until the doctor cleared his throat insistently. "Oh, get on with you all now," Addy said, reverting to her more usual severe demeanor.

"I'll thank you to remember I do the predicting here, Gwyn," said Dorsey Dibdin. "Come along, Baldwin. Don't gainsay a Leo. That is her ladyship's sign in the zodiac." The astrologer glanced sourly at Adelaide Seton as he gathered up his charts, inkpots, and quills. "You and all us here, lad, will lift a goblet of claret together and have us a good swig or two of wine to celebrate your son while I'm charting his stars."

Baldwin glanced from the little balding old man to the midwife, who had repossessed the infant, then to Kat again. He shrugged and grinned at her as if to say, *What am I to do?*

"Cross my palm with coin and I'll read the child's cards for you, Beaumarais, quicker 'n Dorsey can get his quill dipped," Bessy Mortlock wheedled.

"You've been telling the babe's cards all day for nothing but your own curiosity, eh, Bess?" Baldwin said, teasing her with a smile and his far-famed rogue's wink—two of the tools in his arsenal that had won him particular favor with the ladies in his bachelor days. Now they brought an almost girlish blush to the old Wise Woman's lined face. "Tell me his future is bright and you shall have a whole purse filled with shillings cast of the true old gold—and Dorsey will get the same, if I like what I hear. By the time you're both done with your foretellings, there'll be precious little I won't know about . . ." He hesitated. "Kat, love, what do you mean to name our son?" Baldwin asked.

"Beau, for you, Paul, for the saint upon whose day he is born; and Harry, for his godfather Norland. Will that please you?" asked Kat.

"Beau Paul . . . Harry?" An almost imperceptible narrowing of Win's eyes and the shadow of a scowl, though replaced nearly at once by his sunny grin, hadn't escaped Kat's notice. "Beau, it is! Now come, everyone. I'm providing the drink for the rest of the night!"

"Win! Don't leave me just yet!" Kat exclaimed as he was about to be swept along by the others. Her voice was edged with an urgency that stopped him, and he turned him to face her again.

"I'll just have one toast with these lads and be here with you again while I leave them to their fun."

"Win, I love you. Always remember."

"How will I forget with you beside me forever to tell me so?" he replied instantly, as earnest as she. "Are you fretting again over naught? You had best not be. Your milk won't come down sweet for Beau."

"Win?" Again Kat's voice held him. "I've never been as happy, not ever before in my life, as I am this moment," she said with tremulous sweetness. "I'm so happy that I'm afraid it may not last."

"My own sweet love, our joy will last forever, I promise."

He sat at the edge of the bed and rested his hand along her face. "There's always some vicissitudes in life. Every family has 'em, sure. But for us, there'll be more good times, like this, than troubled ones," he replied, "because you'll be giving me more sons, and even a daughter or two for me to dote upon as I do on you, eh, my pretty Kat?" She nodded and offered her dear crooked little smile, which made her seem to him as trusting and vulnerable as a child.

"Wondrous, rare man that you are, Baldwin Beaumarais, you tempt fate with such talk. How can even you promise happiness forever? The future is a closed book."

"Ah, Kat, you know I can do *anything* I put my heart and mind to." Win laughed. "And these soothsayers are about to open the book of the future for us, and for Beau, soon's we have a bit of a tipple, so . . ."

"Well then, I'll let you go if you promise you'll hurry back to us." Kat yawned.

"Nothing in this world could long keep me from you and the boy, Kat. Sleep now. I'll be here at your side again before you know I've gone."

But Kat did know. It was not until full noon next day that Win returned, and when he did, he was dressed for travel. As her eyes flickered open, they at once found the storm of bronze curls at his nape and then his broad shoulders, curled forward protectively. He stood at the window, holding the swaddled baby in his arms.

"I told you I was fearful the joy of it was too fine to last. I was right, was I not? I see you're leaving us, Baldwin," she said. "Tell me why."

"I cannot yet say," he replied gruffly.

"Will you say leastways what you are thinking on so hard?"

"Not . . . now," he answered, his mind reeling with the information given him by Andrew Danter and what had been inadvertently revealed to him by a man in the tavern last night, a courier in the livery of Harry de Morely, Earl of Norland.

"You look winded. Have a drink, man," Baldwin had offered as he descended the stairs from Kat's room. Though he was never pleased to be reminded of Kat's former suitor, de Morely, he would, of course, be gracious to his messenger.

"If you think me winded, sir, you should see me horse," the courier had commented. "His lordship sends for word of your lady wife, sir," he said, "and of the child."

"They both thrive and are beautiful," Baldwin replied, pointedly ignoring Andrew Danter, who, already in his cups, was dancing about trying to get his attention.

"Glad to know it, as his lordship will also be," affirmed the messenger. "Is it a boy or girl, sir?"

"We've a son. Beau Paul Harry."

"Ah. In that event, I'm to hand you this, sir" —the man put forward one of three letters he drew from beneath his cloak, sealed with the red wax imprint of the earl's crest— "and be on my way at once. I've another message to deliver in London, to his lordship's solicitor, and then I'm to take the good news, sir, to the Earl of Norland, with all possible speed."

Soon after, Baldwin strode into the public room, the letter clenched in his fist, Danter, who had been shown the missive, following with a grim and gloomily helpless expression. The tight, determined set of Win's mouth and the blaze of his eyes sent a chill of silence through the noise and merry chaos of the room. The lute player rendering "Light O' Love" continued for a few notes before he, too, fell quiet

"Blast it, Beaumarais. You must listen to me!" insisted the staggering actor in the sudden silent tension in the room. "I've words of wisdom to impart to you."

"Wisdom isn't what I require this minute, Andrew. 'Tis truth I need," Win growled at the actor, who was bearing down upon him with two mugs of brew. An instant later, drenched by beer, Danter was sprawled on his back halfway across the room, where Baldwin's unintentional angry blow had sent him. "A thousand pardons," Win apologized, helping his friend to his feet. " 'Twas caused by hot anger, and I'll need your wisdom later."

"Think naught of it. I'm on my third goblet of drink—that which is called *sheep wine,* for it stupefies a man and causes him to bleat nonsense" —Danter fingered his jaw—"not to speak out truth or wisdom. For that, go to Bessy."

"Old woman," Baldwin said, straddling a chair opposite Bessy Mortlock, "deal those cards for . . . for the boy."

The tavern was dimly lit. The lantern hanging over the table swayed, casting somber shadows on the faces of the people who gathered close. The only sounds in the room were the hiss of a log on the fire and the Wise Woman's gravelly voice interpreting the meaning of the cards as they fell.

"The Lion tells the child will have strength. The Emperor card predicts greatness. The Sun is the power of the universe." Bess hesitated. "The child born this day, who will grow to be strong, great, and powerful, is of noble blood."

"No!" Baldwin rasped, leaping to his feet and hurling the chair aside. "Read the cards again, old woman."

"I'll read them all night as I have been doing all day" —Bessy shrugged—"but nothing will change. The cards don't lie. You know that, Beaumarais."

"There's always a first time," he had insisted, shuffling the deck and placing it on the table in front of her.

"Win?" Kat implored. "Do not close me out. Tell me what troubles you so."

"Beau Paul Harry. He's a quiet boy."

"That's naught to worry over, my darling fool. One day he'll roar like the tide at London Bridge. He will make his mark on the world, as you have." Kat's voice imparted pride and great tenderness. Her eyes, the same clear green as her husband's, were filled with foreboding.

"Bess Mortlock said the same. Kat, tell me the God's truth," Win said very softly, his expression one of chagrin and misery when he turned to her. "I must ask you this: Who fathered this boy?" Kat's expression went from surprise to pain to sadness to anger in the space of seconds before a blankness settled over her features and she lifted her arms for the baby.

"You didn't think to ask me that when you implored me to take your name and insisted upon giving it to the child I was carrying so he'd not be born a bastard like you and me. You must tell me now, *please,* what has occurred, what seed of foreboding is taking root in your heart?" Kat asked.

"You're my best friend. I love you, Kat. And I *will* rear the boy as my own, as I promised," he replied, "but I've learned something which makes it . . . I needs must know for a certainty who sired him. Speak now and I will never mention or even think on this again, no matter what your answer."

"You will. You'll mull and ruminate forever. I know you. No matter what I say, you'll never again be at peace with me or the boy, not ever. Oh, Win! How have things come to such a pass between us?" Kat asked with a sad, stricken look. Baldwin, cursing himself, moved away to lean on the mantel and stare into the fire.

"It began that winter day you asked a 'small favor' of me, as you termed it—that I relieve you of the impediment of your virginity to save your intended husband the bother. I did." Baldwin shrugged.

"Yes," answered Kat, "Oh, yes, you did indeed."

Chapter 1

London
January, 1542
One year earlier

"Those ragamuffins will be gobbling up the inn's profits, Katesby Dalton, if you don't have a care," Baldwin Beaumarais whispered in Kat's ear, leaning over her as she knelt stirring a fire on the kitchen hearth. Taken by surprise at the very small hour of the morning when her day's work began, she gasped, arose, and swirled about with the iron poker swinging even though she was protected by a mismatched pack of milling mongrel dogs. Some were growling at the intrusion. Others, who recognized Win, wagged toward him in greeting. One old terrier, the house favorite, aptly called Deaf Jack, snored on at the center of a baker's dozen of sleeping children, all curled together under blankets amid the fragrant rushes covering the floor.

"Hold, Katesby, you fierce damsel!" Win laughed, easily evading her blow with his swordsman's lithe feint, first to one side, then the other. "Desist, wench, 'fore you raise a goose egg on my skull!"

"Oh, by the breath of garlic eaters! It's only you!" she gasped in a whisper, one hand protectively at her throat, the other keeping the poker aloft. "Baldwin Beaumarais, you near scared the life out of me. Your feet made no din at all crossing the floor."

"*Only* me, your greatest friend? I've been abroad six months and more since the harvest, and that's how you greet me?" He shook his head in mock despair. "I'm crushed!"

"Crushed? You? A man with the vainglory of a peacock and wealth to waste garbing yourself like one? It's not blasted likely anything I say could make a dent in your conceit!"

Teasing banter had always been an element of their long friendship, of the affectionate, loyal camaraderie they shared as partners in a thriving commercial enterprise that might otherwise have become strained by quixotic complications. On this unseasonably chilly May morning, though Kat stood brandishing the poker at Win, she was immensely gladdened to see him, as usual after he'd been away for a time. She didn't even try to contain her elation as she thoroughly looked him over. He was more splendid than ever with his long, bronze hair and wide shoulders.

"Come back to marry me, have you?" she twitted, grinning.

He grinned back at her. "You needn't settle for a rogue like me, sweetheart."

"Rogue or gentleman, I could fall in love with you, Win, if I was of a mind to." She shrugged, smiling even more broadly.

"Balderdash." He chuckled as he looked sidelong at his lovely partner. Her best features were her full lips and her huge green eyes, he thought. At any rate, not much more of her was visible beneath the shapeless work smock she wore.

"It only seemed right and natural to tell you—warn you—I've been mulling on the prospect of marriage. I want babies. You *are* my best friend. I've always told you everything, so I'm giving you the right of first refusal," she said casually, a shrug in her voice.

Win took her work-reddened hand and kissed it with a flourish and a bow. This was his own Kat talking *to him* about marriage *again.* He'd been away from her nearly half a year, and it was the first subject to come up. It had been the last before he'd gone abroad. Of course he loved her, but not *that way.* He decided to take it as part of her customary banter. It had best be.

"You're still the jester, as always, eh, Kat?" he asked. "I'd consider fathering your babes . . ." He smiled with exaggerated lechery.

"But you'd not consider wedding me first, I take it."

"I appreciate the honor and courtesy you do me with your offer, Katesby. And because I know how much you yearn for little ones of your own, I've searched half the world round on my recent travels for a likely husband for you."

"Oh? And did you discover one? Where is he?" she asked, peering over his shoulder toward the open door with feigned eagerness.

"I haven't come on the precise right man for the job—yet."

"Don't you trouble yourself further on my account, dearie. I've had an offer. I've found my own gent to marry with," she replied. "Now then, tell me. Did you not miss me at all during your travels?"

Baldwin frowned at her question, more especially at her unexpected tidings. "Well, indeed I missed your warmth and smile and your Sunday roasts and . . . all. Who's made you a marriage offer, eh?"

"I thought certes you'd arrive home this time positive I'd be the perfect wife for *you,* Win," she said blithely, with a casual shrug.

"It would be convenient for us to be wed, what with our

shared ownership of this inn and our other profitable enterprises but''—he paused, then winked to lighten the mood and show her he wasn't taking her offer seriously—''I'm going to dash your hopes.''

''Drat!'' she said, affecting his jester's tone. ''You turn me down without the slightest qualm, I take it?''

''That's so. You've another offer leastways to fall back on.'' Kat had, of course, anticipated Baldwin's reply, but not the strong stab of disappointment and pain she felt.

''Have you discovered a likely wife for yourself while you were looking for a man for me?'' she asked, unaware that she held her breath while awaiting his reply.

''I'm in no hurry to take vows. Nor should you be.'' His eyes narrowed. ''You're a woman of some means now, Kat. Go slow, at least till I've looked your boy over, made some inquiries about him. Speak his name.'' Kat was, Win knew, no fool. She was a girl well endowed with grit and verve, usually sensible and practical, but sometimes her heart went as soft as butter and was as easily melted. ''You're not in love with this . . . whoever he is? Could you be?''

''No. See, I could fall in love with you now, I conjecture. With him, love perhaps will grow over time. I do like him remarkably well. Oh, and he is not a boy but a man, full grown,'' she answered.

''Do I know him? Blast it, what be his name?'' Baldwin was faintly riled.

''I am not at liberty to say just yet, not till 'tis a settled thing.'' Kat looked away.

''If you don't mind telling me, when might that be? I'm the nearest thing to a family you've got in this world, Katesby. Don't you think my participation in your marriage agreement would be in order?''

''In a fortnight or thereabouts, when the gentleman returns to London, I'll tell you all. He might dispatch a messenger sooner, of course,'' she answered his first question, avoiding the second about the marriage agreement.

"I take it you've already consented and he dithers, keeping you in doubt? No gentleman, that," he gibed.

"Actually, I'm the ditherer," Kat answered, hanging a kettle from a hook over the fire."He's a true gentleman to the bone, born noble, Win. He's gone away to his north-country estate to give me time to ponder on it all."

"Still a virgin, are you, Kat?" Win abruptly demanded, then struck his brow with the heel of his hand. "I beg your pardon, truly. I've no license to ask you that."

"When have *you* needed leave to ask me about *anything?*" she replied.

"Well, *are* you?" he shot back, taking a step closer to her.

"Am I still a maid? In actuality, Win, I'm relieved you brought that up, glad that you mentioned it. I *do* need the benefit of your experience in . . . all that realm," she replied and gave him her luminous, slightly askew smile.

"That's not an answer. 'Tis neither a yes nor is it a no," he said, his brow furrowing. "Perchance could it be this matter progressed with you and your gent just so far that you are left unsure of your condition? Is that it?"

"No," she protested with an indignant laugh. "That's not it."

"So what is it? Speak to me, Katesby."

"Later, when I've done with the morning chores and you've eaten and rested and are more at your ease. And Win—that about me falling in love with you? Just put it right out of your mind," she said as if she had made a great jest in her idle chatter.

"The notion wasn't *that* absurd," he replied, a bit miffed, but also relieved, for he had, fleetingly, considered the advantages of being loved by Katesby Dalton. They already knew each other well. There'd be no unpleasant surprises, no secrets, no bothersome familiarizations and accommodations. But no! It would not do because Kat was his foremost friend, the nearest thing he'd ever had to a little sister, though she was no longer "little," he reminded himself, looking into her immense eyes, which were almost on a level with his own.

She had shot up like a cornstalk at fourteen, to his wonder and her own mortification, to near his own six feet of height, less perhaps two inches, measured, as was English custom, with three barley corns to the inch. Over the next few years, while he had been away from London but for brief, infrequent visits, the leggy sprig of a girl had continued to grow more gracefully and in every direction *but* up. She had developed a certain comeliness, with her strong features and an endearing, inadvertently come-hither smile. Some men, it was true, took notice of her, were drawn to her—there was no doubt of that. But what nobly born gentleman, the holder of a north-country estate, no less, would be offering marriage to the plain proprietress of a small inn, even if she was something of a gem, a jewel in the rough?

"Merely tell me if I am acquainted with your admirer, Kat, as you won't reveal his name to me," Baldwin asked.

"He thinks I'm pretty. I know 'tis flattery but . . . I do like hearing that." She blushed fiercely and turned away toward the fire.

"Never trust a flatterer," Baldwin answered shortly, again furrowing his handsome brow.

"If you're so quick to name my new friend a flatterer, you must not think me in the least pretty," she challenged.

"You twist my words. I merely said: 'Never trust a flatterer,' " Baldwin protested. "Of *course* I find you pretty and I hold you more dear than anyone else."

Kat, who had yet to acknowledge her blossoming beauty, was always surprised to discover the tolerably fair young woman with large eyes reflected in a darkened window as she passed, or at the bottom of a shiny pewter bowl she was polishing. But she had neither time nor vanity to ponder on it and rarely gazed into a mirror. At nearly nineteen, she still went on wearing the shapeless, coarsely spun work dresses and floppy kerchiefs in which, as an ungainly fourteen-year-old, she had tried to conceal her awkwardness.

The ploy hadn't worked for the coltish girl she had been, and it didn't work now. The elegant contours of her willowy figure were often revealed as she went about her daily business, reaching, bending, lifting a child, scattering feed to the inn yard hens on a breezy day. But Baldwin, if he took note of it at all, considered her statuesque figure a fine bargaining tool in the marriage market. Of course, she'd have to get out of her slack clothes once in a while and learn to dress to her advantage in more appealing garments. She'd refused his suggestions about her attire, insisting she was a busy working woman dressed for comfort and ease of movement. "Of course you're pretty, Kat," he reiterated, "but—"

"But I'm not pretty enough to be a wife to you?" she asked in her appealingly foggy voice. It enhanced the impression she gave of earthy bravado that was actually a self-protective veneer that Baldwin knew was fostered by early misfortune. He knew, too, that her seemingly stubborn willfulness was often belied by the curiosity, expectation, and humor in her steady green eyes. There was a deep, sweet wisdom there, too, beyond her years, and hidden from all but those who, like Baldwin, knew her well, there was a tender, romantic girl longing for love. He was bent upon helping her find it—with the right man. She was hinting—damn, she was near proclaiming with her marriage talk—that *that* man was he. It wasn't.

"Blast it, Kat!" he roared in a whisper so as not to awaken the children. "You're my full partner in a thriving London inn and high-stakes gaming house. I've depended on you to run this establishment since the day I bought it. Verily, I named it for you. The Sign of the Kat hangs without, does it not? You made a success of our venture because you're wise to the wiles of the street, hardworking, ambitious. I am obliged to see you don't make a match with a mountebank."

"You neglected to say that I'm also loyal, resourceful, energetic, and honest—good traits in a business partner who's the proprietress of an inn. But not in a wife for you. Win, *I* know I'm not a fine lady, not the gentlewoman you dream of taking to wife, not a dainty, spoiled squire's daughter. You warn me of mountebanks, but you're an easy mark for a merchant's pampered, privileged, indolent child with soft hands and unknowing eyes. Have a care *you* don't make a bad marriage bargain."

She was right, as always, Baldwin admitted to himself. And as always, she read him like an open book, looked right into his heart and soul. He valued such insight, in a friend. But in a wife? He had his doubts.

"I know *I'm* not dainty," Kat continued with a shrug, leaning to wipe the surface of a table, "not like some of the bevy of belles—silly chits at that—who've chased after you. And usually caught you, I'll add, in bed if not in church."

"You are more a lady than any woman I've known," he said simply. "You realize, Katesby, we *will* marry someday and . . ." he began. She stopped what she was doing and looked straight at him. "No, not each *other,*" he added quickly, exasperation in his tone. "We'll both make good matches to better our positions and enhance our modest fortunes. And as for my belles, Kat, I care not if they be of exalted rank or no, witless or clever, so long as they are amusing and eager. I would not be so be unkind to any lady as to deny her the pleasure of my company in bed," he said, the humor back in his voice.

"I've noted well that you deny no female that pleasure. What of me?" Kat asked with a sweet and mocking air. She tossed back her tawny hair, which had been framing her face and cascading over her shoulders. "Oh, don't answer that, and let us be done with this quibbling. You're *here!*" She laughed, twining her arms about his neck as she so often had. Her pleasure at having Win home was so vast, she glowed. And then she kissed his mouth. His lips were firm and warm and smooth, more delectable than a perfect summer apple.

"You're trembling," he said, not moving a muscle except to turn his head before he passed an arm about her waist. He'd forgotten how narrow it was. Whether she was trembling or no, her cheek against his was hot, either from the fire or her blush, and her breasts against his chest were full and soft. This had to stop *now,* he thought, but he didn't stir. Nor did she.

"Of course I'm shivering," she answered, her sweet breath warm at his ear. " 'Tis deep January, man. The wind cuts like a knife and 'tis swirling snow in here. Shut the door, why don't you, Baldwin?"

"The door of this inn was unbolted, Madam Proprietress. I strode right up behind you and you heard naught. What if I'd been a cutthroat or a robber?" He set his hands on her arms, which were still enfolding his neck, intending to untwine them.

"You *are* a robber."

He winked. "Aye, and you're my mark."

"Sure, I used to spot your gulls for you, but we did no one injury ever."

"Quite the opposite. We put our spoils to good use, not like some other foisterers and ferrets I could name. That's why you must keep the door bolted or chance being taken by surprise by a culprit."

" 'Tis those costly boots you wear—that's why I didn't hear you, Win. Spanish leather is soft as silk. What have you got under there? A gift?" she asked, sending a hand under his cloak.

"For you," he said, setting a quick, wholesome kiss on

her brow before stepping back and producing a small plant sporting one brave and jaunty wine-red Levantine rose. "I sailed home on the *Conquest.* Jim Bolling sends the plant to you. He sends these to Gwyn to use in her stews and bakes and for planting," Win added. He spilled the contents of a silken pouch upon the table—cloves of pungent-smelling garlic. "And I've brought you these, Kat," he said, carefully emptying his pocket of dry twigs and sticks, stoppered vials of fragrant liquid, and six flower bulbs. "They are *lilium chalcedonicum* and *lilium martagon*—beautiful lilies for your garden, more rare than jewels. These are seeds of aromatic spikenard. The root there is of the calamus plant. It makes a good elixir, I'm told, for colic and cramp."

"And the vials?" she asked, opening each of the three in turn and inhaling.

"One is oil of cinnamon, one of rosewater, and the third is oil of olive for your hands, to make them soft and smooth, eh?"

Kat, ashamed of her ragged nails and callused red hands, hid them behind her back. "What, no aloes and frankincense, as are extolled in the Bible, in the Song of Solomon? 'His cheeks are as a bed of spices, as sweet flowers: his lips like lilies, dropping sweet-smelling myrrh.' "

Kat's wide smile was wonderfully warm and happy, and Win found it delightful. "I missed you," he divulged with a blink of surprise.

"Good," she responded, meaning it. "And I you. And so your ship has come in again with another rich cargo and you aboard, too."

"We touched at Plymouth, then came up to anchor at Deptford. And here I am, as you see me."

"Indeed. And there's no finer sight to these eyes of mine. Where did young and dashing Captain Bolling find you?" Kat lowered her face to inhale the scent of the rose.

"At Malaga."

"Where's that?" She fingered the branches of the plant. "I hope it isn't frost-blasted," she worried.

"Malaga is in the south of Spain, a sunny, warm city not long since ruled by Moors."

"Warm? It is not warm here. Shut the door *please.* The wind will chill my babies." Kat pulled the cover over one of the sleeping children.

"Your orphans of the storm, Kat, wrapped as they are and well fed, won't feel the cold *this* cruel night, thanks to you. Where did you find these tykes?" Baldwin glanced about at the dark heads and the fair, which was all that could be seen of the youngsters; then he looked at Kat amid her strays, the dogs and children at her feet. She seemed to him a fusing of mindful mother and defending warrior angel standing over them all. At that instant she was not merely pretty, but *beautiful.*

"I discovered them in the niches we well knew and made use of along Tower Bridge. I always find some there."

"If not for you, more than one of them would have frozen this night."

"So shut the door, eh?" Kat asked softly, feeling his eyes touch her as she moved away from him, remembering suddenly, for no cause she could imagine, a night months ago when, hesitating outside a room of the inn, she overheard a renowned London beauty, Marjory Faunt, an actual-born *lady,* sighing with love over Baldwin and making the most brazen suggestions.

Kat hadn't meant to eavesdrop, but she just hadn't been able to abandon her post, not until the talking stopped. She had heard a chair overturn and other sounds that brought unruly images to her mind and a blush to her cheeks. She tried to forget what she'd heard, but by early the next morning, when she was already up starting the day's chores and Win was just coming in, she knew it wasn't going to be that simple. He stopped in her kitchen on his way to his rooms upstairs to break the night's fast and chat.

He stood tall at the mantel, his lean face, usually smooth-shaven, showing a night's growth of stubble. His doublet of black brocade, cut upon red velvet, was lacking the fine copper lace ruff that had been embellishing it last evening, she took notice.

"Have a good night, Kat?" he had asked, pouring thick cream on the steaming gruel she set on the table for him.

"Very. The tavern was so busy, patrons were jostling against each other, and the gaming room was full. By closing time, my apron pockets were heavy with coin. And you, Win? Did you have a good night?" She watched him nod and smile to himself, his manly profile silhouetted in a slant of dawn sunlight that lit his long, bronze mane. She was compelled to brush an errant curl from his brow, and when her hand stirred the scent of the woman's perfume from his hair, she was awash in a wave of jealousy. And appalled. She'd known Baldwin Beaumarais since he was a small, slight, quick, and clever young rascal, a skilled pickpocket surviving on the streets of the city. Now, at twenty-seven, he was every inch a man, slender but well made, strong, and tall. The red hair of his boyhood, which had earned him the byname "carrots," had turned a gleaming dark bronze. He had come into some property and a modest sum of money, which he had increased many times over. He now moved at all levels of English society with ease and grace, though not by dint of wealth alone. Baldwin had acquired book learning and courtly ways from his patrician mentor, Lord Monfort, Marquess of Falconbridge, who had taken the brash, clever, scrawny boy out of the slums of London and, with the help of his marchoiness, made a gentleman of him.

By the time Baldwin began his twentieth year, by then studying rhetoric at Clare College of Cambridge, women of all ranks found him irresistible. The phenomenon had astounded him at first, as he had told Kat, and pleased him immensely. And if, over time, he had grown somewhat accustomed to all the admiring feminine attention, it continued to gratify him immensely. He never lost a certain boyish manner of deferential, unassuming awe, which made him all the more appealing to jaded ladies and innocent maidens alike. Though honor and a determination to keep his freedom kept him from the beds of virgins, the former urchin, who had so craved love, had yet to find a reason to disappoint a generous and affectionate practiced woman. After a tryst or two, he would usually extricate himself from a liaison but with a generosity and good nature that left his lovers sighing, sated, his proponents ever after. Marjory Faunt was merely one of his many devotees and friends, the one who doubtless had kept his costly lace ruff as a memento of a night of love.

"I'll have to close the door myself, it seems," Kat announced, frowning as a strong gust of wind set the fire dancing and drew her back to the present.

"Drovers from the docks are waiting to unload wagons filled with goods from Malaga, same as your rose. I've presents for Gwyn, the Goodkind ladies, and a few others."

"Trinkets for half the ladies in London, what?" she goaded. "Let the men take turn by turn guarding the goods and coming in to warm themselves and eat a bite. The job of unloading will be more easily done at full light. Tell 'em that and *then* shut the door, eh, Win?"

"That will suit them, Kat. Oh, and Kat? I've brought you something else. 'Tis also without. A surprise."

"From . . . Malaga?" she asked, turning to look at him, alerted by a different fervor in his tone. He shrugged off his cloak, his handsome face serious, and put his sword and dagger on the mantel. Then he squared his broad shoulders, which were made to appear even wider than they naturally were by the fashionably winged shoulders of his close-fitting doublet, which narrowed at his small waist. The padded, slashed sleeves, each with a row of a dozen decorative gold buttons, revealed the rich crimson silk lining beneath the dark velvet. His shirt—of white cobweb lawn—the finest of linens, showed at his throat and, when he set his hands on his hips, at his wrists as well. His tall boots, pointed and heeled, were set wide. Kat was all too familiar with that determined stance. "It must be a very curious surprise for you to behave so mysteriously—that or a very big one. Is it something or *someone* else?" she asked and folded her arms beneath her breasts, her stance defensive.

"Can't fool you, Katesby, can I?" He grinned, looking proud of her, though she saw a touch of chagrin in his expression. " 'Tis *someone*," he conceded. "I know that you'll take to her, that you'll prize her as I do. If not, she'll stay here only a night or two. Then I'll find another place for her. May I have her in?"

"Blast it, Beaumarais, why ask my permission now to have a go with a trollop?" She frowned. "You never have before."

"This is not what you suppose, Kat. I ask because I'd thank you from my heart should you find it in yours to look out for her in London," he said, and her heart sank. He was in earnest about this female, whoever she was. He was so earnest, it seemed he might actually be in love with her. It was bound to happen to him sooner or later, Kat told herself, but why couldn't it be later, and with *her*?

"You'd best bring the lady in out of the weather," she murmured, bracing herself for the meeting, already imagining Win holding some strange girl on his knee, saying things she longed to hear but that he'd never told her. Worst of all, she probably *would* like his sweetheart and what a quandary she'd be in then!

Chapter 2

"Women and gin made me old before my time, wot? Women, gin, and the scurvies. I was lamentable sick with the scurvies. Got a drink, missy?" The person summoned by Win—a broad, tall seaman holding a canvas bundle against his shoulder—made straight for the fire. His ears were scarlet, his face sallow beneath a fading tan.

"Blaidd Kyd, cabin lad to Captain Bolling," Win explained to Kat as he relieved the large boy of the bundle.

"What are you toting, Mr. Kyd? Work for the washing girls? Give it over," Kat said. Win gestured her away.

"Old before his time is Blaidd Kyd, at fifteen."

"And large," said Kat.

Kyd glowered. " 'Tis a hard life at sea. You was not with us, sir, when we ran down to Cape Verde. It was three men to a rat at every mess, and the grog was more water than rum."

"Be cheerful you had as much. It was more'n we did, this damsel and me, much of the time we were growing up," Win answered. "Take off your cap, mutt, and be presented to Katesby Dalton, landlady and half owner of The Sign of the Kat inn."

"Cheerful is not in me nature, sir. I'm a dour Welshman, do you recall? What's them?" asked Kyd, gesturing with his chin at the mound of children and dogs on the floor, before he snatched off his cap to reveal a sparse new growth of prickly blond hair on a pale skull. "My pleasure, miss." He bowed to Kat, bending nearly to the floor. "The want of leisure and the carefree life kept me ignorant of certain niceties, but Win Chance taught me to do that, to bow, on introduction to a lady. I mean to say, Baldwin—uh, Mr. *Beaumarais.*"

Kat and Win exchanged glances. "Why does the boy know you as Chance?" she asked.

"He's sworn to secrecy. I trust him, eh, Blaidd?"

"I'm a hunted man, same as . . . that other I'm not to name," said Kyd. "I pledged my life to Mr. Beaumarais. He's been hiding me from my enemies."

"A boy his size is not an easy thing to conceal. I got him out of England for a time, but he wants to clear his name."

"I will 'less they catch me first."

"Have you got a secure place for him to sleep, Kat?" Win asked.

"Vouched for by you or no, it's perilous, him letting slip *that* name," she worried.

"A rare blunder of the tongue. Blaidd rarely misspeaks. Find him a bed, eh, Kat?"

"He can crawl in among these other youngsters if Deaf Jack will abide the loose-talking Goliath," she replied. "That old dog never is wrong about the true character of man or beast." Without waking, the animal, as if feeling their glances, stretched his short legs, quivered all over, then curled himself back into a tight ball. "Right there's the safest hiding place in London for a fugitive from justice, even if magistrates and officers of the Crown do frequent this inn. Lucky for us and others, they never see what's right under their pompous noses."

"There's also a goodly number of predatory women, roaring boys, card sharpers, usurers' touts, and the like give us their business, Kat. Do you think my young friend will be able to keep out of *their* way, also?" Win asked with a wink at Kyd.

"On these premises, everyone behaves decent and gambles honorable. I won't allow sharping or touting here," Kat replied firmly with a toss of her head. "Certes, I could keep a particular watchful eye on this oaf of a lad, just to be sure he comes to no harm—that is, if he doesn't misspeak again and give himself away, and you, too."

"It's the varlets he's after I worry about, not Blaidd. He took care of himself so well, the authorities and certain swaggerers and felons are all after *him* now," Win explained.

"I can't abide pettifoggers," grumbled the boy, clenching his fists.

"Some of my best friends are pettifoggers, and I cannot abide loose-lipped, self-righteous oafs," Kat teased. "Ah, but hark, lad. If you are too downcast for too long, you may lose all taste for pleasure. Tell him so, Win, and give over the washing, eh?" she said, reaching for the bundle he still held. Win pivoted and strode away from her.

"Why call me oaf, miss, when we've only just met?" asked Blaidd peevishly.

"Don't fret, Kyd. It's just a bit of raillery—Katesby's way of discovering if you've got a clever tongue and an aptitude for banter," Win explained, walking up and back before the great hearth with the bundle held securely against his chest.

"I already said I wasn't given to cheerfulness and idle chatter," Blaidd said brusquely.

The boy was a natural, unintentional clown, Kat decided, watching him knock into an empty copper cauldron hanging from a beam behind his head and then catch it with a lunge before it hit the stone hearth with what would have been an ear-shattering clatter.

"Would you prefer I call you oaf *after* I get to know you?" Kat asked Blaidd with a friendly, scoffing smile as she again went after the canvas bundle Win held. He waved her away and turned his back.

"Most girls do." The lad shrugged, blushing. " Call me oaf. See, a real ladylike little thing, all beribboned and lace-frilled, ties my tongue and makes me feel cumbersome of person."

"You *are* oafish, just as I said," Kat heckled sweetly. "I'll do my best to put you at your ease."

"But *you* don't affect me thus, Miss Kat," the boy answered, rising to the bait, trying to play her game by offering a wrong-handed compliment. To his chagrin, *she* flushed.

"Of *course* I don't affect you, or most men, surely not Baldwin, that way. Not being a petite, beribboned, lacy, helpless sort of female person, I'm treated like one of the knaves, part of the throng. Even so, actually *because* I'm plain and, I'm told, down to earth, I've had a very favorable offer of marriage from a fine gentleman, believe it or no, Blaidd."

"Why wouldn't I believe it?" puzzled the boy.

"Come, Kat. You can trust us. Who *is* this 'gentleman?' " demanded Win. "And say again, what was it exactly you wished information about that you wanted to *practice* with me in that regard?"

"Not *now,* Win," she said with a blushing glance at the boy. "And as for you, Blaidd Kyd," she continued, "I'll call you worse than oaf if you ever again utter Baldwin Beaumarais's secret name. Now, get some rest. You appear to need it. First, tell me who's hunting you so I can be on my guard."

"You're already on watch for some of Blaidd's enemies.

They're mine also. The king's main spymaster, Francis Wiltenham, and Rattcliffe, the torturer."

"As notable a pair of wicked, devilish knaves as ever drew breath. If, as 'tis said, a man may be judged by his foes as well as his friends," Kat said with a nod, "my opinion of you has risen, young Blaidd. You may explain to me how so humble a fellow as yourself earned the rancor of those wicked, powerful men." She set a comradely light clout on Blaidd's shoulder, then relieved him of the cauldron he still was clutching.

"I became embroiled with one Francis Flud and his cousin Paul Wadd, touts and foul spies of Wiltenham."

"Also known as Welsh Frank and Paul Penniless. Why don't *they* like you?"

"Lute strings, is why. Them two dastards got me poor dad's bond for a loan of twenty pounds. They gave him but five in coin of the realm and the rest in lute strings for him to sell, deemed to be worth the difference of fifteen pounds. But there was no great need for lute strings in the land, as any but a poor gullible countryman like me poor dad might have guessed. The strings could not be given away. Flud and Wadd hounded me poor dad into debtors' prison. It was there he hanged himself. With lute strings." A single tear rolled down Kyd's cheek. "When I sought to avenge me poor dad, Waad and Flud accused me of vicious crimes they themselves had done. I was dangling on the Tyburn gallows when our champion of the tyrannized and downtrodden, Win Chance, saved me by cutting in on my dance on air."

"I am sorry, Blaidd. You're safe here," Kat said with quiet sympathy. "Sleep secure."

"I need food more'n I need sleep. I'm ravenous hungry," complained Kyd. "Uh, I mean to say please, miss, I need . . . and so forth," he added with a begrudging look at Win. "So does *she.*" The bundle he had brought in began now to wriggle in Win's arms and a thin cry came muffled from it.

"Meet my 'trollop,' Katesby," Win invited, unfolding the canvas packet and a blanket beneath it to reveal a small, oval, fawn-hued face like ivory touched with olive gold, encircled by an umbra of silky black curls. Almond-shaped dark eyes blinked. The little bowed mouth puckered, then rounded into a great yawn.

"Win! A moppet and such a dear little thing. Did you bring her from Spain?" Kat exclaimed with a smile, reaching out for the child. Win nodded, charmed by Kat's response. "Aren't there foundlings enough for you in London?" she gently teased.

"For me, aye. Not for you. She was left at the Alcazar—the ruins of a Moorish castle above the harbor at Malaga. Desperate mothers surrender infants to the Fates there. The outcome could be the rescue of the baby and a more secure, better life than the mother and kin could provide—or . . . not. It's in the hand of destiny, 'tis believed. There are many well-known tales of princes and princesses in danger raised up by humble folk."

"In those tales, noble blood always tells. The royal orphan regains a rightful crown and is ever greatful to the sainted couple who reared him."

"In England children are left to Providence at monastery gates and almshouses," said Blaidd in a dismal tone.

"It was at the Graie Friars in Southwark for me," Kat sighed, brushing a curl from the child's brow. "I was some older than this baby. She's not reached her first birthday, I'd deem. I'd passed my second, or it was supposed I had, though no one knew for a certainty. I had a little golden ring on a ribbon round my neck."

"Was that the last time you wore one?" Win asked and winked at Kyd.

"Do you mean a ribbon or a ring?" she retorted. "I've

never worn either since, but I'm expecting I'll be adorned with both soon now if . . . *when* I wed."

The baby, lying on the table, kicking her legs, took hold of Win's finger. He lifted her to him again. Kat smiled. It was apparent to her that Win adored the little girl. Strong arms, wide shoulders, bronze hair to black ringlets. Made for this.

"Whatever happened to your ring on a ribbon, Katesby?" he asked.

"Friar Truckle has it. 'Tis the only link to my past. If someday, someone kith or kin were to seek after me, the search might begin at Graie Friars, where the ring has waited all these years. Perhaps it will lead me home, wherever that may have been. Has this foundling any keepsake?"

Kat took the child from Win and looked down at the baby girl in her arms, her eyes shining, and Win again saw her as a beautiful, defending angel taking yet another little creature under her wing. Blaidd Kyd, for all his great size still feeling himself to be more lost boy than grown man, was also enthralled by the tableau, and he was made in a moment unwitting Kat's unintended conquest. He didn't realize at once he'd fallen in love with her, for he'd not been rendered tongue-tied and awkward by her—mayhap her lack of frills and bows and other dainty ornaments dangling about her person, had disarmed him.

"Only the figured blanket she's wrapped in, with the Arab squiggles, is all the pretty child has in the world. Win Chance—*uh, Mr. Beau—marais,*" Kyd amended, "called her Roxelana after the first wife of the Turkish Sultan Suleiman, then Chandra, the word for moon in the Moorish tongue—he first saw the little creature sleeping in a beam of moonlight—and also Isabella, for the Queen of Spain. All them names are hers because she was found at the edge of three worlds," Blaidd said.

"She could be of any of those descents or a mingle of them all," Win explained.

"O' course, she has got no family name," said Kyd.

"Chance," said Kat, "if that gentleman doesn't object. It was he who saved her, after all. Roxelana Chandra Isabella Chance."

"Mr. Beaumarais, he settled right off on bringing her to you," the boy said.

"Ah." Kat nodded, pleased by this and that the boy seemed to be warming to her enough to speak at some length. "Well, Beaumarais," she then challenged Win, "howbeit you won't wed me, but you'll give me a baby?" She smiled at him with a suggestion of coyness.

He lifted a brow and smiled with one corner of his mouth, his look knowing. "I've saved you the usual bother."

"And the usual frolic," she quipped.

"A risque rejoinder, Kat. I've never before known you to be the least bit bawdy. I do know Roxelana's plight must strike your heart, as it did mine."

"And me own heart, too," said Blaidd. "All us three victims of circumstance as we be, buffeted about by fate, same as Roxelana. All us three should undertake the foundling's fostering. It will be an abiding bond between all us three and her. *Now* can I have a bit to eat?" he asked, spotting a dry crust of bread left on the corner of a table and wolfing it down. "Oh, and if Mr. Beaumarais is not of a mind to wed you, Mistress Kat, and give you the pleasure of begetting, I *am*."

She flushed. Win looked daggers at the boy with eyes as green and hard as jade. "You overstep yourself, Kyd."

"Win, please don't snarl. The boy jests," Kat soothed. She knew how quick and ruthless his rare anger could be, and she tried to turn it now to humor. "You should thank Blaidd for his gallant proposal, even though I haven't a single hair ribbon to my name. Thank you, young sir."

"It was no jest," said Blaidd affably. He was really challenging Win, Kat realized, and wondered if Kyd had all his wits about him. It was a chancy thing to do. As Win looked from Kyd to Kat, she was relieved to see his lips curve into a smile before he threw up his hands, tossed back his handsome head, and laughed.

"Is it any wonder I had to deliver this ridiculous wag by cutting him down from the gallows? He was already dancing on air," he told Kat. She visibly paled. "He's cocky as a rooster and brave as a bear, is Kyd, and a dumb show all on his own. He gives offense to friend and enemy, to the highborn and to underlings alike with no hesitation or discernment."

"What's wrong with offering marriage to the lady?" Kyd irksomely mused.

"Don't press your luck, Kyd," Win advised as Kat set her hand on his arm, a gesture that always calmed him.

"Now I've at least two suitors to choose from," she bantered.

"I trust your other admirer is not such a crude want-wit as Kyd." Win grimaced at the boy in a botched attempt at a smile. He was more annoyed, he knew, than he should be by this silliness and wasn't sure why.

"My other suitor is also eloquent and gallant," Kat said.

"Who is he?" Win demanded, but Kat shook her head.

"I would discuss matters of a privy nature with you now, Kat, not after you've done the morning chores and the day's marketing, sweeping, baking, and brewing. Stuff Kyd's mouth with food to stifle his babble and put him to sleep. I'm *really* eager to know who the devil has been courting you, Kat, while I've been gone, perhaps taking advantage of you. It chills my blood to think it, but if I'd arrived home a fortnight from now, I could have found you wed to some knave who would have a claim on your means and property. I won't have you ill used or duped."

"Aha. *Again* you imply a man couldn't want me for myself. Is that what you're saying?"

"No, Kat. You're twisting my words *again.* I'm saying love, the stirrings of the heart, can confound the clearest of heads."

"Not mine. Come, Beaumarais. You know I'm not so thick as to make any unscrupulous stranger your partner in our ventures. The gentleman I'm considering has a fortune of his own, one so great he wouldn't covet any of *our* riches. In fact, he offers to write off any debt you feel is owing me for my contribution to our flourishing enterprises."

"Does he now? There isn't wealth enough in the world for that, Kat . . . to repay my debt to you. Your would-be benefactor sounds like an arrogant, insufferable sort. I want to know . . ."

"Our chat must wait, Baldwin," she insisted. "I've this baby to care for. . . ." She smiled when Roxelana wriggled in her arms. The baby was insisting clearly, but soundlessly, that she be set down on the floor. "And I must feed the other youngsters when they awaken. There're your drovers out in the storm to be welcomed and served, my overnight travelers will have to be tended to, fishmongers to be bargained with—"

"There'll be no fish caught this day and you know it, rascally clever damsel!" Win's laugh made her heart dance. "The storm's been too wild for small boats to set out. By God, you're behaving just like a woman, trying a man's patience. *My* patience at that!"

"Imagine it, Beaumarais—me, Katesby Dalton, behaving like a *woman.* Methinks that's the most agreeable thing you've said to me since you came gliding in here on your brigand's boots and scared the breath out of me," she twitted. "So I will just go right on trying your patience and see what it earns me!"

"It'll earn you a trouncing, that's what." He grinned and lunged for her, allowing her to easily elude him.

"Someday, you might truly want to get hold of me, Win. But the only way you'll ever be able to catch me is if I want you to. I've always been as quick on my feet as you are." She laughed as she flung back her hair and swirled a long worsted cloak about her shoulders. Grabbing a basket with one hand and a milk pail with the other, then lowering her head against the storm, she set off to the barn.

The milk, hot from the cow, was steaming in the cold winter morning, and the eighteen newly laid eggs Kat collected from the hen roosts in the rafters were warm. She cooked them up with a slab of bacon, a meal ample enough to satisfy six men. Blaidd kept Roxelana, who happily stuffed food into her mouth with her hands, perched on his knee as he and Win shared their heaping trencher with her. The three consumed all the eggs and bacon put before them, devoured a pound loaf of barley bread, and emptied a bowl of pease porridge with honey. Blaidd twice filled the bowl of a wooden dipper with milk for Roxelana, and when she had done and was yawning grandly, he burrowed, with the baby in his strong bear's grip, in among the sleeping dogs and children and soon was shaking the walls with his snores.

Win sat before the kitchen fire, his long legs extended, and gulped hot pear cider. With an exaggerated show of patience, he went over Kat's account books while she and her barmaid, bleary-eyed Gwyn, who'd been roused early from sleep, served the drovers in the front room of the inn.

"Who is he, Kat?" he asked each time she hurried past him to brew more tea, to carry refilled trenchers of steaming gruel to the drovers, or to fetch pewter trays of more elaborate fare for awakening guests anxious to get on with their travels."What's the favor you want of me?" Win knew she'd tell him in her own good time. The girl couldn't keep a secret, not from him, but he liked teasing her, watching her smile or feign exasperation.

"Who's who?" she would reply. "You've no need to know just now, when I'm seeing to trade."

But at last the wagons were unloaded and their valuable cargo stored away, the bustle of the morning rush diminishing, most of the guests happily sent on their way, the children being managed by Gwyn, the dogs being fed by the stable boy, the scullery girls scraping what scraps there were left in the wooden trenchers into the stew kettle for the midday meal and letting Deaf Jack lick the bowls clean in readiness for the next serving.

"You've no more excuses or diversions. I've waited from well before dawn to high noon. So?" Win took her work-reddened hands in his and drew her closer to him. "Who is the man you perchance may wed?"

"I'll say if you will you promise to do one thing I ask of you," she bargained in her faintly hoarse milk-and-honey voice. Her eyes were immense, gleaming.

"I promise. You know I'll do anything for you, Katesby."

"Anything?'

"If I'm able," he replied. She was being oddly mysterious, not like herself at all. It was unsettling.

"You're able, surely." She didn't take her eyes from his.

"Well . . . what is it I must promise?" He felt her trembling.

"Give me . . . a love lesson."

He didn't answer at first. Then he did. "What say you?" he asked, puzzled.

"Good heavens, Baldwin. Are you going to make me beseech you?"

"I don't understand," he said. She couldn't mean what he thought she did.

"Blast it, do I have to spell it out?"

"Just say what you want of me, clear and simple."

"I require *deflowering*. Take me to bed, damn it. Is *that* straightforward enough for you?"

"Oh, aye, Kat." He chuckled. "That's clear, but surely it is *not* simple. My answer, in the unlikely event you're not jesting, is no." He yawned and stretched, the muscles of his chest obvious beneath the soft fabric of his shirt.

"You promised," Kat insisted.

"Bravo!" he laughed. "You excel at acting like an impudent little girl denied a sweet. Love isn't child's play, Kat. You don't take on a man to give you instruction at it as you contract for lessons upon the harpsichord. What in blazes will you come up with next?" He laughed, then brought her hand to his lips. "I'm off to bed now, Kat . . . to sleep. Alone," he added, striding from the kitchen.

She stood where she was until she heard a stair creak, always the fourth one, under his tread. "Gwyn!" she called, setting off after him. "Keep my tatterdemalion gang of little urchins indoors until the storm subsides. And keep them quiet, please."

"Quiet? Them lot? How?"

"Just keep feeding them, tell them stories, teach them to write their names on slates, use your inventiveness. And Gwyn, please heat water for Baldwin's bath and have the scullery girls tote the buckets to his room right quick," she added, her mouth set with determination and her eyes all mischief and sparks.

Chapter 3

"You are no gentleman to go back on your word." Kat, standing with her back against the closed door of Win's room, spoke in a smoky-sweet voice and smiled.

"You are no lady to ask me to ravish you, Kat. What role are you attempting to play now? Humorist or bawd?" Win asked, patting the crown of her head in a patronizing, indulgent way. "Whichever, you're not good at it."

"Neither," she answered.

Her unwavering eyes were the clear green of tropic seas—blue green, aqua green, lovely. Tropical waters were warm and enticing, Win knew, but though a man might see to the very floor of the sea, he could not judge its depth—or a woman's—without diving in. Win rarely passed up a chance to take a plunge. *But not* this *time, Beaumarais, not with* this *woman, not* Kat, he cautioned himself.

"Marjory Faunt is a true lady by birth and marriage. She proposed a like endeavor to you. I heard her."

"I never thought you'd be peeping at keyholes and eavesdropping, Kat."

"Gwyn was frightful busy that night, and I was coming round with the tray of edibles and beverage you'd ordered. I didn't mean to spy on you. I didn't put my eye to the keyhole but . . . I heard."

She blushed so prettily, Win had to smile also. "Be at ease. Such things occur, though more often by design than happenstance. You know, Kat, Marjory Faunt is a seemly, young, wedded woman, no virginal romantic dreamer. She and I were merely pleasuring each other, no more. She was not in love with me nor I with her, not then or now."

"Do you mean to pleasure her again?" Kat asked in a low voice.

"Well, and why not, should the convenient occasion present itself?" Win replied, irked by what he took for a reproof.

"Well, and why not pleasure *me* and allow me to do the same for you? Now would seem a convenient occasion." She slid home the bolt of the door.

"How now, my dear little fool?" He laughed, his fists set on his hips. "This line of talk has gone far enough. It begins to fret me, so harken well to what I say, Kat. You do me great honor with such a simple-seeming, generous offer, but the first time a woman is taken by a man, the proceeding may not be any pleasure at all, painful rather. Now, let us finish with our finances. If we have had profit enough this past twelvemonth, we can buy the inn you want—the one on the Canterbury Road." He turned away from her and strode to the table, where he randomly riffled the pages of a ledger.

"It would not be painful for *you*, Beau, to deflower *me*—I know that much. So why do you fuss so?"

"Quit, Kat, you persevering damsel! You know nothing of the lusty pastimes men and women sport at, no matter what you've imagined or been told by your confidantes or overheard through the closed doors of this establishment."

"You've described my dilemma in a thimble. I've heard a great deal and experienced nothing. I wish to learn. Who better than you to enlighten me?"

"*Any* other man, that's who'd be better. Blast it, Kitten, many a girl falls hard and steadfast in love with the man who rends her maidenhead. If you were even to suspicion you were in love with me . . ."

Kat's heart lurched with joy. He had used his particular pet name for her, something he'd not done in a good while. She was beginning to sway him!

"And what if we did fall in love?" he asked, his eyes narrowing.

"With each other?" she asked. He nodded, his long hair falling forward to shade his brow and conceal his eyes as he undid the fastenings of his shirt.

"I'm counting on it," Kat answered, winking broadly, approaching to help him with his buttons. "Would that be *so* disagreeable to you?"

"It would ruin everything." His voice was rough as he caught and held her hands against his chest.

"I'd be so *good* for you, Win. I know what you need better than anyone, better than you know yourself."

"But you're my friend, Kat." His half-lidded eyes revealed flashes of emerald green heat. It was a serious moment. It passed almost instantly.

"Have you never been a friend to any of your ladies?" she asked, catching his shirt as he dropped it.

"Well, certes, in a way, but not like this. Not like you and me."

"We'll still be friends when it's over—closer than ever. Don't you trust me, Win?"

"I can't take the gamble. You mean too much to me to muddy the waters with an amour."

"Don't be silly, Beau. You of course *know* you're not in love with me even a little and never could be. There's precious little danger I'll fall in love with you. How could I?

I know you too well—all your faults and flaws and stubborn ways. I'm merely asking a little favor of you, is all, as a friend."

"Why?" he demanded with an exasperated frown.

"Why not give yourself to your husband, whoever *that* may be, presumably this suitor of yours."

"He has been thrice widowed, the last time two years ago. The earl is an older man, his raven hair tinged with snow. He's lonely, he has said, and wishes to wed, but not to dally again with a maid. He has had his fill of green girls, he has said also, and of temperamental young noble ladies. He thinks me sound-thinking, he said, and seemly, too, though he assumes I am a practiced woman, not a virginal, romantic dreamer. Is that not the way you described me?"

"Do you mean to wed a venerable old chap?" Win asked doubtfully.

"I'm considering marriage to a mellowed gentleman, not an ancient. Harry has not quite so many years upon him as King Henry, who also now seeks a wife, his sixth, to entertain and comfort him in his advancing years."

"No older than the king? Kat, I mean no disrespect to our sovereign, but Henry is into his fifty-second year—balding, paunchy, huge, wrinkled, and peevish. He took a nineteen-year-old bride and then could not please her. Catherine made a cuckold of a king and lost her head for it."

"Catherine Howard was known to be a most flirtatious and forward virgin at fourteen. By fifteen, Harry says, she was doing more than finger exercises with her harpsichord instructor. Harry says if she'd not been a silly twit, so brazen as to bring the man to court as her secretary, but kept him nearby for her convenience, she might have had her cakes and ale and kept the king. There's more to marriage than huffing and puffing and four bare legs in bed, Harry says."

"Damnation, who is this well-informed, chatty *Harry* you keep citing?"

"Harry de Morely," she said in a voice so small that Win wondered if he had heard her correctly.

"Ah, Harry de Morely, Earl of Norland. *That Harry*?" he asked skeptically. Kat nodded. "I congratulate you upon an outstanding conquest. The earl has been pursued by every aristocratic widow in England and by every well-connected family with a marriageable daughter, some even younger than you. And here's Katesby Dalton, a commoner of very modest means, an unassuming London innkeeper, taking her good time, considering his offer."

"What would you advise me to do? Leap at it?" Kat smiled and shrugged.

"One thing I cannot in all good conscience advise is that you reject the suit of one of the wealthiest, most powerful men in the kingdom."

"So you *are* counseling me to wed Norland?" Kat queried, suddenly aware her heart might break, then and there, if Win was able to tell her straight out to become another man's wife. Kat braced herself to hear the worst. The morning sun was in her eyes and streaking her long, thick, tawny mane. The tilt of her chin was valiant, her willowy body perfectly still even though Win was gazing at her strangely, silently.

How pretty she was and poised, he mused, staring at Kat as though, familiar as she was, he'd never really looked at her before. He tried to foresee life without her, to imagine her anywhere other than beside him. He was finding that difficult, nearly impossible. "Do you . . . esteem Norland?" he asked after a tense silence.

"He is most kind. There's something forlorn about him that tugs at my heart."

"You . . . favor him?"

"Yes, I like him. I am marvelously well pleased by his company."

"And he by yours or he'd not have proposed wedlock."

"That would seem so. We are easy together, compatible, the earl and myself."

"You and he are friends then, you and the earl, as you and I are friends?"

"Not like *us,* Beau, not so close. No one could ever take your place in my heart, but there was an instant warmth and liking with me and Harry. He came to the inn by chance, being nearby at Temple Bar, seeing to a legal matter with one of his yeoman, who is owed a sum of pence by—"

"Has he kissed you?" Win demanded gruffly.

"Harry's yeoman? Heavens, no!" Kat jibed.

"Stop jesting, Kat. You know I mean Harry. Has *he* kissed you?" Win waited upon her answer with particular intensity, Kat realized. It mattered to him.

"Yes," she replied.

"How? Where?"

"Nicely. In the kitchen."

"Kat!" Win cautioned ominously.

"You are going on at me like the king's interrogator in the Tower. Will you put me to the rack next?"

"Worse, if you don't answer directly."

"Harry has kissed me upon the hand only. What's happened to your famous good humor?" she asked as Win exhaled dramatically.

"Does he wish an heir of you?"

"No. He has two sons of his second wife. They are now at Clare College, Cambridge, where you attended."

"I was a sizar, the lowliest of poor scholars, with so small an allowance that I served at table in exchange for my rations at the buttery. Quite unlike Norland's sons, no doubt. If not an heir, what does he require of you, Kat?"

"He wishes me to ease his lonesomeness, to bring 'vivacity and gregariousness,' he says, to his households. Also to manage the daily business of his estates, dairies, breweries, oversee his household servants—"

"Keep count of his pewter goblets and sterling plate. Be his caretaker, housekeeper, his—"

"To be his *wife*, blast you, in every way." It was a rare show of temper for Kat. He had made her angry, Win realized.

"I'm sorry, Kat," he offered. "But what you're asking is passing strange."

"Lady Seton has readily agreed to school me in the proper manner of dress and speech and comportment for the wife of an earl. I only ask that you further my advancement. The earl wants none of the inconvenience of a virgin. My locale, the nature of my vocation, my 'friendly, unaffected manner,' he said, led him to think me . . . experienced. Give me some experience, please, Win. Just take my maidenhead and be done with it."

"There's a mite more to lovemaking than that, Kitten," he answered with an affectionate laugh, "and this conversation is absurd."

" 'Tisn't absurd. Help me, as a kind friend, get ahead in life, as you said I should. Harry wants a worldly woman for his third wife. He thinks I am that. Come, Beau! I'll not likely ever have such an offer again, you know."

"Nor will I, I don't suppose," he conjectured, shaking his head with disbelief.

"I trust you to teach me. We're not in love, you and me, but we are friends. Win, if not you, who can I turn to for help in this? Will you suggest another . . . ?"

"No!" he roared, starting to pace, amused but also bemused now by her persistence. "I won't have any part of your preposterous scheme, and I forewarn you not to commence a union with duplicity. Tell the earl the truth, that you're a virgin. If he can't accept you as you are, don't wed the man."

"Really, Beau," Kat cajoled. "It will mean so much to Harry, and little if anything, to us. Not much, leastways."

"Won't mean anything?" he asked with an incredulous, green-eyed stare. "The girl's daft," he said to the ceiling.

"Win, I think I'm cold. In that way, I mean. I've never felt the least heat for a man. I don't think there's much likelihood I'll become all stirred up and passionate, nor be much pleased by this deflowering activity, so you needn't worry."

"You'll feel more than you can conceivably imagine, Katesby, if you and I were to do this thing." Evidently she'd struck a sensitive place in him, Kat realized. He wasn't laughing at her anymore.

Drat, he thought, he *just might have to* give her what she was asking of him, give her a jolt of passion, make her feel the hot ache of desire building, erupting, the urgency to feel it again and again. After all, he owed her that as a friend. It might be her one chance, if she wed old Norland, to know what a lusty young man could do. "Don't be so certain you'll be able, afterward, to say, 'Thank you, kind sir,' to me and walk off."

"What will I say?" Kat asked, aware Win was seriously considering her request. He had a soft spot, and she'd struck it. She *still had* a prayer, by heaven, of making him fall in love with her.

"If the thing is well and rightly done, as I would do it, you'll be so heated, your iciness, that indifference to men will ever after be banished. Verily, you may find yourself in a condition of recurring craving. After a few lessons from me, I give you fair warning, you'll say forthwith, 'I want more, please, sir," he grinned.

"Do you mean to say that after rutting but once, one is afflicted with a craving such as a drunkard's thirst for spirits?"

"Not precisely, Kat," Win answered, barely able to keep his laughter at bay. She was priceless, dearly naive, and much in need of his care and protection—that or an impish prankster.

"Perhaps 'tis more like to an abiding malady, such as wool-sorter disease or softening of the brain, from which one never recovers?" she pressed. "Is that why the company of women has been your primary diversion since first I saw you with a wanton wench? *Now I understand!*" she nodded sagely. "Win, when I have said, 'More please,' what will you reply?"

"Not 'I love you.' Be warned. If you come crying to me later, I'll comfort you, but all the while I'll be saying I told you so. I've been with girls aplenty, Kat," he added with feigned nonchalance. "You will be one more pleasure, however fleeting."

He was toying with her, ready to teach her a love lesson she'd not forget. She'd be "stirred" by *him* all right, and marvelously well pleased, before he'd done with her. They stood face-to-face, smiling a little, their eyes alight, both knowing some die had been cast, a decision made, both knowing, also, that nothing would ever again be the same between them. "We'll go at it slow and easy, Kitten," Win promised, setting his hands on her shoulders.

"When do we start?" she asked directly, though scared all at once. For some girls, she had been told, the first time was easy and led straight to indescribable, blissful pleasure. For others, it was torment.

"Now?" he asked, lowering his mouth toward hers.

There was a thump at the door.

"Better wait," Kat answered and with immense relief admitted a procession of three prattling scullery girls toting buckets which were emptied into an oblong leaden basin not unlike a laundry tub, though deeper. Win had brought the enormous thing home from his last voyage. It had required near to a dozen men and more than a hundred oaths to get the Turkish bath up the stairs and into Win's rooms, and there it had stood, close to the hearth, unmoved since.

"Welcome home, Mr. Beaumarais," said the first girl in a flirty singsong tone, as she batted her black lashes.

"Thank you, Jeannie," Win replied, smiling broadly. "It's good to be here. You get prettier every time I see you again."

"Did you have a good voyage, Mr. Beaumarais?" asked the younger one with a shy yet seductive little giggle.

"Fine, thank you, Jenny. You know, I cannot say if 'tis you or your sister who is the more comely wench of the pair or you," he replied, sending them both into paroxysms of titters.

"Get on with you, you naughty girls!" exclaimed the third, an older woman in her thirties, as she shooed, then followed the others from the room.

"You've a pair of handsome daughters, Jilly Goodkind!" Win called after them.

"I've got to watch 'em like a very hawk, sir, though neither of 'em yet holds a candle to her mother, aye?" asked Jilly, poking her head back into the room. "If you should be wanting for anything, sir, anything at all, you've only to summon me," she leered. "Don't be standing about half undressed as you are now, nor when you're dripping wet after your soak, or you'll catch your death. I never did hold with this getting wet all over," she admonished, closing the door after her.

"Heaven help the woman who weds you, Beaumarais!" exclaimed Kat. "She'll never have a moment's respite from licentious ladies putting themselves in your way."

"And now I've you, too, to contend with in that way. Is there no rest for the wicked?" He sighed dramatically, glancing heavenward. "Close your eyes Kat, or you might lose all self-control at the sight of me bare naked. Close your eyes and open your mouth. Talk to me before I'm overcome by sleep." He yawned.

"Why close my eyes now, after we've decided?"

"Now that you've extracted this absurd promise from me, to give you love lessons, I must go at it leisurely or risk scaring you off like a startled kitten."

"Try scaring *me* off, Beaumarais," Kat replied with determined, if forced valor. "I dare you."

Chapter 4

"Shall we ever begin or wilt thou soak eternally there in that colossal washbowl?" Kat asked.

She meandered about the room, adjusting a candlestick here, a chair there, trying to appear calm, though she wasn't.

Win had gotten out of his breeches, his back to her, a quilt draped over his broad shoulders like a cape, until he let it drop and stepped over the side of the tub. Living close as Win and Kat did, she mistress of an inn and he a man of unassuming directness, the sight of his, and many another man's, naked back wasn't any novelty to her. But *this* glimpse, in the present circumstance, of Baldwin's long-muscled, bare back and the compact swell of his rounded flanks took her breath away, and she knew their friendship already had changed though they'd yet even to kiss. Perhaps he was right, that it was a mistake to tamper with what they had together. She studied Win's clean-shaven, lean, honed profile as he rested his head back against the rim of the tub. His bronze hair, wet, appeared darker. The lashes of his half-closed eyes were long and cast shadows on his face when he languidly turned his emerald-green eyes to her.

"Please pour in the last bucket of water, eh, Kat?" he asked. "And quieten yourself. Naught will happen—just yet."

"When?" she asked, going to the hearth where the water was being kept warm by the fire.

"These things happen in their own way, at the proper time."

"When's that?" she fretted.

"You'll know."

"How?" she asked doubtfully, approaching the tub, a wooden bucket in hand. "Where do you want this?" she asked. Win sat straight up.

"Pour it over my head, as always." She did and he growled something incomprehensible, shaking his head. Water droplets flew from his hair and hissed on the hot stones of the hearth.

"Water too cool? I'll send for more to be heated and brought up from the kitchen."

"Never you mind. Now stay near, Kat, right where you are, so you can towel my hair, as always."

"Your servant, *sir*," she jibed, dropping a thick turkey cloth over his head and buffing vigorously.

"Ow! Have a care! Be soft, wench, as though you were caressing a valued object, a precious jewel, not rough as a scullion scouring an old copper kettle."

"This is how I always towel your hair. I've done it countless times, and you never have complained before."

"This is a special occasion, aye?"

"Seems the same as usual so far," Kat demurred, though lightening her touch.

"That's better." Win smiled, resting back again, looking at her upside down as she leaned over him. "Now we'll do something a bit out of the ordinary. Just right quick, as if you're testing the warmth of bubbling broth and taking care not to burn your tongue, put your lips on mine, just for a trice.

"Tolerable well done," he said when she pecked at his mouth and pulled away as though she *had* been scalded. "Do that yet again, a mite more leisurely. Oh, and give me a mere dart of your tongue." Win closed his eyes and waited. Kat's long hair fell forward, a silken tent about their faces when she set her hands, one to each side of him on the tub rim, and leaned her mouth to his. When he flicked the tip of his tongue at her rigid lips, they softened and parted. His hand came up to rest on the crown of her head to steady her, and then his mouth opened wide. Her tongue withdrew from the thrust of his before her mouth closed tightly.

"Mmph," she said, swallowing a laugh behind his gorgeous back. "How was that?"

"A slight improvement. Fair to middling, for the outset. Leastways you didn't bite off my tongue."

"Shall I try again?" she asked with a sweetly mocking air. He laughed.

"Not yet. First, set the hearth stool at the head of the tub, sit yourself upon it, and rub my back." When he sat upright and leaned forward, she saw rippling muscles flex down to his narrow waist, where her view became obscured by the sudsy bathwater. It was a temptation to Kat to let her fingers follow, exploring all down his spine. She resisted the enticement.

"And how is *this*?" she asked, briskly buffeting and chaffing him about the neck and shoulders.

"You are not pounding dough for a loaf of coarse oat bread," he protested. "Think you, when you touch either side of my neck, of kneading the most excellent flour for the *primarius panis*, for the finest white wheaten bread, of the sort baked only in the ovens of nobles and high gentry.

Carefully shape the loaf, skillfully smooth it. Ah, yes," he sighed. "Perfect."

"I've always been a skillful baker, you know. Now, what am I to imagine when I am working along *here*?" she asked as she ran a fingertip down his supple spine.

"You must spread wide both hands, like butterflies with gentle wings, and touch as though you were fondling fine velvet cloth. Ah . . . just so." He exhaled, letting his eyes drift closed after stealing a quick look at Kat. Her eyes, contemplating his back and shoulders, were filled with admiration, and something more, a certain warmth. "Now stroke me all up and down and, while you're about it, tell me of the inn you think we should purchase—if you do *not* wed Harry de Morely, that is."

"You cannot mean me to talk commerce and trade, as usual, *now*?" she asked, nonplussed.

"Would you prefer that I rise up out of my bath and rend you like a dragon, Kat?" he asked softly. "I'm not ready, even if you are." Her fingers on his shoulders gripped harder. He reached back and placed his hands over hers and reclined to look up at her again. "Talking business, as usual, will perhaps put you more at ease. If you're overwrought and tense as you seem to be, the love lesson may go harder for you. So relax. Talk to me a while."

"Talk? But what of?"

"Oh . . . tell me about the inn in the countryside."

"It is hard by the Salisbury Plain, where your grazing lands lie, and only a short way from Warminster. The distance to Codford is ten miles, from Codford to Amesbury ten miles, from Amesbury to . . ."

Kat, unbidden, touched her lips to the jointure of Win's neck and shoulder. Funny, she thought, she had never before noticed that particularly inviting curve. She raised her head in time to see a corner of Win's mouth flick in a smile.

"Why'd you do that?" he asked in rich, low voice. "Do you know why?"

"Felt like, that's why," she answered in a murmur. "Because you're a right snout-fair rakehell with *quarroms* to match."

"Do it again, eh, Kat, and then tell me once more, but in right proper English, why. See, I don't mind you slipping back into the street jargon" —he chuckled—"truly, I rather favor it. It stirs me, see, but I doubt your earl will countenance his countess speaking like a *dell.*"

"For truth, that's what I am, a *dell* waiting for you to change me into a *doxy.*"

"Nay, you'll never be a doxy. You're too much a lady at heart. If, in the cant of the streets, a dell's a virgin vagrant miss, you only partly fit the description. You are unbedded, sure, but you're no longer a vagrant and never will be again. Why, just think on it, Kat, you may soon be a genuine titled lady and 'tis possible you shall be thoroughly unsuited to the designation of virgin as well." Feeling awkward now, and self-conscious, Kat nuzzled the other side of Win's strong neck.

"You're a handsome-faced rake with a . . . an outstanding body of estimable muscles to match." She giggled. "There. I've kissed you and said why."

"And you've not even seen the best of me yet. I think there's a prayer, Kat, a decent likelihood, that you could be a mite stirred up by a man, even if you never have felt the least heat for one. I can't promise, mind, but I wager I'll be able to quicken you into something of a passionate condition. Help me, will you, by slipping off that shapeless dress?"

"What? And stand here in me shift?" she exclaimed.

"Or less," he replied. "And not stand there for long."

"Ah. But I've not done talking about trade and commerce, see? Now, from Amesbury to Andover is near fifteen miles" —Kat hurriedly took up where she had left off—"not as the crow flies, mind, but along the well-traveled high road to London and Oxford. The hostelry is one of the choice inns along the way, with beds enough for near a hundred callers, and fine napery for the table, and bed linens enough to give each visitor new-washed sheets unused by any other before, and there's grand stabling and . . . oh?"

Win had taken Kat's hand and brought the palm to his lips.

"Go on," he said. "Don't let me stop you. Grand stables you say?"

"No, you go on," she answered. Her tone was playfully mocking, but there was a quaver in her voice. "See, I think I'm stirring some. Leastways I'm wanting . . . something." Win felt her hands, strong and cool, resting on the muscles of his upper arms.

"You've no notion what stirring is, not yet, Kitten," he said lazily. She liked the remarkable look in his smoldering green eyes and his slow smile, one she'd never seen before but deemed many another women had.

"And are you a'tall, well . . . a mite . . . stirred and . . . ?" she asked with trepidation.

"I'm not feeling quite . . . dragon-like," he said, and smiled to calm her again. She nodded, knelt beside the tub, and rested her chin on her laced hands on the rim. "But I am stirred. Look." He directed her with his eyes. Though he hadn't appeared to move, something stirred below his waist, breaking the surface of the bathwater.

"I think . . . perhaps . . . you should rise out of there," she suggested, dipping her fingers. "Before that cold water chills you to the bone."

"I don't want to affright you," he rasped. Now he was grasping for words, to avoid sounding vain or boastful.

" . . . with the prodigiousness of your full splendor? I'm a virgin, not an unsuspecting, timorous twit," Kat answered steadily, though her heart thundered.

"I know you've seen much, but not, I gather from what you've told me, what I have to show." He grinned.

"I'll look only quickly, to avoid swooning. And perhaps I'll touch if you think it wise and safe for me to do that." The sweet mockery was back in her voice, and there was a taunting twinkle in her eyes. She wasn't taking this with sufficient seriousness, Win thought. It irked him. He grasped her hand, plunged it into the water, and drew it down over his taut belly.

"Feel that?" he asked. She nodded, not speaking or moving except to hesitantly gauge by touch what her eyes had yet to measure. She was not feeling nearly as reckless and sassy as she had been a moment before.

"If you're going to touch, you may as well stroke, eh?" Win suggested helpfully.

"How, exactly?" A faint pink colored her cheeks.

"Don't be shamefast. I'll teach you. That's what we're doing here, is it not? Just . . . so." He nodded, his glowing eyes holding hers as he folded her fingers about him and moved her hand down under the waterline again.

"Could you do it now, the deflowering? Are you ready?" Kat asked anxiously.

"I could, yes," he answered. "But I will not."

"Why not?" she asked, relief and disappointment causing her to breathe an inward sigh. "When will you?"

"When your enthusiasm is greater."

"Oh, come! I've steeled myself for the thing, and now you set new conditions? I couldn't be more eager to have this done with, Win."

"I think you'll be a deal more eager," he promised, "not to have it done with." She flushed again, whether with irritation or chagrin he wasn't certain. "Hand me the towel, eh, Kat?" When she did, he stood, hurriedly enfolding his waist at the same time, but not before she'd seen what he'd tried to conceal. He stepped out of the tub, took her hand, led her to the hearth. She was wide-eyed and unprotesting, though she blushed a lovely shade of rose when he lifted her dress over her head. She wore nothing beneath it. He took a gulp of air. There in the glow of firelight was the loveliest, fullest, roundest, narrowest, most perfect feminine form his eyes had ever grazed. She had wide, though delicate shoulders and long, long coltish legs which suggested a girlishness belied by a shapely indentation of waistline and a swell of rose-tipped breasts. "My God, Kat, why have you been concealing all this . . . this perfection?"

"Don't tease me, not now," she implored, hiding her face in her hands. His parted them and raised her chin so she would look into his eyes.

"I speak all in earnest. You're made perfect and lovely. I've never seen the like." He smiled softly as he drew her against him, then kissed her mouth carefully, gently. She felt the fleeting pressure of his tongue against her lips before she became aware of the pressure of his hand at the base of her spine, his protrusion pressing against her belly, his lips at her ear. When his tongue first grazed the tip of her breast, she felt as if a raw nerve had been struck. She was the one to gasp then. "Oh, dear," she said.

"Put your arms about my neck," he suggested, "if you'd like to."

"I would," she said and did. Now, the kiss was stronger, longer. Her lips parted, his tongue surged, filling her mouth until she stepped away.

"Don't be fearful," he said with tender regard. "What's wrong?"

"Naught. Only I've a curiosity to look at you, all of a piece."

"Look, but best not touch, eh?" he said, letting the towel drop. He grinned and shrugged, confounded to find himself on display, being measured by her innocently admiring eyes.

"I knew you were a well-made man, Beau, but I'd not adequately imagined the strength, nor fully prized the fine proportion and balance of your muscles. And I'd no actual idea of the . . . amazing asymmetry. Why not touch again?" she asked. "I did before."

"Well . . . touch, but not where nor as you did before lest this love lesson end sooner than you'd like, before its purpose is accomplished. If you ask me why, I will think you really are a twit."

"Before it begins, rightly." She nodded with a blink of her immense eyes.

"Enough gawking," he said roughly, reaching for her, drawing her to him so that their bodies brushed at lips and thighs while his hands on her haunches brought her belly firmly against his. "The best kiss, so far," he said in a raveled voice before Kat felt herself lifted from her feet. Again she hid her face, now against his throat as he carried her across the room to the bed. They were both shivering, she with a desire to kiss some more and with a fatalistic fear —it *was* about to happen—and he, still wet from head to foot, with cold. "There's a hot brick here under the comforter, heating the bed," she said, smiling up at him, wan and pale.

"De Morely will find there are great advantages to having a former innkeeper for a wife," he said wryly, toweling off before sliding into bed beside her. She looked like a trapped, frightened little animal as she moved as far away from him as it was possible to get without tumbling out the far side of the bed.

"I don't wish to discuss Harry now," she stated, lying as straight as a stick, her fear revived.

"What do you wish to discuss?" he asked, moving closer but taking care their bodies didn't touch. Leaning on an elbow, he looked down at her. She appeared in equal measure determined and terrified.

"Naught," she answered. Her fists were clenched at her sides. He took her near hand, unfolded her fingers one by one, laced them with his own, and began to talk softly of his recent travels, unhurriedly wooing her, for a time, with his voice alone.

Chapter 5

"We sailed far into the Mediterranean Sea, past Spain and Italy, through the islands of the Greeks, to the clear Aegean. Many of the lands along the shores we passed had been ravaged, in recent memory, by marauders from the sea led by a shrewd, brilliant Algerian, Kahyr ad-Din. He sails as First Admiral under the flag of the Ottoman Sultan Suleiman, designated 'Suleiman the Great' for his supremacy as a ruler of men and his fighting spirit. The admiral ad-Din, who is called by the Italians *Barbarossa,* for his red beard, battles to thwart the Spaniards' great fleet, and the Spaniard King Charles's driving ambition to reconquer lands now ruled over by the sultan. Only some months before we sailed into those waters, ad-Din had halted the most recent effort of Charles to repossess Tripolitania, Algiers, Tunisia, Morroque . . ."

"Such names must fit wondrous places. Speak them over again for me, Beau?" Kat asked dreamily.

"Morroque . . . Tunisia . . . Algeria . . . Tripolitania," Baldwin intoned, brushing a few riotous ringlets back from

Kat's brow, "named together the Barbary States, for they were wrested from the grip of Spain by Barbarossa and his men."

"Where are those wondrous places?" Kat asked, the curls tumbling over her brow again.

"Along the northern shores of Afrique, where we were seized by a grandson of ad-Din, Hasan, a boy perhaps all of seventeen, maneuvering a small, swift fleet of his own. Seeing the young commander in action was an inspiration to Blaidd Kyd, I tell you."

"You—in the *Conquest,* with Captain Bolling, Kyd, and the rest—were seized by the infidel? And you said not a word of it to me until now? And you've been here for hours? Beau!" Kat felt a swell of relief and affection tinged with annoyance that he'd jeopardized himself. She was so distracted by her now irrelevant fear for him that she forgot her qualms and moved closer to him. When he slid his arm about her shoulders, she made no demur.

"Divulge the particulars with haste, if you please, Beaumarais. Say how you got away and came safe home. Tell me all about it."

"We passed hard to leeward of the Isle of Rhodes, where Hasan's ships were hidden in a cove. We tried to outrun him, but game as the *Conquest* is, she's not a match for an oared fighting galleon."

"This Hasan could have made galley slaves of you all, as the infidels have of so many Spaniards. There you'd have been, all alone in a dark cell, not knowing day from night, never hearing a friendly human voice in a familiar tongue. I'd not ever have seen you again, unless I begged, stole, borrowed, sold off all we own to try to buy your freedom. It would have taken *years,*" Kat moaned, shaking her head with disapproval. "How did you escape that fate?"

"I taught Hasan a game of cards new to him—piquet."

"I know you make fast friends wherever you go, but to

rescue yourself and your shipmates with a game of *piquet?* That seems quite the feat, even for so great a charmer as you."

"I'd make a friend of the devil himself, if need be, so I wouldn't have to be alone for long. But you're right. It wasn't just a game of cards which saved us. I also gave the boy captain Dorsey Dibdin's twelve-step alchemical formula for turning lead into gold. I explained calcination, one of the early stages of the thing, and the conjunction of the planets which must occur, also early in the process, about luting . . ."

"Stuff and nonsense! He did not attempt the experiment else you would be a galley slave by now. Surely, if lead could be turned to gold, Dorsey would have done it by now and he'd be rich, not telling fortunes for shillings and always in risk of being collared by priests and witch hunters. And what may *luting* be?" asked Kat with gentle derision.

"I am startled at your backwardness in this, Katesby!" he teased, drawing her closer against him. "Luting means to encase an object in thick clay, to protect it from the great heat needed for the alchemical process to progress."

"A certain heat, I've heard, is necessary for various processes to progress." She laughed softly. "Go on, do."

"I drew the black crow symbol for Hasan, like this." Baldwin's hand traced a shape upon Kat's back. "And . . . the dragon symbol." His fingers moved again, and his hand went below her waist. She quivered. He did not withdraw. Rather, his touch grew firm and his hands encompassed her bottom. "*Perfectly formed,*" he breathed. "*Preferable to gold.*"

"What say you?" she asked fearfully, going taut against him. "A . . . dragon?"

"The symbol of a dragon," he said, not releasing her, "is for imperfect stuff that will never become gold, no matter the sagacity of the alchemist. I spoke to Hasan of augmentation of materials," he went on in a gravelly voice, swelling against her flat stomach, "and about projection, the final alchemical stage when the philosophers' red stone actually transforms dross to gold."

"And your boy-corsair truly *believed* you?" Kat asked, arching her body away from Baldwin. He relaxed his hold reluctantly.

"I will not swear to that," he said with a long, whistling breath, "but Hasan did enjoy our company. In return, he gave us our freedom and a parchment written upon in Arabic and in Latin, stamped with the sultan's seal, to ensure our safe passage, now and always, through Barbary seas. We became friends. He bade me return in a twelvemonth, to rendezvous with him and his renowned father at the Isle of Rhodes."

Watching Kat from a little distance, feeling the loss of her in his arms, Baldwin continued talking to calm her, his tone casual, soothing, yet also subtly seductive. "The place is now governed by Suleiman. It has been since the sultan's forces under Barbarossa chased the warrior Knights Hospitallers from the place. The Hospitallers, who came to be called The Knights of Rhodes, had long before—two hundred years—driven the Saracens from the same island. They had fought off the Turks, been under siege for fifty years, until Barbarossa finally won the capitulation of the warrior knights. They moved on. Now they are the Knights of Malta, and Rhodes has become Hasan's home port, from which he sallies forth in his fast ships to wage war against the Spanish fleet and vessels of other Christian realms.

"Barbarossa and his corsairs continue to sweep the Mediterranean coasts of Christian lands, but Hasan has more ambitious plans, to venture past Gibraltar, sail into the Atlantic, and raid the west coast of Spain and Portugal, for captives. His inspiration is Julia Gonzaga, Duchess of Traietto, said to be the most beautiful noblewoman in all Europe. He took great delight in seizing her from the shores of Italy as she walked along the beach below her castle. She escaped."

"And if she had been pirated away," asked Kat, "what would her fate have been? Not to be made a galley slave, surely."

"Her captor would have been constrained to deliver an aristocratic beauty of great repute as a spoil of war to the padishah either to be ransomed or sequestered in his harem, the seraglio of Suleiman. It confines a thousand women, his wives and his concubines and captives, females of many forms and colors, of differing castes and ranks, from many lands, each one exquisite, it is said."

"Julia of Traietto would have been made a slave of another sort!" Kat exclaimed.

"I know 'tis difficult for you to suppose, Katesby, independent and cool as you are, but some women emphatically wish to be, dream of being, thus enslaved," Baldwin responded, restraining a grin, "by a powerful, adept man, with wealth beyond measure. But of the thousand beautiful females in the harem, all adorned, always in readiness, all schooled in the sensual arts . . ."

"Schooled? Taught, as you have agreed to teach me?"

"Not in the same way. There are no men in the harem but eunuchs. The women all belong to the sultan, but few are ever served by him. To be so favored, often for less than obvious reasons, for all are lovely, a girl must capture the attention and arouse the curiosity of this jaded man in the hope that she will please and interest him as no woman ever before has done."

"How does one female, among a thousand others as beautiful as she, earn a glance?" Kat asked in a tone a tone of skeptical derision.

"You've struck upon the very mystery, Katesby, of the allure between any man and woman. Sultans and slaves are no exception. Suleiman's mood may, on one night, lead him to single out a fiery, red-haired, bold-eyed consort, a great man's wife stolen from her husband. On another occasion, his need may be for a docile virgin, or a sweet-voiced singer of songs, or a clever girl with whom to talk of this and that, or for one less scintillating but more voluptuous." Baldwin's voice was soft and his eyes took on a musing, distant expression.

"Is that every man's dream, to have an infinite selection of women, a sultan's harem?" Kat interrupted Baldwin's reverie. He smiled.

"I can't answer for every man. My own fantasy, Kitten, is to find all the qualities I require embodied in one perfect woman."

"Impossible," she declared.

"Perhaps not," he countered. "I can dream, can I not? Well, and howsoever he chooses her, Suleiman's companion is bathed and groomed and polished and perfumed even more exactly than she usually is. Then each begins her night in the same way. She is left at Suleiman's door to enter his chamber alone, to find him abed, awaiting her. On her knees she approaches, lifts silken covers at the Sultan's feet, slips in, slides upward very slowly, using her hands and mouth as she goes, as she has been taught to do. Her object is to arouse his lust, her great hope to engage his more abiding interest. 'Tis a challenge to a girl, eh?" Baldwin's eyes were full of mischief as he observed Kat try to contain her indignation.

"A challenge indeed. How did the Duchess of Traietto avoid such a widely sought-after fate?" she asked with disdain.

"Hasan wants her for himself. He helped free her from Barbarossa. Now the love-struck boy swears to take the lady and run with wind the next time she is in residence at her Fondi castle. She has agreed to signal with a torch and await him at the edge of the sea, or so he boasts."

"Perhaps she has not heard what I have. It is said by

travelers stopping here at the inn that infidels are cruel and . . ."

"Can you not guess that she is in love?"

"In love with a marauding bandit who does not fight honorably, as do we and our forbears, the Romans, the Franks, the Gauls, the Knights Crusader of Briton, King Richard and others of his renown, who searched among infidels for the Holy Grail?"

"Where gods converge, honor, like beauty, is in the eye of the beholder. Would you deem it honorable of the Roman general who blinded all the hundreds of conquered men of Zagoria, all but the one, a boy who was left with sight in one eye so that he could guide the others wandering to beg about the world, as a warning to Rome's enemies? And what of the Spaniards, followers of the true faith, who make galley slaves not only of infidels but of *Englishmen*, taken prisoner in land battles or on the sea?"

"The Papist King Charles, who has been anointed emperor, wants to rule over all the world as he now rules over the Continent. I have heard statesmen and other travelers talking of it, in the tavern. He is Henry's chiefest rival for power, a foe and threat to our England. If it becomes bantered about and generally known, Beaumarais, that the wanted knave, Win Chance, avowed enemy and humbler of spymaster Wiltenham and of Rattcliffe the torturer, does consort with England's other enemy, infidel looters and plundering corsairs who take our ships and goods, Chance may have 'traitor' and 'pirate' added to his list of villainous by-names and misnomers. Chance has foes enough as it is. He is wanted as a cutthroat, a cutpurse, a highwayman, and a rabble-rouser who scoffs at the law of the land, makes laughingstocks of London bailiffs and jackasses of hangmen by snatching men from the very gallows." Kat was seething.

"And I've delivered a woman or two as well," Baldwin said teasingly.

"You've confounded your share of powerful, wicked men who feed on corruption as kite birds and crows feed on decay, but take comfort. When Chance swings at Tyburn, the balladeers and pamphleteers of London will ensure his everlasting fame, akin to that of the hero Robin Hood, so much do the tyrannized common folk love Chance," Kat said with an ironic shrug.

"Win Chance will never hang, Kat. I promise you that."

"And what of Baldwin Beaumarais?" she asked. She received no reply. "Well, is it Chance or Beaumarais who will go, in a twelvemonth, to meet his new heathen friend at Rhodes?"

"Beau will go if Chance does not encounter Hasan before the year is out. Rather than return to Rhodes, where I've heard my footfalls echo upon ancient stone, I would sail away to look upon a new world—*Espanola.*" Win's voice, almost purring, lingered on the word and a longing look came into his eyes. "Hasan told to me the tale of a Moorish corsair, Dragut, once a galley slave of the Spaniard, now a lieutenant in Barbarossa's service. Dragut has seen the Isle of Española. He has agreed to escort Hasan and the willingly abducted Lady Julia there, after a rendezvous with me in England. The three will try to come ashore near Maldon at about the time of St. Swithin's feast day."

"In summer, when the light lasts long, Hasan, Dragut, and the runaway Duchess of Traietto will flaunt themselves just a few miles from London? That would be biting their thumbs under King Henry's Roman nose. There will no doubt be a handsome ransom or reward for the return of the duchess—that is, if she and her escort have avoided French and English warships while passing through the Dover Straights, hard by fortified English Calais. Why would sensible men or a sane woman do it?"

"For love and glory, of course. Kat, I cannot attest to, nor deny, Dragut's rationality, but Suleiman has signed a treaty with King Francis. Now the Turks and French are allied and fighting together against Charles. The sultan's ships have left French trading vessels in the Mediterranean unmolested, and the corsairs have naught to fear from the French. Dragut will smuggle Hasan, Julia, and himself ashore in England for the bravado of the adventure, and to further his plot against the Spanish, for whom he harbors an abiding hatred."

"But what can Baldwin Beaumarais, or Win Chance for that matter, offer these international intriguers? Indeed, what have they to tempt him?"

"I am acquainted with a number of influential English merchants and nobles. I have a circle of rich and powerful friends, soon to include your earl husband, de Morely. I am connected, positioned to enlist investments of riches in a trading venture to launch a galleon, outfit her with guns and cannon, staff her with English seamen, the fiercest sea fighters there are, to play a part in Dragut's assault on Española. There is vast wealth to be gained by loosing the New World from the Spaniard's stronghold."

"You actually do mean to become a pirate!"

"Not a pirate, Kat, a patriot. I will immeasurably enrich England's coffers," Baldwin explained, excitement in his voice and flashing eyes. "The Frenchman, Jean Fleury, took three Spanish galleons just off the Azores. They were loaded to the gunwales with New World gold and jewels. There was an emerald as large as my fist." Baldwin raised his clenched hand.

"And how will you find this new world?" Kat asked skeptically.

"With Hasan and Julia. And Dragut, who has drawn a chart from memory, a representation to guide adventurers to the shores of . . . Kat?" he questioned.

"Enough now of your bold ambition. Here am I, a would-be alchemist in need of heat to change an unremarkable girl into a woman, an adventuress of sorts, with no chart to guide me, only you," she whispered as she caressed him. "You must be my guide. Direct me, illuminate me, demonstrate how this part of you is . . . well, augmented," she said, her hand venturing about at the base of his belly. "Why are you not upright like a signpost as you were before?"

"Do you wish me to be?" Win asked with an intake of breath when her hand came to rest.

"I don't know. *Should* I want you . . . it . . . to rear up? Will it, if I so desire?"

"You may cause me to do your pleasure, once I have again got . . . like a signpost."

"Ah. Before you can pleasure me, this part of you must stand. What will induce that? Oh!" she whispered, pulling away her hand as she felt him stirring beneath her fingers.

"A word, a sigh, a pleasing sight. Particularly a deft touch. Don't stop now." He smiled, now as hard as a pikestaff beneath her caress, the memory of her perfect body guiding his own hands.

"Will it—this part—always stand at your whim or your command?"

"It has never failed yet," he boasted. "But now I'm at *your* command."

"Ah. And have I any like response you may call up in me?" She sighed dreamily, a bit breathlessly as his agitating of her breasts began to have its intended consequences.

"You have indeed," he whispered, brushing his lips to hers. "My effect upon you will be as governing, if not so conspicuous, as yours upon me," he promised.

"Do you mean a mere thought or view will pleasure me also?" she marveled.

He nodded.

"A thought or a glance may rouse sweet sensations in a woman."

"Sweet sensations? In truth, I've been feeling something unsettling odd and agreeable, for the most part," she mused, "since you . . ." She sat bolt upright. "Allow me to look upon you again, Beau, to determine if the sight of a man, entire and unclothed, will strengthen and sweeten these feelings I have. Stand and turn about, slowly."

"A look at just *any* man won't do the trick. Nor will *just* a look. I'd rather warm and please you by touching, just so, than posing."

"Let me look again, Beau, just for a moment, just to determine if a mere glimpse of you has a noticeable effect upon me." With a growl of protest, Win removed himself from the cozy quilts and bedclothes and the warmth of her body, stood, turned once about, and was ready to dive into bed again when she said with awed admiration, "See! It rises!"

"Because of the look in your eyes, your stare, your hungry voice. Because what I've seen of your body commands it." He was beside her again, pulling her nearer, moving against her.

"It never fails you, you said?" Her voice was low, her eyes half-lidded

"It will never fail you either." He laughed softly, seductively, before he lowered his mouth to hers, pressed her back and down, and slid closer to her. Her lips didn't part until he sighed, "In future, you will always and forever recall I was the one who taught you to . . . kiss, eh?" His hand, resting on her breast, moved to her waist, turning her to him, then slid down her back and deep between her thighs, his fingers going into her, the heel of his hand pressing in a way that made her weak and wild, and soon her legs enfolded his hips.

"Open your eyes and look at me, Kitten. Keep looking hard at me, into my eyes, no matter what you feel . . . pleasure or pain. . . ."

"Now?" she asked. " Now you're going to do it? Wait. Hold off. I fancy what you're doing to me at this moment, but I don't know if I'm ready for the rest of it, all the other. I . . . "

"*I* know. You are ready," he answered. He moved over and into her, forcing her body to slowly begin to soften and expand to take him in.

"What in blazes do you think you're doing?" she protested. "Blast, but you're hurting me, Beau! Stop this at once, do you hear?"

"I'm doing exactly . . . what you asked of me," he rasped, "and there's no stopping now." He thrust hard, harder, burying himself inside her as her fingernails imprinted his shoulders and she howled once, with pain and fury and elemental passion, just once, before he felt her spasm with pleasure and release beneath him.

"Well, there," he graveled, moving in and out of her with growing force and speed, until he, too, exploded, or so it seemed to Kat, with a deep-throated roar before, to her dismay, he stopped, still atop her, heavy and warm, sighing.

"Beau," she whispered. " Beau, I had no notion . . . of this."

"So. 'Tis done," he answered, his mouth against her ear, his arms about her as he rolled her above him.

"Is it?" she asked with poignant, innocent disappointment "Why?"

"Why?" he roared, this time with a bark of laughter. "Because you've been deflowered, that's why. Isn't that what you asked of me?"

"Isn't there more?"

"Well, there could be, if you'd like another, more advanced love lesson. Shall I illustrate further? Would you like me to?"

"I *would* like. Go on. Do that again and show me what more there is. Show me all of it . . . . everything."

"Not just yet." He grinned, raking back her long, silky hair with both his hands. "I'll demonstrate again. I'll soon teach you some more, show whatever you want to see, do . . . whatever, but all and everything? That would take time. How many nights do have we to practice?"

"Harry's been gone but three days. That gives us nearly a fortnight. Is that time enough?" She tossed back her hair and peered into the hot green glow of his smiling eyes.

"It will take all night, every night, but you'll likely get it right, I wot."

"What are we waiting for? What do you mean, you'll *soon* go on? When? For how long? Why not now?" She sighed, kissing his mouth. He was inside her still, and she felt him tauten before he pulled away. "Your conjecture was correct, Beau, don't you see? I *do* want more, please, sir," she teased, rephrasing his words.

"That was no conjecture, rather a matter of fact gleaned from prior experience in this. Ease off a mite, Kitten. It will be for the good to wait a bit. So, as you were saying, if you decline Harry and we do buy the inn on the Bath Road, who'll manage this place?"

"Gwyn Stark, if you agree. Oh, rats and plagues and speak of the devil! I'm being ranted after now, of all moments," she said with dismay and sat up as Gwyn's agitated shouts grew loud. "Well, I'm not a lady of leisure, am I, with the luxury of lying abed all day? I'm a working girl."

"Ah, but once you're a countess . . ." Win said, drawing her down beside him again, "countless luxuries will be yours."

"Why must you dwell upon that now, when I'm beside you?" she asked with annoyance. "Let me loose. I'm needed belowstairs."

"You're needed here," he insisted. "You importuned me for 'more, please, sir,' did you not? Well, now you can have it. Quick as you like."

"Truly? Now? Again? How quick?"

"In a brace of shakes, fast as two rolls of the dice."

"You know as well as me that I must see to business. Furthermore, methinks 'twill be for the better if we do not hurry through these lessons, if I am to learn properly . . . and also . . ."

"Ah" —he nodded—"and also, what?" She *was* a rare one, his friend Kat, as transparent as gossamer, as amusing as a pretty kitten discovering her own tail.

"And also lest the enjoyment end sooner than it might. Wait just as you are. I'll hasten back," she promised.

"See you do," he relented with a parody of a frown as, regretfully, he watched her dress drop over her shoulders to envelop her fine body in overly ample folds of coarse fabric. How lovely she would be in the choice, form-following silk her earl would drape her in, the fabric clinging to every swelling curve and hollow. Damn, but she was lovely even in plain heavy flannel, if man took the time to notice, which *he'd* not done before, and should have. This indisputable realization was accompanied by a great stretch and yawn as Win debated with himself what next to teach her. He was still pondering, a half smile curling the right corner of his mouth, when she had done brushing out her tawny hair and was ready to quit the chamber.

"There's an altogether wicked look in your eyes, Beau," she noted, laughing softly with restrained merriment. Inexperienced as she was with men in bed, she could read this supine male as clearly as a Latin scholar could interpret Virgil. Baldwin Beaumarais *wanted* her!

"I'll show you wonderful wickedness when you return," he replied with a ravishing grin, a promise—or threat—in his voice. "Be quick, Kitten. Remember, I'm waiting here at the ready to provide further tutelage."

"Has any woman ever forgot to remember you were waiting for her in bed, Beau?" she teased before scurrying off in response to another howl from Gwyn.

Chapter 6

Kat, with an intake of breath, followed by one of her renowned expletives—"Weasels and moles!"— bolted through the assembly of youngsters and dogs, straight across the kitchen to save a piglet, roasting on a spit in the hearth, that was in imminent danger of being charred to a crisp by a fat-fed roaring fire. How would Gwyn ever manage the inn, Kat worried, if on her first unsupervised day on the job, the main meal had to be rescued from incineration?

The groaning board at The Sign of the Kat drew a goodly crowd every day, the fare she presented deservedly acclaimed all over London and beyond, as equal to, even better than that served in many a nobleman's great hall, save only, perhaps, the king's, whose kitchens were presided over by a French cook—"chef" as the debonair fellow preferred to be called. Kat's roasted suckling piglet, her hams smoked in the spring in one of the inn's four chimneys, her stewed kid and roasted capons were rivaled only by her joint of marsh mutton that was of a unique, delicate flavor, for she offered only the meat of sheep fed upon the salt hay of the Essex lowlands. Except in the four warm months, those with names lacking the letter R, Kat served her midday meal, be the main course venison, fish, or fowl, after first offering her guests mounds of Colchester oysters delivered in barrels to London within hours of being plucked from their briny beds. It was Gwyn's dispute with an oyster cartman which had caused the girl to neglect the roast and to pluck Kat, after a manner of speaking, out of Baldwin's bed.

When Kat came upon the belligerents in the main room, the five or six waifs still at the inn, their faces flushed with heat and pleasure, loudly egged on the terrier dog, Deaf Jack, who had a secure hold of the man's boot toe and shook it as if it were a rat, growling fiercely on Gwyn's behalf. The cartman, doing what looked to be a dervish dance about the kitchen in an effort to shake free of the tenacious dog, alternately shouted, protested, and beseeched Gwyn who, also shouting and red in the face, was holding Roxelana on her hip and following in the footsteps of the dancer and the dog.

"Don't never try to dupe me, you . . . you . . . shellfish monger!" the girl asserted. "Asking me, 'cause I'm not shrewd as the mistress, for double the usual price of a barrel of oysters! 'Tis an insult to me!" To try to free himself of the dog, the man spun about, suddenly changing direction. The animal still held fast as the despairing visitor came face to face with Gwyn, who clapped a hand on his shoulder. "Got you, you goat's blister," she announced with spurious triumph. Roxelana, burbling with delight, tangled her baby fingers in the beleaguered fellow's forelock and pulled.

"Help, oh, help!" the boy howled, unable to move, held fast by the baby, the dog, and the outraged girl.

"Katesby! Come quick!" bellowed Gwyn once more, not

yet aware of her mistress standing in the doorway, arms folded over her bosom, observing the farcical scene.

"Gwyn, prithee, do not shout and disturb the household further. I *have* come," Kat answered calmly. "What is all this? Who are you, sir?" she asked the oysterman.

"Caleb Shute, here today in place of me uncle Potter Shute, who is laid low by ague and could not come out in the storm. 'Storm or no,' coughed me uncle Potter, 'Mistress Kat must have oysters for her boarders and herself, she loves 'em so.' So I come on up to London in the storm, and now, if you be she, Mistress Kat her own self, save me, please," he beseeched, "from this scourge of hell hounds, imps and vipers afore I need a draft of dragonwort to cure me of their cursed stings! Leave go of me," he entreated Gwyn. "Call off your minions, you sorceress, and you shall have all the shellfishes in the barrel for nought!"

"Cal Shute?" asked Kat. "Last I saw of you, you were a mere tyke and now, here you are, all grown—or mostly."

"Yes, mistress," Potter, still held prisoner, answered politely.

"Your uncle won't thank you for giving away the fruits—fishes rather—of his labors for nought," Kat said.

"I'd rather any day face Uncle Potter's displeasure than deal with the fury of this lot here in your establishment, Mistress Kat, assumin' I ever see me Uncle Potter again and I am not carried off to hell on me way home by the fiend that was coming after me in the storm all the ways here from the Essex damps. I prithee, leave loose of me, wench," Caleb lamented. "I got woes enough without you."

"A fiend followed you from the Essex marshes?" Gwyn asked with intense interest. "Sorry about lambasting you, then," she added and backed a step away from the boy after untangling Roxelana's little fingers from his hair. Kat tapped her toe before Deaf Jack, a signal for the dog to release his clenched jaws.

"As I recall, your Uncle Potter told me you have a jittery nature and a lively imagination, young Cal. There was no fiend after you, I'd venture to say, just blowing snow and drifts," Kat suggested to allay Cal's agitation. "Tell me the price of the oysters so's I can pay you, but first come warm yourself at the fireside, be soothed by a draft of hot mulled cider, and wait out the storm here with us. When you're able to see the road, you'll have no worry about spirits and the like."

"Certes, in fine weather all I'll have to disquiet me is dread of brigands and cutthroats," Cal ruminated, inclined to accept Kat's appealing invitation. "And me Uncle Potter always says 'tis better to abide the trouble you know" — he regarded Gwyn warily—"than go about lookin' for a new one."

"If actually you was chased by an unnatural fiend, that's all the more reason to stay put here, 'taint it?" Gwyn shrugged. She was offering a restrained apology and tentative friendship. "What'd it look like, the demon? Were it floating about in air like a ghost, slithering like a dragon, howling?" she questioned eagerly.

"The demon was wrapped about and about in a hooded shroud, sitting a great tall horse that was breathing out smoke," Cal answered earnestly. "The pair of them was silent as the grave. I heard not so much as hoof fall or a snort. They just came on at a steady pace, not gaining upon me or dropping back, but fading now and again."

"Disappearing, do you mean?"

"For pity's sake, Gwyn, with his own qualms and mental fancies, the lad needs no prompting from you. I think we should let the whole subject be," Kat said. Neither Gwyn nor Caleb seemed to have heard.

"Once, before the spirit vanished wholly, I looked over me shoulder. His hood had blowed off but I could see no face, only rime and hoarfrost, 'neath a blood-red jewel dangling in a dark void, betwixt where a man's eyes should be." Cal's voice ceased. There was an edgy silence but for the hissing of wet wood on the fire when suddenly the baby squealed. Gwyn gasped, and Cal steadied himself against the wall. When Roxelana reached up to the towering Blaidd Kyd, who had silently appeared in the room with a grin and a long knife held in his teeth, Caleb Shute fled into the storm, vowing never again to come up to London, most especially not to the environs of The Sign of the Kat, where demons were more numerous than flies on dung in summer.

"I do hope the poor dear don't catch his death on the way home," Kat said.

"From them ghosts?" asked Gwyn.

"Which ghosts?" asked Blaidd, lifting a laughing Roxelana high in the air, then setting her down, eliciting an imperious little yelp of protest from the child.

"I do not much hold with the notion of ghosts. I mean to say the boy could catch his death of ague, or freeze, Gwyn, in the storm." Kat sighed. "But the Shutes are not fools, not even twitchety Caleb. Living down on the low coast, they recognize a perilous storm when they see one. Cal will be likely be just fine. I do wish you hadn't encouraged his demon terrors."

"What demons?" Blaidd demanded.

"Dorsey and Bess will be here 'fore long, Kat. I'll talk to them about headless snow ghosts. 'Tis their area of mastery. And if any harm should come to Caleb Shute, it'll be *Kyd's* fault," Gwyn said sheepishly, "not mine. I was gettin' the weak-kneedly thing calmed some."

"*My* fault?" Kyd asked.

"For putting another fright in 'im that caused him to run," Gwyn replied.

"Whatever did I do to that piteous spectacle of an Englishman?" Blaidd wondered with a wicked grin, conspicuously setting his long knife on the mantel before he began playing peek-eyes with Roxelana.

"You just stepped in here is what you did. The mere sight of you frighted him out, you being so broad and tall and fierce-faced. You got those red ears sticking out like pitcher handles and them few prickly yellow hairs on your pate baring your skull. And the dagger didn't help a wit, neither, to put Cal at his ease. Blaidd Kyd, all and all, you are not a pretty sight."

"Odd you should say so. Ladies usually think me a handsome devil," Blaidd remarked blandly as his ears got redder. "Aye, is that not so, me lovely Roxelana?" he asked. The baby gurgled with pleasure when he gallantly kissed her little hand, and Gwyn smiled at that. In her own contrary way, Kat realized, the barmaid was flirting with the big, intense Welshman. What was more, as pretty as Gwyn was, and ornamented with baubles and trinkets, shy Blaidd was flirting also, if indirectly, saying words to Roxelana he could not speak directly to Gwyn.

"Sorry I scared off the boy, Mistress Gwyn. I'll go get him, if you wish."

"Then there'll be the two of you out in the snow, and the demon besides," answered Gwyn.

"*What* headless ghost demon? And who's Dorsey and Bess?" Blaidd asked, beginning to sound peeved.

"Dorsey Dibdin and Bessy Mortlock are a magus and a Wise Woman. She reads the Tarot. He reads *everything*," Gwyn answered. "He's a Cunning Man—an aeromancer who reads clouds, a tiromancer who divines with cheeses, an alchemist, though most renowned as an astrologer."

"John Lambe was lynched by a mob at Southwark for calling himself an astrologer," Blaidd frowned. "The church don't hold with such devil's work. Neither do a good many folk."

"Enough magic talk, for now," said Kat firmly, regretting this time away from Win, who was waiting for her. "I've more interesting things to do than chatter of ghosts, and we've practical matters to attend to before I can do them—

the more interesting things." She blushed, Blaidd noted with bemused interest, as she went on. "Gwyn, there's a lesson in this, my girl, for an aspiring innkeeper such as yourself. To have oysters fetched the several leagues from Colchester on such a day as this is worth twice—nay, thrice—the usual price of a barrel. Old Potter well knows how I relish the ugly things, as do half the folk in London, many of them our customers. Now we'll be the only inn in the city to offer any sea fare this wild day, because Potter Shute treats me as if I was kin to him."

"Oh, goat's blisters! I did wrong to beleaguer the lad and not heed what he tried to tell me!" Gwyn wailed. "But you know I've a doubting nature. If demons get him, it *will* be all *my* fault."

"Gwyn, catch ahold on yourself," Kat said wearily. "You'll learn to value your honest mongers and loyal tradesmen, to treat fair with them, to pay suitable prices for their wares, and to send the swindlers packing."

"I hope I'll learn," Gwyn said doubtfully. "But I dunno. More'n anything, I fear being taken for a dupe. I haven't your cleverness, Katesby, nor your steady good sense. I don't know how to dicker and deal and make good bargains and the like."

"You should have some notion how it's done. You've been beside me since the day I took charge of this place," Kat said, dismayed. At once she was sorry, her friend looked so crestfallen. "There, there, Gwynny, my little helper, don't fret. You know I could never manage without you even if you are not yet a confident tradeswoman. You're sure to become one in no time and make skillful bargains and barters. You *are* better than a fair to middling cook as it 'tis, eh, girl?"

"Well . . . yes, so I am," Gwyn agreed, brightening. "That's why Captain Bolling brought the bag of garlic to me."

"See to the roast, so's it don't burn while I tote up Mr.

Carlyle's reckoning, else we shall soon, the both of us, be attempting to appease a disgruntled guest. Today I've no time or wish to be smoothing feathers. I've other things to . . . handle." Kat smiled to herself, turning on her heel, happily anticipating her return to Baldwin's embrace and a few instructive hours abed on this wintery day, deep in his downy mattress, before the inn's evening trade began in earnest. The snow was letting up, and soon as it stopped, there'd be a throng under The Sign of the Kat.

"Say there, Ninny—I mean Gwynny—I've got a barter for you you won't be able to spurn," Kat overheard Blaidd flirting with Gwyn.

"What could *you* have that might interest *me*, you blunt-Blaidd, lack-brain jackanapes?" Gwyn bantered, the sugar and spice in her voice belying her uncivil words. It could be that the feisty, pretty, outgoing girl and the shy, dour, overgrown farmer's boy would develop an interest in each other, Kat mused as she hurried to tend to her own affairs.

"I'm back," she sparkled at Baldwin after tending to her guest, Mr.Carlyle, with such charming alacrity that the man complimented her on the speedy send-off. "What will you have me learn from you now, Beau?" she inquired, bolting the chamber door and starting across the room. She paused to feed the fire, and, without thinking, run the hem of her apron along the edge of a low chest to test for dust there, a good housekeeper's habit. There was none. Baldwin watched her from the bed, braced on one elbow, the light of the candle on the side table sparking green heat in his eyes.

"I've been thinking on that," he answered lazily, revealing a flash of white teeth in a luring smile. His lips, marveled Kat, hesitating where she stood, his lips were so . . . *full.* But not pouty, not a bit—pouty was too soft a word to describe a mouth shaped to such manly perfection and able to bestow such vigorous pleasure.

"Have you been thinking as well, Kitten, about what you'd like to learn?" he asked, casually containing his inclination to surge up, capture her in his arms, carry her back to his warm lair, and proceed with pure passion and instinct, not step-by-step planning, as their guide. But he didn't want to frighten her and she looked so—not timid, that was never a word that would characterize Katesby Dalton—rather, demure, genteel, and a mite shamefaced.

"Well, I hadn't dwelt on the thing," she fibbed, "but I did wonder, why not start again from the . . . start?" She blushed endearingly.

"There's only one first time, Kat. And moreover, you've considerable to learn in a limited time," he said, arching a brow. "We'll progress to lesson two now, perhaps even three, if you'd care to." They were smiling, each upon the other, the desire which had been stirring low in Kat's belly becoming a stunning stab of need. Win lifted the quilt invitingly. "I'm willing, if you are."

"Besides willing, I'd aver you're ready and able as well," she answered. "I mean, espying what you're wielding, I'd surmise you're . . . oh!" She flushed more deeply at her forwardness. Her cheeks blazed and she dropped her eyes, only to raise them once more when he spoke her name in a velvet-soft tone and beckoned her with a nod and a wink. She sprinted to the bedside, tugged her dress over her head and, shivering, leapt in beside Baldwin. She hid her hot face in the curve of his neck.

"There's no cause for you to be abashed about what you're feeling," he whispered, husky-voiced. "Not with me, nor any man." He rolled her in his arms, wrapped them both in the toasty quilt warmed by his body heat, and took her mouth in a slow, long, strong kiss. "What are you wanting?" he asked and she sighed.

"I want you to make me feel as you did before. Will you?"

"Even better."

"When?"

"Presently," he whispered.

"Soon!" she insisted, parting her legs, moving beneath him, situating herself to ease his way, ready to feel him hard in her, as before.

"Not too soon," he answered, taking her mouth again. He pressed against her belly and her thighs, furrowing, not going into her, pleasuring her most amazingly with the movement of his limber hips and muscular body, his mouth and fine hands, for what seemed to Kat an immeasurable time, until she erupted beneath him in long, unending waves. He waited, letting her endure the marvel of her pleasure, while he himself marveled at her responsiveness and sensuality that had brought her such absolute release. He'd never seen quite the like, and he prized his friend Kat more wonderfully than ever, in a whole new way. He held her to him. Her head rested on his shoulder. Her enlightened and adoring eyes soon opened upon him.

"Not bad, Kitten, for a wench who . . . ah, how did you phrase it? Never had felt the least heat for a man?" He chuckled.

"Don't *tease* me," she implored. "I was a simpleton before, a fool. I knew nothing of lovemaking and the like, or so I thought. Now I recognize some of these sensations. I've felt them before, mildly, in an uneasy, unsettling way, never so strong. I had no notion of what was perturbing me so, with restless longings. I made no link between such feelings and . . . you. So now you've got me all stirred up, as you, of course, knew you would. . . ."

"I did *not* know," he assured her, laughing. "You've been a true surprise to me, a most pleasing one. As this thing's gone thus far, I can warrant I've not ever experienced the sweet like of you before, Kat, for swift stirring and heating, nor for so jubilantly boiling over."

"That pleases you?" she asked thoughtfully, like a little girl pondering a puzzle. He nodded.

"It would please any man to give a woman satisfaction such as that."

"Ah. So you're saying I will be as pleased by *any* man as I have been by you, that there is nothing exceptional about you?"

He frowned. " 'Tis not precisely what I mean. Not a few women *have* said I am . . . very good."

"Not a few? How many?" asked Kat. The vanity of the scamp was boundless, she thought. He thought himself the deity's boon to womankind.

"Countless," was Win's reply. She had to be jesting, he thought, stealing a glance at her.

"Oh, dear, I'm afraid I don't understand all this," Kat sighed, hiding an indulgent smile. "You *are* exceptional, you claim, but any man would do as well by me?"

"No," he answered through clenched teeth. "Give credit where 'tis due."

"Certes, once I understand what credit is due who," she spoofed. "Now Win, were you pleased this time even though you did not spend yourself but only gave me the opportunity of . . . ?" She giggled

"I was waiting so that I could pleasure you again, prattling wench," he explained with a low laugh, "but I've decided now that turnabout is only fair play."

"I understand! Now it's my turn to serve you!"

"Just so. Cease chattering. And put your tongue to better use, eh?"

She looked puzzled for a moment until her eyes lighted with comprehension.

"As you told me was done by the chosen woman of the night in the sultan's harem?"

"I'd had in mind a kiss," he answered in a slightly hoarse

voice, finding her astonishingly unpredictable and direct. But if she was so about other things, why not this? he asked himself. "I'd be pleased to play the sultan to your kadeem, as the chosen women are called, if you wish it."

Without a word, Kat wriggled to the bottom of the bed, to Win's feet, and began to graze upward with her lips. He felt her breasts soft against his legs, her mouth whispering along the inner sides of his thighs. Her hands came to rest on his hips, and he caught his breath at the flicking of her tongue. Her lips were nibbling and encircling him. He moaned, holding on until he drew her up, felt her warm, soft, hard-tipped breasts glide over his hard belly and chest until his lips were parting hers, tasting. He thrust up into her once, twice. She was riding him as he bucked and snorted, his legs enfolding her hips. Even after he was still, she rode on before she too subsided.

"Well done," he murmured.

"Quite *lovely*," she whispered against his brow. "I've got the idea now, I think, and all it took was three lessons. Or was that number four?"

"Got the idea? You?" Win chided. "You're just a beginner, you little twit, a neophyte."

"Beau, you've already done me a greater service than I asked of you, that your promise obliged you to. You've not only pierced my maidenhead as I implored, but under your tutelage, with your encouragement, I've learned that I *am* receptive to a man's touch, not cold at all! Thank you, dear friend, for teaching and *demonstrating* that a man indeed may give me pleasure in this way." She planted a noisy, warm kiss on his furrowed brow. "So, there's no need now for us to continue thus, not with each other leastways. You've done exactly what I asked of you, as always, and . . ."

"Do you actually suppose any man will be able to give you the same pleasure?" His eyes were brimming with incredulity, irritation in his tone.

"Yes, that is my assumption. Is that not so?" she inquired with, to Win, a maddening innocence. "All men are similarly endowed, or so I am wont to imagine. Am I in error about it?"

"You are wrong if you suppose that all men are comparably apt and similarly equipped or equally deft and tender in this endeavor of bestowing pleasure on a woman, and if it happens that there is love on one side or the other or both, it adds to the delight, it is said, of the participants." He closed his glorious green eyes, which had been holding her gaze.

"Verily, Beau? Love fosters the fun of the sport?" She smiled with love and longing he didn't see.

"So I'm told. I cannot swear to it, as I've not been in love."

" 'Tis impossible for me to imagine more prodigious pleasure than what we've shared, or leastways what I felt, and we aren't in love at all. More's the pity then, that we shan't ever be loving together, not that romantic way, we two. But I have learned what I had need of knowing to content his lordship. You have been as good and loyal and generous a friend to me as always. Thank you, Win."

"You've naught to thank me for, Katesby, if you think Norland will be intrigued with your new-learned prowess as a lover." His eyes flashed open, and he surprised a soft expression on her face that he had never seen before. It vanished under his gaze before he could construe its meaning.

"Harry will be assuaged, leastways, that I'm not altogether a beginner, but why will he not be very pleased?" Kat asked lightly, exhibiting mild surprise. "How many more lessons might I require from you, if I wish to become truly enthralling to Harry?"

"Stop counting, blast it. There's so many more love lessons I could give you, you'd not be able to run a tally so high," he replied, a frown line appearing between his eyes. He felt vague misgivings begin to dawn, about going on with the game they were playing.

"Ah, as many lessons as that?" She yawned, pleased with his answer, smiling secretly, drowsing in his strong, encircling arms. Win felt her long, languid body curling against his. She was so at her ease that she purred against his chest, as amorous and sated as any woman he'd ever bedded. He found it inconceivable that, well served as she'd been, still lying in his embrace, she could even think, no less speak of, going from his arms to Norland's. Or anyone's, for that matter. *Besides, he didn't want her to, not yet.* In fact, he didn't want to hear another word about damn Harry. "Kitten, hear me," he murmured in his lulling, velvet voice against her brow, "I would speak to you of a man's heart and spirit and his dignity and of the prudence of not wounding him after he has pleasured you, whether or not you're in love with him."

"Wounding?" she mumbled. "Did I wound you in your heart and spirit and so forth? But how . . . ?"

"I don't mean *me,* twit," he protested, patting her head and ruffling her hair as he always had. "I was thinking of your future. Don't go prattling on of . . . of another man so soon after a lover has pleased you. That's not a suitable subject for a woman to broach. Her appropriate demeanor, her display of warmth after loving, may do much to sway the future of the affair, of the friendship."

"Mm-hm," she breathed against his chest.

"Now, a word, if I may, about love and friendship. No one, not even a Wise Man, can divine the habits of the heart. Neither you nor I can know how a sweet friendship and harmony, such as ours, may be transformed into something else by the hot lust we also, by happy coincidence, happen to share." She didn't reply, just nestled deeper into him.

"You recall the true, abiding love I spoke of hitherto, which men and women all seek and some find? Methinks, on reflection, that we, you and I, should not resist it overly much nor dismiss it out of hand. Blast it, Katesby, I'm saying there's a possibility, however unlikely it appears now, that we—you and I—could yet fall into it—love. There's naught to absolutely thwart it happening, in truth; but your damned duke and our own pair of resolute heads and hearts. I know I'm not the man of your musing, nor you the genteel lady I crave, yet methinks my heart could be . . . vulnerable to you. What do you say to that?" he whispered. "Could you fall in love with me, do you conjecture?

"Ah, well, never mind, then," Win said at once, before she could possibly have answered. "I was merely testing your determination to wed this Harry of yours. Forget that, what I said, about you and me falling in love. Lust will do for us two fine, eh, Kat?" he rasped, sliding his thigh up between hers and awakening her slowly, carnally, from a sweet sleep made especially agreeable by the warmth of his body and the hum of his caressing voice.

"What say you, Beau?" She smiled before she stretched and yawned like a kitten, her mouth wide, her little tongue aflutter, her eyes narrowing into mere shiny slits of green.

"You didn't hear one word I spoke, did you?" he asked and laughed aloud with the irony of it, and with relief, but also, if truth be told, and he never lied to himself, a trace of disappointment. He'd actually hazarded his bastioned heart by offering it to Kat, offering to offer it, rather, *and she'd been sound asleep,* thank heaven. Zounds, but he'd had a close call! By pure luck he'd got out of danger unscathed, but a jot more quickly than he might have wanted if he admitted the truth, which he did, with a long audible sigh. He had, fleetingly, actually wished to risk playing the true love game with Kat, for if ever he was going to fall under the mad sway of romance with any woman, it would be she. Distrustful as he was, guarded in his feelings, he doubted *he'd* fall, let the barriers down, even for Kat.

He had no doubt, however, that with the slightest encouragement, *she* would love him. Likely that was all he really wanted, now that she was about to wed another—to know he could own her heart for his own pride's sake. It would be damn wicked of him, to jostle her heart at this juncture and chance ruining her future with a great earl. Loving one man, he doubted her sense of honor and her tender heart would permit her to wed another unless she was in the most dire circumstances.

"I heard you sigh just now, but little of what you said before, about something doing for us fine. I heard you say that. What will do for us?" Kat inquired hopefully.

"More diligent, luscious lechery. There's no end to what you can savor with me now, and use to enthrall de Morely later."

"Oh." She now sighed, disappointed, wanting, almost expecting something more from him. "Well, I'll settle for that, then, for passion. Will you pleasure me again?" she asked, sleepily seductive. "Oh, weasels and moles," she fumed at the sound of a knock at their door, "*and* bloody goats' blisters as well," she added, bounding out of bed. She nimbly donned her dress, ran her fingers through her stormy hair, and called, "Come!" as she perched on the edge of a tall chair near the fire.

The door rattled in its frame until she remembered it was locked and went, after a regretful shrug at Win, still warm in bed, to draw the bolt. He lifted the quilt in teasing, beckoning invitation.

"Show-off! Cease to display your attribute," she whispered before he dropped the covers to conceal himself just as Jeannie, Jilly, and Jenny bustled into the chamber shaking snow from their cloaks, all three agog and puffing with cold and eagerness to deliver the latest tidings.

"Well now, out with it. Let's hear what great news you've got to report that's so momentous you dare to disturb my . . . sleep. I warn you, girls, it best be urgent or you'll all really catch it from me," Win grumbled before he grinned, he was that happy.

"And from me, too," Kat mimicked him, almost frowning, her hands set firmly on her hips, her most commanding stance, before she loosed an irrepressible laugh of pure exhilaration.

"Well, if you two are not a giddy pair of dearlings, I'll be Bess O'Bedlam," said Jilly indiscreetly, rolling her eyes heavenward.

"We always said you was a touch daft, Mam," commented Jeannie, taking in the scene in one knowing glance, "even if you haven't never been locked up in the madhouse."

"Stop gabbing and tell 'em what we come here to tell," giggled Jenny, the shy one, blushing as she too assessed the situation they'd blundered into.

Chapter 7

"There's a rider half a league up the road, asleep or near to it, froze to his saddle," Jilly reported. "And his mount's stumbling in circles upon the frozen ground, going this way and that and come up lame in the left forefoot, limping. Cal Shute, the oysterman's kin, you know? He came to the inn gate to say so. Odd, the boy would not step inside to warm himself at the fire."

"He seemed scared of something, Jen?" Jeannie asked.

"Yes. Fair terrified," answered her little sister, nodding so vehemently that her head kerchief slipped down over her round brown eyes.

"So much so, he moved neither this way nor that. And him so cold, his eyelashes were froze in little stiff spikes. Such lovely *long* lashes, he has," Jeannie sighed.

"Oh, you minx!" Jilly glared with disbelief at her daughter. "You fret me, with your craze for the lads. Imagine, just imagine, noticing a boy's lashes at such a time."

"It was Gwyn put a scare into the oyster boy, with some help from Blaidd Kyd and the eerie-blowing snow. Where is Cal now? And what say you of the mysterious frozen rider?'' Kat asked.

''We went stumbling out a way, we three, sliding and laughing, leaving the irresolute boy behind after a few steps, his warnings in our ears of evil spirits and the like, crouching in the storm. We saw not one living mortal, only a few muddled imprints nearly covered over by falling snow,'' Jeannie explained, ''tracks what could've been made by anyone, even Cal himself. But we did find this, with a light frosting of snow upon it. It could not have been dropped much before we got to the place and its owner can't have got far.'' She put forward a worn leather pouch such as a courier might carry. ''It was empty but for this one odd coin, not English. There's foreign writing on it, see?'' Win, his quilt tucked about his waist, revealing his bare, broad chest, beckoned her to the side of the bed and struck a flint to fire a candle.

''A Lowlands coin, Dutch, a false one at that. It has been dipped in a weak silver wash, but 'tis pewter. See?'' he said, scratching the coin's surface. ''This leathern case was not in possession of any ghost, but likely a spy or secret informant. He must have important information, to be riding in this weather.''

''He probably came ashore before the snow began, then followed Cal Shute through the storm up to London.''

''The country is swarming with spies,'' Jeannie said, ''or so it would seem if you eavesdrop on the king's bailiffs who come here, and also watch the dodgy young students, the 'university wits' as they call themselves. And other such sturdy beggars and loons stopping here at the inn, some of 'em sitting all hunched over their tankards, heads together, eyes shifting.''

''Gwyn thinks them to be Papist priests and Englishmen of the Roman persuasion, fomenting rebellion.''

''Gwyn overstates the Papist menace. The shifty-eyed rogues you see are not all spies and agents. Many, as you well know, ladies, are usurers' touts, cutpurses, dicers, nippers, foisters, among them some of the wittiest knaves God ever made, not a few friends to me."

"Such friends as that, Mr. Beaumarais, will beguile you of your life and your wife, if you had one," argued Jilly. "Have a care, sir."

"Even such men as that may find some respite here from the wicked world, if they do not practice their nefarious trades under *my* roof," said Kat. "Under The Sign of the Kat, they know they must behave honorably."

"Send for the boy Cal, please. I would learn more from him of his ghost," said Win. "Whoever lost this" —he tossed the leather bag to Jeannie—"whether he be spy or king's courier, is himself now lost in the storm."

"The oyster lad's fled. He told the stable boy he'd be seeking sanctuary, safe from demons until the storm abates, with Brother Truckle at the Graie Friars' monastery."

"The good friars, I wot, already have a hall full of poor folk and beggars, but they'll turn no one away on such a day as this," said Kat. "We must send provisions, bread and salt-beef treacle for brews, at least. I'm certain they've exhausted the monastery's scant supplies." At once in command, she began issuing orders. "And we must search again for the lost traveler, perhaps even now expiring under a snowdrift."

"You yourself needn't go just yet, Katesby. A good manager must allot to her hirelings certain tasks in need of doing, so she may concentrate on truely consequential enterprises." Win winked. "Acquiring another inn, say. Did you not report to me that the Plough Inn outside Temple Bar in the legal district was bought within the past twelvemonth for one hundred and twenty pounds? Tell me *more*."

"Herm's Rents at Holborn went for half that sum. But that's just poor lodgings, not a fine establishment such as ours, which requires the constant attention of the proprietress, me, to maintain its high standards and reputation." Kat smiled, hesitated, yearning to stay, but left Win alone in bed, frowning in earnest. "I'll be back to discuss . . . Herm's Rents," she said with a regretful little shrug.

"Jen, please light the fire under the cauldron in the barn," she directed, "to melt ice for the injured horse. Jill, you are to tell the stable lad to walk out the animal till it is calmed. In this weather the horse will be steaming and blowing. And help the groom feed the poor beast. And blanket him. You might become our first stable *girl*, eh, Jenny?

"You, Blaidd, please stop babbling at that baby," she said as she rushed through the warm kitchen, "and come along with me to try and deliver this mysterious rider from the storm."

"You've no cloak. I'll go myself," said Kyd.

"I'll just dash up and get a wrap and follow right after you," Kat said, starting for the stairs.

After Kat went off with the Goodkind girls, Win had drowsed voluptuously, keeping ready for her. Happily, he hadn't had to wait long.

"Well, there you be," he smiled with sultry pleasure when she came bursting into the room within minutes of her leaving. "Have you delegated?"

"Win, I've only come for a cloak—and a kiss," she made haste to say. "I've no time to undress and frolic with you, no matter how much I might like to. Duty before pleasure, the maxim says."

"There's no need to unclothe and scant time required for a hasty lesson," he answered, gliding from the bed to kiss her lips before he turned her to face the mirror. He tied her apron strings into a bow at her little waist, then tacked up her dress to expose the fullness of her bare derriere to his view, setting hands upon her there, then grazing her from knee to belly along her thighs and down again to test the moistness between them already flowing in readiness.

He leaned forward to kiss her ear and inhale the fragrance of her skin as he undid a few of the upper hooks of her bodice, just enough to free one pale breast and see the nipple tauten in his fingers. He felt the other, fabric-draped, spread and harden, and a waft of heat, as warm as a tropical zephyr, rose from her skin. In the mirror, he saw her delicate nostrils flare. Her chest heaved when she lifted her arms to reach back to entwine his neck, her other breast rising full and free of her bodice.

He drew an oaken chair before her, set her hands upon the elaborate carving of its high back, and set his own hands on her coltish hips to steady her before he commenced moving into her and out. She caught her breath, tossed her tawny mane, and arched her back, keeping the curve of her bottom against his belly—like a wild mare, he thought—able this time to anticipate gratification, and wanting it all. Their nerve endings were still alive, almost raw with the imprinted recall of delicious lust recently shared, and their bodies were instantly attuned, their give and take synchronized so that the effluence of her spasm promptly commingled with the flood of his. He didn't want to release her, and so he fastened up her bodice, still holding her hard to him before he let her skirt drop and smoothed it down over her hips and flanks.

A quarter of an hour by the clock after Blaidd had gone off on what would prove to be a futile search for a thing he was convinced was a ghost, or worse, the snow had stopped falling. Church bells tolling vespers rang, muffled by layers of white. And Kat was back in the kitchen, striving to appear casual though she was flushed with elation. "Storm's ending," she commented.

"Where's the cloak you went for?" asked Jeannie mischieviously

"Forgot it again," was Kat's blushing answer. "I'll just

leave the investigation to Blaidd. He'll have plenty of help from others now, eh?"

A hint of low sunlight showed in the western sky as dusk came down and people began to appear on the street, a few shopkeepers at first, cautious, tentative, to brush off their doorsteps, happy to see others of their kind put testing noses to the diminishing wind. Dogs bounded free, barking, elated to discolor the pristine snow. Cats came on tiptoe from snug hiding places to examine the altered white terrain. And a dun-colored, lamed gelding, riderless, came limping into the inn yard and was led to the stables where melted ice water and a warm stall awaited him.

Mulled hot cider, strong ale, claret, and mounds of food greeted stranded travelers who came in out of the cold to the warm comfort of a blazing hearth and voices raised in greeting and discourse, in prayerful thanks for survival. It was an innkeeper's nightmare *and* dream, a trying but also a most profitable time as overland coaches, delayed by the storm, pulled up at Kat's door, one after the other over several hours, freeing relieved, tired, agitated folk to be greeted and succored, thawed, comforted, fed, and eventually bedded down, often as many as three or four to a mattress not counting children and infants in arms. The inn's workers were run, almost literally, off their feet.

As the tavern filled with both itinerants and regulars, a festive din was raised. The storm had ended, they had come through it safe to again enjoy a fine meal and the warm company of their fellow creatures, to share good spirits, both gregarious and alcoholic, and cheerful, if tipsy, song.

As soon as Kat could pause for a breath, a bit of broth, and a sip of claret, she thought of Win waiting for her and darted for the stairs.

* * *

If Kat were a rose, she'd be the reddest in the world! Win came abruptly wide awake with that thought foremost in his mind, to find himself alone in the near dark, the sheeting tangled and the taste of Kat on his tongue. His body throbbed and his heart pounded as he sat bolt upright in bed, clinging to wisps of a dream of uprooted flowers drifting on a stormy sea. The details of the elusive dream floated away, leaving him with a sudden, compelling determination to discover from whence Kat had come and learn what storm of emotions had caused her to be cast adrift in the world.

He'd slept long and deeply. The afternoon had gone and the day had moved well into the shank of the evening. There was music of lute, cittern, and drum, and a din of voices and laughter rising from the tavern below, and here he was, a man who never passed up an occasion for merrymaking, alone when a gathering was under way. Blast! By the sound of it, he was missing some lively revels, he thought, feeling as he used to as a small boy when the others kept him from joining in their street games and ran him off with gleeful taunts, as bigger boys were wont to do to smaller ones. Where the devil *was* Katesby? he brooded, when he wanted her—in more ways than one.

The girl was neglecting him, he silently grumbled. She'd let the fire on his hearth die down, and she'd forgotten to bring, or even send up, food and drink.

He arose in the cold, got the fire blazing to warm and light the chamber, and returned to bed. Anticipating Kat's arrival at any moment, he occupied himself with recollections of their bounteous day together. He smiled to himself, thinking how freely she had flexed her body against his, at her abundant sensuality . . . responsiveness . . . curiosity, the verve with which she'd followed his every instruction and responded in kind to his moves and caresses. She had even devised some notable maneuvers of her own, without any hint of chagrin. No doubt of it, Katesby was a resourceful amateur! A shameless, wonderful, wanton wench, he'd called her in joyful jest, at the time being pleasured by her busy mouth. He'd reciprocated and made her whisper *Beau! Beau!* again and again, breathing and sighing the name she most liked for him, and the sensation of her breath was as a warm, caressing Mediterranean breeze on his skin.

Where *was* the girl? he grumbled to himself again, now that, in truth, he craved her again and, at the moment, no other he could think of. He'd had sundry and diverse bedmates, among them some of the most notorious mistresses in London, women touted in the highest circles for their skills, yet Kat the novice, his inexperienced sensual apprentice, could, by instinct alone, teach some of those London courtesans a thing or two. He grinned. Then he began to frown, perplexed. Something was not quite genuine in this. She was keeping something from him, leaving something unsaid. He sat up again and struck a candle alight as misgivings began taking form in his mind, about innocence so complete as Kat's and guilelessness so unworldly. After all, she was a clever street girl turned innkeeper who'd seen and heard much in her young life But what need had she, though, to dissemble with *him*, her fastest friend, to whom she exposed all her thoughts and feelings—or had until now, leastways.

His hands clasped behind his head and eyes narrowed, Win lay back and thought harder, trying, though it wasn't easy, to find Kat blameworthy of something more than making him wait for supper.

Had she been *using* him? Obviously, dolt. She had been straightforward about it from the start and besides, in the using she had done *him* no harm, but had given pleasure, rather. No, that was not the answer he sought, not the cause of his disquiet about her.

She might have been at bed play with some other before she'd come to him. Perhaps that was her secret. The reason she was so apt and free spirited at the love game was that she had played it before. Win tried to conjure the presence of another man in Kat's arms, to imagine her romping with a stranger, frolicking, performing, laughing with delight, as she had done with him, then putting a stop to the venture *before* she gave up her virginity.

"Impossible!" he objected aloud, unable to picture her with any man but himself, nor imagine her curbing her excitement at the critical moment. Why would she? She wasn't preserving her maidenhead for her future husband. In actuality, she wished to spare the earl that nuisance. And she had! Certes, he himself had deflowered Kat. One corner of Win's mouth slowly curled in a smile of appreciation. He was ready to abandon his whole line of thought when another possibility occurred to him.

Perchance the aristocrat de Morely was a licentious old fellow with a predilection for petting and fondling, but lacking the hard drive to breach a virgin? No good, Beaumarais. Win frowned, pursing his lips, narrowing his eyes, his habit when he doubted his own logic. The lady had not even been touched, much less pawed over, by any man before him. She was too spontaneous for that to have been so, too obviously on an exploration of discovery with him, fool that he was.

Zounds, but *something* was askew between them, he knew, though try as he might Win could fix on no cause. He also knew Kat was utterly incapable of being in any way false for long. It was not her way to be conniving. The truth would soon come out, and it was likely nothing of any import at all, so why was he feeling dejected and . . . forsaken? No, that couldn't be. He was rarely subject to those emotions, but he did feel a definite twinge of . . . hunger! *That* was it. All he lacked was food and good, raucous company, and here he was missing out on the festivities downstairs!

Damn, but that intimation of an unmanly ache had

caused him to feel defenseless for a moment. In other circumstances, for example if Kat had been present, it might have interfered with clear thinking, even have rendered him vulnerable to other soft sentiments, such as love. The thought shocked Win right out of bed to pace the cold floor and, for one of the few times in his life, to set about deceiving himself in earnest.

This bother had started with the preposterous promise Kat had extracted from him, to give her love lessons. He'd been duped, he told himself, then found he couldn't accept so self-serving an excuse. No, it wouldn't do, for he had taken Kat's declaration of frostiness and indifference to the caress of a man, her proclaimed lack of sensual appetite, as a direct challenge to his manhood. If truth be told, his own pride and vanity gave him leave—nay, obliged him, to be caught in the gossamer snare of her ill-begotten, playful promise. He *would* prove to her, and prove yet again to himself, that his virile prowess was irresistible. He could, if and when he chose, turn any constrained girl into an amorous woman, have her helpless in his arms in a trice. Verily, he'd shown that to Kat, but it wasn't all his love lessons had done. They had also shown him weaknesses in *himself.* To phrase it forthrightly, he had discovered a possible susceptibility to possessive, inane, imprudent, romantic *love.*

"Devil fiddle it, it cannot be!" he grumbled. *"I am not even near to falling in love,"* Baldwin proclaimed, diving back under the covers. 'Tis lust, is all. I'm not the first man, nor the last, to let good bed sport sway his good sense. Best get up right quick, you gallant you, he warned himself, before Kat gets back.

Again vaulting from the bed, he made haste to get into his smallclothes and leggings. That done, he selected from his oaken cabinet a richly brocaded doublet. He would, in high style, leave the hooks unfastened to show the beauty of his linen shirt, embroidered all down the front and along the deep cuffs with gold and silken threads. About his narrow waist, much admired by members of the fair sex, he cinched a jewel-studded belt, set his dagger in its scabbard, raked back his shining copper hair, and took a fast glance in the mirror. Good. All he needed now was a diversion from Kat. He'd find that in an old friend, or make a new one among safely wed noble ladies who, of an evening, frequented the gaming tables below. Another woman, any woman, in his bed would keep Kat out of it, and things between them would be the same as they'd been before. Always. Being the rational, resolute pair they were, each would wed another, as planned. Kat already had captured an earl, but he had yet to make the acquaintance, as suggested by his friends Lord and Lady Seton, of a well-provided-for young widow whose lands near Bath adjoined and might well be joined to his own property there.

Kat and Win met, one rushing up, the other down, on the creaky fourth stair of the inn.

"I must fix that one day," he said with a self-conscious smile.

"Sorry to have been so long." She smiled, pulling off her head kerchief and letting her tawny hair tumble about her shoulders. "Leastways, here I am now, Beau."

"I realize your services were required elsewhere and still are, from the sound of things. We've got a full house tonight, eh, partner?" He went down one step. Now they were of precisely the same height. He pursed his gorgeous lips, and Kat kissed them.

"Mm." She nodded. "I've a crowd to tend to, sure, but I won't be missed if I'm temporarily gone. Gwyn and the Goodkinds are in charge. I've delegated, as you told me a good manager must." Kat danced up a few steps, expecting Win to follow.

"I'm ravenous, Katesby—for food," he said, not moving.

"Well, why not just do as we did that last time?" she suggested with a low, throaty, nearly irresistible laugh, extending a beckoning hand, reaching for his to lead him back upstairs. He bounded a step above her, blocking the way.

"You fancied being occupied in that fashion?" He winked, raising her chin and looking into her clear, smiling green eyes. "Your earl husband will relish taking you that way, I wot. He'll have me to thank for that particular bit of his wife's carnal knowledge, though he'll not know it." Win watched Kat's eyes turn a deeper green, reminding him of tropical waters darkening under errant clouds.

"If . . . when, I mean to say, I wed the earl, he will have you to thank for *all* his wife's carnal knowledge and *she* will know it." An expression of confusion replaced the happiness Kat had been radiating as she read Win's face. There was a hard set to his jaw and a look not unlike reproach in his eyes.

"That particular manner of a man and woman joining will be of especial usefulness when you and the earl are standing on a balcony or stair landing, smiling beneficently down upon your dancing guests in his great hall below or . . ."

"I must be certain to remember, in such a position, not to unfasten more than one or two hooks at the top of my bodice, lest the earl and I put on an unseemly display." Her answer betrayed her distress at Win's tone and subject manner.

". . . or perhaps you will be at the rail of the earl's barge on the Thames, the moon half shrouded in mist," he pressed, "on your way to a court ball when . . ."

"Blast you, Baldwin Beaumarais! Don't dare to speak more to me now. Just keep silent, I prithee," Kat insisted. "Say nothing unless it's to explain what's gone wrong and how I've displeased you."

"Naught is wrong, Kat. You've never displeased me," he replied, thinking, "Not until now that you've got me wanting you so, it pains me." He was tempted to shout out those words, then say, "Kat, keep your distance or you'll have me in bed thinking I'm in love with you, and what would we do then?" He hesitated, watching her, his deep green eyes caught in her beautiful, turbulent, sea-green glance.

"Why are you are looking at me odd?" she asked. "Oh, go on, Win, better say what you're thinking. If you quell hurtful thoughts, they may turn inward to corrode your heart. You know me, you rascally rogue. I can deal with anything, 'specially you," she jested, aiming a comradely feint at his chin with her fist.

Why *not* tell her he wanted her? Win mused, his determination wavering. If he didn't, he might always regret it, and all he had got to lose was his heart. Win cleared his throat. "Attend to me, Kitten. I've something that must be said, whether or no you wish to hear it." His insistent manner and the blaze of his eyes took her aback. He was about to desolate her, dash her hopes of love for good and always. She vehemently shook her head and set her fingertips upon his full, warm lips to silence him.

"I've changed my mind. Keep your thoughts to yourself for now. With this sort of cantankerous temperament upon you, Win Beaumarais, you'll likely speak words you and I both will later rue."

"Yes, of course. You're right," he agreed, taking a deep breath, bemused that Kat had yet again stopped him from making a fool of himself.

"Please say no more until you've considered your thoughts well. During the next love lesson, when we are alone together, and close, *then* tell me what troubles you. Now let us go down."

He wanted her! She could feel it, see it in his desirous eyes. She *would* have the man loving her if only he gave her time enough, if he remained in London just a while longer. The foremost way to keep him there, Kat reasoned, was to play her only strong card, by keeping him in bed and busy and heated, but leave him always wanting more so he'd not want to go away, ever.

"There won't be more lessons, Kat. I've kept the pirated promise you extracted from me by trickery," he said, distorting the truth. His practical nature was in command again of his instincts. He knew the best way to keep her at a distance was to provoke her defensive, fiery temper "Your duke's been saved the effort and bother of deflowering a virgin. That done, I've other kettles to stir."

Kat's heart reeled as if she'd been struck, but she didn't show her distress by as much as the flicker of an eye. He wasn't fooling *her.* Win never did. He longed to lie with her again, but no matter how strong his desire, his self-command was stronger. Beau had a will of iron when he made up his mind to something, but she was no weakling herself, no silly romantic at the mercy of her emotions. She'd play along with him until she could learn what the devil he was up to now.

"How now, Baldwin?" She sighed as if with exasperation, then added with genuine ire, "You're an inconstant, rascally knave, maybe *not* the true friend to me you claim you are. You do try my patience sorely, sir!" Her hands were set on her hips, her eyes shading from green to stormy indigo.

"I beg a thousand pardons, to be sure, Katesby, but you know I get churlish when I'm hungry for my supper. Come on down now, eh?" His face was impassive, his jaw and his mind set.

"I'll detain you just long enough to say a thing worth your attention, Win," she answered with feigned indifference.

"Yes, what is it?" he replied shortly, waiting at the bottom of the stairs, tapping his elegantly shod toe, his back to her. One glance now and he'd take her upstairs, have her right here, *somewhere,* and soon. He'd not have a choice.

"Harry's an earl, not a duke," she said and giggled, and Baldwin spun on the heel of his Spanish leather boot to stare up at her with amazement. Here he stood battling his strongest impulses, and the imp was laughing! "Also," Kat went on, "know that I love you just as I always have, in loyalty and friendship. By my troth, I thank you for demonstrating to me the various ins and outs of that other sort of love, but now, as you said, that must be done between us, for good and all, else . . . who knows what might happen to our well-laid plans to clamber higher, to achieve greater substance and fortune and . . . the like?"

"Exactly." He nodded, narrow-eyed.

"And if we never again speak of this day's events, not even think on them," she added with a frozen smile, "we'll just be confidantes together as we were before, will we not?" For a mere second Kat thought she glimpsed the lonely eyes of a lost boy in Win's manly, handsome face before he shrugged and answered her smile with his radiant, glinting white grin.

"We will be as before," he agreed, wishing it so but bothered by a shade of doubt. Would he, could he, be in her proximity and not take what he so wanted? "Howsomever, are you seriously suggesting that *I* never muse tenderly upon what has passed between us today? Will you dictate my thoughts now, Katesby?"

"Of course not," she replied in a heartsore whisper, knowing she'd never forget today, nor stop longing for what might have been, unless she could make it what *was.*

"I've a thing to say to you, too, wench. Hearken to me well. Nothing, not lechery" —he leered and winked— "*not even love,* will ever come between us. And no matter how far we are apart, however many miles lie between us, if ever you have need of me, all you must do is call. Blazon it, whisper it, utter it, *think* it. Your word will find me. Now, are you going to fill my rumbling innards or must I venture out in the night after curfew to Thavies Inn to have my hunger sated?''

"I'll not hear of no such thing!'' she replied, tripping lightly down the stairs, proffering her indulgent, dear, crooked smile. When she came beside him and Win raised her fingers to his lips and bowed, as if to a fine lady, she snatched her callused hand away to conceal behind her back.

"Don't be shamed by your hands, Kat,'' he admonished. "They evidence the good hard work you've done.'' His hand claimed hers again and, shoulder to shoulder, they strode into the boisterous tavern as the yard door burst open. A tall figure shrouded in fur from chin to heel stood on the threshold. At his left was a squire, a man of sour expression, and to his right a grimacing young aristocrat got up in red velvet and scarlet silk, shivering so his teeth rattled in his head.

"My lord earl!'' gasped Kat, clutching Win's hand and leading him forward. "What a surprise. I'd not expected your return to London till several days hence.''

Chapter 8

Harry de Morely, an austere-looking man of middling age, didn't quite offer a smile, merely a hint of one.

"I'll not be long in London. We are passing only a night or two here in the city," de Morely answered in a measured voice. "On the way to Caen. Being so close to The Sign of the Kat, I thought to take advantage of the inn's many comforts," he added impassively.

The squire relieved the earl of the thick ermine cloak, revealing Norland to be of wiry build, so slim of form that the blades of his shoulders were discernable, like vestigial wings beneath his doublet of plain dark wool. The coarse canvas shirt beneath showed a modest white ruff with only a tracing of simple lacework at the throat and wrists. His waist was belted in plain tanned leather, and an unadorned steel sword glinted against narrow dark leggings. A single gold earring set with a large pearl was the only rich ornament on the earl's person. He brought to mind a penitent monk or atoning lay brother, and Win would not have been surprised to learn the man was wearing a horsehair shirt against his skin. De Morely had close-cropped, iron-streaked dark hair which grew along his jaw line to form a small beard. Barbered to a fine point, it exaggerated the length of the earl's worn, still-handsome face, in which a pair of indentations appeared to have been hand-carved above an aristocratic nose, and parallel tracks deeply hewn down leathern cheeks. The eyes were autumn gray—curious, calculating, and cold.

"My lord," said Win with an almost imperceptible nod of his head.

"Mr. Beaumarais," de Morely replied with equal remove. The two regarded each other, Kat thought, like a pair of stallions on the scent of a mare, one tough and venerable, the young challenger lithe and quick, both canny as each assessed the other's strengths and susceptibilities.

"You conform well to Kat's description, Beaumarais. Does he not, Charles?" de Morely asked the shivering boy dressed all in scarlet. "My son Charles, sir, a future Earl of Norland, *if* he outlives me." The earl glanced about the tavern dubiously and, lowering his voice, beckoned Win and Kat to lean in close. "Charles ponders over blasphemous tomes, logarithmic tables, matters of the occult, *magick*. He toys with heresy, I've told him. He will find himself in the Tower one day with vile Ratcliffe the torturer, and there'll be nought I'll be able to do when they lop off his head."

Charles blinked at his parent, sniffled, and smiled diffidently, his expression apologetic and entreating. "My l-l-lord," the son stuttered, "I'll not risk rousing your choler with explanations I've already proffered."

"Be off with you, Charlie. The sight of you rouses my choler," the earl sighed.

"Go to the kitchen, why don't you, Charlie?" Kat smiled, patting the boy's shoulder. "A drink of Gwyn's broth and the fire will warm you, afore you're taken again with the sneezes and ague." Grateful for the means of escape offered, the boy bolted as his father watched with morose disdain.

"He's a pathetic, bookish creature, always taken up with his tomes full of lines and circles and odd characters when he should be out wenching, ruffling, and roistering in riotous company as I was at his age.

"Now, Beaumarais," the earl addressed Win, "I've heard much about you from Katesby. Will you join me for a bit of sup and a pitcher of claret?"

Kat looked on with a bit of uneasiness. She hadn't expected these two to meet so soon nor in these circumstances, and she'd no idea what might happen.

"I am given to understand, sir, that you intend to take Katesby Dalton to wife," said Win abruptly. "Is it so?"

"Yes. If she'll have me," de Morely replied, finding Beaumarais offensively blunt.

"Why?"

"Why *what*, sir?" the earl snarled in displeasure.

"Why do you propose to make a countess of a commoner?"

"So that I may transform her into one of the great ladies of the land."

"And if perchance that is not *her* ambition, if she prefers to remain here with . . . ?"

"With you, Beaumarais?" The earl's smile was mirthless. "If you are supposing that I will leave her future in your hands, forget about it."

"Apparently neither of you realizes that I, and no other, am the arbiter of my own destiny," Kat said with blazing indignation as the two men turned simultaneously to stare at her.

"Now do be seated, good sirs, so that you may enjoy to the fullest the hospitality of this place." Both men seemed taken aback and a mite indignant.

"If either of you had understanding or regard for me

in this, you'd be looking right sheepish about now, for discussing me as though I were a commodity—a bolt of silk, a blooded mare, a barrel of oysters—to be disposed of at your will and whim. Neither of you, I perceive seeing you together, has a propensity to be other than conceited, commanding, contentious, bold, stubborn, and proud of it! Methinks I might prefer the company of a kinder, gentler man, such as Charlie de Morely," Kat announced before she strode off.

"Men!" she said, stalking into the kitchen. "They are illogical, paradoxical, irrational, self-centered . . ."

"Are you only just discovering that?" Gwyn Stark laughed. She was mounding bread pudding on trenchers for that night's kitchen full of hungry waifs. Among them sat Lord Charles de Morely, sharing his pudding with the dog in his lap, Deaf Jack. The nobleman was deep in discussion with Blaidd Kyd, who dandled Roxelana on his knee.

"Dice and card play are the chiefest means by which rich gentleman such as yourself, Charlie, are induced to part with their money," Blaidd was helpfully explaining. "I'll keep my eyes upon you if you like, while you're here in London. You must have a special care not to play among strangers who act as if they are simple of mind or in their cups and are neither."

"Even gullible, fainthearted, and flimsy as I appear, and also more like my father's fool than his heir, got up thus in scarlet silks, lacking only pointed cap and bells for the role, I'm no mark for coney catchers, Mr. Kyd. I have an aptitude for numerals and formulas. It enables me to count cards, to know when a pack has been shuffled cunningly. I keep a chronicle in my mind of which cards and numbers have been played and which not, and I know when there is an oversupply of a particular card signaling a cheat. Also, I distinguish false dice from fair by noting the lack of randomness in the toss of the false or the excessive frequency with which certain combinations of dots do or do not appear. I am as well a wizard at chesse-play."

"Do you discover lead-weighted fullums, hollow gourds, even them wee hair bristles that keeps the dices from landing on one side?" Blaidd was both impressed and skeptical. "Mumchance is me own favorite game. You know that one, milord, I'd suppose. The players sit about the table, each calls out a card—Red Eight, Black Knave and so on—and then the deck is distributed, card by card, all 'round until the first man to be dealt the one he named takes the coffer."

"Indeed I know the game, Kyd. There's a plenitude of possibilities for a swindling dealer and one ally to cheat at mumchance."

"So, if you're so clever, milord, why *are* you attired in the toggery of a finicky popinjay?" the massive Kyd asked the slight, overly tall, stooped, squint-eyed young noble.

"My earl father demands I make myself more pleasing to members of the female sex, so I dress up gaudy, but it doesn't serve me well, not even with a codpiece of a contrasting shade embroidered with fine pearls. I fear I will never fulfill the earl's wish for an heir of me, to ensure the continuation of his name, line, and title together in a single mortal. He nurtures uneasiness that I shall succumb to the pox before I set seed, which is not so unlikely."

"Why has the earl not arranged an appropriate match for you?" asked Kat, making a space for herself on the bench beside Charles. She took a child on her lap, a small boy who had been racing about in a frenzied manner, unable to wedge his way to the table as the others sat close, blocking him out. He urgently began spooning pudding into his mouth, fending off the dog with his elbow.

"I've no way with ladies," complained Charles. "No daughter of a noble family has ever yet agreed willingly to have me. My father can be a harsh man, one not easily dissuaded of a thing once he has fixed on it, but to my surprise and comfort, in this matter of my marriage he has shown forbearance. He will not have me enter into a compelled match. My mother, you see, was foisted upon him when he loved another. Forced to wed, the pair soon came to loathe and despise each other. Father likes to tell he abided Mother just often enough to beget one debacle of her, a botch of nature—me. When Mother died of the pox, I lost the only person on the face of the earth who could ever have loved such an inferior thing as I am." When Charlie hung his head, the dog Jack licked the nobleman's narrow nose.

"Oh, my dear, *dear* Charlie, you are entirely lovable and no such thing as inferior! Methinks the quandary is you have yet to find and use your actual strengths," said Kat emphatically.

"He'd get strong quick enough, and sturdy as an ox," said Blaidd, "if he was to heft crates and barrels aboard a ship, climb masts, hoist himself hand over hand along the rat lines in the rigging. By the devil's purple-hued malt worms, I'd get you bulked up, Charlie, milord, so's you'd have no need of stuffing cotton batting in your leggings and codpiece." Blaidd's eyes lit with delight at his brilliant idea and the prospect of having a future earl under his control.

"I will never ever go to sea, not even to build brawn and muscle. The rocking of a vessel on water undoes me," sniffed Charles.

"You truly are the poor map of woe your noble parent thinks you to be, eh, Your Excellency?" sneered Blaidd affably. "Good worts and ghosts' blisters, get a grasp, Charlie. You wallow in self-lenience. Don't be trumpeting your finicky failings. Subdue them, Your Honor."

"My father advises the same," answered Charlie with a helpless shrug.

"Harry has been so kind to me, I would not have supposed he could be so hard on you. Does he never say a good word of you, or admire anything about you?" asked Kat.

"He asserts, 'My son and I are as much alike as an egg is like an oyster.' Thus he disparages me to all and sundry He esteems me somewhat only when I win large at gambling, for he cannot understand how I so customarily do it. 'Be off to the gaming tables, boy,' he orders me. 'Put your one capability, that arcane arithmetical astuteness, to some *use*.'

"I never knew my father," sighed Kat.

"I envy you that," answered Charles miserably.

"Nor did I know my mother." She smiled wistfully. "My first memory is of Brother Truckle at Graie Friars. He has kept my ring on a ribbon, expecting someone, someday would come seeking after me. It's yet to happen," Kat added.

"I am sorry," said Charles. "Oh my word! Whatever is the matter, Mr. Kyd? What ails thee?" he asked sympathetically, seeing a tear role down Blaidd's cheek.

"Ah, me own poor dad, the best of fathers, was hounded into debtors' prison, and there hanged himself with . . . with lute strings," asserted the large boy with a catch in his voice.

"Lute strings?" asked Charlie. His jaw dropped.

"Two dastards got me poor dad's bond, Your Eminence, for a sizable loan. They gave him but five pounds in coin of the realm and the rest in lute strings, which they deemed to be worth fifteen pounds. They were worth nothin', there bein' no market for lute strings. The strings could not be given away and them curs demanded payment of fifteen pounds in the king's coinage." On hearing this, Charlie shoved the dog from his lap, took up Roxelana, and patted Blaidd's prickly blond head, now lowered to rest despondently on the table.

"What foul, marble-hearted villains were at work in this fraud upon your father, Blaidd?"

"They are called Flud and Wadd, sire, also known about as Welsh Frank and Paul Penniless, card sharpers, usurers' touts . . ." Blaidd's voice came muffled from the crook of his arm.

"Card sharpers?" repeated Charlie, his myopic eyes opening wide.

"Aye, and also foul intelligence gatherers of spymaster Francis Wiltenham, and Rattcliffe, the torturer."

"No!" exclaimed Charlie. "Why, my father the earl threatens me often with this Rattcliffe."

"Why and wherefore, Your Worship?"

"My library is the cause. Besides my cabinets of measuring instruments, my globe replicas of the earth and such, I have in excess of a thousand books written in many tongues—the Latin, Greek, Hebrew, Arabic, French, Castellan Spanish. More. There are chests filled with books, many containing occult philosophy so called, but in reality explicating science—geography, chemistry, the conjunction of planets, and the like. The king and his bishops forbid such study as blasphemous and heretical, a danger to the civil peace of our country. If it becomes known that one studies such things, he may be at risk of his life."

"Your earl father is trying to protect you, Charlie, in these strange times in which we live," Kat said. She and Gwyn were spreading blankets for the children upon the reed-covered floor near the warm fire.

"Strange times indeed," Gwyn interjected. "We are imperiled by secret sects, Papists hiding in every crevice, keeping private worship, Brownists creeping about, talking against the Established Church, evil spirits and demons roaming the land. This very day a ghost followed the oyster boy's cart from South Essex!"

"Gwyn, do at least *try* to be sensible!" protested Kat. "A ghost doesn't ride a flesh-and-blood horse such as the one that arrived here unmastered."

"True, Kat," agreed Blaidd. "Ghosts ride phantom horses, I wot."

At that, she shook her head, set down the well-filled child, threw up her hands, and left the table to stand in the entryway to the tavern, curious about what was transpiring between Harry and Win.

They sat head to head across a table, leaning forward, locked in intense talk, neither favoring the other with any hint of friendly warmth—nor even thinking of doing so, she worried. Certes, but they were more than something alike, Kat thought. The men were almost of a height, both well made of light, though strong and wiry physiques. Each watched the other like a hawk now, as they conversed, a similar reserved, stark wariness on both handsome faces, and Kat dearly wished she could hear what was passing between them.

"I'm aware that perhaps I might have asked her hand of you, sir, who are all the family, in a manner of speaking, Kat may ah, well . . . *boast* of, let us say, though that's not quite a precise use of the word. Lacking blood kin, Katesby claims you as her protector. But you were not available to me, being absent from England, when I discovered her. My eagerness to claim this unpolished jewel prompted me to act in haste. I ask you now, only as a courtesy to Katesby, mind, who wishes it of me, to smile upon this marriage I propose, and give her away."

"I cannot 'give her away,' nor am I prepared to smile on this match as you request. Kat is more of an age to be matched with your son," Win answered, unsmiling.

"I'd not inflict a sad thing such as him upon our lady, Beaumarais. Charles is not a man such you are, sir, but a timid creature, raised up by his mother, whom I detested. I was too much absent during his youth. She had overmuch influence upon him."

"What mean you by *our lady*?" Win bristled.

"In a manner of speaking, Katesby is *ours*. I talk freely to you, Win, for we share a regard for her well-being and happiness. I wish to have her near me to protect, to cherish, to *mold* into a great lady. I will provide her all the comforts and prizes this world has to offer. You would want her to have no less, she being as an affectionate sister to you."

Win scowled. "She should be as a captivating daughter to you."

"Yet she is neither sister nor daughter to either of us, Beaumarais," commented de Morely, "rather a wholly desirable young woman to *both*, I now realize. You want her yourself." Win neither confirmed nor denied the earl's supposition, but his silence was answer enough for Harry. And if his stilled tongue had not given Win away, his tense expression and the muscle flexing along his right cheek would have confirmed as well as words his true feelings.

"Of course I want her," he thought and silently cursed himself for a fool, for he'd gone precisely where the earl had been leading him, down a primrose path of self-revelation.

"Ah, so that *is* the way of it!" Harry said with an exultant, knowing, cold smile. It transformed him in Win's eyes, from ascetic monk to gloating devil. "I had no thought before meeting you, Beaumarais, of fomenting your jealousy, for I'd not supposed you to be a rival for the lady. Now that I have discovered the truth, I'll be on my guard. I warn you, I'll fight you for her by any means, fair or foul, and I'll win. Give over now, while we are all yet friends," Harry suggested.

Win barked a cold incredulous laugh. "Come, come, Beaumarais, be sensible, man," Harry pressed in an almost wheedling tone. "I will do more for her than you ever could, lad. My intentions are honorable. I will settle an independent fortune upon Katesby even before we are wed, to dispose of as she will, even give to you."

"You can't buy me off, de Morely. You've all England

from which to choose a companion for your declining years. May I make so bold as to ask why you have singled out Katesby?"

"You know the old wives' tale of the girl saved from her life of drudgery by a prince. I want with all my heart to rescue Katesby," the earl replied flippantly. "Seriously, sir, you, who know her well, should be the last man to ask why methinks, but I'll tell you nonetheless. Kat's story touches me—an abandoned orphan who survived, unembittered no less, on the streets of London, with a compassion for children in similar straits, her charity and kindness to them, her skill at graciously administering this inn so that one and all are welcome here, and at ease. 'Tis all impressive."

"And should Kat have no wish to be 'saved' from 'drudgery,' as you describe the work she loves? Moreover, you are no prince."

"I *want* her, Beaumarais. She brings to my mind and heart one I loved, who loved me, long ago. Kat enlivens my heart and allows me to relive my frittered youth, for she is able to give me the love I have lacked in my life. I have yet to claim her heart, I know, but I *will,* in time."

"You don't have all the time in the world. You're no longer a youth, you know. Harry, I mean no offence, but what of *her* yearnings? I am loath to say it, sir, but I have a concern about your . . . well . . . ability to . . . to satisfy . . . You know, sir, do you not, to what I allude?" Baldwin, on the counterattack, kept his tone polite, chagrined, kindly sympathetic.

"Men have found themselves dead for lesser insults than yours, Beaumarais," said Harry evenly. His deep-set eyes locked upon Win with a measuring fierceness bordering on fury "So, you think Kat will find me . . . lacking? Go on, if you dare."

"On short acquaintance" —Win grinned boyishly—"I find you lacking in little, sir, except perhaps a measure of youthful vigor. Mayn't be that a man of your years will not be able to keep pace with so young and spirited a wife?"

Baldwin asked. "But of course, as you've previously mentioned, you are able to compensate a lady with other amenities—wealth and ease, gowns and jewels, servants, visits to court, the excitement of the hunt in royal preserves from which starving men are forbidden to 'poach'. Such things *do* go a good way, for *some* women, to make up for other deficiencies in their husbands."

Win was pressing the earl, testing to find the limits of the man's temper, trying to provoke him to draw a dagger or challenge a duel. But though fury burned ever brighter in de Morely's gray eyes, he made no move. "I can give her something she wants, Harry, which you perhaps cannot."

Win took a full minute to drain his tankard of ale. The earl waited, then asked, pale with cold anger, "What . . . may . . . that . . . be, if I might make so bold?"

"A child of her own," replied Win, his tone implying the obviousness of his answer.

"Give me leave to put your apprehensions to rest, Beaumarais," was the earl' s response, his voice thick with sarcastical humor. "The girl stirs more than my wistful boyish hopes and longings. The mere sight of Kat, even in her workaday duds, heats my blood and touches me to the quick of my manhood. You've no cause for concern on that score." De Morely's confident hard smile was heat and ice combined. "I'll please her and in so doing give her yet another thing you never will be able to offer her—a noble, titled son."

"You may *try* to get a son of her but . . ." Win shrugged and left the sentence unfinished, his unspoken doubts about the earl's potency dangling dangerously in the air between them.

"My younger brother is a sluggish dullard and my son a frail. I *will* pass my estates and titles to my own male issue. As my lady wife, Katesby, as I have said, will be well gratified in every way. You, of course, Beaumarais, have pleased her in bed, I take it? That is your inference, is it not? You *do* know, then, what effect she has on a man, do you not?''

As Win now grappled to restrain his own temper, the earl leapt into the breach of silence between them. ''I anticipate that bedding Kat is an experience akin to mating with an adolescent lioness, or coupling with a wild mare, eh?'' de Morely asked. His nettling smile impelled Win to his feet, hand at his dagger hilt.

''I will make no reply to your discourteous question. You are unmannerly to pose it. Methinks I could teach you better decorum,'' Win growled. In the silence that fell upon the room, Kat's step could be distinctly heard as she dashed forward to prevent swordplay. The sound of benches scraping and boots clattering on the wooden floor filled the tavern as men moved to line the sides of room.

Chapter 9

When the tense hush again settled, Kat stood in the abandoned center of the tavern, the only sound the rattle of coins and dice from the gaming room. The earl's retainers, coachmen, outriders, and guards—a baker's dozen in all—stood at their lord's shoulders in a blaze of red-and-blue livery, the Norland colors.

A different sort of band was grouped opposite them, standing with Win—men in the unbleached stockings and short cloaks of yeoman, laborers, sailors, chapmen, and others whose occupations could not be so clearly discernable by their attire, shabby fellows, threadbare pamphleteers with dangerous opinions. There were also young men in plumed hats and buckled shoes, who lived by their dishonest wits with no other mission than to fill their own purses and dress in the latest fashions. Among these were a man burned through the gristle of the ear for petty thievery, two men branded upon their brows for vagrancy, others showing the blue marks of Bedlam set upon their wrists by dagger pricks rubbed and enduringly stained onto the skin with burnt paper.

"*My* retinue," said Win with a flourish of his dagger, standing with feet planted wide apart, his ornamented belt reflecting many-colored spears of jeweled light. Kat turned to him, set her hands upon his wide shoulders, and fingered the rich brocade of his doublet.

"Win," she whispered, "stop now lest I lose both you and Harry!" He set her aside as though she were of no more weight or substance than a feather, and she looked fiercely into the faces of his men, stepping up before each one to search his eyes—Jeremy Edge, gambler. Perkin Thyn, pickpocket. Francis Wyggington, spy. Hugh Wyld, highwayman. Tom Spratt, agent of the Crown, or not, she didn't know for a certainty. Her favorite, Jake Feake, poet, and others, frequenters all of Ram Alley, Damnation Alley, Devil's Gap, and other London slums where the streets, lined with tilting, crowded, reeking tenements and bawdy-house stews, were little more than runnels of mud. These men, damned by poverty, were lovers of streetwalkers, champions of orphans, saviors of madmen, sworn enemies of the king's corrupt sheriffs, bailiffs, torturers, gaolers, and hangmen. These were her people and there was naught Kat would say or do to hinder them. She stood with them, and turned to face Harry de Morely, Earl of Norland

"I withdraw my question, Beaumarais," announced Harry. "I was testing you only. You have shown me your mettle and devotion to Kat. Do sit down with me again, you gallant hotspur, before you suffer grave damage, get run through by my squire there." De Morely glanced at the man poised beside him. "Will Warbeck's speciality is the *coup de grace,* Beaumarais, the gash to the face, and the thrust *alla revolta,* the dagger in the eye. It pierces the brain and brings swift death."

"My man there," Win answered calmly, "is Giles Hather,

King of the Derbyshire gypsies. Like others of his tribe, he will be satisfied with no less than the heart's blood of his enemies."

"How did you lose your ears, Egyptian, if that's what you be?" demanded de Morely's squire of an olive-skinned, black-haired, muscular man holding a double-edged dagger in each hand.

"They took 'em when I was in the pillory," Giles replied. "I was put on display for reading palms. While I was caught there, among my possessions was found pewter plate said to be stolen and a license deemed falsified, so they stuck me earless comely head in the hangman's hempen window. Lucky for me, Chance came . . . by lucky chance, my pardon came to Tyburn Hill in time to save me from dancing on air."

"Read me fate and doom in the lines in me hand, eh, Giles, when we've done throwing out this lot?" asked Blaidd.

"Get thee out of sight, oaf!" wailed Gwyn, who with all her strength was trying to shove and drag Kyd into the kitchen again. The boy was as immovable as a boulder.

"Out!" roared Win, exasperated to see Kyd show his face in public.

"Aw, you know how hard it is for me to pass up a good fight," Kyd muttered, skulking off to the kitchen with Gwyn shoving and Deaf Jack snapping at his heels, to collide head to head with Charlie, peeking round the doorjamb. On impact, the slighter boy went down screeching but was caught before he hit the floor and taken off effortlessly by Kyd.

"I think you to be a counterfeit Egyptian, a lawbreaking English vagrant got up like a gypsy. Can you talk in the Romany tongue? Can you do the morrisco dance?" Warbeck persisted, badgering Giles Hather, waving his long sword.

"Giles is able to do both. He is no sluggard with dagger

nor saber neither," said Baldwin, setting a hand on the man's shoulder. De Morely, who had not moved but to blink with disgust at his foundering son, sat back in his chair, stretched out his legs, and looked up at Win with cool but enlarging regard.

"Hold, Warbeck!" he ordered his squire, then said to Baldwin, "Whilst you're up on your feet, Beaumarais, get us each another tankard of ale, if you please. I'm a touch stiff in the knees or I'd do so myself."

"Quite common a complaint in a man of your age, de Morely." Win shrugged, sheathing his dagger. "Poor King Henry has been on the hobble for some years," Win taunted, but this time with his sharp, fast white grin. A mumble of approval went round the room and Kat, with an angry exclamation, bolted for the kitchen, and the men dispersed.

"Henry's the elder," de Morely grumbled. "And the fatter. With his bulk 'tis no wonder his knees are giving out."

"I know a Wise Woman with a recipe for gout. Shall I summon her to the table?" Win asked ironically. He received no answer to the question but was gratified to see the earl's flush of annoyance and decided not to press his advantage just then. He would keep in mind what might well become a significant bit of useful information—Harry de Morely, clever, contained, highborn, devious, had finally revealed one weakness at least—he was afflicted with gout.

"To me and, I trust, to you, Katesby is worth her weight in pearls, sir," said de Morely when Win returned to the table and set down the refilled tankards. "Do I glimpse a look of displeasure on your lean countenance, Beaumarais? A thousand pardons, sir, if I gave offense earlier, but I *had* presumed, and correct me if I err, that you and I were not rivals for Kat's hand, that you've had ample opportunity to take the girl to wife, if you had so wished or ever intended."

"Indeed, you are correct, sir. That is a thing I have never wished for, nor intended," Win answered. He turned on his heel, about to stride off to the gaming room.

"Wait!" called Harry. "Tell me what you know of Kat's history. She has certain patrician qualities which, despite some unburnished edges, first attracted my attention."

"Ask her."

"I have. She knows nothing of her beginnings. I hoped you could . . ."

"I cannot. She was a foundling, as was I. We, the pair of us, come from the streets."

"I know *your* origins. I've uneathed much information about you. In your youth you came into an inheritance left you by a father who never claimed you in his lifetime. My informants also have told me that you then remade yourself from cutpurse to gentleman, not so much by dint of the altered facts of your true lineage, but by your own efforts and a bit of help from a pair of noble mentors, Lords Seton and Montfort, who saw to your education. I know as well that you saw to Kat's secure future by purchasing this inn for her, that together you and she have doubled the modest fortune left to the boy who was known for a time as Baldwin the Bastard Heir. That was before you left London to travel abroad . . . to Italy."

"Your meddlers and agents have done a thorough job," said Win, with begrudging respect for de Morely's capabilities but satisfied that no connection had been made between Baldwin Beaumarais and Win Chance.

"This practice of young Englishmen, noblemen's sons, and those sprigs even of common gentlemen of means, of going into Italy distresses many of the king's advisors and clerics. Some scholars, of course, go to complete medical studies and others to read Roman law, the basis of our own, but most visit Italy to frolic. Some of our countrymen, such as yourself, Beaumarais, return with a lively grace and charm and are for the most part good men. Others become transformed by the licentious and corrupt behavior of the foreign populace."

"You refer to the English Italianates, Harry, such as Langton, Lord Hesketh? He who renamed himself Ludovico and went about London with silk-draped page boys at his clacking heels."

"Hesketh, who had been a frequent visitor to my son's library, is now imprisoned in the Tower as a heretic for having the indiscretion to proclaim at court, 'He is a fool that maketh account of any religion . . . but he more the fool that would part with any . . . of his pleasure or wealth for his obsession.' Others, the very same sort as Hesketh, friends to Viscount de Morely, are known to import atheism and easy infidelity into this land. When they return to our England, many of those voyagers are kept under furtive surveillance. Did you know that, Beaumarais?" asked the earl. Win disliked this turn of the conversation, wondering if, after all, de Morely knew more of Chance than he'd revealed.

"I'd heard as much, and that some of these so-called heretics are in actuality working for spymaster Wiltenham. Is there anything more you care to tell me, my lord?" he asked, with brusque boldness, on guard for any sign that de Morely knew more than he was saying.

"Indeed. With all my sources and resources, which uneathed much about you, I cannot find a trace of Kat's origins. Her annals begin and end at the gates of Graie Friars."

"You've questioned Friar Truckle, I take it?" Win's eyes sparkled with amusement.

"That dedicated, pious old fellow is deaf and doddering, with no memory left to speak of, or so it would seem," complained Harry.

"That's as I've heard," Win answered with a wry smile,

knowing full well Truckle heard only what he wished to. "The good brother may grasp some of what I say. He knows me and has been known to answer my questions—on occasion. I'll go to him myself, Harry, on your behalf," Win offered, failing to mention his own newly stirred interest in Kat's history. "I suspect Truckle will be forthcoming in light of her possible marriage."

"*Possible* marriage?" the earl scoffed, offering an almost warm smile. "You're an outrageous optimist, Beaumarais, if you suppose, now that I've found her, I'll ever let her go."

"I am often termed outrageous, de Morely, and I'm widely known to be a confirmed optimist," Win answered. The two men were aware they were drawing battle lines acceptable to both in the contest to come.

"I was rather outrageous myself, Beaumarais, and like you, widely known but as a sporting, hard-living, reckless man. Lately, I've wearied of the usual preoccupations of the aristocracy—hawks, hounds, horses, apparel and drink, and of my mistresses with their sweet flimflams and empty heads. The halls of my of manors and castles echo with silence. I have come thither seeking the hand of Katesby Dalton," declared Harry with a nod in her direction, "for I crave concord, integrity, and a good measure of merriment in my lonely life. Kat will give me those and more."

"I'll make you privy to a matter which will be of interest to you. I have hitherto counseled Kat to accept your offer."

"Have you indeed, Beaumarais? I'm glad of it. And?" replied the earl, his tone amicable. He sensed Win had more to say, and waited for the other shoe to drop. "You know, I'm coming to think I could be persuaded to abide you, Beaumarais. Call me Harry, why don't you?"

"Uh—if you wish, Harry."

"Of course, we—you and I, Beaumarais—will both continue to hold Kat very dear, I know, whatever the outcome here, but if truly you want the best for her, encourage her to marry me, man!" Harry's gray eyes were fervent, almost feverish.

"Compromise is sometimes necessary in these things, and, all in all, she won't do better than to become a countess. Howsomever, ne'er forget she has a mind of her own. She's a headstrong female. She doesn't always follow my counsel." Win shrugged, a tease in his tone, humor in his eyes. "In fact, Harry, she has often been known to do the precise opposite of what I advise. If she supposes I am strongly against this match, that may drive her all the more quickly into it."

"Not too quickly," cautioned the earl. "I wish her to be quite convinced she wants me to take her away from . . ." He glanced about the tavern at the King of the Gypsies, with a Cunning Woman and a Wise Man, together poring over Tarot cards. At a near table, amidst the odd assortment of humankind—ladies and gentlemen quitting the high-stakes game room, the students, artisans, and musicians contributing to the merry noise and chaos of the tavern—he found a glum, round, pink face that jogged his memory. A name. Sharp—Something Sharp—came to the earl's mind. He knew it to be wrong but couldn't dredge up the right one and he could not recollect the circumstances of their paths having crossed. It nagged at his memory as he turned his preoccupied eyes back to Baldwin.

"Do you see the pink-faced man there, the one scribbling in a book? I know him for some reason, but I can't recall why. His name is Sharp or Keen or some such. Know him, Beaumarais?"

"I've never seen him before. He has the smug look of a covert agent but in whose service he operates I'd not even venture to speculate what with all the plots and counterplots and accusations of treason being hurled about now in England."

"Who he actually is will come to me, sooner or later. Older minds don't work as quickly as young ones, eh,

Beaumarais? Now, back to the subject at hand. Kat must be sure she wants to give up all *this* just to become a great lady," Harry finished sarcastically.

"Time alone, and Kat, will tell, eh?" Win replied. "I won't speak to her against your suit, quite the opposite. To be made wife of an earl would be an immense advantage to Katesby. Howbeit, I'm ready to wager, Harry, you'll not succeed in making her your countess," Win challenged confidently.

"Your wager's taken," answered Harry forgetting, for the moment, about Sharp. "What would you venture?"

"My life. That not being practical, I'll bet the *Conquest.* She's a good ship. And you? What will be your pledge?"

"Oh, it matters little to me, for I will not lose," the Earl declared confidently. "Name your preference—land, gold, goods, whatever."

"If I were you, Harry, I'd offer to play for the lady's heart." Win laughed in goading jest.

"Would that be to your liking, Beaumarais?"

"Certes, if I was in the love with the wench as you are. Howsomever, I'm not. If you'd chance one of your houses—any manor house will do, or a parcel of land. That would also be acceptable."

"Will my acreage on Cottswold Hill suit? Yes? Good, I want you to know, Beaumarais, I will always respect and reward you in whatever way I am able, for your loyalty to my future wife," de Morely answered, also confident.

"Don't patronize me," Win protested. "I will always do what I deem best where Kat's happiness is at stake."

"We're of one mind there. I'll drink to that," said Harry, raising his tankard in a toast to Win, then to Kat, who was poised at that moment on the kitchen threshold. Both men looked at her with a certain pride of possession, she thought, and both beckoned. Her own smile glowed.

"Later," she mouthed across the clamorous tavern. "Busy now!" Then she strode back into the kitchen.

"Are the Earl Harry and Win Beaumarais behaving civilized?" asked Gwyn.

"As though they've become fast friends, it appears," Kat answered, relieved yet bemused. They were up to *something,* that pair of gallants, *together,* and her curiosity was intense.

Chapter 10

The table had been cleared and Kat sat near Blaidd and Charlie while she carefully brushed out the long, tangled, and matted cornsilk tresses of an uncomplaining little girl whose eyes teared at every unavoidable tug of her hair.

"How will you avenge your father's death upon Flud and Wadd?" Charlie asked Blaidd.

"I will kill 'em, Excellency."

"I've a superior suggestion. In appreciation for your helping me to become more strapping in body and build, I will turn you into the best card sharper in England. After me, of course."

"Of course, after you, Your Regency. And then?" asked Blaidd, his interest piqued.

"Then you and I shall bilk the bilkers at card-play. We'll both take them on and win all they have, and more. They will owe you so many pounds silver that you will be able to have them incarcerated in debtors' prison for so long, they'll forget the color of sky!" Charles was impressed by his own plan. "I've not been so pleased with myself in a long while, Kyd, not since I bested my father—by fair means of course,'' he insisted, ''at a game of chesse-play.''

''Of *course* by fair means, Highness, '' Blaidd answered dubiously. ''I want to do 'em in, the curs.''

''Kyd, I hold only my father's second title, Viscount de Morely. I am not a highness, a grace, a regency, or an excellency. I am not excellent, nor even much g-g-good.'' Charles smiled shyly at his attempt at a jest. ''I am addressed as my lord.''

''I wish to treat with my father's tormentors in my own way, my lord. Kill 'em.''

''Of course, but move one step at a time, my good Kyd,'' suggested Charlie. ''First get them jailed, then find a way to get them murthered. There are cutthroats aplenty for hire, such as Mean Mack Flick. I observed him, as I was passing outside Herm's Rents, to strangle a man with a towel, cast him a blow with a ten-pound pressing iron, then deliver a gash in the face to be certain his quarry was killed quite dead.''

''I will attend to Wadd and Flud on me own, and it must be before I'm caught by the sheriffs.''

''You're a fugitive, are you?'' Charlie asked, and took a keener look at Blaidd.

''Why do you suppose, Your Grace, I'm loitering out here in the kitchen with children and dogs when I could be in the tavern swilling and carousing? I'm keeping out of sight, lying low, hiding until I clear my name.''

''Here? Hiding here at a place frequented by constables, sheriffs, tattlers, traitors, crown spies? I've another thought, good Blaidd. Come with me to my manor—my father's manor—in Sussex. There we may instruct each other and labor to improve ourselves undisturbed. We will stay gone from London until your pate is well covered by a growth of long hair, and you sport a beard and mustaches. You will be attired as my gentleman's man or my steward, in the Norland livery. That will help to disguise you from the king's constables when you return to London. It's your height that could be a bother."

"I'm no taller nor longer'n you," Blaidd said, "if you'd unfold yourself and stand perpendicular to the ground instead of bent over."

"Right!" Charles slapped his palm on the table and winced. "And I shall tell Father I am taking on a retainer of my own. I never have done it before." Blaidd, intrigued and enlivened by his new prospects, stood suddenly, hit his head on a low beam and, near to tumbling, neatly flipped backwards over the bench, eliciting peals of laughter from the children and applause from Kat and Gwyn.

"Kat told about you being a natural, haphazard sort of clown, boy," tittered Gwyn, "didn't you, Kat? But I'd not supposed you to be droll as all this," she managed to say between giggles, helping Blaidd to his feet and adding, "I'm sorry. I know it t'aint kind to laugh at a oaf but you are *just . . . so . . .* funny!" Scowling at Gwyn, Blaidd adjusted his breeks. "How 'bout a smile for Gwynny, so she knows there's no hard feelings between us, eh?" she asked sheepishly.

"I'll tell you same as I told Kat, Ninny. I'm a dour Welshman, not a clown nor a oaf given to frippery," he replied. "See, cheerful is not in me nature," he insisted even as his scowl reversed to a smile and he, too, burst into laughter.

"Who dubbed you 'oaf'?" asked Charlie, rocking back and forth with mild merriment.

"Certain small and dainty female persons. See, a really ladylike little thing, all beribboned and lace-frilled, ties my tongue and makes me feel cumbersome of person. Oafish, Kat called me, though she being not small and bare of ribbons has no such effect upon me," Blaidd jested.

Kat smiled. "That was all in fun. I really don't find you oafish."

"Gads, but I understand Blaidd only too well," Charlie said, clasping his hands. "It goes the same way with me as with him, except it matters not to me whether a lady is wearing ribbons or no. My t-t-tongue ties in the presence of . . ." His eyes repeatedly darted to Gwyn's pretty face, then dropped again to his hands, now folded in his lap, ". . . of winsome women."

"Have you never been with even one girl, not a single tumble in the hay with a kindly country wench, or an encounter in a doorjamb with a scullion in from your father's kitchens?" Blaidd asked with a forlorn expression.

"Do you dance at all, Charlie?" Gwyn asked kindly. "If you held a lady's hand and moved about with her in a formal way, mightn't that be . . . helpful?" She took one of his hands and he stood.

"Can't dance. Too much vaulting and leaping for my poor legs."

"There you are again, Your Excellency," Blaidd said with annoyance, "advertising another of your weaknesses. When you have labored under my overseeing, you shall show a fine unpadded leg and leap high as a morrisco dancer."

"It pleases me to have you all enjoying such a grand time, but someone, Gwyn, must refill the goblets of the players in the game room," said Kat, taking on her role of manager. "Take a large wineskin of good claret and a pail of oysters, please."

"Gamblers are a queer lot," Gwyn said. "The inn could well burn down around 'em and they'd give the fire scant notice. There'd be never a break in the dice-play, just a shift of the locale."

"So . . . s-s-so I've observed," stammered Charles.

"Right, that, about gamblers," Blaidd said, as if he'd just been graced with a revelation. "Earlier, not one of them budged or even glanced up when there was a near altercation in the tavern between the earl and Chance." He slapped a hand over his mouth. "Agh, blue malt worms! I didn't intend . . . I should nay have said . . ."

"Say no *more,*" hissed Kat, and Blaidd clenched his mouth shut so hard, the others heard his teeth click. Kat glowered at him, Gwyn shook her head, and several of the children looked curiously in Blaidd's direction. Charlie, but for an extra eye-blink, Kat observed, took no notice of Blaidd's gaffe and made no comment about Chance, as if he hadn't heard or, if he had, didn't understand what had been revealed.

"Well, if you won't dance, Charles, will you not take a place at the gaming table?" Gwyn asked in hopes of distracting and getting him out of the kitchen.

"If you allow me to help," he replied, relieving her of the heavy pail of oysters tilting her to one side. When the pair had gone, Blaidd turned to Kat looking so forlorn and sorry, she hadn't the heart to castigate him.

"Don't worry, Blaidd," she sighed. "Young de Morely has little experience of the world, nor interest in it, particularly that part containing London's low life, spies, bailiffs, frauds and cheats, and other so-called culprits of that sort."

"Win put it perfect, didn't he, when he said I was a dumb show all on me own?" Blaidd, slumped at the table once more, held his shining head in his big hands.

"He also described you as cocky as a rooster and brave as a bear. Keep an eye on him, eh, Kyd?"

"Sure and don't I always?" the boy asked, cocking an ear toward the tavern. "Aye, Kat, call in the gypsy, if you please. I require a true moon man to read me future in my palm."

"Is it so you never had any lover, Charlie? A virgin man you are, then?" asked Gwyn in a whisper, her lips close to his ear. She and young de Morely occupied a table tucked against a wall, close to the tavern hearth. His answer to her question was one quick nod. "What's your age, Charlie?"

"Eighteen, on my next b-b-b-b-birth anniversary." His face turned a close shade to the scarlet of his attire.

"I also am untouched, a chaste maid, at sixteen," Gwyn volunteered.

"Imagine that."

"I've had offers, mind you," she added with a slow, prideful smile.

"Blaidd Kyd?" Charles ventured.

"Oh, no! He's near as timid as you, excepting when he's with wantons and bawds, he tells, if they be not too pretty, only sufferable in appearance."

"He likes *you*. I've watched him watching you. Who else has sought your favors?"

"Jim Bowling—Captain Bowling, that is, master of Baldwin's boat *Conquest*. Ship, not boat, they tell me I must call her, the vessel. The captain is a well-made, handsome man of great good humor. Also of good repute and with a good income. He'd make a good match for me and me for him, I decided, but he's asked only for me favors, never for me hand in wedlock. I'm delaying. I require more from Jim. I want his name." Gwyn raised her chin proudly. "Can you fathom it, Charlie, why I deny Jimmy my favors and would surrender to you?"

"No, not unless . . . you . . . it cannot be that you . . . are in love with me?"

"No, not a bit! I love Jim. Understand, it is a reach for an undowered barmaid to catch a ship's captain, but Jimmy t'aint altogether outside the reaches of my net. You are, though, a noble viscount and future earl. I do like you, Charlie, and I wish to be a friend to you, and of service. I've declined other men, and I've had to fend off a few, but with you I'd not resist. The opposite's true. What say you?"

"Are you bestowing yourself upon me just to . . . be kind?"

"I'm drawn to you, Charlie. I think you a lovely, mild

boy. I expect you'll be kind to me also, when we are abed. But 'tis more than that. You're Viscount de Morely, one day to be Earl of Norland! A girl ne'er forgets her first man, it's said, and if he's noble, why that should render the milestone even more splendidly memorable."

Charles made so bold as to lift his disbelieving eyes from the tabletop and look at Gwyn. She was a pretty thing, with just that bonny bit of a nose and a cupid's-bow mouth. She was also pleasingly small of stature, her slim form girlish, not bursting the seams of her dress with soft protrusions and overhangs.

"If we do lie . . . together, then I'd know if I was . . . manly," he said wistfully.

"No matter how it passes with thee and me, I *know* you are a fine man. I'm certain of that, whatever your father has told you. Come with me now?" Gwyn whispered before her seductive, deep-throated chuckle filled the room. A few guests, the usual late-night predatory women and roaring boys, turned in their direction, and Charles moved a little away from Gwyn. She might be small of person, but she could guffaw like a goliath, he thought, alarmed, and if she were to laugh at him? He couldn't chance it.

"I . . . I would . . . wait until another time, tomorrow night or the next even. Father and I are to be at court to have an audience with the king in the morning. I wouldn't want to . . . I mustn't oversleep," said Charles, sidling for the inn door, where a carriage, he knew, well warmed by a brazier of slow-burning charcoal, was waiting to take him to the earl's townhouse near Charing Cross.

"Warbeck, do tell Father I shall send the driver back to fetch him," he called over his shoulder to the squire, as he went slipping and sliding on frozen snow in his haste to escape. He hurled himself into what he expected to be the dim solitude of the carriage. To his annoyance, it held an occupant.

"Good evening to you, sir," Charles, shivering, greeted

the pink-faced man, Burgess Blunt, furtive agent of the London constabulary. "Did you observe anything within the tavern of interest to your keepers and overseers?"

Blunt did not deign to glance up until he had finished writing in a small leather-bound book, replaced it and his quill and ink pot in a writing case, snapped it shut, and turned the lock with a gold key on a gold chain which he dropped into a silk pouch dangling about his neck.

"Indeed, my lord. The establishment is patronized by university wits and threadbare law clerks as well as by eminent men and women. It is also a lair of spies, traitors, Egyptian moon men, dice cheats, heretics, and criminals of all sorts. I espied an escaped felon there, called Blaidd Kyd. Doubtless, Wiltenham will, at dawn, send a troop to apprehend the young cuffin. He will be passed to Rattcliffe for the torturer's amusement before the hangman claims him, for the second time."

"Twice hanged? How can it be?" questioned the viscount.

"The outlaw, Chance, made so bold as to cut Kyd down during his first jaunt to the gibbet. Likely the reckless Robyn Hood of London will attempt the same daredeviltry again, to save his friend. This time, we shall be ready," Blunt said smugly. A small man whose feet barely touched the carriage floor, Blunt was smooth-shaven, round-faced, and pink-skinned. He had thin, light orange hair receding from a high brow and a bulbous nose between close-set, pale hazel eyes. He was reputed to be a sneering, boastful, dangerous man, whom Charles expected might be a useful one as well.

"And what of the other of the low folk drinking under The Sign of the Kat?" he asked.

"We will leave them at liberty for a time, to steer us to the leader of their ring of outlawry, insurrection, and—"

"And lead you to him you designate the Robyn Hood of London, Win Chance," Charles inserted.

"They are one and the same man, the outlaw leader and Chance, the foremost of these villains! What have you learned of him? Do tell me! *Tell me* all," squealed Blunt, quivering with excitement.

"I've learned nothing . . . exact. His name was uttered, then silence fell," Charles tormented Blunt. "What know you of the proprietress of the inn herself? She will become mother to me unless I am able to malign her in some way—even, if necessary, arrange for a fatal accident to befall her." In his intensity, Charles had lost his hesitant manner and halting speech.

"The lively landlady, Katesby Dalton, is much loved for her good works. She is well connected, and protected, by some significant personages, I know not who. If I am to stalk her for you, milord, fabricate a charge against her, perhaps even arrange for her to meet with a mishap, shall I say? Well, I must have great care and considerable coin as well as a damning accusation founded upon some scrap of hearsay, gossip, even fact . . ."

"I'll get all that for you, Blunt. I know just where to begin—at Graie Friars with an aged monk called Truckle. She told me so herself."

"Good Brother Truckle? He is uncle to Arthur, Lord Seton, and to Lord Seton's sister, Lady Cary, who herself is wife to Lord Monfort, he a first cousin to Seton's wife, Adelaide!"

"Indeed? Do tell," said Charles in some confusion. "Well . . . so?"

"Can't follow all that, can you, my lord? Bookish creatures often have little common sense, I've noticed," Blunt said in a nasty, mocking tone. "The bloodlines of our English aristocrats run every which way. Those I just rattled off for you all do some of their *noblesse oblige* by donating alms to Graie Friars, to which you say Katesby Dalton also has some connection. They—the Setons and Montforts—

could be her high-placed friends. I wonder about . . . Chance."

"All I am able to advise you there, Blunt, is to leave Blaidd Kyd at large, the quicker to seize Chance. Moreover, I wish to make some use of the large boy," said Charles. "He's to do me a service."

"If this leviathan of a Welshman eludes me, you'll pay a forfeit, de Morely," warned Blunt.

"Spare me your threats, Burgess. You, Wiltenham, Rattcliffe, and the hangman will get Kyd when I've done with him. The young giant will not escape again. Now, I'm wondering, Blunt, mightn't we get Katesby Dalton hanged, along with Chance and Kyd?"

The inn door had just closed after Charles when Baldwin and Harry, jingling his winnings in his pocket pouch, stepped from the gaming room into the tavern to be joined by Kat.

"Because I'm feeling graced and expansive this night, I wish to share with you, Beaumarais, a most superior wine conveyed from Portugal," said Harry. "I've only just collected a skinful from the dock where it was unloaded in the small hours of yesterday morning. I try never to travel the roads without a supply. Warbeck, good man, fetch the wineskin of port from my carriage," Harry ordered the squire, who was coming in from the frigid cold of the winter's night.

"It is not there, sire," answered Warbeck.

"Not?" questioned the earl coldly, raising a brow. "What barbarian has swilled down my rare and precious wine?"

" 'Tis your carriage which is not there, though manifestly the wine contained in it is gone as well. The Viscount de Morely vowed to send the driver right round for you, sir, on the instant he arrived at his destination."

"The carriage may perhaps return, but doubtless it will

have been plundered of my port, if I know Charlie,'' snorted the earl.

''Allow me, Harry, to pour you a goblet of the very same wine,'' suggested Baldwin, ''carried to London in my ship *Conquest,* landed yesterday.''

''Your holdings are more substantial than I'd been informed,'' remarked Harry, narrow-eyed with interest. ''Be that as it may, you'll of course join me, Beaumarais, in a quaff to our wager?''

''One swallow, then I must be off. I've other business this night,'' answered Win.

''Perhaps you'll join me to break the fast at first light? Lacking a carriage to take me home, I shall spend the remainder of this night under The Sign of the Kat.''

''We're full up, Harry.'' Baldwin's cool shark grin flashed.

''I'm confident Katesby will find a place for *me.*'' The earl offered his own fierce twitch of a smile. ''Is it not so, my dear?'' He smiled upon Kat as she joined their circle.

''You shall have my chamber, milord,'' she answered happily.

''And where will *you* spend this night?'' Win asked her.

''Don't fret about me, Win. I'll find a nook or cranny *somewhere.*''

Kat's full smile lit the room as she looked from Win to Harry and back to Win, who lifted an interrogative brow, shrugged, then nodded as if to say, ''Go after him, girl. It's perfectly acceptable to me.''

''I must to bed at once. I'm not so young as I was, as Beaumarais has reminded me.'' Harry winked and yawned extravagantly. ''I wish to be sprightly on awakening. I have an audience with the king on the morrow. I go to the royal palace in the Tower to seek permission of Henry to wed, to ask his leave to take you to wife, dear Katesby.''

''Because I am an insignificant commoner?''

''A commoner, yes, but not insignificant. That is some

of the cause of my going to the king. Also, there is the constraint laid upon all peers of the English nobility that the monarch must grant leave to his nobles to wed whomsoever. Thus the king is secure that aristocratic blood will not run so blue and true in any one family's veins that it may lay claim to the throne and crown of England, should the opportunity ever present."

"Your proposal of marriage does me the greatest honor, dear Harry, but do not go to the king too hastily," Kat said, troubled. "I haven't yet . . . I have not given you my answer."

"And I will not command it from you till you feel free to speak. I wish to be able to act quickly on the positive answer I anticipate from you, my dear."

"Wedding is destiny," commented Win. "So goes an old adage."

"Hanging likewise, says the same proverb," snapped Harry. "'Hanging and wiving goes by destiny.'" He saw his two companions exchange swift glances. Win's expression was enigmatic, Kat's appalled. She placed a hand at her neck and gasped, as if feeling a noose, and turned away from the men, clearing her throat.

"Love and a cough cannot be hid," Win commented softly, patting her back. "That's another good old saying."

"Well, well, and *tempus fugit,* time flies. Shall we to bed?" asked Harry.

"I'll show you up now, my lord," Kat offered.

"Will you return soon again, Katesby?" Win asked hastily. "I've a matter to talk of with you."

"Shall I keep running up and down, like a bucket in a well?" she asked, hands on her hips.

"You gave me to believe, Beaumarais, you had other business to do this night," said Harry with a scoffing, vapid smile.

It suited the powerful earl not at all, decided Win, though he found Kat's smile fetchingly wicked when she added, "*And* you've other kettles to stir." The fourth stair creaked as she danced up to it and waited for Harry, who followed more slowly.

"I *will* get to fixing that stair one day," mused Baldwin absently, as if his mind were already elsewhere, stirring that other kettle. In truth, he was urgently trying to think of a way to keep Kat with him and away from Harry de Morely.

"By chaff and bran, let her bed him if she will! 'Tis of no moment to me," he said under his breath, striding out the door into the night.

Chapter 11

Later, when the new day was a quarter hour old by the clock, Kat's kitchen was at last still. Roxelana was asleep in her arms as she sat rocking in a chair. The fire crackled. The children and dogs were curled together, asleep. The inn under The Sign of the Kat, full up to its rafters, had settled into quiet but for the creak of old timbers under the rocking chair, the lowing of a cow from the barn, and the random, slumberous call of a guest from deep in dreams.

Kat was thinking of Beau, wondering if he was, at that very minute, in the arms of a woman; if whoever she was, was pleasing him, amusing him, running her fingers along the long cord of his spine, tasting his firm, full lips as she herself had done, nibbling on the bounteous, swelling lower one.

His lips were red, and one was thin,
Compared with that was next his chin,
Some bee had stung it newly.

She smiled wistfully, whispering those lines of poesy to herself. What must she do to persuade the man he loved her? And what must she do to convince Harry de Morely he did not?

The second question should have been the easier for her to answer. She had told him, when she bade him good night at the door of her chamber, that she did not love him but loved another, that in fairness and good conscience, she must decline his proposal, for he deserved a devoted wife, not a silly twit pining for the love of another. Harry would have none of it. He'd not take no for answer—not so soon as this. Furthermore, he cared not if she loved another *this* day.

"On the morrow, or on some more distant morrow," Harry had said, his cool, pale hand resting along her cheek, "you will perhaps have a change of mind and heart. I esteem your honesty, Katesby, and thank you for it, but say nothing more to me just now. Mull longer over this and allow me to keep my happy expectations. I've not felt so . . . fond and doting in years. I'm a patient man, my dear." She'd agreed to mull.

The baby Roxelana stretched her little arms, gurgled, fluttered her long, dark lashes, and went off to sleep again. Jack the dog vigorously scratched at a flea, yawned, yawped, wriggled his way into the center of the sleeping mound, and settled down again.

The little boy Kat had spoon-fed, a child of about seven summers, she decided, had tentatively situated himself near the others, at the outer edge of the cluster. He didn't sleep but stared into the fire, his dark, unblinking eyes flat and glowing, reflecting light. Now he rose and began to roam about the room, first along the lines of the walls, looking into containers and bins, climbing on chairs only to jump right down again, then lift himself up to the ledge of a frosted window to peer out. The latched shutters confined his view to his own reflection, and his pace, as he resumed circling the kitchen, grew faster. When he came to the great oaken door, he scratched and pulled at it, leaped up at the latch and bolt but could not reach them, leaned his back against the door, and looked at Kat.

The boy brought to her mind a street kitten of six or seven months she'd taken in last winter. It had eaten greedily, purring, drunk deeply, then explored its confines, lingering over what caught its interest—a shadow, an apron tie—until it had rounded the kitchen several times and then begun to appear trapped within four walls, seemed to grow larger with each circuit of the room as if, soon, the space would not contain it as it moved restlessly, seeking a way out to the freedom of the street despite the cold and danger awaiting it there.

"Do you want to leave here?" Kat asked the boy. "Shall I slip the bolt for you?"

"Yes, please, miss." He nodded, flattened against the door.

"Hold," she answered, placing Roxelana into a down-lined basket and tucking a coverlet round her. Then she raised the lid of a large chest and rummaged through it until she produced a pair of black boots, a hooded cape, and a woven kersey-wool scarf.

"There!" she commented when the child wore the boots, which came above his knees to meet the cape, the hood resting low on his brow and secured by the scarf wound twice about his throat, covering the lower part of his small face. Only a pair of dark eyes was visible.

"Thank you, miss," he said as the great door swung open, dwarfing him. "I'm all got up just like Win Chance, amn't I?"

"Yes, you are," Kat answered, surprised at what she had created, a miniature Chance. The full-size original *did* dress and wrap all in black and show only his eyes.

"I will be like him when I'm grown, and do as he does."

"Steal and rob?" she asked, tongue in cheek.

"He don't. It's not so!" the child said stubbornly. "Chance helps the poor with what the rich don't know they got and don't miss."

" 'Tis warm here, my chivalrous Little Chance. Stay. Where will you go this cold night if you leave?" she asked the child.

"To look for me mum," was the answer.

"Where?"

"On the bridge or at Graie Friars. I saved her a bit of bread, see?"

"Hold a minute. I'll give you more food to take," Kat said, piling sausage and cheese upon a cloth and tying the four corners to make a neat bundle. "There," she said, handing it over. "Will she, your mum, feed and care for you tomorrow, boy?"

"No, miss. I must do for her. That been so since she was put in pillory at Cheapside. She never been the same, after. She t'aint bothered to do nothing much for herself since."

"What was her offense?" Kat asked in a low voice.

"Forsaking her child in the streets of Southwark. That was her crime. It was *my* fault, what they done to her."

"Your fault?" Kat asked, pained. "How?"

"If she had no tyke—me—to forsake, she'd not have been pilloried, eh? I'll be going now. She frets awfully when she don't see me for a time."

"Come here again tomorrow. Bring her with you."

"Right, miss," he said. She saw the dark eyes smile.

"And watch for the bellman making his rounds, that he doesn't grab you for being on the streets after curfew," she said in a whispered shout as the small figure in black was silhouetted against the snow before it vanished into the night.

She closed the door, thinking of the real Chance, wondering if he was on the ramble this night, up to some good, or if Baldwin, up to no good, was asleep, safe in some bed somewhere in London Towne. Goats' blisters! She would not be wondering and worrying, running after him forever, trailing her heart's blood! She repeated the words of a poem scribbled on a scrap of paper and left by some aspiring poet in the tavern.

Why so pale and wan, fond lover?
Prithee, why so pale?
Will, when looking well can't move him,
Looking ill prevail?

"No," she said, tossing back her hair and lifting her chin proudly. She looked at her reflection in a shiny copper cauldron and forced a glaring smile. It wouldn't do to go about appearing tired and low. Kat picked up Roxelana's basket. She cast a glance at the sleeping children and whispered the first prayer she had ever been taught by Brother Truckle.

St. Francis and St. Benedict
Bless this house from wicked wight.
Keep it from all evil spirits
Fairies, weasels, bats, and ferrites.

The fourth step creaked as she started up the stairs. She paused there to add, "And bless the old man, too."

At three in the morning, Win bypassed the creaking fourth step as, holding a candle aloft, he took the stairs two at a time to his rooms. He dropped his furred cloak, placed the brocade jacket over a chair—the same oaken high-backed one upon which, earlier, Kat had set her hands while he set his upon her hips. His body reacted to his thoughts, and he stripped down directly to release the bulge uncoiling against his leggings. The fire was low and steady, and in its light he washed his face with the near-frozen water in the pitcher on the mantel, then sponged himself all over to cool down. He raked back his coppery hair and, pursing his lips, he puffed out the candle. He braced himself for the chill of cold sheets and slithered between them. They were warm. Kat was in his bed.

"What are you doing here? What do you want of me now?" His tone was exasperated, his voice thick with desire when his body pressed to her warmth and folded about her.

"I want to know where you've been," she replied in a sleepy milk-and-gravel voice, jostling against him. She wriggled in his arms to bring them face-to-face, one of her long, warm legs overlapping his, wrapping about him.

"Stirring kettles, you toasty wench," he breathed against her brow, his strong arm enfolding her waist, his hand dropping down, filling with the soft, lean swell of her, to secure her against him.

"No!" she sighed. "I don't believe you."

"I was visiting with the good Friar Truckle," he answered, feeling her lips pressed to his shoulder.

"Why?" she asked.

"To talk of you." His hips swiveled, thrusting him against her.

"Why?" she asked, baring her teeth and nipping at his lower lip with some measure of restraint.

"At Norland's bidding. Harry wishes to know your derivation."

"As do I wish, but the friar doesn't know. He's oft told me so. What took you and him so long, conversing on a subject about which neither of you had much to say?"

"I found him at New Inn, a considerable walk from the monastery for an old man on a frigid night. He was, he said, seeking sinners and drunks to save from the cold at least, if not from hell and the devil. He was deep in his cups himself."

"As he has been known intermittently to be, poor man 'Tis one of the hazards of his vocation. Go on, Win." Kat's head rested on Win's shoulder. His hand cupped her breast. During the lull, a pause on an agreeable and comfortable plateau of passion, they rested, skin to skin, easy together, friends.

"I managed to get Truckle to say that though indeed he does have your ring, he could not give it to me this night. 'Tis put safely away with other objects of possible pertinence to you and others like you who were left orphans at Graie Friars." Kat leaned up on one elbow to look into Win's face.

"So, he did not give the ring over to you? Did he make any speculation or even a rash guess as to from whence I came? And do I want to know? There are matters in this world best not known, some rocks which should not be lifted."

"I can't answer that. I learned little. Truckle has your ring, as I have said, put well away for safekeeping. The only difficulty is, he cannot remember *where*. He vows that on the morrow, when his mind is enlivened, he will recall the hiding place of the ring. I'm to return to Graie Friars in the morning. He said a revelatory thing as he waved me good-bye."

"Tell it," whispered Kat.

"He says he will take with him to the grave secrets he has sworn to keep regarding more than one child's actual parentage."

"Is there no way around this quagmire? Cannot he find any excuse to reveal the truth? If the mother and father have passed over, or turned derelict, or if a life depended upon a revelation only Brother Truckle's to make, would he speak?"

"Only one predicament would allow him to break his word and reveal a confidence. That would be to stop someone going against the teachings of the Church or breaking a commandment."

"But he will give us my ring, you say? That is, if he finds it? Nothing else?"

"The old man might have offered me a clue or a hint, along with one of the toothless grimaces he uses for a smile. He asked to be remembered to you, his sweetheart with a sweet tooth, for the yield of the sugar islands. What does that mean to you, Kat?" They had released their holds upon each other and were separated by a few inches until Kat again slid into the curve of Win's arm to rest her head upon his shoulder.

"I've a liking for sugar treacle, for honey from the hive dipped in sundry fall and summer fruits, but I crave such sweets to no greater degree than most. I find no hint or clue in the sugary words of a tipsy old monk."

"Mm-hm," mumbled Win, his eyelids heavy. "Will you let me sleep now for a bit, Kat?" he asked in a drowsy undertone, pulling the quilts up to his chin.

"No, I will not," she answered, flipping the covers off his long form.

"What do you want of me, wench?" he grumbled, the next actor in their bed-bound tug of war. He stripped the covers from Kat entirely and rolled in them to secure them around and beneath him. On her knees straddling him, she hauled and yanked. She could not budge the quilt, but the sight of her splendid body bared, the swell of the muscles in her arms, the tightening of her flat belly as she grappled, most of all the flex of her breasts poised above him, brought Win very wide awake.

"Kat . . ." He grinned, a teasing threat in his tone, murder, mayhem, and lechery in his eyes." What do you want?"

"A lesson."

'Kat . . ." He stopped grinning. "We agreed—no more."

"Ah, but you took me by surprise, talking there on the

steps. After we came to that agreement, I recalled what you had said when we were . . . into the thick of it. 'Stop counting,' you said. There were so many more love lessons you could give, I'd not be able to run a tally so high."

"Oh? As many lessons as that, did I say?" She nodded down at him three or four times over, as a little girl might do, but when she sat back, on his thighs, her knees to either side of him and set her hands on her hips, it was no little girl he was staring at, rather a slender young Venus with high breasts, the hips of a woman. And a waist so fine he could encircle it with his hands if he could extract them from the cocoon of blankets he'd rolled himself into.

"What else did I say?" he asked slowly.

"You said if you were to teach me all the various and sundry ways, one night at a time, it would take until forever before we'd get in a rut and tedium would beset us. Now you sidestep. You promised I could have countless lessons," she scolded, in a silky-voiced whisper before she leaned to kiss his lips. "Are you not a man of your word, then?"

"You are not . . . in need of . . . more lessons," he rasped at spaced intervals between which he parted his lips to tap the succulence of hers. She was pleased. He might relent. Then he turned his mouth away.

"You are tangled in a web of your own making. Promise to do my bidding, or I'll never let you go," Kat tenderly threatened.

"Hark now, Katesby. I've had a few bedmates, some notorious women extolled for their carnal expertise. By your natural predisposition alone, in my expert opinion, you could teach many courtesans a thing or two." Kat saw his quick white grin gleam in the semidarkness. "You know as much as you need to know now. You've got glorious ah . . . underpinnings on which to proceed, fine instincts, creativity, warmth. You're mirthful and merry . . . in bed and out. That's all to the good. Get off me now, before you regret your sassiness."

"I must have done *something* wrong, Win. There must be *some* room for improvement," she bantered, stretching along his full length, feeling him hard under her.

"Not that I can think of. What is it, precisely, you want to learn?" he asked, tensing his muscles, preparing to spring. He'd teach the imp a thing or two, take her by surprise all right, not with words this time, but with the flat of his hand.

"I don't *know* what I don't know. That's the trouble. Can we not just . . . make merry?" she asked with an adorable little laugh. He sprang, uncoiled like a great cat, and had her pinned under him.

"I was going to spank you as soon as I got the upper hand, but now I find there's another thing I'd rather do with you."

Kat shivered with anticipation, and her voice was hoarse with passion when she asked, "What may that be?"

Kat's low voice quavered with eagerness and also with a reverent dread. Win kissed her nose. It wrinkled when she smiled.

"Make merry," he answered with laughing eyes before his mouth plunged down to hers.

Chapter 12

When Win awakened to find Kat's place in his bed empty, he had an urgent need to find her. He pulled on what garments came quickest to hand. The fourth step creaked beneath his weight and Kat, at the kitchen hearth, looked up to find him standing barefoot in the doorway in shirttails and breeches, smiling at her. The warm kitchen of the inn was quiet but for the crackling fire. The waifs, fed, could not be restrained from running out to see the snow-covered city, and the dogs had poured out with them.

"You're looking content with yourself this morning," she remarked, smiling back at him.

"Aye. And you're looking . . . pretty. What are you doing?"

"I'm stirring kettles," she bantered. "You've not ever said that to me before, that I looked . . ."

"I should have," he replied. The fire behind her was shining in her long, flowing hair, turning it to golden flame. Her cheeks were pink with heat, and her immense green eyes were dancing with a light all their own. They were *beautiful*, Win marveled, wondering how it could have been he'd never seen her thus. He straddled a bench and she stood blushing under his long scrutiny.

"You're not merely pretty. Today, you appear to be exceptionally . . . merry, also," Win said as Kat set a brimming pewter bowl before him and a mug of hot cider.

"Not without cause. I've been well merried half the night." Her lips curved up at one corner, suggesting a flirty smile. He grinned. She raked a shaft of his coppery hair from his brow and traced his stubbled jaw, fleetingly kissed his lips. He captured her hand.

"The lovely fragrance . . . ?"

"I've just tossed perfumed cakes into the fire. Soon the room will be fragrant with the same odor, dried buds of damask roses, rose water, civet, and ambergris, crushed all together in the mortar, dried, and stored in summer for such a moment as this. Why look you at me with such deep amaze, Beau?" Kat asked.

" 'Tis not amazement you see in me but regard rather, for your . . . housewifely talents."

"Eat while it's hot, then," she answered with that familiar, crooked little smile of hers that he liked so well. He did eat, watching her all the while glide about the kitchen attending to chores so all would be in readiness for the next guests to awaken hungry and anxious to be on the roads again.

An accustomed, pleasing silence settled on the kitchen again; a warm quiet and ease enveloped Kat and Win. All was the same as it had always been with them, he mused. Nearly the same. Better, for they were even closer now, friends in more ways than one. Here he was, home after months at sea, sipping cider while Kat kneaded bread, shifting a stray curl from her eyes with the back of her hand, humming to herself. This moment was entire and flawless as none had been before it, Win decided. He had the ridiculous notion that if he could stop time and progress, build a bulwark against all the intrusions of the world and be always thus, with Kat alone, he would.

"Kat . . . ?" She looked to him, longing to hear him put into words what she read in his eyes. Her heart thudded so in her breast that she thought he must hear it beating. She longed to touch him, set her hands along his broad shoulders, brush her cheek to his, taste his mouth. She didn't move. It was too perfect a moment to interrupt.

"Aye, Beau?" she whispered.

"Would you . . . do you . . . did you collect what was owing from the ones who've gone?" Some of the travelers, those caught by the snow with a long, hard, white road yet to travel, departed The Sign of the Kat before first light. They had been fed by the innkeeper on trenchers of hot gruel with pools of butter melting into thick cream. There were fresh bread, salt cod fishes, and smoked eels, too, and hot barley water to wash it all down. Kat's departing guests had been sent off with full stomachs rumbling, some to attempt going on by carriage or cart, others on foot.

"They didn't all settle up," she sighed, letting go of the perfect moment. "Stopped as they were unexpectedly, one couple pleaded lack of ready coin. The husband promised to make good their debt. They are gentlefolk, but threadbare poor and so slight they must endure a pinching diet. I asked that they bestow whatever pence they could spare upon the Graie Friars, should they pass that way."

Her thoughts turned to Friar Truckle. So did Baldwin's. Though he had himself taken the man home, he hadn't put him to bed and he couldn't help but wonder if, in fact, the friar had gone safe asleep. There was the possibility the old fellow had slipped out again. He'd been known to do exactly so more than one time before. Win drained his goblet of cider and stood.

"I'll be off soon as we do our numbers, Kat. Friar Truckle may need me to help in the search for your ring," he told her, recalling Truckle as he'd seen him last. The brother's cowl had been blown from his head. Fingering the bare, cold skin of his shaved tonsure, he watched from just inside the gates of Graie Friars Poor House as Baldwin had gone slipping and sliding down along Hog Lane.

"Nice lad, Baldwin," Brewster Truckle said of his friend, "to come out on such a night and escort an old inebriate home from the tavern right up to his own portal."

For years, Brewster Truckle had been babbling to himself in undertones usually incomprehensible to others. When this comical sign of old age first began to manifest itself, Truckle, ashamed, took every care to stop his tongue. He couldn't and so instead he pretended to be speaking to cats, dogs, horses, the fire, even to inanimate objects. That made him as much a butt of jest as talking to himself, and so eventually he put it about that he was perpetually at prayer. Thus he turned an embarrassing quirk to an advantage.

It was wondrous useful, what an old man could overhear and put to good use, if he was thought to be a pious simpleton, harmless, and deaf to boot. By wandering the aisles of St. Paul's Cathedral, the great meeting place of all ranks of London folk, Truckle learned the names of those who had recently inherited wealth, found money in the streets, bilked a country bumpkin, or cut a fat purse. By sipping tea at Lloyd's, where merchants, traders, and ship brokers gathered, he learned exactly who had landed a shipment of fine silks and spices, sold a load of English sheep's wool at profit to the Belgies. He went round at first opportunity to such a man's gate to beg alms for the Graie Friars. A person recently and abundantly blessed was more inclined to generosity. Truckle looked up, counting in his mind the alms he'd obtained in just that way. He was smiling as a few snowflakes from the rooftop sifted down past him.

"Aye, bless me, Baldwin! Come back!" he shouted. "I just recalled something, a piece of information I learned yesterday—yesterday, when the snow was starting!"

He had been walking the aisles of St. Paul's, a virtual miniature London, with its collection of folk both high and low, honest men and felons. Much jostling and turning this way and that went on and such a confusion of languages was spoken that the cathedral seemed to Truckle a veritable Babel. There the old man had overheard the name of a butcher who, at great profit was secretly smuggling English sheeps to Spain. In Truckle's opinion, English sheep, like all things English, were superior to foreign ones. There might be no law against wearing fancy foreign styles, or reading foreign books—*some* foreign books, leastways—nor against preparing food in odd ways. Nor was there any law against getting rich by vending superior English wool, already wove, to foreigners. But *sheep* shipping, *that* was a crime, a specially vile one, same as selling English horses into Scotland. It was punishable on first conviction by forfeiture of all possessions, a year's imprisonment, and loss of the left hand, which was nailed up in the marketplace. For the second offense, the punishment was death.

Truckle had tucked away in his memory the name of the butcher, which had been coupled with that of Beaumarais, one Alberic Scoggin. He had intended to put Win on his guard and make good use of this information at an appropriate time, but then promptly forgot the whole subject until his mind was jogged by a few snowflakes. He had best pass on his bit of information to Baldwin now, before he forgot again. He called out to his young friend, who was navigating the narrow passageway called Hog Lane, which was otherwise deserted. Not even a Winchester goose, as streetwalkers were called, though he knew not why, was abroad fluffing her soiled feathers.

"Beaumarais!" he called again. "Listen!"

"Tell me tomorrow, brother," Baldwin had called, making his precarious way down the hill.

"I'll forget again, by then," complained Truckle, but Baldwin, swearing to himself under his breath, hadn't heard.

"Blasts and fogs," Win exclaimed when his leather boot heel rang and he slid on an icy patch of cobblestones cleared of snow by a brisk wind. "Get yourself inside, Rooster. 'Tis not safe out of doors this night for man nor beast nor half-drunk monk neither!" Win again shouted over his shoulder.

Brewster Truckle was called Rooster for his cackling laugh and dangling chins. This appellation was used behind his back by some of his most cherished, if disrespectful orphans. And to his face by his friends, one of whom he watched spread his arms like a rope dancer keeping his perilous balance. "Inside, d'you hear?" Win ordered as he secured his equilibrium, paused and turned, returned the old man's wave, and stamped off around the corner on his way home through deep powdery snow.

"Baldwin said I wasn't to go out again this night, did Baldwin," Truckle told a gargoyle above the door of the poorhouse. "He told me to keep to the safety of my own hearth till he returned in the morning to see me again. Pshaw. By me troth, I'll be as safe under merciful heaven as a babe in its mother's arms." Rooster grinned at the glaring stone beast. "Who would harm a shuffling, penniless old friar doing his last round of the neighborhood in search of the freezing, poor, and needy? I'll just get me a final little tipple, this one from Alice at the Dew Drop Inn. I might get alms from slothful drunkards still there after curfew." Truckle licked his lips. "Alice pours freely of her brew, especially for a man of God such as myself. It might be that a jot will jiggle me memory once more and help me dredge up the cause of Beaumarais's promised return in the morning."

Rooster Truckle's befuddlement, like his deafness, was intermittent, and as he stepped off into thick darkness, heading toward the Dew Drop Inn, precise numbers began rolling through his fleetingly well-focused mind. He knew to the halfpenny the outlay needed for culled gurgeons—bran and chaff—to bake the course stuff named cheat bread, served at the poorhouse. Lacking enough, he had often made a bread of beans and peas or oats leavened with acorns. He also knew the number of rotting marrow bones and half-decayed turnips he had collected to make a broth substantial enough to sustain life in his needy little charges.

"Praise be to God for Katesby Dalton," he proclaimed. " 'Tis been her generosity saved many a child we couldn't feed nor hardly find a space for, inside out of the cold." Truckle paused, thinking of the first time he'd seen Kat.

She had been four or five years old, if that, gripping the hand of a fellow Rooster Truckle took on first glance to be a man of the sea. Potter Shute was an oyster-catcher and shellfish monger from south Essex, Truckle was soon to learn. The little girl in her blue velvet dress had looked up at him with wide, sea-green eyes, showing courage and fear both, as with her free hand she clung to a pretty ring dangling on a ribbon about her neck.

He had taken her in, of course, and put away the little dress in a chest in the dank cellar of Graie Friars along with other such worthless tokens, the only ties to the pasts of his charges, children lost or abandoned, wrenched somehow from the arms of mothers, the protection of fathers unknown. But there, too, in the cellar, was a thing of value, or so it had been said by the oysterman in his telling of Kat's story. It was a tar-coated leather skin of rare old wine, which had been pressed from Mediterranean grapes and carried to England in one of the last of the Roman ships to ply the seas between Gaeletha and Dover. Rightly, it belonged to Kat, but Truckle had not yet gotten around to telling her of it. In fact, he'd forgotten all about the old wine by the time she had run off, after three years at Graie Friars, to strike out on her own. She had come back with gifts and friends in tow, among them, one day, Baldwin Beaumarais.

"My mind is no longer sharp as it was, but I will try to remember in the morning to tell *him* of the wine," Truckle, with a glance over his shoulder, promised his gargoyle. "I think the boy told me he'd be here again on the morrow—or was it the next day? No matter. Just thanks be to heaven for Beaumarais's charity, giving me goods to use or peddle, as need be, every time his ship comes in. Those two are good to us, very good, but above all, I must laud the Maker of us all for his avenging angel sent down disguised as the outlaw Chance. It's the fruits of that one's endeavors that truly are our mainstay," Truckle said.

He was by then making his unsteady progress down the icy lane, finding his way more by habit than sight. To get his bearings, he took a few deep sniffs, searching the air like a dog for a familiar scent. Truckle missed the usual homely, sharp reek of his street. The garbage and offal and their odors were masked this night by frost and snow.

"Blanes, pox, blotch, and biles," shouted the friar as he slipped on the same patch of icy cobbles that had nearly brought down Baldwin. The old man was neither as agile nor as fortunate as his young friend. He landed hard on his stiff, bony, weak old knees, knowing at once they would never be the same again. Unable to quickly get his clasped hands free from the sleeves of his robe, he listed to one side, then the other, before he fell forward to bury his prominent Romanesque nose deep in powdery snow. He blasphemed and at once begged God's forgiveness as he struggled to raise himself. He was sprawled on his belly, foundering in the snow like a splay-legged horse, when he felt himself grasped beneath the elbows and lifted to his feet.

"My heartfelt thanks, to you, sir. If not for your fortuitous passing, I might have lain there all night and not been found until daybreak, by then a frozen corpse." Rooster Truckle peered uphill into the shadows where his rescuer now stood, draped in black from head to toe but for his eyes. He was reassured by the lack of a scythe that the hidden figure was not the Angel of Death. "That you, Mr. Chance, by some chance? 'Tis a relief to see you, sir. I thought it might have been a phantom sent by Heaven or Hell to claim a sinning old monk at last," the friar jested and stepped forward, up the hill. "No, you can't be he, not Win Chance. You're too puny," commented Truckle, who was by then on a level with the silent stranger over whom he towered, though he was himself a person of modest height.

"Are you here to rob me? I've nothing, nothing, naught. I long ago took a vow of poverty. If you would rob for profit on the streets, you must choose the better neighborhoods. Here, we are all paupers."

"You possess an object of value I will have of you, a child's ring of gold set with coral stone and mother of pearl. Give it over."

"Eh? Sing, you say?" yelled Truckle, abruptly hard of hearing. "At the Dew Drop Inn, where I was just on me way to going, there's singing." To attract help, the old man began a rendering of the popular ballad "Light O' Love." His attacker struck the first blow.

"Don't toy with me, old man. You have for years had the ring I speak of. I've been sent to confiscate it. Give over."

"I don't carry such trifles on my person. What do you want with it? Who sent you?" asked Truckle, sidestepping the next buffet only to fall again, this time his feet flying out from under him. His mind racing, eyes rolling, he stared up stupidly, flat on his back, helpless as an old tortoise. If this pipsqueak, he found himself musing, as pink as a boiled shrimp, which was one of God's creatures after all, had been sent to confiscate the ring—odd word that—it had to be of some value beyond its own slight worth. It might hold a message to Kat!

"It's not for you to ask who or why, brother." Truckle felt the kick and heard his rib snap. Then the man was leaning close over him, exposing a round, smooth face, crimson with cold. "Remember me," he said. "I'll return at first cockcrow. If you don't have this particular trifle about your person by then, you *will* meet Death, replete with a scythe. And I shall arrange for not a few of your dear, *dear* friends to be introduced to Rattcliffe the Torturer and his ingenious machines in the Tower dungeon."

"Stop! What you kicking Rooster for? You're hurting 'im," Burgess Blunt heard a small voice ask. He raised his face and peered into the dark eyes of a small boy who was got up as he himself was, to look like the outlaw Win Chance. Blunt snatched the black scarf that hid the boy's the face and committed it to memory before the child turned and ran.

Rooster Truckle moaned when he was roughly dragged to his feet and shoved forward by Blunt uphill in the direction of Graie Friars Poor House. His head throbbed, his ribs pained fiercely, he could barely gasp in a breath, and his eyes would not focus. As he struggled up Hog Lane, he saw black-garbed Chances, a baker's dozen of them, dancing about him, large and small, everywhere. Though one of them seemed to be leading him by the hand, he did not quite make it all the way home before he fell again.

Little Chance ran this way and that, distraught, wondering what he must do now. The Rooster would freeze in the wet, cold snow if left there until morning. The child scrambled the rest of the way up the hill to gates of the poorhouse. He reached for the bell cord only to find it was way above him, beyond his reach. He leaped and jumped until tears of frustration coursed down his face.

He kicked and banged small fists at the gate, winced in pain, looked about, and decided to try a running jump this time for the bell cord. Turning to walk a little way down the hill, he heard the rustle of taffeta in the dark, then saw "the fine strapping lass," as he'd heard the woman called, half carrying, half dragging the old friar up the hill toward home. The woman gently propped the monk against his own gatepost and watched him as he slid down along it.

"Saved, I'm saved by a Colchester hen," gasped Truckle.

"Winchester goose, sir, is what you mean," the woman replied softly. "Though I'm not from neither one, but from Candy Island. Nan's me name."

"Colchester . . . Winchester. Whatever. God will bless you, Nan, for the *good* turn you've done this night!"

"Think so, sir?" She smiled sadly, then spoke to Little Chance.

"You saw who did this hurt to Rooster?" she asked. He nodded. "As did I," she said, glancing about fearfully. "That pink-faced, wicked shrimp of a man. He saw you, too, but he didn't spot me. I had the sense to keep to the shadows until he'd gone." She touched the boy's cheek. "Here, Robby, we must be quick away from this place after you give the alarm for Rooster."

She lifted the boy. He grabbed and reached the bell rope; then he held on to it with both hands to swing back and forth laughing, jerking, and twisting to make the bell peal out its loud cry. For a long moment Nan, smiling, watched the boy at play. Then she paled and sucked in a breath. "Rob, leave loose at once!" she cried before she turned and ran. " 'Tis an horrible omen!" she whispered to herself. "It means I'm to see him hanged one day." The child rotated on the rope to see the vacant place where she'd been standing. He let go and dropped to the ground.

"Ma!" cried Little Chance, on the run after her. "Wait! I was searchin' for you everywheres. I been bid to come back to the inn at The Sign of the Kat and bring you with me."

Chapter 13

"I spread cloth upon the table three times in a day," Kat told Win, sitting opposite her. She opened a bound book on the table and handed it across to him. Its pages were covered with numbers written in columns, in ink, in her neat hand. "There is a meal to break the night's fast, another beginning in the forenoon, dinner, the day's prodigious meal. I offer nuncheons of cheese and beer later, then supper at six of the night. Frequently there is yet a resupper for lingerers and late-arriving wayfarers."

"As you have done regularly heretofore, eh?" Win asked, his arresting glance rising from the book to her face. Her eyes, always candid and clear, were radiant when they met his, and her lips, that perfect bow, spread in a smile bright as the sun. Win came around the table to sit beside her. "So's we can look at the numbers together," he explained. "Continue."

"From two bushels of flour, if they be free of weevils, I am able to cast forty loaves of the finest white manchet bread." Her eyes slid sideways as Win moved closer to her.

"Each loaf goes in to bake weighing . . . eight ounces and comes out . . ." Win's arm came over her shoulders and his fingers traced over a page of the book before he turned her face to him to kiss her mouth.

"Eight ounces?" he asked.

"Win!" she exclaimed after warmly returning the kiss, then trying to look severe. "This is neither the time nor place for lessons. Now hear me out. Breads go into the oven weighing eight ounces and when they come out are only six ounces."

"Interesting. Can you explain it?" He raised his hand from the book to clasp her breast and graze the nipple. "The finest . . . you say, white bread?" Kat felt a shock of desire knife through her. She shook his hand away.

"The Goodkind ladies help me with the brewing, two or three times in the course of each month," she went on hurriedly, a bit breathless now. "I obtain eight bushels of choice malt, well turned and dried, a half bushel of wheat meal also, ground oats, two pounds of the best English hops . . ."

"Oats?" Win set an elbow on the table, leaned his head to one side and, resting his cheek upon the palm of his hand, looked up at her. She snapped shut the book.

"Baldwin Beaumarais!" she began, finding it nearly impossible to sit so close by him and not touch him, difficult to keep her feelings hidden and not to blurt out, "I love you, blast it, and what am I to do about that?"

"Oats!" she said. "Yes. To temper the beer. The mash is all mixed so evenly together, you cannot tell the malt from the other grains, but if it is not done just so, there will be lumps and clots. One must have great care in the boiling of the grains and draining off not once but three times over, and the mashing . . ." He took the book and randomly spread it open again.

"Please . . . show me the figures?" he asked, passing his

arm about her waist. He drew her against him and tongued her ear.

"I pay out ten shillings for malt each month, four shillings and six pence for the wood to boil the water . . ." She turned her face to his. She'd already told Harry the truth, that she'd not be wed to him for she loved another. *Be forthrightly with the 'other' and speak out to Win also,* she told herself.

"The cost to brew ten score gallons of my golden yellow beer is twenty shillings, all in all, encompassing the girls' supplemental wages for their added hours."

"Betimes it occurs that your beer is more alike to the color of your hair, which is a mite darker than gold, more a tawny shade." He rested a hand along either side of her face, then gathered back her long hair to her nape and set his lips at the curve above her shoulder, below her ear.

"Come, now again, with me upstairs, eh, Kitten?" he asked, husky voiced.

"I've not even a fleeting moment to spare just now," she sighed, aware the house was stirring, servants awakening and guests moving about.

"If a maltster were to deliver brew to the inn, would you find more time for me?" Win teased her, not only with his words but with his stroking hands. "Damn," he groaned when the stair creaked. He swiveled to turn his back to the door, leaned against the table, and extended his bare feet toward the fire.

"No brewer's beer for my borders!" Kat exclaimed, springing up and smoothing her apron. "Indeed, not all waters are of like goodness in brewing and we are hailed for ours. I, myself, secretly mingle half a quarter of an ounce of bayberries, finely powdered, with each new batch. That gives our brew a distinctive taste. The Lord Mayor of London, an august and rotund epicurean person, you will agree, comes hither and praises our beer."

"Also he compliments our fat capons, of which he has

eaten aplenty, as he has of our beef and mutton, all washed down with oceans of claret," said Gwyn, entering the kitchen with Roxelana on her hip.

"Yes, but the lord mayor always demands our strong beer with venison, whenever we serve it to him." Kat smiled, reaching out for the baby. "Good *morrow!* Good morrow, pretty girl," Kat cooed and the child gurgled with delight, her little plump arms waving, legs kicking.

"What is amiss with that man, Beaumarais, sitting there?" asked Gwyn, glancing at Win's back, handing over the happy baby to Kat.

"He has cold feet, I suspect," answered Kat, sympathetic but also a mite bedeviling in the same breath.

"If there be a man who knows how to warm his feet and his every other bodily part, 'tis Beaumarais," noted Jillly Goodkind, who had just come on the scene followed by her sleepy daughters. "Think you the vendors and markets are dug out and unfolded yet after the snow?"

"Some stalls in Cheapside Market between St. Paul's and Carfax Road are doing trade in bread, turnips, even some cheesecake from outlying Holloway," announced Dorsey Dibden, arriving with Bessy Matlock to occupy their usual corner table. "On Fish Street you may buy only salt stock fish, nothin' yet fresh-caught."

"Forsooth, there's piemen on the streets shouting their wares—*Hot Pies! Hot Pudding Pies from Pimlico!* Passing by Thavies Inn making our way here, we saw the keeper out shouting his wines—*White from Alsace, Red from Gascoigne.*"

"Ladies," said Kat when they had done with their gruel and cider, "a pair of you is to go off to strangle and pluck chickens for supper, another must collect soiled linen, and the last will heat the washwater for it."

"What of Roxelana?" asked Gwyn with a yawn. "Shall I take her up for a nap?" The baby, sitting in her basket near the hearth, was banging a wooden mallet against a pewter bowl. She looked up and laughed at the sound of her own name and yawned in imitation of Gwyn.

"She doesn't appear tired in the least. I'll see to her," answered Win, turning with a smile at Kat, then gathering up the baby. "I'll see to you, you tiny, pretty girl," he burbled at Roxelana "We shall play at winks, eh?" he asked, closing one eye.

"Nobility, gentry, even students begin to dine before noon on the day's principal meal," a guest, one Mistress Wilt from Halifax, remarked with a frown. The woman and her family were the last guests to come down to table the morning after the snow. The others had all left The Sign of the Kat, either to go about the business that had brought them to London or, having completed that business, to return from whence they had come. "Why, prithee, innkeeper, do you serve in the kitchen and provide us with only gruel, beef, pork, bacon, eggs, butter, and fish broth?"

"Our beef, pork, and bacon are not too much powdered with salt, I trust, Mistress Wilt?" asked Kat. The woman shifted her shoulders.

"Is any beverage provided here but cow's milk and claret?" she asked.

"We press apples in the fall for cider, and pears for nectar. I also offer a very flavorful perry swish-swash of honeycombs and water, infused with pepper and spice. It's not merely tasty but also good for cough and stomach complaints."

"I expect pasties, mutton, fowls, and fine claret, for my *dinner.*"

"Is Mr. Wilt noble, gentle, or a scholar, madam?" asked Win of the perpetually displeased Mistress Wilt.

"He's a clerk inspector," she replied, scowling.

"Not nobles, gentlefolk, or students dine upon their

large main meal at eight of a morning. I've never known a clerk to, either. Am I not correct there, madam?" Win asked with his quick, charming grin.

"And the poor dine and sup when and where they may. Out-of-term university scholars, of which I am one, often eat not a bite until ten of the night," commented a young man who kept spearing the best and largest pieces of bacon with his knife and urgently stuffing the food into his mouth faster than he could swallow it, which distended his cheeks and hindered his speech. He gulped, coughed, gasped, then smiled as he speared half a loaf of Kat's best white bread.

"The customs of the world are wonderful diverse. In some lands there is one meal a day. In England in summer we begin with salad. Elsewhere they finish with lettuces, even mulberries," noted Kat.

"Most students and scholars, other than rich men's sons, eat but one meal a day, even in term. For me to break the fast at eight in morning, and so abundantly as this, is a singular treat." The young scholar smiled at Kat, as well as he could with a full mouth, then glanced at and then quickly turning away from the Wilt girl, who was seated beside her mother. Both women were dark-haired and dark-eyed, had full, round moon faces, and were attired in black linsey-woolsey which concealed them from head to heels but for an occasional lump. The husband and father of the pair, an actuary's clerk and sometime inspector of market weights and measures, peered about coldly. A wary man, he sat to the other side of his girl from his wife, both guarding her against imagined hordes of despoilers.

"Are you crammed in there on that bench, sir? Will you sit on *this* less crowded side of the table?" suggested Kat.

"I'll remain as I am, thank you. One must keep a strict watch over a headstrong daughter, until she is disposed of," Mr. Wilt replied with a sniff and a sharp nod at his wife.

"Disposed of?" echoed Kat indignantly.

"Married off. Then it becomes the chore of the husband to keep a woman to the straight and narrow. May it please God the world should last so long that I may behold her another man's responsibility before she turns wild and wayward and ruins her chances of marriage by running off on a rash and impulsive escapade with a rogue." At that, the wife nodded once, sharply.

"Has she ever shown any inclination to do so?" Kat asked, more than indignant now. She was irate.

"Some children fear witches and dragons. My girl has a healthy terror of the constable's cart behind which bad girls are hauled through the streets and whipped," Mistress Wilt pronounced. "My girl has been often reminded of the other portions of the punishment for harlotry and adultery in this land. The malefactor is made to stand naked but for a sheet outside the church door for a month of Sundays, bearing a sign, 'Harlot' or 'Adulteress,' as may be the case." Young Miss Wilt, expressionless, kept her eyes lowered as she had been taught, and looked only at the fire.

"Adultery within the court or its near environs," intruded the student, garbed in a frayed doublet decorated with the spots and splashes of many previous meals, "may result in the perpetrator being dragged across the Thames, from Lambeth to Westminster, at the tail of a boat. 'Tis terrifying, I'm told."

"You are a student of the law, sir, I surmise," said Win, sitting at the end of a bench, dandling the baby on his knee as she gnawed earnestly on a bread crust.

"I am that, at Gray's, at the Inns of Court," the young man answered pleasantly. Though shabby in dress, he was pleasing of appearance, with warm dark eyes, long brown hair, and a friendly manner.

"Know you much of crime and punishment in England? Would you speak legal to us, sir?" asked Jeannie, bustling into the room, trailing sticky feathers after her. "That would be thrilling, sir!" she added, exuding flirtatious admiration. "I'm done with plucking them cacklers now, Mr. Beaumarais. I'll take a hold of that precious baby so's you can eat in comfort," she told Win, who handed over Roxelana, making space for Jean and getting himself closer to Kat. He searched for her hand under the table, captured it and placed it on the hard swell in his lap. Kat never blinked or turned her head. She blushed, coughed, sipped wine, and went to caressing him, moving only her fingers. She wriggled out of her shoe and entwined her leg with his, aware of the coldness of his foot through her stocking. His foot ran up between her calves and she pressed them together, to warm him.

Bess the Wise Woman, at the far end of the bench, was advising a farmer who had come through the snow to consult her about his poor fall crop. "When the last flocks of cranes pass going south in winter and the new moon of January rises, twelve ears of corn, one for each of the months of the year, must be laid upon the hot hearth to ensure an ample crop for the next growing season."

"Conjury, sorcery, witchcraft," hissed Mistress Wilt. "That is heresy the old woman talks, I tell you!"

"Witches are burned alive slowly, while heretics are cooked quick before they lead others astray. 'Tis the law," said the student. "And scolds are ducked." He scowled pointedly at Mistress Wilt.

"Tell more law, sir. Please do," gawped Jen.

"Felon is a word derived from the Saxon *fell,* meaning evil. It is given to those of untamable nature—those who poach by night with dark painted faces, sellers of horses or mares into Scotland, conjurers, sorcerers, witches, and wizards, as Wife Wilt has remarked. Stealing of hawks' eggs, cutting purses, letting out ponds are capital crimes. There are more, two hundred hanging offenses, but I fear to bore you."

"Not at all, sir. 'Tis most . . . interesting, is it not, Baldwin?" Kat asked with a smile.

"Poisoning, sir. What of that?" Jilly asked. The room was still, all eyes on the student, who drained his goblet and cheerfully went on.

"A man who poisons another is boiled in water or lead for such a deed. A woman who does the same to her husband is burned. Robbing by highway, sea, or dwelling is dealt with by hanging. Perjurers are pilloried, branded on the brow with the letter P, and suffer the loss of all their movable goods as well as of all the trees on their lands."

"We English abhor to question with pain and torture, for our nation is free, stout, and haughty," Mr. Wilt said with pride. "That is why the English condemned go cheerfully to the hangman to meet death."

"Men take to robbing along the highway when they are too poor to buy britches. They are forced to poach to eat and feed their offspring," Win growled.

"As for hailings and tearings of the body by the tormenter in the Tower," croaked Dorsey Dibdin, "I have known of some who have had firsthand experience of it and survived."

"And them that were hanged after, was quaking in terror," said Jilly," though it is the ambition of every felon to die game and be remembered ever after in them flash street ballads the bad boys make up and sing."

"I make it a practice to observe hangings as often as practical, scullion, and I beg to differ," Wilt pronounced, swelling with indignation. "And as for indecent songs and immoral gutter tunes . . ."

"Aha, is it a gallows hound we have here?" asked Blaidd Kyd. With a bundle on his shoulder, he thrust his thinly capped blond head into the room and sang in a rough tremor:

Six highwaymen to carry me,
Given them broadswords and liberty.
Six blooming girls to bear my pall,
Given them gloves and ribbons and all.
When I am dead, they'll tell the truth:
He was a wild and wicked youth.

"How now?" demanded Mistress Wilt as her daughter's eyes lifted and the girl's face came alight.

"I'm off to Sussex," said Blaidd, "with Charlie de Morely, soon as he and the earl are done with their call on the king," announced Blaidd, meeting the intense, unsmiling gaze of the plain and ribbonless Miss Wilt.

"You do make a fine sweet nectar," Win said softly to Kat, "of pear." He drained his cup. "Certes, pear pressing is a country woman's occupation, the product ofttimes named mead."

"Here, I'll pour more for you," Kat answered, trying to disentangle herself from Win. "Do budge yourself a mite, Baldwin. I must be away upstairs at once to see to . . . housekeeping." He grinned and let her stand.

"Do you require an assist with the housekeeping?" he asked.

"There *is* a heavy oaken chest in your chambers too weighty for me to shift without help."

"I'll help you, Kat," offered Blaidd, who had been lingering, observing Miss Wilt.

"Never you mind, boy," Win snarled. He and Kat had put each other into a fever of need. The situation was wearing on his patience and good nature—and hers also, Win gauged from the heated look in her eyes.

"Certes, you can help the lady better'n me," acknowledged Blaidd with a broad wink to which Win did not respond as he followed Kat toward the stairs. Before the two had quitted the kitchen, the fourth step creaked, and Harry de Morely, Earl of Norland, strode into the room.

"I'm so hungry, I could eat a horse. Or a barrel of oysters," announced the earl.

"I can provide that to you," sighed Kat with a helpless glance at Win. "Not the horse—the oysters, I meant to say, and perhaps not a full barrel. I've been at them. I like oysters as others do sweets."

"I haven't slept so long or well in a long while," noted the earl. "I was most content and comfortable in your bed, Katesby."

"Only think how much more content you'd have been, Norland, if she had shared it with you," grumbled Win, passing by Harry on his way upstairs, alone.

Chapter 14

"I was a hotheaded young man, the heir to an earldom, all of twenty years old and in service to the powerful Wolsey, who was then cardinal," Harry told Kat who, listening with attention, sat beside him, the two alone in a private dining room of the inn. De Morely paused in his talk only to wash down his oysters with quantities of an icy-cold white wine. "Now, whenever Cardinal Wolsey would repair to court, his young men would escort him, and when Wolsey was in attendance upon the king, we blades would remove to the queen's chambers. There we would amuse her maidens and ladies in waiting. And there I lost my heart."

"Do continue, my lord," said Kat, refilling his goblet, then folding her hands in her lap.

"I gave my heart to one who did exceed all the other ladies there, in charm and beauty and liveliness, Lady Mary Wyat. And she loved me. And we wished to be wed."

"You, my lord, would have married for *love?*"

"And I did, then, secretly. And would again now, my dear, wed for love of a different sort, for I am no longer a boy, but love I feel nonetheless. You are mulling still?" His deep-set eyes were intense, curious.

"Harry," sighed Kat, "I am. But I do not expect, nor should you, that my answer will change. Tell me more now of your Lady Wife Mary."

"My earl father would not hear of the alliance. Mary was the daughter of a mere commoner. Wyat had been knighted and enriched by the king, it was true, but yet he was a small landholder of modest wealth. I had already been matched to the daughter of the Earl of Shillington, Lady Ellen Margeaux. The thing had been smiled on by King Henry."

"Yet you married with Mary?"

"We ran away together to Essex and were wed there by the priest in a village church, the marriage duly recorded in the record book. Two days after, we were caught by Wyat's riders. Mary was torn from my arms."

"What did you then, Harry?" Kat's voice was low and sorrowful, the tale of true young love cruelly thwarted touching her heart. Harry lowered his close-cropped gray head, and Kat set a hand on his shoulder by way of comfort.

"Enter," she responded softly to a knock upon the door, and Win strode in to find the pair posed together in, to him, a tableau of companionship, perhaps even of love. Without glancing in Win's direction, Kat filled him in quickly and bade him take a place and hear out the earl's sad tale.

"My earl father made complaint of me to Wolsey, who in turn spoke of the matter to King Henry, who was 'much offended.' The red-robed cardinal berated me, telling me I had offended God also with my entanglement and folly, that it was my duty to God, father, and king to wed with a woman 'of matched estate and honor.' I defended Mary who, though a commoner herself, was related to several ducal houses. I said I would not deny or forsake her, that

I thought myself sufficient to take me a wife where my fancy served me best."

Win glanced from Harry to Kat. She was listening in rapt attention, her hand resting now upon Harry's on the table. "The corpulent and corrupt cardinal, his red cap covering his ears, coming down to his trembling jowls which, I remember thinking then, seemed like to explode in his apoplexy at my willful defiance." The earl laughed with dark pleasure.

"My noble father was summoned. He came right quick to the court, I'll tell you. 'Son,' saith he, 'thou hast always been a proud, presumptuous, disdainful, and very unthrift waster. Therefore what joy, what comfort, what pleasure or solace should I conceive in thee?' I have never forgotten those words. I have berated my own son in the same manner with near the same words which, too late, I now would unspeak and take back."

" 'Tis never too late to do and say the right and just thing," said Kat. "Explain now to Charlie, how you feel."

"A man may not unspeak, sir, or turn back time, but he may make amends where he has done harm," Win offered. "What of the fate of your lady love?"

"I never saw her again after she was seized from the carriage. In the church ledger, the page on which our names were writ was ripped out. The priest himself who joined us together, like Mary, vanished forever from my life. I heard once that Mary had been sent away, into France. I dispatched men hither and yon to search for her. I went myself to our English city of Caen in Normandy where her mother's cousin resided, then on the Continent. I journeyed into France. In Spain, it was rumored she was one of many girls taken from a coastwise convent and sold into slavery by Algerian corsairs. I offered a great ransom, but to no end. Later, it was said she died in England, of a broken heart, within a year or at most two of our separation," the earl concluded.

"My apologies, Beaumarais, if I have bored you with my unmanly narrative. Love, as you and I are aware, is only a kind of madness that causes one to wail, sigh, and groan, being alternately and simultaneously in conditions of longing, elation, dejection, and the like. Fortunately, more often than not, it is a temporary thing. Nothing more.

"I will be off to the court to speak with the king before his two or three hours sitting at meat and drink render the sleepy glutton insensible. His majesty daily indulges in a banquet and, withal, he has grown so bloated he has difficulty arising from table to attend evening prayers. Such excess and sumptuousness profit only physicians," added the gaunt earl with a bow to Kat before his parting. He had an ill-disguised grimace of pain on his narrow face and left with a faint limp as he favored his gout-plagued knee.

"Have you given the earl your answer?" Win inquired as soon as Harry had gone off. "Have you two made your plans?"

"Win, you're dressed to travel!" she exclaimed, taking account of his leather leggings and over-the-knee boots, the gauntlet gloves and short riding crop in his hand.

"I thought you'd never notice," he answered with a forced laugh.

"But you've only been home two days," Kat protested. "When will you return?"

"In a fortnight or thereabouts. Will that be in good time for me to be present at your wedding?" He turned away to hide his expression, awaiting her reply.

"But . . . where are you going?" she asked, avoiding his question with one of her own.

"Firstly to call on Rooster Truckle. After, I'll ride on to Bath."

"But . . . why must you?" Kat inadvertently asked. "Not that I care, but . . . the highways and roads will be deep in snow still."

"I go on two matters of business, the first to see how my sheep and their shepherd, Andrew Danter, are faring. He has written to report an inexplicable loss of lambs, rams, and ewes, the best of the flock, even the bellwether that the rest follow."

"And is your other matter of business to do with the inn of which we spoke?" she asked expectantly.

"Perchance I will add that to my agenda, though I won't have need of another establishment, once you are a countess, for . . ." He left the sentence unfinished. "No, my second enterprise which, I expect, might merge pleasure, is to be a meeting with the Widow Pebbles, Gail Pebbles. Her property abuts mine on its western border."

"How convenient and advantageous for you. Do keep me informed, Baldwin, of the progress of your courtship of Miss Pebbles," said Kat, also turning away, plucking her eyes from the copper curl at his nape, and the wide shoulders plunging to a slim, bejewelled waist.

"Indeed, I will," he answered as they stood, back to back, on opposite sides of the room. "Ah, Kat? You neglected to answer my question. If some idiot cause of sentiment or concern about the disparity between you and the earl has prevented you from giving Harry your answer, I again urge you to accept his proposal. Don't risk your once-in-a-lifetime prospect of becoming a countess by playing coy with the earl. Tell him yes, and be right quick about it—that is, if you haven't. Accept him when I've gone and he returns from the court with the king's consent. Publish the bans, announce the vows, whatever."

"By cock and pie, what mean you, accusing me of 'idiot sentiment' and 'playing coy'? I haven't been coy or sentimental in my whole life, sir!" Kat proclaimed with indignant bluster. "And as for any disparity of our years and positions, if Harry cares not, why must I?"

"I merely wondered, is all. Of course, my lessons . . . the *love* lessons?"

"What of them then?" she snapped, sounding thoroughly out of sorts. Peeking over her shoulder, she saw he had set himself down and had laced his hands behind his head, but she could not see his face. She stood near the mantel, staring into the fire.

"The lessons you inveigled from me were all you lacked, you said, to meet the earl's requirement for an experienced mate. Howsomever, being bedded—well bedded," he insisted, "by one partner—me—while contemplating marriage with another—Harry—may have been a distraction to you and caused you some confusion?" His tone of voice, she noted, was quizzical, hopeful even.

"Wrong, sir! To the contrary I'm not confused in the least!"

"Ah. Well . . ." Win took a deep breath before he went on. "He's a good man, Kat. A powerful one, and proud, and inordinately fond of you and an aficionado of women, competent at pleasing them, he says, and of course, now you are somewhat seasoned in that way also, and you'll come to the right decision if you haven't yet. But I ramble on, eh? So . . . so you've given him it, your answer?"

"Yes, I have," said Kat, omitting to say what that answer was.

"You *have?*" Win felt stunned, clouted to the heart, regretful, foolish.

Instantaneously he accepted the possibility of being in love. He felt deranged with it, mad with love, just as Harry had portrayed the condition. He barely managed to suppress sighs and groans. He felt longing, elation, and despair all coinciding. As if he . . . loved Kat! "What if you *are* in love with her?" he anguished. Was it possible? Ah, but now he'd lost her forever, he would never know for a certainty one way nor the other. "Nay, you've not *lost* her, fool," he corrected himself. "You gave her away, handed her over like a worthless bauble to another man and without a fight. Fight? Blast, but you were too stubborn, blind, and doltish to even admit you perhaps should have entered the fray, too lily-livered to risk your damn heart on the field of battle, too dense to enter the lists of love!"

"Ha!" he exploded in a self-derisive laugh.

"What think you funny, Beaumarais, my cuffin?" Kat asked in her feisty milk-and-gravel voice, the one she used to invoke her self-protective veneer of earthy bravado while her heart ached and her eyes welled with tears. When they faced each other to say their farewells, Kat saw yearning and read regret in Win's eyes. All he discovered in hers, which were glinting green, was humor, curiosity, expectation. By the time she walked with him into the main room, he saw an expression of jubilation on her face as well, and Win attributed it to thoughts of her impending marriage. Actually, knowing she hadn't lost Win, not yet, put joy in Kat's smile when she proffered her hand. He took it in both of his.

"So, it seems we are, the both of us, on the way to fulfilling our ambitions, eh, Katesby—to reaching those goals we set, of climbing the ladder of fate out of the streets?"

"Indeed, Baldwin. And we've kept the promise we made. Whichever of us stood on a higher rung would forever reach down to pull the other along."

Still clasping her hand, Win suddenly hauled Kat forward into his clasping arms, crushing her to him, his mouth hot and hard, toiling on hers as though he were starving, his tongue surging into her drawing mouth, his body, in upheaval, working against hers.

"Am I to give you a token to take with you, Win?" she breathed as his hands moved over her.

"A token such . . . such as a garter, mean you?" he growled, going down on a knee, drawing her to him with one hand and sending the other riding up under her skirt, searching, as he talked in a low, heated undertone. "The Order . . . Order of the Garter was founded by . . . by King

Edward, the third King Edward who . . . who, riding after his Queen, did . . ."

"Win!" Kat gasped.

". . . the king did espy a garter fallen in the road. His grooms disdained to stoop to take up so lowly an object but he, King Edward, knew to whom the blue garter belonged—to his queen." Win spoke in a steady, low tone while his hand fondled and played upon Kat. "The king, being most familiar with the region of the queen's person which the garter had encircled, and the near environs of the queen's person . . ." Kat had let her head roll back and her eyelids flutter while Win's fingers stroked and furrowed, deft, precise, strong ". . . bade his man to take up the ribbon garter. And the king's man did but did remark upon the trifling nature of the thing and forthwith . . . forthwith the king held the garter aloft and told his men, 'I will make the proudest of you reverence the like.' "

Kat rested her hand upon Win's shoulder to steady herself, and her breaths came fast. "Not long after, Katesby, the king founded the noble Order of the Garter, to join which small, elite circle a knight to this day has to be nominated, elected, installed . . ." Kat moaned softly. Her body arched back, curled forward, and was still being assailed by a long tremor when Win arose. "Forget the garter. Now I'd rather you give me something else to remember you by," he rasped, sweeping her off her feet and striding to the stairs.

"Methinks you are a honeysuckle villain, Beau, to want to use me so, now . . . again . . . for no sound reason, since we've done with love lessons."

"I did just give you a sound reason, wench," he told her with a low laugh. He made the fourth step creak, but barely, he went so quickly over it. "I've more to give and take so's you recollect, at least for a time peradventure, after you become a countess, what a man may give to a woman."

"Fool! Do you suppose I'll ever forget what you've already given me?" she whispered. "Win? Listen. Someone below requires my services." She sighed. "There's a knocking at the inn door."

"I require your services."

" 'Tis the proper duty of an innkeeper to make all welcome by unbolting the door to 'em all. Leave off this recreation now, Beau. Set me down and be on your way."

"Be on my way?" he demanded, incredulous, standing still on the landing, not even contemplating setting Kat down. "You needs must learn your proper duty, my girl, not as an innkeeper, but as a woman. I'm prepared to give a lesson and not in love. I will teach you that you mayn't lead a man so far as this and then say to him, 'be on your way.' "

"Lead you on?" she demanded indignantly, trying to wriggle from his hold.

"You didn't say me nay, did you, Kitten?" He laughed. "And you're not saying it now, are you?"

"No! Yes! No!" she said and laughed, the sound a sensual purr low in her throat. He grinned. Then his mouth tasted hers two, three, four times over until, downstairs, the inn door burst open with a crash.

"Help, oh help! Villains! Cutthroats and devils!" arose a great hue and cry. With an oath, Win took to the stairs once more to descend, still holding Kat in his arms.

Chapter 15

"My horse, my horse! Murtherers and thieves have stole my mount . . . left me in out'n the storm!" declaimed a disheveled courier dressed in the Norland colors, the livery stained and torn. His hair and short beard were thick with hoarfrost. His lips were blue, his teeth clattered in his head, and his entire body was in a violent tremble. "I've come up from Essex with a message for Lord de Morely."

"Where's your dispatch case, man? Was it taken?" asked Win.

"Taken . . . yes." The fellow nodded.

"I think we have it. It was found in the snow, with naught left inside it but a counterfeit coin."

"The witless scoundrels! All they got for their trouble and mine was me scrap of old green cheese I was toting, in the event hunger o'ercame me before I got to a residence or inn on my travels. The coin is evidence, all I need, to act against certain parties in whom the earl has taken an interest." The courier staggered a few steps.

"Did you lose documents?"

"The information . . . for his lordship? 'Tis in me head. I must ride at once to Norland," the man croaked as his legs gave way beneath him and he collapsed to the floor in a swoon.

"Jean! Jilly! Jen!" Kat called when Win finally remembered to set her down. "Bring warm blankets, and more firewood! Hurry! Put the kettle of stew on to boil! Give a hand here! We've got Cal Shute's 'ghost' that followed him from Colchester!"

"He's no ghost yet," said Win, kneeling at the courier's side and starting in to peel off the man's wet clothing. "But he will be, judging by the ashen color of him, if we don't get him warm right quick. Who's still abed?"

"Gwyn is abed. What matters that?" asked Kat, helping Win lift and hoist the courier to his shoulder.

"Don't ask me questions now. Which room's hers?"

"Last at the back, at the very top of the inn, more a cabinet with a small hearth, four flights up, tucked under the eaves," Kat answered, leading the way. "I understand! Her bed will be warmed, ready to start this poor wanderer thawing at once."

"Fie upon you. Hell gnaw your bones," grumbled Gwyn when they came into her chamber. She opened one eye and tussled with Kat for possession of her quilts.

"Up and out of there, Gwyn, or you'll be sharing your bed with a man you never saw before now."

"Aye?" answered Gwyn, stumbling to her feet, more asleep than awake, though fully dressed but for her shoes. "Who be that?"

"Cal's ghost, or soon to become him," Win replied, lowering his burden to Gwyn's rasping straw pallet, rolling him in the quilts before Jilly, who had followed them up the stairs, layered on more blankets.

"He's lookin' a nicer shade of gray already," she noted, "with a hint of rose in it."

"De Morely, I must go to de Morely," groaned the courier.

"There, there, lad," Jilly soothed.

"Tell us your name. We'll send for his lordship to come here, for you are not in a condition to venture forth," said Kat, examining the man's face.

"Horace," the man answered.

"That's a decent-lookin' man in Gwyn's bed," said Jeannie, prancing into the room with a steaming trencher.

"He's Horace," Jilly told her daughter, "and near to froze. He's not in no condition to be flirting with the likes of you, miss."

"We are not come to flirt, me and Jenny. We have come to spoon-feed him." The sisters placed themselves on either side of Horace.

"Horace? Hungry, are you?" Kat asked, leaning over him to pass a spoonful of broth beneath his nose.

"Where am I?" he asked, opening his eyes wide.

"Well, you're not gone to heaven yet, boy," teased Win, "though you are surrounded by angels." Horace smiled weakly, then frowned in consternation.

"Norland!" he said. "There's plotting aplenty afoot he mustn't fall afoul of. He must be told."

"I'll have him fetched here, soon as he's done at Court. You may inform him then. Now I'll take my leave of you, Horace. I'm off to Bath. Rest easy, man. I leave you in good hands. Fare thee well, ladies," added Win, touching a hand to his brow in a salute.

"You shall return to London in a fortnight, then?" inquired Kat in an offhand way.

" 'Tis my plan, give or take a day, if heaven be willing and God grants I live so long. Will I find you here, Kat?" he questioned casually.

"I'm always here, ain't I? Where else on earth would I be?" she asked and smiled with overly honeyed charm.

He set a kiss on the top of her head.

The fourth stair creaked.

The inn door slammed. Not until then did Kat sigh or even move. Turning her attention to Horace once more, she observed him to be making a miraculous recovery, slurping soup from the spoon Jeannie put to his mouth while her sister patted his lips with a linen cloth after each swallow.

"I see I'm not needed here," said Kat, already missing Baldwin, wishing to be by herself in her misery. "I'll just go down to the kitchen and bake bread, should anyone want me . . . ever."

"He'll be back, Kat. Want to wager on it?" Gwyn asked.

"And bet against myself?" Kat shrugged, slipping from the room and closing the door behind her.

The boy, Little Chance, was waiting for her, perched on a chair in the kitchen.

"Hullo, friend," she sang out. "Where's your scarf I gave you, and where's your mother? You said you'd bring her to me."

"Lost me scarf. Mam wouldn't come, for she is fearful and hiding in a cellar off Hog Lane."

"Oh? That so, Little Chance?" responded Kat, taking the boy's jacket. "Why's your mother hiding? And what be your actual name?"

"Robert, but I fancy you calling me Chance. Ma and me, we both saw the one who did injury to Rooster . . . Brother Truckle, I mean," he corrected himself. "Now the friar's near dead and Ma is scared, like she always is, but worse, about Brother Truckle. See, he was near to murdered in the street last night and he is on his deathbed now, and all the king's men are about hunting after Win Chance."

"Chance?" asked Kat, appalled, reaching for her cloak. "But he wouldn't . . . Why Chance?"

"The friar only said, 'Chance, Chance,' before he stopped speaking entirely. The man who done it was dressed just like me, and I'm dressed up like Win Chance. Maybe that's why Rooster thought it was Chance. It matters not, miss. Now the old man has forgot even his own name. He don't remember where he is, or nothing."

"What else did Rooster say before he stopped speaking? Think hard now, Little Chance," Kat implored.

" 'Shrimp, shrimp.' I heard him say that. Nothing else."

"You did set your own eyes on the robber, you and your mother both? Do you know him? Does she?" The boy nodded.

"It was not Chance, but it weren't a robber neither."

"How do you know that?"

"Firstly, Win Chance is a champion man, like knights of old. He would not do such a base deed. Secondly, the one who did it was a little bit of a man, too stunted to be Chance. He appeared big enough while I was crouching down and Rooster was lying flat out. But when The Gnome—Mam named him that—dragged the friar up on his feet, Rooster was head and shoulders over The Gnome. Mam said he was not any robber for he didn't take nothing, not even the few silver coins Friar Truckle spilled about when he fell. Me, I never have seen The Gnome before, nor did me Mam, but sure it is we'll both know him if we meet up with him ever again."

"Silver?" asked Kat. "Brother Truckle spilled silver?"

"Aye, and Mam gathered them from the snow and gave me one to keep, in the event I get myself into a predicament or disaster." The boy stuck out his fist, which he unfolded to reveal the coin he was clutching—a match, Kat saw, to the counterfeit pewter piece found in the bottom of the courier's bag.

"Come! Let us be off, Little Chance. There's a brutal waylayer loose, with a cache of fake coins. First there was Horace, the courier, knocked from horse. Now, poor

Take A Trip Into A Timeless World of Passion and Adventure with ensington Choice Historical Romances! —Absolutely FREE!

Rooster is knocked senseless. We must go quick to the dear monk at Graie Friars, *and* find your mother, then get her and you somewhere safe before the cruel counterfeiter strikes again!"

Kat took Rob's hand, then pulled open the inn door and stopped, frozen in place, confronted on the threshold by a troop of the King's Palace Guard, the commander with knuckles poised about to rap for entry.

"Katesby Dalton, Innkeeper?" he asked.

"What's amiss, sir?" she asked with a nod of her head.

"We are come with orders to escort Katesby Dalton, Innkeeper, to the Tower," proclaimed the commander in a stentorian voice. "There's a cart in readiness to convey you as you admit by a nod of the head that you be she."

"Run fast as you can to Graie Friars, *please,*" Kat whispered to Rob. "If Win Chan—Baldwin Beaumarais lingers there still, tell him I've been carted off to the Tower!"

"What if I don't find your friend there at the poor house? What am I to do then?" Rob asked with a sob in his voice. Kat, being led away, hesitated.

"Save your mother. You and she both must leave London, take to the roads, lose yourselves among a swarm of beggars or a gang of gypsies while you follow the signposts to Bath. *There* you will find Beaumarais! And Rob, don't fret. Just hurry. Pray for me!" she said with a brave smile.

Kat was taken through the anthill slum streets of London, where the white glare of snow was already dimmed, the surface fouled and refuse-strewn. Snow, melting in the sun, ran in rivulets past leaning, half-timbered houses. As the procession passed, doors were opened and faces peered from windows. From small, precarious-looking balconies, silent people stared. Shutters flew open. Folk looked down from garrets, and up from gutters as the cart went by, and soon many began to follow behind it. The crowd swelled at each cross street and turn, and the odd silence of the people in the ordinarily teeming lanes seemed ominous to the mounted men of the King's Guard.

Kat was standing in the cart, not being hauled behind it as she had expected to be and as was customary during the arrest and transport of a miscreant to gaol. The two-wheeled conveyance rocked from side to side, lurched over ruts in the snow and mud, and Kat, gazing at the sky, wondering when she might see it again, held to the sides with both hands listening to the thud of hooves and the occasional shouted orders of the commander to the guardsmen, the only sounds to be heard. As the cart made the turn at Rat Alley, the squall of a baby ripped the silence, and a low rumble, like the buzz of an angry swarming of bees, arose from the throng.

"Where you takin' 'er?"

"What's to be done with Kastesby Dalton?"

"What's her crime? What her offense?"

"Generous is what she is! Cares for old and young, feeds the poor of London Towne, defends good, speaks against injustice . . ." These assertions came louder, thicker as the mob's number, and anger, swelled in the wake of the cart as it rattled across London Bridge.

"Free her! Loose her! Liberate Katesby!" people called as the Tower came in sight. Men and women swarmed about the big wheeled cart, some jamming clubs and sticks between the spokes to stop its progress. Young apprentices grasped the bridles of the tall, matched chestnut mounts of the King's Guards.

"Back! Back, you wretched rabble!" shouted the commander of the troop, flourishing his halliard. "This is sedition and horse thievery you engage in, louts, both hanging offenses! Fall back!"

But the crowd did not. Finding himself ignored and, to his growing unease, roughly jostled, the commander shouted, "Troop, present arms." The men drew their swords nervously, not quite in spit-and-polish unison, for they were house guards not field soldiers and had rarely faced a foe more intimidating than an arrogant, drunken nobleman looking for the castle gate. Even so, the chilling hiss of steel against steel and the sight of twenty waving blades glinting in the sun cast a momentary hush over the mob which stalled, but only momentarily, before it surged forward again with a bellow.

"Loose Kat! Free Kat!"

The cry went up so loud that the roar, if not the words, carried to the top of the Tower, where a handful of men stood peering down from a high balcony. Burgess Blunt, spy; Jack Fletch, hangman; Francis Flud and Paul Wadd, foul spies of Wiltenham, who himself stood with Rattcliffe, the torturer, and Viscount Charles de Morely, who was at the moment a most unhappy, nervous nobleman. Below, in the Norland barge anchored on the Thames, Blaidd Kyd, perhaps the most wanted men in all England at the moment, waited for his new friend Charlie to begin a voyage upriver to the viscount's country manor.

"Here's a means for us to lure the cutthroat, Chance, into the open!" piped Blunt. "Capture Katesby, whom I have long suspected of collusion with the rogue."

"Not all our inquiries, tortures, rackings, and torments, nor our hunts and searches conducted door to door in Southwark, not all the rewards and bribes offered, would so effectively lure Chance out of hiding as would the news that Katesby Dalton is in the Tower! You said yourself, Viscount, the lady innkeeper and the outlaw were acquainted."

"B-b-but she isn't in the Tower," stuttered Charles, "nor will she ever be if . . . if my father has his way." His tongue tied totally when his companions, a mean-countenanced lot, all turned at once to glower at him.

"The earl may not get his way. King Henry foiled your noble parent's marriage plans once before and could do so again. Perhaps the girl isn't headed to the Tower *this* day, Charlie," cold-eyed Blunt snapped with all the high-pitched, dainty peevishness of a little Maltese sleeve dog. "Nor will she likely be taken there on the morrow, but I promise you, the girl and your new comrade, young Kyd, will find themselves in the Tower ere long, and perhaps so will your eminent arrogant parent, with his penchant for offending the king. And the dauntless outlaw Chance will use all his derring-do to rescue them as he did Kyd before. And we will be ready for him and his subterfuge then. Oh, and he will die a very, *very* beastly death."

Blunt sighed, drooling with depraved anticipation. "I think, Charlie, you had best cast off with that Kyd before we change our minds about letting you have him, even for a short interlude. Thinking about the terrible slow death of Chance, at my own hands, with a little help from my colleagues, has got me and some of these others here, I'd wager, into a mood for some instantaneous gratification. Abusing that hulking blond boy of yours would do much to satisfy our aroused appetites."

"*Our*... appetites? What—whose?" asked Charlie. With a wave of a pudgy hand, Blunt indicated the group on the balcony. Each member nodded in agreement. Charles looked down at Blaidd in the barge below, then at the approaching crowd. "Z-z-zounds!" he exclaimed and took his immediate departure, heading for the stairs.

"Good people, hold!" Kat was calling out, trying to be heard above the clamor and roar. "Hold. You put yourselves in mortal danger, interfering thus with the king's men!"

"You're one of our own, Katesby!" a woman shouted. "We won't let 'em have you, not for no reason!"

"We won't let 'em have at her, *now or ever*," a young man shouted. "Clubs, boys, clubs!" he sang out, the cry known to every apprentice in London as a call to arms—a signal that a street fight was in the making.

"Go back!" pleaded Kat, reaching out to touch the hand of the woman. "Go back before . . ."

She looked suddenly toward the sound of a blood-curdling yell from the rear of the mass.

The crowd quickly parted, as a flood flowing over a boulder divides, and she saw a group of mounted horsemen surging through the gap, riding at full gallop. There were Jeremy Edge, Jake Feake, Perkin Thyn, Francis Wyggington, Hugh Wyld, among them. So were Tom Spratt and Giles Hather, surrounded by his gypsies. And there were more, some known to Kat by sight though not by name, and yet others she knew not at all, hardened rogues, villains, intermixed with honest, hard-working townsmen, all mingling to form a small, united, determined army following Win Chance. He was in the lead, dressed all in black, riding his wild-eyed gray stallion, Dash, the pair of them looking to have ridden straight from hell, so fearsome were their aspects.

Kat breathed a sigh of thanks to the heavens as the men of the King's Guard scattered, a mounted trio going up and over the embankment into the river, the others racing for the safety of the north Tower gate. Only one, the trumpeter, stood his ground and blew the call to arms again and again to bring more armed men into the roadway.

Racing alongside the cart, Win leaned low, and with one strong arm swept Kat up out of it, into the saddle before him.

"What are you doing here? Are you mad? Want to get hanged, do you?" she asked, near tears of anger at his recklessness, and of relief and happiness, for she was in Win's arms, where she felt safer than any other place in the world.

"I told you, if ever you have need me all you must do is blazon it, whisper it, utter it, think it. Word will find me where e'er I am and soon you would look up to see me at your side," Win answered, turning Dash, who reared and snorted and pawed the air seeking a path of escape through the surrounding sea of humanity. There was no way clear and no horse, however well trained and loyal, would ride down a man. Win and Kat were encircled by His Majesty's Beefeaters. The indoor guards who usually watched the king's silver plate, but who had been standing in ranks on Tower Green had, at the sound of the trumpet, come pouring out to the aid of their fellows.

"Got 'em! Damn, I've got the pair of 'em, Chance and his moll!" Blunt squealed, looking over the parapet. "My brilliance is boundless!"

"If they are indeed 'got,' it is due more to a fluke of happenstance than to your scheming, Burgess," Rattcliffe snorted.

"Rattcliffe, I caught them, just like that, snap . . . snap," crowed Blunt, clicking his fingers, doing a few dance leaps in place. "I *knew* Katesby Dalton had been summoned hither by the king, did I not? I *knew* the House Guards had been dispatched to escort her. I knew also that a carriage or litter chair could not be maneuvered through the snow-covered streets. I *knew* a cart with two large wheels, such as is used to drag malefactors though the town, would be more serviceable. I *knew* Chance would likely get word of the vixen's arrest, and I strongly suspected he would come hither, bold and reckless outlaw that he is, to rescue his friend and ally, Katesby Dalton, who perhaps is the rogue's lover, too. *Knowing* all that, I had the King's Beefeaters standing ready in ranks on Tower Green, and there they go now to capture Win Chance!"

"Kat is mistress of Chance, say you, Blunt?" queried Hangman Fletch with interest.

"You're counting chickens, Blunt, before they have quite hatched," said Wadd.

"You are swallowing gurgeons ere they're catched,"

added Flud. "Listen and look down. No one's been catched yet!"

A great blare of horns and trumpets was sounding as Charlie de Morely, squinting against the winter sun glaring off snow, stepped almost briskly out Tower Gate at the head of a contingent of Norland outriders.

"Unhand that damsel, man!" shouted Charlie with some authority. Coming to Dash's side, he whispered, "Struggle, Katesby, as if . . . as if you be his . . . captive. Uh, Mr. Chance?" Charlie went on, whispering. "Threaten Kat with your d-d-dagger at her throat, sir, if you please, Mr. Chance, and we, you and I, shall negotiate in loud voices over her freedom—and yours."

"Why is she here?" murmured Win. Then in a loud, rough voice he ordered, "Stay back, Viscount, or the girl's good as dead!" He held Kat close against him for pleasure and also so she would not fall from the dancing horse.

"It's the king and the earl who have sent for her, not the Warrant Officers. King Henry demands to see my father's intended young wife," Charlie replied *sotto voce.* "Chance, what will it take . . ." blared Charlie before he gained control of himself and went on in a carrying, though more regulated tone. "What will you take to free Katesby Dalton?"

"Your word, and your father's, that she'll be safe and your promise there will be no arrests or hangings in retribution against these people for uprising and sedition!"

"Agreed, Chance." The viscount nodded.

"Also my men must be allowed to ride from here across London Bridge and out of the town free, unfettered, and unfollowed."

"Agreed, Chance," the viscount said again.

"Order the king's men to withdraw into the Tower. I'll dispatch the people home and my men on their way." In a softer voice, he added, "We three will stay just as we are, me holding Kat hostage, you waiting to rescue her, Charlie, until we are altogether alone on this bank of the Thames.''

"If you would save the innocent life of Katesby Dalton, go now! Evacuate! Desert this place,'' ordered de Morely, pointing guards in the direction in which they were to march, gesturing at the crowd,

"And what of your safety, Win Chance? How will you get away free?'' Kat asked.

"Just watch me.'' He grinned behind his mask, letting her see the smile in his eyes.

His orders and Charlie de Morely's flew thick and fast, and people, guards, and soldiers began scattering, running, riding away. After a great rush and scuffle, after the blare of horns sounding military retreat, after the passing of near an hour of the clock, the horseman astride his dancing gray mount, his captive still clasped before him, and the viscount were alone. Charlie lifted a hand to help the hostage dismount. She showed some reluctance to be freed at first, and when Kat stood, finally, on the ground beside Dash, her hands gripped the saddle.

"When will we meet again?'' she asked, her raised eyes showing a glaze of tears.

Chance unmasked his face and leaned to her lips, his arm going about her, lifting her a little off the ground. The deep, desperate parting kiss seemed to last an eternity yet wasn't enough for the parting lovers, who clung together a moment longer.

"I told you I'd soon return, in a fortnight, no longer. We're being observed. Let loose now and cuff me a good clout, Kitten. Strike as if you mean it,'' ordered Win, "or suspicions will be roused.'' She pulled back her right arm and brought her open hand forward fast, checking her swing only at the last moment so the slap wasn't nearly as resounding as it might have been. Then she burst into tears.

"Oh . . . Win!'' she gulped. "Hide your face, blast you,

lest you be seen and named!" Kat glanced up at the Tower where Blunt and his henchmen still stood peering down.

"They have gotten no glimpse of my features, for I have not raised my face. Only Charlie has seen me." Win laughed, readjusting his disguise so that once more only his flashing green eyes were visible. "De Morely, protect my secret. Also, protect my Kat!"

"I will, on my honor I will! Go now," answered Charlie. "Blaidd and I are all the defense Kat will need!"

Dash reared, pawed the air, and pivoted, and as his rider leaned well forward over the withers, the horse leapt into a full gallop. Kat looked after them for a long while, watched until Win had ridden out of sight and the clatter of Dash's hooves on London Bridge faded. By then her tears had dried and she turned to set a kiss on Charlie's cheek.

"Thank you, Charlie," she said. "How brave you are! You are my champion and protector, a veritable knight as of olden times. My own pure, sweet, noble Sir Galahad. You will not give away the secret of Win Chance and . . . ?"

"The secret of Chance and Beaumarais, that they are one and the same? I swore on my honor, did I not?" he replied. "I will be true to my word to you, as the dial is true to the sun, for as long as I walk this earth."

Kat grinned. "Do you hear yourself, Charlie de Morely? Your tongue hasn't tripped over even one word, not in a while now."

"Becoming your Galahad, Katesby, your virtuous knight errant, has cured me, untangled my tongue, wot?" He smiled, shy but happy, and crooked his arm as a resting place for Kat's hand. "Let us go now. King Henry and all the inner circle of his court await you."

"I'm to be presented now, as I am?" She held back, dismayed. "What will they think when I appear in a work dress with rolled sleeves, wearing an apron, my hair unkempt, all loose and . . ."

". . . and with white flour smudges on your brow and cheek? Yes, you are to be presented exactly so." De Morely nodded while Kat wiped at her cheek with the back of her hand, only making matters worse by spreading the flour over a wider area. "They shall think whatever the king expects them to. And they know he is an impatient man. When he learned of the purpose of Father's royal audience—that he would, with the king's consent, take a young lady to wife—Henry insisted upon setting his own eyes upon her . . . you. At once."

"Was his majesty favorably disposed to the earl's petition, do you suppose?" asked Kat.

"I . . . I s-s-suppose the king was not disinclined to consider Father's request, b-b-but with wily King Henry the Fox, t'aint easy to know his true and actual predispositions," replied Charlie, the return of his stutter, however slightly, betraying his inner conflict. He was answering Kat with less than full honesty as he mused upon the ludicrous scene he'd witnessed earlier in the king's apartments.

Chapter 16

Winter morning light played upon walls brocaded in gold fabric, on hangings aglint with gold threads, tapestry weavings depicting gold-cloaked nobles mounted upon gold-bridled horses departing for the hunt. Light flickered upon golden tassels, goblets and ewers, danced on the gold plate with which the king's table was laid, flamed the cloth-of-gold robes which encased Henry's massive person slumped in a small throne at the head of the laden table.

The balding, paunchy, huge, and disgruntled monarch was clearly out of sorts, a condition that struck fear and dread into all who came within range of his sight or voice. Those few who dared speak at all did their best to distract and amuse the peevish king, among them his ten-year-old daughter Elizabeth.

"I am reading, Majesty, of the king of the ancient land of Pella," the princess began, her intelligent eyes bright in her small, anxious face. Elizabeth had her father's coloring, pale skin and light orange hair, brows so faint they were close to invisible.

"Always got your nose in a book, daughter. Damned odd," grumbled the king. The child was a diplomat by nature and necessity due to her precarious situation at court and in her father's affection, and she said no more. The Earl of Norland, a man secure in his power and less inclined to tact, made the next attempt to amuse King Henry.

"My son would make a highly suitable match for the Princess Elizabeth, preferring, as does she, the company of books to all other amusements and diversions," offered Harry de Morely, his usual subtle drollery discomfiting those who didn't recognize it for humor of a sort.

"Match? But I will never wed," said Elizabeth firmly.

"Silence, daughter! You'll do as you're commanded by me, your father, lord, and king. You will do your duty to England when I choose a husband for you from among the great princes of Christendom. You will thus secure for me and for England a powerful ally who will get offspring upon you—earls and dukes and lords aplenty. Tudor blood—the blood of the Conqueror—will course in their veins as it does in yours and mine!" roared out the king, knitting his pale brows.

"My own boy, Charles there, is of Plantagenet lineage twofold, your grace." De Morely pressed his jest with a narrow-eyed taunting glance at his son, who blushed. "There is no nobler blood in all England than that of the Plantagenets." This thrust was directed at the king himself, whose Tudor ancestry didn't quite equal the Plantagenets', or so the Plantagenets posited. King Henry rolled his eyes heavenward.

"I've not enjoyed the, ah—pleasure, shall we say? Yes, pleasure will do, of your company, de Morely, in some time. You've kept your sinewy form and youthful slimness, I observe," the king admitted grudgingly. "I do espy iron-gray streaks in your dark hair, yet your eyes are as calculating and cold as ever I remember them. Yes, you are much unchanged, Norland. You are the same vexatious Harry as of yore, waxed even more brazenly belligerent methinks, and surely not the most pleasing company for a king," Henry grumbled. "Why did you request this audience with us, Norland? To the point, man. Present your petition and let us be done with this audience."

"I shall get to my own affairs with alacrity, sire, if only you take even some slight notice of Charlie. My son is a shining example of a perfect nobleman-scholar, Majesty, a fitting mate for a bookish girl such as your daughter, the princess. Doubly noble-blooded as is Charlie, he would never pose a threat to Prince Edward or the throne. Charlie's greatest, perhaps only, ambition is to lie beside a book on a grassy riverbank, drowsing in melancholy."

"Father!" wailed Charles before turning to the king. "Majesty, my f-f-father saves himself the expense of both a jester and a whipping boy by using me to serve him in both capacities."

"Harry! Charlie! Do keep this tedious squabbling and scolding to your own house and get to the business which has brought you hither," sighed the king with exaggerated weariness. "And I thought *our* domestic jousts were outrageous, eh, Elizabeth?"

"Just say you'll consider Charles as a husband for the Lady Elizabeth, Your Grace, however fleetingly, and we'll get on with the actual reason for my being here," de Morley goaded.

"I'll say anything to be quit of you, Harry. You irk me as you always have done. Yes, I shall, howsomever momentarily, cogitate upon Charles de Morely's fitness as royal consort. There. Now make haste to declare your own business before my displeasure in your companionship turns to exasperation," Henry carped. Before de Morely could reply, Jasper the Jester leapt forward. The king groaned. "Oh, shall I never have a moment's ease? Must I be vexed incessantly by gadflies, nits, and fleas? What is it *you* wish to plague me about, you moldy gargoyle? Out with it, Jasper, thou weed. What wilt *thou* say?"

"A noble monarch, the noblest king in all Christendom, had best choose for such a daughter as the Lady Elizabeth a man of sufficient nimbleness of mind to match her in wit and astuteness, Your Majesty," lectured Elizabeth's fool, lauding his mistress.

"Do you presume to edify and command me, Fool?" flared Henry.

"By me troth, Majesty, I have no such intent nor any purpose at all but to serve my lady. He who will be consort of *this* Princess must be not only quick of wit but strong as well in spirit and body, for brilliant scholar as my young lady be, she is as brilliant a rider—as were you at her same age, sire," the jester inserted, an appeal to the king's vanity. "Elizabeth the princess is indefatigable in the dance and at the hunt, as you know well, Majesty, and thus—"

"You flatter me overmuch, Jasper," interrupted the politic Elizabeth, smiling fondly upon her harlequin fool. He, in happy response, jingled the silver bells at his wrists and ankles and turned two rolling somersaults for her.

"I, too, was indefatigable at the hunt at her same age, and for many years after," nodded King Henry, seeming somewhat cheered at the memory until he sighed and was engulfed again in gloom. "Oh, I was indeed indefatigable at the hunt, at the joust, at dancing, at games of all sorts, particularly at the game of love. But so fatigable have I now grown that my last queen, the harlot Catherine, dealt with me in dastardly fashion and brazenly made a cuckold of a king." The king pouted like a great baby, then glowered daggers at his fool, who cut short a hurdy-gurdy rendering of a street tune, "Cuckolds All in a Row."

"And she lost her treasonous head for it, sire!" said Jasper Fool, stamping his belled, pointed boot emphatically.

"Catherine Howard was known to be a most flirtatious

and forward virgin even at the tender age of fourteen, Majesty," interjected elegant Adelaide, Lady Seton, as she offered a cool, knowing, patrician smile. One of the favored noble ladies of Henry's inner circle, his closet, she was often in attendance at the King's dining and gaming tables.

"I know. I *know now* what she was known to be by everyone but me. By fifteen, Catherine was doing more than finger exercises with her harpsichord instructor, Henry Manox. It was he who boasted he commonly used to feel the secret and other parts of the queen's person. Oh, I've heard that told time and time again, but not *in* time to warn me away from her. Why did no one of you here, not one of my nobles nor of my clergy speak to me of Catherine's wanton ways *before* I made the jade my fifth queen?" demanded Henry, looking about accusingly. "Oh why, *why* is it that none of my wives have ever understood me?" he queried.

"Come, come, Great Harry. Mawkishness ill suits your regal self, sire," chided pretty Lady Montfort, another frequent visitor at court. "Your third lady, Queen Jane, who gave you Prince Edward, your heir, understood you, surely. And as for young Catherine, who could have so much as hinted ill of her, once you had lost your great heart and settled upon her as your fifth queen? Any who had dared counsel you caution, Majesty, would swiftly have been invited to take up long residence in the Tower prison. Admit it, Your Grace."

"You, my dear Lady Cary," the king answered with a fond, rather sly smile, "likely could have got away with it."

"I respectfully beg to differ, Majesty," flirted her ladyship. "Unlikely is more like it."

"Oh, woe, woe! I am the topic of gossip in every court in Europe. The French King Francis, famous for his lewdness and for the ribaldry of his court, writes to avow that he feels my grief as though it were his own. Yet I have been told he relished all the wicked facts, remarked with glee that the queen had been wondrously naughty and had wondrously abused me."

"Have you also heard, Majesty, what many members of your own nobility relish repeating," Henry's own jester, Clarence Kite, began, "that if Queen Catherine had not been a ninny she could have had her cakes and ale and kept her king? Of him—you, that is, your noble self, sire—'tis widely remarked, though not by me, that he—you—would have been none the wiser."

This dark and dangerous sally was made, to his own peril, by Kite, a man of snide and biting, brilliant, and brutally honest wit. The fool's compulsion to speak with veracity no matter how provoking his utterances might prove as often won him the admiration as the wrath of the unpredictable king, and all present waited with bated breath for Henry's reaction. It was mere seconds before Henry's notorious temper flared like lightning in his small, pale blue eyes and he roared like the lion in the royal menagerie. Laboriously hauling his great bulk half out of his throne chair, the irate monarch propelled a golden goblet through the air toward Clarence. The jester, much practiced at dodging articles hurled at him by the king, ducked and received no greater injury than a splatter of red wine upon his gold-and-white jerkin. He smiled and the outraged king, rising to his full impressive height, drew a dagger from his belt and stood poised to fling it at Kite. The jester froze, the smile fixed and deadened on his face, an easy target.

"Ah, our Tudor domestic tranquility certes is a comfort to heart and soul, is it not, Father?" said little Elizabeth, with a seraphic, yet satirical smile which brought a look of surprise, then appreciation, then finally humor to the king's countenance. There was general laughter then, the tension of the moment dissolved by the child who had an adeptness at manipulating her volatile parent.

"Oh, and is it any riddle, my lord king," the little girl

went on, "that privy as I have long been to all the base particulars of marital treachery among the aristocrats of our land, you and your queens not least among them, that I would choose, given my druthers, sire, though not yours, never to wed, not ever?" she asked with a drollery that evoked her father's slow, deep laugh.

"Ah, Lizzie, you've a way about you, now and again, that brightens my dark moods and thwarts my baneful inclinations. Well, tell us now as you would have before I silenced you, what it is that so intrigues you about the king of the Land of Pella, of whom you are reading?" The child, rewarded with her father's attention at last, nodded sagely, a tiny smile revealing her pleasure.

"The king in the Land of Pella had in *his* stables, Father, three thousand mares and three hundred stallions. You, sire, who are a greater monarch than the King of Pella do not have as many mares or stallions. Why so?"

"Before you were born, Elizabeth, I caused to be built my own noble studdery. I imported into England, to be bred with our great English stock of horseflesh, the finest and most magnificent equines from abroad—Flemish roils, Scottish nags, Spanish jennets, Naples coursers. I obtained some splendid results in the progeny—splendid, that is, till my stud officers grew lazy and let the breeding go all this way and that, as the beasts were naturally inclined. Soon all I had was a mixed brood of ungainly bastard stock, neither fleet nor beautiful nor strong." Henry frowned and sighed. "Another of my memorable disappointments."

"There you go, Majesty, indulging in piteousness again," said Lady Montfort sympathetically.

" 'Tis no rollick being in your company, Great Harry," commented Lady Seton. "Not so long ago all was wont to be gaiety and merriment where you were, sire. Is there no way we may cheer you? Will music or dancing or feasting or madrigals lift your spirits? A good bear-baiting, perhaps?

Jugglers? Minstrels? Mimes?" The king only pouted and shook his head at each suggestion, setting his great jowls aquiver, while drooping lower in his small throne.

"Oh, buck up, Majesty. Great men are not *always* wise in all they attempt, nor do all their undertakings flourish as they might hope. Take hold of yourself," offered de Morely, looking bored and sounding almost disdainful. He and Lady Seton exchanged weary glances.

"Harry, Harry," scolded the king, wagging a fat finger, "methinks you are a prime proof of your own theorem. It is not wise of any man, great or otherwise, to offer affront to his king, even roundaboutly. Have a care, Norland, that you do not provoke me overly much with your arrogance and nonchalance. A noble Plantagenet you are, but I am king here. Speak your piece, man, and leave me in peace, before you go too far."

"I am come here today to beg His Majesty's permission to wed," said de Morely with a smile. Henry sat up straighter, his interest piqued.

"Have you a particular damsel in mind, de Morely, or shall I arrange a match?"

"I would take a particular woman to wife, Majesty. She—the particular woman—is the sole reason I would willingly enter into a state a matrimony again."

"I'm looking for a wife myself, you know," answered Henry with a narrow-eyed stare, which evidenced some workings of his mind.

"Indeed I do know, Majesty. How is *your* quest proceeding?"

"Not as well as your own, apparently, Harry. Methinks I may steal your lady. Who is the favored dame you have set your mind upon? Anyone I know?"

" 'Tis my heart, sire. I have set my heart upon her." De Morely's narrow face was softened by smile lines at the corners of his eyes, which were now uncharacteristically soft and warm. " 'Tis no one of your acquaintance."

"Your heart? Oh, Harry, Harry, I've been in love myself," said Henry, "and I know the condition to be most troublesome. It tosses things all upside down. What might be the age of your lady love?" asked the shrewd king, observing an exchange of glances between the de Morelys, father and son.

"She has reached her nineteenth summer, Majesty," answered Harry with pride.

"Oh, Harry, Harry, I must warn you to look ere ye leap, man," said the king with a lecherous grin. "I had a young wife myself, you know. When *I* took a nineteen-year-old bride, no one warned *me* of the pitfalls. My sages and doctors only quoted to me the works of some poet or other who wrote: 'Spare diet is the cause love lasts/ For surfeits sooner kill than fasts.' Not true, I learned. When 'spare diet' did not satisfy my young queen, *I* was then advised that fish dinners would make a man leap like a flea. Not true, neither, de Morely, and so my young Catherine brought lovers into her royal bedchamber. The brazen harlot had lovers swarming like bees here, at my very own court. Why, Thomas Culpepper, a man of my Privy Chamber, confessed he intended and meant to do ill with the queen and she with him, though he averred the matter never came to a head."

"Whether the boisterous, wild young man ever did or no come to a head in bed with the queen, the queen lost her head, Majesty!" interposed Jasper Fool in a failed attempt to comfort the king.

"Must you start him up on *that* again?" asked Lady Seton with an exasperated heavenward roll of her eyes.

"I reproach my ministers for keeping me in ignorance of her true nature," moaned the king, "and my doctors for deceiving me about my own, suggesting a young wife would be a nostrum for a man grown bald, paunchy, and wrinkled."

"I would wager that your advisors also suggested, Majesty, that, 'tis not the meat, but 'tis the appetite makes eating a delight,'' said Harry de Morely. The king, again slumped disconsolately in his gilded chair, nodded, setting his chins quivering. "Methinks," continued de Morely, "you indeed were misled, sire, for in my experience, a woman's appetite needs be satisfied by ample rations, whether of meat, fish, fowl, or whatever. Her satiety after plenty is but a transient state. 'Tis meat which gives true delight that in turn gives rise to even greater appetite."

"And that, Majesty, is altogether *meet,* is't not?" punned Clarence Kite, returned to the royal chamber attired in a fresh, spotless jerkin, and ringing his fool's bell softly. The king nodded at Kite in appreciation of the fool's word play, his recent rage at the man forgotten; then he turned his attention to de Morely again.

"Could your young woman give you another heir, de Morely?" Henry demanded. "A second son who, unlike his brother, could pose a threat one day to my own progeny? 'Tis my God-given duty, you know, Harry, to ensure that aristocratic blood does never run so thick in a male offspring of yours, or of any noble, that he could one day lay claim to the throne of England."

"No need to worry on that score, Majesty. My lady is a commoner," de Morely assured the king.

"A commoner? How common, Harry?"

"She is an innkeeper, Your Grace, howbeit a most uncommon one."

"Harry, Harry! An innkeeper, forsooth?" bellowed the king with an incredulous laugh, more animated than he'd been in days. "Mean you a bawdy housekeeper who has besotted a goatish old man with her voluptuous wiles?" At this, de Morely paled with rage.

"If any but you, Majesty, had spoke thus, his blood, thick or thin, would be flowing from his corpse. You err, sire, in your assessment of my lady," he gritted as the king's rumbling, rolling laugh filled the chamber. "The lady in question is above—"

"Toy with the chit, man. Dally to your heart's ease, but do not be so foolish as to contemplate taking the cunning creature to wife! I won't permit it, Harry, won't allow the noble Earl of Norland to make a duchess of a trollop and a damn fool of himself!" Henry's face had gone bright red with mirth as he clutched his heaving sides.

"You made Nan Boleyn your queen," protested de Morely.

"For Anne and for me it was young love on both sides, de Morely. Besides, the creature bewitched me. Oh, I do beg your pardon, Elizabeth, to speak so of your mother, but truth's truth, aye. And the Boleyns were not altogether common, not tavern keepers, certes."

"You'll not again deprive me of a woman I love, Henry Tudor, I swear it!" roared de Morely, his hand grasping his sword hilt as, again, a taut silence fell upon the chamber, the denizens waiting to learn if Norland had, in an instant, sealed his own doom. Would King Henry issue the command that he be dragged off to the Tower to await trial for treason?

"Harry, Harry," murmured the king, his little, narrowed eyes almost obscured in folds of flesh, "you've always been defiant."

"And you've always been fair, Majesty," responded the quick-witted, nimble-tongued Norland with a fast, easy smile, his hand still on his sword hilt, though just resting there now as casually, as innocuously, as it would linger on his hip or belt buckle. De Morely went on speaking as though nothing untoward had occurred and no threat to the king had been so much as contemplated. "Before you deny my plea, only see my lady, speak but fleetingly with a true flower of honest English womanhood, and you will comprehend my delight in her. You will know she is not trying to entrap me. In truth, you will know the opposite to be true. She has yet to give her answer to my proposal, yet I live in hope it will be 'yes.' Only just see her, sire, I implore you."

"Zounds!" shouted Henry. "Send a troop of my own guard to fetch hither this female paragon! Send now. I would see at once, with my own eyes, the proud barmaid, the glorious tavern wench Harry de Morely, my noble Earl of Norland, would make his countess and who makes *him* wait upon her reply!

"Old men do foolish things, Harry," warned Henry once the troop of guards was dispatched. "Misery might follow, misery upon misery. I know from my own experience with . . ." Stifled groans rose from several corners of the room simultaneously. "Well, you all know about that, about . . . Catherine."

"Catherine who lost her head? *That Catherine?* Yes, yes, Majesty, we do know," Lady Seton reminded him impatiently.

"Harumph," said the king before again focusing his keen attention on de Morely. "So, you're at it again, eh, Harry, wanting to marry beneath you?" asked the monarch, enjoying the situation immensely. He liked nothing more than bringing a headstrong nobleman to his knees, and in all his realm there was no more noble, nor more headstrong a man than Harry de Morely.

"Just as a nobleman may not take too elevated a wife and thus overly thicken the blood of his offspring, neither may he wed too low and mongrelize my aristocracy. I discovered, during the episode of my failed studdery and stable, how disastrous may be the results of indiscriminate breeding. I will not allow the thick and ancient de Morely line to be thinned overmuch by . . . how now? What be the fuss and commotion without? Insurrection, uprising, riot, and revolt?" worried Henry on hearing the roar from below of the throng accompanying Kat to court.

He hurried to his balcony with surprising agility to

observe, from beginning to end, the scene played below by his Beefeaters and House Guards and the angry populace, a cross section of London's citizenry it looked to be, with gypsies and thieves cheek by jowl with shopkeepers, apprentices, artisans, students, even lawyers. The drama was most dramatically rendered, thought Henry, by a willowy girl being held hostage, and her captor, Win Chance. The bold, ingenious outlaw was got up in black cloak and masking scarf, his usual outfit, as readily identifiable as a goldsmith's hallmark.

The king was watching still as the crowd dispersed, as Chance, almost reluctantly, it appeared, released his hostage and rode off, free as the wind as always. The outlaw's audacity was marveled at by one and all in the realm even, though somewhat grudgingly, by the King of England himself. The outlaw gone out of sight, Henry watched his former captive square her shoulders, toss back her wild, wind-blown mane, tilt her chin, and set a hand upon young de Morely's proffered arm. From his vantage, as the pair stepped toward the Tower gate, the king could not see that the lady's hand was floury from kneading bread, nor that it clutched her escort's sleeve urgently.

Neither Kat nor Charlie saw, though Henry did, the seizure and arrest of a tall, thick, nearly smooth-pated lad, who was taken from a barge at dockside and dragged off, fighting like the very devil, in shackles and chains, to the Tower dungeon.

Chapter 17

Charles de Morely squired Kat through the king's Great Hall, where folk were gathering for the meal served there each day to hundreds of the king's subjects—his many courtiers, household servants, soldiers, guards, clergy, distiguished visitors to London, even peasants in the town on business. Also a horde of paupers and beggars.

"These are daily fed by the king, who is bound to care for the poor souls of his realm, impoverished by circumstance, through no fault or delinquency of their own—the aged, blind, and lame, fatherless children, wounded soldiers, ruined householders. These folk rely upon the king's daily charity, and the charity of the collection plate in every parish, to persist. Excluded only are those the king deems the thriftless poor—rioters, lazy vagabonds, rogues, and strumpets.

"There are street musicians here I recognize," Kat said. "That man with the patch upon his eyes is often performing outside Graie Friars on Hog Lane."

"A man may sing for his supper here, or play upon a

lute or lyre. As for the young gallants present, this is a locale, like St. Paul's aisle, in which to be seen, to exchange talk and gossip."

"I see the same sort at the inn. Those of means, men about town, are more interested in being seen than in supping. See, Charlie, how seeming careless they toss their rich cloaks over their shoulders when really they wish to show off costly silk linings beneath brocades."

"These other young men here, who do not flash and flaunt, are would-be cavaliers of slender means, hiding frayed elbows beneath their close-held poor melton-cloth mantles."

"I am familiar with their like, too, the lads who show mannerly restraint but who secretly salivate in anticipation of much-needed edibles."

"Over all looms the Lord Steward, George Hatton, manager of the King's Court and households. His spies keep suspicious, gimlety eyes upon the regiments of cooks, turnspits, scullions, dishwashers, and kitchen louts, each and every one, the steward is certain, only awaits a opportunity to purloin a fat capon or a tub of butter."

"Imagine how much must be lost in wastage, breakage, and spillage, besides theft. I keep a reckoning of the goods in my small larder at the inn, but to keep a tally of this enormous domicile seems daunting," said Kat, gazing about. Unacquainted as she was with the vast spectacle, all seemed chaos, pandemonium, and din as she and de Morely passed through the hall.

"In truth, " Charlie explained, "there is a method in this seeming madness. Each rank and clique of diners is careful to take its proper place at table, the poorest and least of them below the salt, their betters above."

"Be that as it may, Charlie, all and sundry, wherever they've settled themselves, fall still and gawp as we go by." A wave of quiet in a sea of curious eyes did follow in Kat's wake. " 'Tis like a devilish dream I've had, in which I lost all me garments while all about me kept theirs and gawped. I feel a sight, Charlie."

"You are a sight, Katesby, an unusual one here, and most charming," whispered Charles, "with your hair flowing free and flour smudges dotted"—he wiped at her brow with a silk cloth he drew from his waistcoat—"dotted here and there. Unusual and wonderful is what you are."

Kat, heartened, held her head higher, looking exceedingly self-possessed, her consternation belied only by her biting grip on Charlie's arm.

"As I live and breath, I *am* relieved to be out of that crowded large chamber with all those eyes!" she whispered to de Morely. "Oh, but the dear save me! Where must we go now? Are we to walk this gauntlet now?" she asked, looking down an endless corridor lit by flaring torches in golden sconces, the flickering light fallling upon two rows of very tall sentinels all dressed in cloth-of-gold pataloons and gold-crested jerkins. Each man stared straight and unblinking before him, clutching a halliard in his right hand, and none showed any sign of life as Kat and Charlie strode by. Though she tried not to, Kat stole a glance at each face as she passed. "Are they *alive*, Charlie?" she whispered with a giggle. "There's something rather . . . well, comical about grown men in such attire standing about like statuary. Have you never been tempted to pinch one? I am. Let's!"

"I prithee, Kat, do not!" he replied, alarmed and intrigued simultaneously by her suggestion. "All hell might well break loose."

When they reached gilded double doors at the end of the corridor, Kat was trying, unsuccessfully, to stifle her low laugh, which was causing Charlie to chortle. The pair of guards flanking the doors did their best to remain stone-faced in spite of Kat's infectious gaiety, and crossed staffs to bar the way.

"Who goes there?" bellowed one, struggling against a grin.

"What business have you with the king?" bawled the other with a short guffaw.

" 'Tis Viscount de Morely and Mistress Dalton, summoned hither by his majesty. Stand down—uh, if you please," said Charlie with just enough firmness, to his own surprise, to instantly get his way. Snorts and barks and gurgles of laughter rolled from man to man back along the corridor, and Kat smiled over her shoulder as the massive doors to the king's chamber swung inward. Looking ahead once more, she was nearly immobilized on the threshold, dazzled by the golden splendor that struck her eyes.

Courtiers and guards and servants, wall hangings, drapery, napery, and tapestries, the plate upon the table, the robes upon the imposing king's person, all looked to her to be made of gold. A short fanfare played upon a trumpet announced the arrival of de Morely and his charge. No one paid them the slightest notice. As Charlie guided Kat into the room, the ladies and gentlemen of the Chamber, richly dressed and wondrously bejewelled, Kat thought, were, as if of a single mind, fixedly gazing upon Henry, who as fixedly gave his attention to a courier so recently arrived that the man yet stood in a spreading puddle as the snow upon his boots finished melting.

"A princess was born in Scotland, Your Majesty!"

"Ha! A princess is it, not a prince for King James and his Queen Mary?" Henry laughed with nasty glee, slapping his thigh. "Mary, Princess of Guise, turned me down when I offered for her hand, to make her queen in England. I wrote saying I was 'a big person in need of a big wife.' She replied that though her stature was large, her neck was little. She would not risk it at my court, a reference to the fates of some of my earlier queens—begging your pardon, Elizabeth, your own mother one of those. Now I see 'tis as well this de Guise chose Scots James, for she makes girls, not boys. She has not given her husband a prince, not yet leastways, though 'tis possible she will yet anon and there will be a king upon the throne of Scotland after James."

" 'Taint possible, Your Majesty," said the courier. "King James will ne'er produce a male heir, for the Princess Mary that was is even now Mary, Queen of Scots, and has been since the sixth day of her short life. King James, Majesty, is dead."

"My discourteous nephew James, dead at thirty, survived but six days into his daughter's life? Zounds!"

"Yes, Majesty. He died of the melancholy, 'tis said, from which he had long suffered, brought to acute despair by the disgrace of his great loss to your forces at Solway. He stopped briefly after, with his pregnant queen, at Linlithgow Castle, where the baby was later born, before withdrawing himself to Falklands Castle, his favorite residence. There, surrounded by his lords and nobles, he died in his own bed. It was when the news was brought to him of his daughter's birth. He heard the messenger, 'turned upon his back . . . gave up a little smile of laughter, and thereafter held up his hands to God and yielded up his spirit.' So it was written by his chronicler."

"James himself had not attained the age of two years when he became king. Dissension in the land was rife, and now a little, little Stuart, Mary, is queen in Scotland," mused the king, thoughtful and shrewd, the personification of his unofficial title of "Henry the Fox" as he was known for his canniness.

"What? Mary Stuart is a queen at six days?" Elizabeth exclaimed. "How unfair when I am not a queen at ten years and will never be."

"You will be a queen somewhere, though never in England, mind," warned Henry, "after you are wed. Anon you will ascend one of Christendom's great thrones, for you will be espoused to a king or at least to an excellent prince.

You will learn, when you rule, that power and prerogative shift and slide this way and that, Elizabeth. On this day there has been change in our favor. With a mere babe on the Scottish throne, insurrection will easily be fomented in that land to our north as it was when the baby James assumed the throne. Certes, our ambition for dominance over the wild Scots will be advanced. My armies defeated theirs but a fortnight ago at Solway Moss when there *was* a king in a castle at Edinburgh. Now James's death has set the stage for intrigue and betrayal in his realm, for political and religious discord, all to our good. We will bring the Scots to heel, throw out the French and Papists, and then turn our eyes and guns to invading *France!* What think you, my Lord Montfort?" asked Henry, turning to one of his favored advisors, Thomas, Marquis of Montfort. "Are we to leap into the void at once, Tom, with our armies or shall we first dispatch our spies, our secret *agents provocateurs* and other connivers, to sew seeds of unrest and dissension?"

"All of those at once, Majesty, and more," answered Montfort. "Persist at battering the Scots' borders and marches with our regiments led as before by the Earl of Hertford. Also offer bribage to penniless lords of crucially situated castles, Chrichton or Liddesdale, whose wealth has been depleted by continuous hostilities. Our Lord Dacre on the north border at Askerton will know with whom to treat.

"We should be liberal with coin for the disaffected among the clergy who have been seeking a Reformation in Scotland," Montfort went on. "Mary of Guise, mother of the infant Queen of the Scots, is loyal to France, as you well know, Majesty, and has with her in Scotland a sizeable retinue of her countrymen. She will keep her daughter to her own religion and Popish ways and deliver Scotland up to France as swift as ever she is able."

Henry nodded. "My prime statesman you be, Thomas Montfort. What more would you have us do?"

"While you batter at the borders, stir trouble in the lawless Highlands and burrow from within at the Scots. I think it would be useful for you to assume a royal demeanor of magnanimous support for the little queen, your niece. A regent to rule for baby Mary doubtless will be appointed by the Scottish Parliament. Likely 'twill be James Hamilton, Earl of Arran, is my conjecture, a reasonable man. We will suggest to him a parley, sire, only veiling a little a threat of invasion."

"Only last fall I awaited James in vain for nine days at York, for talk, and now you say we should dicker with 'em? Conquer 'em, I say! The young men of my court are desirous of both spoil and glory that can be got only in battle."

"Majesty, to fight a full-scale war which may be won in other ways is a waste of blood and treasure. Now that your discourteous nephew James is dead, negotiate a treaty between England and Scotland. Bind the agreement with the betrothal of Prince Edward, your heir, Majesty, and this new little Mary, Queen of Scots. Both lands will thus come under the English crown and rule."

"I have many good, if common men about me aspiring to advancement and ambitious for wealth. Thomas, recall you that all knights are not to the manor born as you were. Men are created knights by their king, me, before battle to encourage bravery, and after, to reward them for valorous service most excellent."

"And there's estimable riches to be made at ransoms. A king's lieutenant may bring a thousand pound," said Sir John Clere. "Even a common man will bring his captor some revenue."

"But the high taxes imposed on the people, sire, to finance war cause grumbling among the populace," interjected Lord Seton.

"Let 'em grumble. Even common soldiers must be given a means to earn a livelihood at their trade, and gentlemen and younger sons enabled to profit. In providing the means, war, we at the same time rid the realm of its most wild and savage element—ruffians, vagabonds, masterless men, common players and the like—who are commandeered to pull oars in our galleys. Lord Monfort, foreign war is like a potion of rhubarb to cleanse choler from the body of the realm."

"Your Majesty, your domain must be cleaned and rid forthwith and without delay of a particular wild and savage member who has perpetrated a deed most foul!" a short man with a round, puffy pink face addressed the king in a squealing voice.

" 'Tis Burgess Blunt," Charlie whispered to Kat, who had been looking about her and listening to all that was said. The little man, she now saw, was quivering with excitement as sweat ran down his high brow to hang in a drip at the end of his nose. Francis Wiltenham and Rattcliffe also stood before Henry, prepared to amend and amplify upon Blunt's tidings.

"There has been a pitiless attack upon Brother Truckle. The old man is near to his death, Majesty!"

"Truckle, of Graie Friars, Majesty," intoned Wiltenham somberly, "struck down in the street by some offender most foul."

"Old Rooster Truckle known as The Good, sire, is he of whom we speak," added Rattcliffe.

"Rooster Truckle, the tippling old monk of Graie Friars? Assaulted, say you?"

"The very same, sire," affirmed Blunt.

"Gads. Only yesterday that good man, Truckle, was in our royal presence begging alms for his orphans and wards. Howsomever often we hold public audience, to hear appeals direct from our subjects, Truckle is always among the petitioners, plaguing . . . entreating us, rather, for contribution, as if the royal treasury held the riches of Cynras, Croesus, Crasus, and Midas put together. I was already wearied from listening to pleas all the day long when that crotchety old holy man began his usual babbles, upbraiding us, *me,* for my long and stately sitting at meat. He intimated we were a 'sleepy glutton.' He faulted us for pampering our belly! When he'd done with his harangue, we felt so blameworthy, we suffered him to lead us off to evening prayers, for the good of our soul. He accompanied us and kept us so long upon our knees at the chapel, I had to make haste back to my chambers, else miss the late supper." Henry downed a serving of wine and pounded his goblet upon the table for more.

"Did you donate to Brother Truckle's cause, sire," asked Lady Seton, "for the good of your soul?"

"I passed him along to my almsman, frugal Algernon Willett, who sees to my soul without emptying my coffers. That aged monk and my grandame, the dowager queen, are an alike pair of scolds, adept as no other in this world at causing us to feel contrite, much as we did as a boy. We do not favor feeling so." The king frowned. "Ah, what gay air is it you play now, Fool?" he asked.

" 'All joy to Great Caesar,' sire," the man answered, fingering a guitar expertly. " 'Tis one of Durfey's Musical Pills to Purge Melancholy."

"Yes. From the Italian harmonic sequences *La folia,*" agreed the king.

"Your musical knowledge, Majesty, is without equal," said the fool, a man valued by Henry for his unequivocal honesty. The king accepted the compliment as truth and smiled for the first time that day.

"Render now one of our lively English tunes, 'The Merry Companion,' " he suggested pleasantly, but then Burgess Blunt cleared his throat and did an impatient dance in place, recapturing Henry's wandering attention. "All right, Blunt," Henry snapped, miffed to be reminded of an unpleasant occurrence. "Hear me. Though 'tis true Rooster Truckle is frequently a tiresome person," rumbled Henry, gulping wine and smacking his lips, "he is a good old soul. To assault so godly and benevolent a man, however wearisome he may be, is monstrous vicious and an affront to the king's peace. I'll not have such crimes committed in our realm," roared Henry, nurturing outrage. "Who did the dastardly deed? Any notion, Blunt?"

"Indeed yes, sire. None other than the cutthroat cowardly outlaw, Win Chance!" At this pronouncement, a great murmur of doubt went round the king's chamber.

" 'Tis not that scoundrel's pattern, to batter old men," mused the king, doubtfully.

"We have evidence—a black scarf discovered at the scene by a street urchin. The lad was an onlooker during the robbery, Your Majesty. Merely by happenstance he saw it all. For his own safety, we are searching all London for him. We will hunt the boy down—uh, hunt *for* the boy so we may protect him from Chance, get him and keep him secure in the Tower," reported Wiltenham briskly.

"Charlie!" whispered Kat, "I must unearth that boy—Little Chance—before they do, else I'd give not a tuppence for his life."

"A search for the villain Chance is also under way, Your Majesty," offered Blunt.

"Word has gone out. Town to town, door to door, all across the land," explained Rattcliffe the Torturer. "We are invading his usual haunts, keeping watchful scrutiny of every establishment he is known to frequent, questioning all persons reported ever to have had dealings with the felon. We are incarcerating street louts, miscreants, gypsies, Winchester gooses, and the like, all we can get our clutches upon, for some among them are certain to be cohorts of Chance, and some of those his close comrades. One or two at least will be persuaded to give the dastard up. We *will* get him this time."

Rattcliffe had begun speaking calmly enough, but gradually his tone changed, his voice grew louder, his words came faster, and his eyes gleamed with anticipated pleasure. "We will get him and when do, he'll die a traitor's death. He'll be racked and broken, half hanged, cut down from the gallows yet alive to be unmanned, gutted, and quartered. His four parts will be fed to the dogs and his head shall adorn a pike on London Bridge, to be picked and pecked by kites and crows till it rots away! His skull . . ."

When, slavering and obviously titillated by his description of the fate awaiting Chance, Rattcliffe paused for breath, the ghastly silence of the chamber was rent by a terrible wail.

"No! Oh, no!" All eyes snapped to the back of the room and fastened with incredulity and curiosity upon Katesby Dalton, standing with her fists clenched at her sides, a single tear making a faint runnel through the floury smudge upon her left cheek.

"Weasels and moles," said Kat softly to herself, startled and troubled by the attention her spontaneous outcry attracted. She knew she should keep a discreet silence now or risk revealing that she was, at the least, acquainted with the outlaw Win Chance. But it often occurred that what Kat Dalton knew she should do, in her own best interest, was not what she knew to be the right thing to do for truth and honor. Now, she quickly decided, no matter what the consequences, she must not, could not, waste so rare and momentous an opportunity to vindicate, or at the least to defend Win Chance before her king and his court, and so she did.

"Begging your indulgence, Your Majesty," she said after a quick curtsy, keeping her eyes downcast, "but the perpetrator of the vile, cowardly attack upon Rooster Truckle could not have been Win Chance!"

Burgess Blunt, his eyes like icicles, fixed a hateful yet inquisitive glance upon Kat.

"You seem very certain of that, young woman. *Why* could it not have been the outlaw Chance?" asked King Henry, beckoning her forward, grateful for the distraction from Rattcliffe's harrowing discourse.

"Chance is neither vile nor a coward, sire. Firstly, he is brave. Secondly, he is a generous champion of Graie Friars Poor House and a good friend to Brother Truckle. Brother Truckle has told me so, and—"

"Friends have been known to fall out," said the king, looking upon Kat with curiosity. "Prithee, who might you be, mistress, and what is your business here?"

"Kat Dalton is my name, sire, and I would say more about—"

"A Kat may look at a king, you know," jested Henry. "Come closer, young damsel. I will hear what you have to say." He extended a large, heavily ringed hand. Servants and courtiers stepped aside to open a path for Kat through the chamber. Harry de Morely, with a flicker of a proud smile, stepped to her side to escort her.

"Ah, now I understand. This is *your* girl, Norland, I take it—your tavern maid?"

"Yes, Majesty," answered the earl.

"She is tall and pleasingly proportioned, from what I can see of her in that kitchen smock. There is fine bone structure in the face and I spy a flag of hair, a pretty, tawny curl creeping from beneath her headcloth. But prithee, Harry, say . . . "

"Majesty, I would say more of Chance!" Kat broke in upon the monarch, something that was rarely tolerated. "Excuse me, sire," she added, "but I would not have been so bold as to intrude if what I must say were not of great urgency. An innocent man, Win Chance, is being falsely accused of a cowardly deed and is being hunted and hounded unjustly. Word has it the assailant was a . . . a gnome-like little man. Chance is tall."

Blunt, Wiltenham, and Rattcliffe leaned forward, keenly interested to hear what Kat Dalton might next declare.

"Go on. Say what you will, then," responded Henry with

only a slight hint of displeasure at her interruption. He was as eager as the villainous trio to know more of the notorious and elusive latter-day Robyn Hood, Win Chance.

"He did not assail Brother Truckle, as I have said, Majesty. 'Tis a matter of mistaken identity, of subterfuge. It's a ruse by the actual assailant, dressed as Chance, to shift the guilt," Kat insisted adamantly.

"How come you to suppose so?" the king rumbled, finding Kat's passion and intensity winning, thinking she might actually be pretty in a fresh , uncommon way, if she was tidied up and dressed like a lady. "Harry," said Henry in a whispered aside heard by one and all, "you may indeed have unearthed a diamond in the rough, or leastways a pearl." The king addressed Kat once more. "On the matter of Chance. Have you made the outlaw rogue's acquaintance? 'Tis said he has quite a way with ladies. Are you, perchance, under his sway, one of those very ladies with whom he's had his way?" Kat blushed beautifully, at a loss for words.

"Ma . . . Majesty," she began, not knowing how to go on without revealing too much about Win, or lying to the king, something she could not bring herself to do. Henry himself inadvertently rescued her by posing his next eager question.

"Do not be shy, sweetheart. Speak up. Tell us, Mistress Dalton, are you offering an alibi for the scoundrel? Was he in your charming company at the dark wee hour of the night the monk was laid low?" The king offered a sly, suggestive wink.

"Sire!" bristled de Morely. "You besmirch Mistress Dalton's reputation with such an inference. Methinks you are trying to bully her, Henry."

"If I am, I'm not succeeding, am I, Harry? Let her answer for herself."

"Majesty, I have proof positive Chance is innocent of this charge," insisted Kat, again adroitly sidestepping the king's question.

"Even if he is innocent of *this* crime, he is a culprit guilty of many another offense."

"He preys only upon the wicked, cruel, and corrupt, sire."

"He preys upon my dignitaries and officers," Henry growled in earnest anger, a sight that would have intimated a less devoted advocate than Kat was for Win.

"Only upon those of your officials guilty of cruelty, wickedness, bribage, injustice, and such like, Majesty," answered she, looking directly at Blunt, Rattcliffe, and Wiltenham, a gesture not lost on his majesty.

"How brave you are, to speak out thus, in this place especially. Such courage and loyalty cannot be bought, even by a king," Henry mused, scrutinizing Kat with narrow-eyed regard. Princess Elizabeth, captivated by the outspoken young woman who had won her father's praise, sidled up to Kat and tugged at her dress.

"I would make your acquaintance and invite you, when your audience with his majesty is done, to come to me at my residence, Hatfield House. I have several dear little dogs there, many singing birds, a pair of parrots, and two small apes."

"I would be honored to meet them one day, my lady," replied Kat with a curtsy. "At my residence I, too, keep many creatures—dogs and cats and the like. I invite you to visit me at The Sign of the Kat. My favored pet is an old terrier, once a famed, heroic ratter, called Jack in his youth, now Deaf Jack, for his affliction that afflicts him but little."

Elizabeth's eyes lit up. "Have you a pony and books? If you do . . . even if you do not, I would come there and stay for dinner," she said and clapped her hands.

"No pony. A cow and a number of books, milady," said Kat, smiling.

"You have a way with children as well as with beasts," Henry noted. "To win my daughter's favor so quickly as you have is not customary. Elizabeth has many, many books, but also, be warned should she take up your invitation, a delicate digestion and a predilection to toothache," said the king. Elizabeth nodded.

"A tooth-drawer once wished to dress my paining tooth with fenugreek, to cause it to loosen and fall out, but there was a danger other teeth would fall as well, alas. I was affrighted of the only other cure offered for my pain—jerking the offensive tooth from my head. My good nurse permitted the tooth-drawer to pull out one of hers, to demonstrate to me that the operation did hardly pain one at all, and so I allowed the withdrawal of my own throbbing tooth. On another occasion—"

"That is sufficient, Elizabeth. Be off with you, child. I would speak further with this miss on the subject previously under discussion—the outlaw Chance," said Henry. "You do agree, Kat Dalton, that he flaunts all rule and authority, leads the king's high sheriffs on fruitless quests, makes fools and dupes of our hangmen and gaolers. Don't he, Francis?" the king pointedly goaded his spymaster, who had frequently been made a laughing butt by Chance.

"Indeed, Majesty. Thus, the wench should accept, does Chance affront the king and scoff at the king's law and at good order in the land," lectured Wiltenham.

"Harumph," agreed the king. "If you are able, tell us how to ferret out Chance and I will reward you most handsomely, Kat. What say you?" wheedled the king with narrowed eyes.

"I say no, Majesty," answered Kat, resolutely polite. Gasps filled the chamber. Wiltenham sputtered in speechless ire and beckoned a pair of house guards forward.

"To the Tower! The Tower with the insurgent wench,"

he croaked as Henry struggled to his feet and pointed a heavily ringed finger at Kat. She drew back and her eyes skimmed about the chamber, like a roof-trapped bird seeking a path to the sky. Finding no route of escape, she stood her ground and awaited the worst.

Chapter 18

"Keep thy tongue between thy teeth, Wiltenham, and back off," Henry ordered with weary contempt. "I've not done with Katesby Dalton.

"Katesby Dalton," he rumbled, fixing his stare upon her, "when you say, 'No, Majesty' to us, an utterance rarely heard in reply to a request, or tolerated, mean you 'No, you cannot help us,' or 'No, you will not?' "

"Certes, Mistress Dalton would do her very best," came a voice familiar to Kat from the rear of the chamber, "as a loyal subject of the king, to foster truth and justice in the land. Is't not so, Kat?"

"Oh, it is indeed so, Mr. Beaumarais!" she agreed, feeling a lurch of the heart and producing a dazzling smile as Win strode through the great gilt doors into the royal chamber. She was struck anew at how wonderfully tall and slender he was, and elegant in his close-fitting doublet of black brocade. The broad winged shoulders of the garment exaggerated his fine, narrow waist, thence directed the eye to the manly, muscled fullness of his thighs and calves as he strode confidently, swiftly forward to kneel before the king. A lock of Win's bronze hair fell forward on his brow, and Kat had to curb a desire to reach out and brush it back in place.

"Mr. Beaumarais, our boon companion, we bid you welcome!" exclaimed Henry, as glad to see Win, it appeared, as was Kat. "I have looked forward to again sharing your rousing good company, sir. I have been most downcast of late, since the queen—ah, we all know since when and which events transpired and how the queen gave offense," Henry said, hanging his large head.

"And lost her treasonous head for it, sire!" said Jasper Fool, stamping his belled, pointed boot. The king grimaced.

"Thou hadst best get thyself a new act, Fool. You weary me. Fortunate for you Beaumarais is among us. What brings you, Beaumarais?"

"I was riding north, Majesty, to my lands near Bath, but turned back quick as ever I could when I was advised of the arrest of my friend and associate, Mistress Dalton."

"You were misinformed, sir," muttered Blunt." The lady is not arrested but is here at the king's invitation."

"So I am gladdened to discover. I've postponed my journey for naught, it seems."

"Not for naught! Not for naught," insisted Henry with the enthusiasm of a child. "You, Beaumarais, and Montfort and Seton shall sup and drink and hunt and play at backgammon tables with us!"

Win bowed his acquiescence to the king's invitation, and Kat moved closer to Win.

"You have walked of your own accord into the lion's den, fool," she said in a scolding whisper. "What are you doing here, really? You knew I was not seized."

"Methinks I perceive, Katesby, that you are not pleased to see me. Am I right in that?" he also whispered, grinning down at her.

"Yes. No. Blast, Beaumarais! Twisting my words as usual. Just *tell* me what brings you so quick back to London," she murmured, hoping it was herself.

"That kiss, the one taken from you by force by Chance, recall?" Kat nodded. "It needs improving upon. I'm here to give you one more lesson before you take on Harry."

"I enjoyed it thoroughly. What, may I inquire, did Chance find lacking in my kissing?" Kat asked indignantly.

"That can only be demonstrated, not told, the lesson learnt in the doing, not in theoretical explaining," Win teased. "I am glad, though, that *you* found nothing amiss in that kiss. A man likes to know he's served a lady to her liking." At that, Kat blushed and looked so defenseless and pretty, he was suffused by a wave of tenderness and took mercy upon her. "In truth, Kat, there was nothing wrong with the kiss. It was outstanding. I came here to free young Blaidd from the Tower prison," he explained.

"What? Not again! How, now? Why? When?" she asked aloud.

"Wiltenham snatched him after you and the viscount went into the royal palace. The lad, waiting to go upriver to Sussex with his host, thinking himself under Charlie's protection, was lolling in plain sight on the deck of de Morely's barge when he was seized."

"How did you do it this time? Free Blaidd?"

"I did not. I hoped it would be easier than heretofore, but the satanic three"—Win gestured toward Rattcliffe, Blunt, and Wiltenham—"while here reporting to the king, had Blaidd under the guard of ten stout men, of whom five were not easily befuddled and less easily unarmed. I gave Blaidd to know we would soon try again to save him from the rack and ruin, pardon the pun. Well, when I again found myself in your locale, I thought to look in upon you, to see how you were faring in high society."

"Well enough, thank you. So please go from this place at once, while yet you may," Kat urged.

"Now I'm here, I'll stay," he shrugged, smiling broadly. "Methinks I'm safer within the lion's den than without. Truly, Kat, they'll not think to look for me—for Win Chance, rather—in their midst and under their noses."

"Beaumarais," bellowed King Henry suddenly, " 'tis arranged with Montfort and Seton. We four will go off on the hunt soon as we resolve what to do about the outlaw who accosted a monk. Leave off bantering with Mistress Dalton and tell us how *you* would go about ensnaring our nemesis, Win Chance."

"I'd lay a lure he couldn't resist, Majesty," Win answered in a flash, smiling happily. "And I would set a trap he couldn't spring."

" 'Tis not that we haven't thought of just that, Mr. Beuamarais," said Blunt with a superior, disdainful look.

" 'Tis not that we haven't tried," added Rattcliffe righteously.

"We will hear you out, sir, on this. Hold forth. What irresistible lure, which fool-proof trap do you mean?" asked Wiltenham, wickedly intent.

"It is well known about that Chance will give his all to save a friend from the torturer's toils and the hangman's noose. At any cost to himself, he will also come to the aid of a stranger he deems to be worthy of saving and falsely accused. I would wager, Wiltenham, that you are detaining even now in your gaols and clinks, men who fit these descriptions. If not, capture—if you can that is," challenged Win, "this Chance's very near comrades. Capture two, three, or four, as many as you are able, and then announce with criers and broadsides all up and down the length and breadth of the realm the hanging of the whole lot, all at once. The event will be akin to a feast day, to which Chance will be drawn as is a moth to a flame. The site must be carefully selected and readied—the edge of a cliff perhaps—and surrounded by a troop of the king's soldiers in uniform and others, disguised and hidden from sight."

"Aha!" roared Henry. "Let us do it! What say you, Blunt? Rattcliffe?"

" 'Tain't easy to get hold of and keep hold of Chance's men, but by fortuitous coincidence, Majesty, we have just now secured one of the outlaw's favorites, a boy brigand he snatched from us before, called Blaidd Kyd," said Wiltenham, who was fascinated with Win's plan. Kat and Win traded fast glances. Charles de Morely, as Wiltenham bragged, opened his mouth to speak a protest and could utter no sound but a dry rasp of outrage as he began inching toward the spymaster.

"I offer you my services, gentlemen, in your attempts to corner Chance," Win volunteered. " My past as a child nipper and cut-purse on the streets, now happily behind me, qualifies me still to select from the prison rosters the names of men who will bring the outlaw to the trap. I'll pick out a few women, doxies and dells, for whom Chance is known to have a weakness." At this, Kat glared at Win. Win grinned in return. "What say you, Majesty?"

"You, Baldwin Beaumarais, by my edict on this day and onward, from here and now, are to regulate the enterprise of entrapping Chance. Blunt, Rattcliffe, and Wiltenham and all their resources and men will be entirely at your service. Fathom that, sirs?" the king asked the unsavory trio. "Yes or no?" Each man assented with a clear, though disgruntled yes, already plotting Win's ruin and downfall from his position of power.

"One exception, Majesty, if I may," offered Wiltenham. "The boy, Kyd, must not be in the group hanged. I would hold him back to bargain over if the plan to capture Chance miscarries."

"Can you find cause to object, Beaumarais?" asked the king.

"It is this very prisoner whose hanging is most certain

to bring out Chance. I suggest we leave the fate of this Kyd to a later time, after I gather information from the street about Chance's favorites. I shall be able to do so more effectively away from the Tower. I'll proceed with the venture from under The Sign of the Kat, sire, where street people will more freely seek me out," Win told the king. "That is, if Mistress Dalton has no objection." Kat and Win, sharing in the wonderful irony of Win's new position, exchanged jubilant grins.

"I've none," she readily answered. "I'm ready to serve you, Mr. Beaumarais, in this as I have in other of your endeavors before, in any way I am able."

"You shan't be able to serve 'im in no way," proclaimed Henry with a foxy smile. "I've other plans for you altogether, Mistress Dalton."

"Am I to take it, Majesty, that your other plans for Katesby Dalton include granting my request and giving the lady to me for my wife?" Harry de Morely asked with a rare grin, reaching for Kat's hand. She held back, awaiting Henry's reply, her gesture not lost on Harry. "If she will have me, that is," he added, his smile gone poignant and forlorn, though there was yet a spark of hope in his handsome face.

"No, Harry. We are not granting anything of the sort," snapped Henry gleefully, seeing his old rival's expression change from one of expectation to wariness and the gray eyes turn calculating and cold on the instant.

"Attend, Harry. The monk, Corbie, centuries ago, warned that choosing a wife, of all the decisions of a lifetime, must be made with sound advice. Only gaze upon me to see a prime example of a man who took no advice in choosing any of his wives and is now suffering sorely." Henry sighed deeply before he continued. "Rashness now may cause long sorrow. A man must cautiously seek a woman of nobility, wealth, looks, health, intelligence, and character to make a wife. So wrote Corbie."

"Perhaps, but . . ."

"The lady ain't noble, Norland, no buts about it!" Henry bellowed gleefully. "And 'tis true, is't not, as you are wont to tell me at the drop of a hat pin, that your Plantagenet blood is as noble—nay, nobler say you, Harry—than mine own?"

"Corbie, Majesty, valued character and intelligence above all," commented Harry with a flare of impatience. "Of the monk's list of desirable attributes, Kat lacks only nobility and wealth, and I've enough of those for us both."

"Granted, Norland, this Kat Dalton seems a comely young woman of character, courage, and loyalty. Of these, loyalty above all cannot be bought, not even by those in our high position. Perhaps by us least of all. The girl's got it."

"Well then, sire, I prithee, tell me why you will not grant me leave to wed a woman so fine as she?" Harry asked, standing tall and slim in his doublet of plain wool and black leggings, his only ornament the single earring with its orient pearl, a striking figure in that deathly silent, gold-lavished royal chamber amidst his peers, all dressed in colorful and rich silks and satins. He spoke with cold, controlled dignity, though there was a demonic fierceness bordering on fury in his eyes.

"Harry, Harry," intoned the king, wagging his finger, relishing de Morely's stifled and futile rage, "you should not gaze upon your monarch with so fierce a mien. Your aspect alone, man, could be taken for high treason. Howbeit, sith I know you wish me no ill"—the king's pale, foxy eyes narrowed—"I will tell you why you may not wed Kat Dalton straightaway. With all her fine points, she is yet a most humble commoner, an insignificant underling who, as she is now, would make a suitable wife for a burgess or a merchant such as Beaumarais, not for a man of aristocratic sensibilities such as yourself, Harry. No, I cannot permit you to wed a—a scullion, no matter how lovely and heroic and promising she be. Just think on it, Harry. When you bring her to court as your countess, how much she will be out of harmony with other ladies. She is unlearned. She divines no Greek or Latin or Hebrew. She cannot soothe you by playing upon the virginals or lute and so forth. Howsomever . . ."

"Majesty, Queen Catherine excelled at playing upon the harpsichord and what pleasure did you derive from it? I care not a fig for music," growled the earl in exasperation, offering Henry a scouring look.

"Do not interrupt me, Norland!" thundered the king, outraged at de Morely's affront—mentioning the queen's harpsichord exercises. He determined to make the earl suffer sorely for remarking upon the harlot, Catherine. "Howsomever, as I was about to remark, Norland, I know a hawk from a handsaw when I see one. 'Tis not impossible this modest lady could make you a good wife. If she is got out of her work dress and groomed and polished some, given a veneer of courtly manners and polite refinement, then . . . "

"*Then* may I make her my wife, Majesty?" asked Harry skeptically, supposing the king had something up his voluminous sleeve. He was right.

"A Kat may look on a king, yet, perhaps, not wed an earl if the king looked upon by the Kat peers back at her and is intrigued by what he sees. Yes, intrigued by what he sees and considers offering for her hand himself. As you know, as all England knows, I, too, seek a wife, Harry." Gasps, grunts, and mutters went swiftly round the room like a wind through wildflowers.

"Sire?" hissed Harry in the total silence which then descended.

"Eh?" asked Win at exactly the same moment, cupping his ear.

"Begging your pardon, Majesty . . ." began Kat simultaneously.

"You heard me arights, all of you," grumbled the king. "Women are the baggage of life, Harry. They hinder us, but we cannot do without them. Thus, if God will once again lend me health and high spirits, I will again take a wife, and if I do, and if she is young, and if it please God the world should last so long, she might well give me another son." Princess Elizabeth rolled her eyes, Lady Montfort breathed a sigh of weariness, and Clarence Kite the Fool again played a few hurdy-gurdy notes of the cuckold's song.

"Think you Kat Dalton is the woman you would make your queen?" asked Win sharply, stepping close to Kat and passing a possessive, protective arm about her trembling shoulders.

"Perchance," pouted Henry. "It 'tain't unthinkable. As Norland aptly said of himself, I've wealth and blue blood enough for two, but I *would* see the damsel remade before I decide. I would see the fair barmaid transformed to a lady. *Then*, and not before, I will determine if Katesby Dalton may become wife of Harry de Morely, his Countess of Norland, or if she will be made wife to Henry Tudor and Queen of England."

"And what of my feelings in this?" Kate asked forthrightly, with dismay and a tinge of vexation in her voice. "If I wish and determine to become neither countess nor queen, Majesty, what will you say then?" The king stared at her in disbelief, smiled a little, then grinned before he was possessed by a deep, rumbling, bone-shaking fit of laughter that left him weak and sniffling, with a servant dabbing tears of hilarity from the corners of his little eyes.

"What a clever jest, Kat! With your other virtues you possess a gift for humor. After loyalty, that's my favorite trait in a wife! Oh me and oh my!" he said with another outburst of giggles. "Lady Montfort! Lady Seton! I give this girl over to you for remodeling. Present her to me when you're done and satisfied with your work. How long will you require, do you reckon?"

"Methinks in a fortnight or two or thereabouts the work will be accomplished," said Lady Seton, looking at Kat with measuring eyes. "Lady Montfort and I have long known Win—Kat, too, of course. I have always thought that as elegant of carriage, proud, and clever as she is, 'tis as though she were wellborn and bred, so 'tis an easy task you set us, Majesty."

"If I didn't know the contrary to be so, I'd hazard she has more than a trace of the aristocrat in her blood and bones," added Lady Montfort thoughtfully.

"Shall we go, Katesby?" the marchioness queried.

"Go . . . where?" asked Kat, holding to Win's arm as she earlier had to Charlie's.

"To my lord's estate, Rockingham Castle in the north country," Lady Montfort replied.

"When?" Win asked, sounding almost brusque before he added, "My lady.

"Now," Lady Seton answered. "Come," she said to Kat, who stood still, her mind in a whirl, her heart aching at the apprehension of being parted yet again from Win.

"I am not ready, quite, to quit London this day. I must arrange for the running of the inn in my absence," she demurred.

"And Brother Truckle has called out for Katesby from his delirium. I fear," said Win, "if she does not go to him, there will be dire consequences. Lady Seton, Lady Montfort, if you must start at once for Rockingham, I will bring Kat north myself in a few days' time."

"No!" Kat cried out suddenly. "Charlie, no!" she repeated, springing toward young de Morely, who had made his way to the front of the room and, dagger in hand, struck out at Burgess Blunt. Pierced through the cheek, the little man jigged about wildly, squealing like a stuck pig.

"You—you broke your word, Blunt, you pragging false knave!" brayed Charlie loudly, finding his voice. "You gave the boy over to Rattcliffe after you promised him to me! Release him or—!"

"Charlie! Hold!" Win shouted, leaping to push the viscount out the trajectory of Rattcliffe's hurled dagger, which he did, only to be caught himself in the arc of Wiltenham's slashing, whistling sword. The weapon sliced into Win's left shoulder, the strength of the blow forcing him to floor, then came to rest jutting from Charlie's back. The boy crumpled beside Win, and the two lay still, side by side, one face up, the other down. In the ensuing mayhem, some women shrieked, others fainted. Noblemen dashed about with brandished weapons not knowing where exactly, or to whom, to apply them. And Princess Elizabeth peered cheerfully out from under the banquet table, where she hid with her fool.

"Brawling in the king's rooms is not countenanced!" sang out Henry with wicked glee. He had drawn himself to his full height and looked on with excitement sparkling in his little eyes. As a precaution against accidental hurt to the monarch, the House Guard surrounded the king who thrust them aside when they obstructed his view.

"Norland, stay your hand!" the king cackled when Harry, howling a war cry, went leaping over the prostrate form of his son and thrust an iron fist into Wiltenham's nose. There was a crack of bone, a spurt of blood, and a scream of pain from the spymaster, who turned to run. He was prevented from fleeing the chamber by Clarence Kite's extended, belled boot and sent sprawling. The fool shook his tambourine in triumph.

"If you've murthered my son, Wiltenham, your goose is cooked," hissed Harry.

"Father, I didn't know you cared," groaned Charlie.

"Please, Win, please be all right," Kat whispered as she sank to her knees, leaned over him, and set desperate kisses on his brow and cheeks and parted lips. His tongue thrust at hers, his eyelids fluttered open, and he winked, then grimaced in pain.

"I'm fair to middling, Kat," he said, sitting up and shaking cobwebs from his head. He winced when Kat pressed her apron to his shoulder and tied it tightly to stanch the bleeding. "What of Charlie de Morely?"

"He's hurt, not kilt," said Harry, who sent for a litter to bear away his moaning son and waited, kneeling, holding fast to the boy's hand.

"We shall take the wounded to the inn straightway," said Kat as she helped Win, who leaned heavily upon her, toward the great doors of the king's chamber.

Chapter 19

"Sith my jaunt to Bath is delayed, there's time for another love lesson or two," said Win. "Fancy one now?"

It was nearly a week after he was hurt in the melee at court, more seriously than anyone at first realized. A plentiful loss of blood before the flow was stanched had left him weak and pale. Even so, Kat had had to fight off the efforts of Dr. Turner of the King's College of Physicians, whose much-touted cure-all, cupping and bleeding, no matter what ailment was being treated, could have been the demise of Win, she protested.

"Cure, for sure," Kat complained to Lady Seton, who'd insisted on bringing Turner to the inn, "if you deem death a remedy for all this world's ills!"

Dorsey Dibdin, the astrologer and Cunning Man, a friend to Kat and Win, treated the gash with an herbal concotion of his own devising, which purged the wound and thus kept Win's fever at bay and hastened his recovery.

And so it was, before the week was out, in his rooms at the inn where Kat had newly strewn the floors with clean, dried rushes and meadowsweet, and where the fire was blazing up, a shaft of winter sun cast its light on Win, who sat propped against pillows in a great chair. He was out of bed for the first time. His left arm was bound close against his chest in a sling, as the doctor and Cunning Man had both ordered.

Win cocked one brow at Kat and gave her a slow grin as she entered the chamber, carrying upon a tray a steaming tureen of thick stew of rabbit, a warm loaf of almond bread, a goblet of beer, one of claret wine and a flagon of aqua vitae, a distilled brandy he favored. Fancied a lesson, she surely did, but good sense and a sense of self-preservation for the moment prevailed. Start *that* again and how would she let him go when the time came for him to leave for Bath and another woman?

"Eat while your food's hot," she answered shortly.

"All my appetites are restored. I'm hungry for something more than food, an *hors d'oeuvre,* the French say."

"No," Kat answered, setting down the tray and standing back, hands on her hips to look at him. "How's your shoulder?"

"Paining me somethin' fierce, Kat, truly," he answered, his handsome face contorted in a burlesque of agony. "And I've been abed till today, and confined to this room so long, I need a bit of distraction. It would do me a world of good. What say you, Kitten?" His come-hither smile was wickedly sweet and his gravelly voice, with a beseeching little-boy lilt, stirred Kat despite herself.

"I'll send up Dorsey and Bess to play at cards with you, if you'd like," she answered, needlessly dusting the mantel. "That'll distract you."

"The company of a Cunning Man and an old Wise Woman is not the sort of amusement I crave. Moreover, one-handed backgammon 'tain't my game. What would be the harm, Katesby, in you and me enjoying a bit of bed sport together? It pleasures us both and 'tisn't as if we're amorous and tender about each other—merely lustful. We agree, do we not, that possessive, imprudent, romantic *love* is ephemeral, fleeting? *We* won't allow a distraction so impermanent and inane as love to divert us from our goals or interfere with our plans, eh?"

"Speak for yourself." Kat lifted the lid of the tureen, spooned out a trencherful of stew, then came to Win's side to tuck a napkin at his chin.

"Speak for myself? Does that imply you *are* amorous about me, perchance even a little in love with me, then, Kat?" Win teased with a purpose.

"No. What I said *implies* naught, me fine bucko." She laughed, speaking also with purpose, hers to keep him at a distance. "I'm declaring right out, plain and blunt, *I'm* not lustful, not in the least." He took her hand and looked up at her with boyish desperation in his imploring eyes. She laughed again but with less fortitude.

"Not lustful? Well, do you fancy being so? I know from experience 'twouldn't take me but a trice to get you that way."

"No, thank you. I don't favor being all stirred up when I've got a inn full of invalids, besides guests, to be tended to."

"I told you, you must delegate chores." He shrugged. "Well then, tell me, how are the other shut-ins progressing?" Horace the courier, Win, Charlie de Morely, and Harry—who had got the ague—were all abed at the inn. So, too, was Brother Truckle, who had been moved there from Graie Friars for the comfort and Kat's ministering care. They were being tended to as their conditions demanded except in the case of Win, who got what *he* demanded, which was a deal more than his condition did. He had been taking up most of Kat's time and attention, night and day, with one request or another—for fluffed pillows, special favorite foods and drinks, for music, talk and gossip, now *this*.

She sighed inwardly, for it was the first time he had made so bold as to offer a lesson. There had been suggestive hints earlier on, mostly tongue-in-cheek when he'd been too feeble to do anything but hint. A day or two later came straightforward, one-handed, affectionate fondles and well-placed pats more difficult for her to ignore.

"Come sit here by me on the bed, Kat, to discuss a bit of business," he suggested. But when she drew up a chair to the side of the bed, he quickly lost interest in business and tried another gambit. "I'm feeling a chill, Katesby. Share your warmth, eh? Warm me a bit like you used to do when we were tykes, with a cuddle up?" he asked, mischief in his green eyes.

Her response to that had been to add a log to fire and a quilt to the heap already covering him, and soon he'd taken to grumbling that a window must needs be cracked to cool the boiling-hot chamber. "Or do you think I'm raging with fever? Just feel my burning brow with your lily-soft hand, or better, set your own cool brow to mine," he had slyly suggested. When, out of concern, she did, he grasped her about the waist, pressed her breasts to his chest, and brushed her cheek with his lips.

"You think youself to be one cagey cuffin, don't you, Baldwin?" she had jovially protested, wriggling away from him, by then steamy herself. "If you're too warm, t'ain't from a sickly fever, good sir!"

So that now, when sitting in his chair, he took her hand, for safety's sake she had had every intention of taking it back. That was until he brought to his lips, all he needed to do this time to set feathery flutters alive in her belly and a familiar dampness seeping. Her determination wavering, to protect herself her she tried to substitute anger for her wrecked composure. She doubted that would work. She was right.

"You have once already accused me of inveigling the lessons from you. Was that not the word you used? Then you said there was no more you could teach me. Now . . . this?" She scowled, or tried to. Her expression was closer to a pout, for she was thinking how hale and handsome he looked and that he'd soon be well and on his way to Bath and that rich widow, Gail Pebbles.

"I won't say such a thing ever again," he promised, raising his right hand. "This time, it will be a fair good swap between us. I tutor you and we pleasure each other." She was flushed and fretting and extraordinarily lovely. He nearly told her so.

"Well . . . but what is there you're able to teach me, injured as you are and heeding doctor's orders, and Dorsey's, not to bounce about else you open your wound that's healing well, for if you do, why, then you'll likely be laid up here abed for the dear knows how long, needing nursing, and haven't I other fish to fry and better things to do, eh?"

Her outburst, Win reasoned, meant one of two things—that she wanted him to leave, or she didn't.

"I'll teach you how to do all the 'bouncing' wanted to suit us both to the full. It would be practical for you to know that, sith you're to wed one old nobleman or another, earl or king." Win frowned. "I supposed you'd not do better than become a countess, Kat. Now it seems you might be a queen." And he'd not even chance meddling or standing in her way, he thought.

" 'Tis not bloody likely I'll be queen. Henry is too canny a fox to carry out that nonsensical scheme. Regardless, his nobles, his bishops, and his counselors won't allow it, if verily there be the merest hint of a true intention in what he said. No, he was intent on plaguing Harry, is all, goading his old rival. And I will not be any countess neither, if the king keeps on pricking at the earl to provoke a rash act so there would be cause to send the foremost noble in the land to the Tower. And forsooth, Win, King Henry perchance could deny his consent for the marriage. If none of those events transpires, it may to come to pass that I will have to persuade Harry . . ." Kat went silent and gnawed on her lower lip. *Persuade him that 'no' means 'no,'* she thought but did not say. "But whatever befalls me, Baldwin, you will go off to Bath and wed a lady rich in lands and sheep and cows and become a country squire, and we'll never be together more, you and me, except in decorous ways, will we?" *She* would never wed any man but Win, Kat knew, but that was not justification for her to endeavor to keep *him* from making an advantageous union.

"When you are a countess and I am a country landlord, hunting fox with the squires who will then be my crass, good-hearted country neighbors, we never will be together, we two, except as you say," agreed Win, drawing her to sit upon his knee, "so why not be indecorous now, while yet we may?"

"Perchance for the last time?" replied Kat in a foggy voice before she kissed his mouth. "Your soup's getting cold," she whispered.

"But I'm warmed, just thinking about . . . indecorousness," he growled, resting his head against the chair back, his eyes half lidded. "What say you, Kat? Where's the harm in granting we're powerfully drawn to each other and making the most of it long as we don't become . . . confused?"

"Confused? About love? No chance of it. So, where's this bouncing to be done?" she asked with a resigned sigh and a glorious smile. Not waiting for his answer, she straddled his thighs and engaged his lips again and found his mouth hungry under hers, warm and soft and strong. She set one hand on his uninjured shoulder, slid it to touch the back of his neck, while undoing the fastenings of his breeches with the other. He raised her skirts and she slid over him, fitting him into her, settling slowly, sheathing the thickness of him, feeling him drive deep until he was wholly taken inside and consumed, proding at the core of her. She moved, raising, lowering, shifting, and billows of pleasure spread through her, became barbed shafts, then exquisite tremors. His release twined hers, merged so totally with hers that there was no gap between them, no separation left at all They were altogether unified, closer than ever before, in every way.

They didn't speak when it was done. They remained as they were, she caught in the circle of his arm that was holding her to him. Her mouth was at the warm curve of his neck, and the rasp of his breath was a storm in her ear, underscored by the thunder of her own heart. When finally she looked with appreciative awe into his eyes, she surprised a softness in their green depths, a glow, perhaps of love, she hoped. She smiled.

At once, as if a curtain had fallen, the bright warmth was eclipsed and Win was looking at Kat with a cool, appraising remove. *Devil fiddle it, I am not even near to falling in love,* he belabored himself before complimenting her, though in an aloof, almost condescending manner which was not easy for him to assume.

"Well done. Another lesson efficiently learned. You're a quick study, Kat," he said, not unkindly, but with dispassionate aloofness meant to conceal from her the strong emotion he was feeling then—love, perchance, he brooded. "But Kat, methinks we had best keep some distance each from the other now," he grumbled, saying the exact opposite of what he felt, "else *you* might get to confusing passion for love, and whatever would we do then?" Win's deep green eyes held her turbulent, sea-green stare.

At another time, in a different circumstance, Kat might have read his true feelings, as though he were an open book. She would likely have been aware of his inner debate, and she would have disarmed and charmed him with a bit of teasing banter. Now though, so soon after her fortresses of body and spirit had been so gloriously stormed, and with their two bodies yet joined, her soft heart was all exposed and loving. Win's manner of indifference, which she took at face value, struck hard and roiled her emotions. She felt downcast and sorrowful and grieved, yet emboldened, too, by churning love and by anger at his swift dismissal. He could have waited till they'd disengaged, at least, before asserting his detachment.

The mix of her sentiments rendered Kat tongue-tied. She could think of nothing to say nor to do but shut her eyes to avoid the indifferent look in his, and kiss him silent. When she set her mouth to his again, she was reckless, ravenous, intemperate, and he responded in kind with open-mouthed ferocity. She drew his thrusting tongue into her mouth and, feeling him inside her still, tightened her inner muscles around him again. He took long, rasping breaths, distended and surged and filled her.

"You're right. This must stop," she sighed, rocking. "Not for the danger of confusion. 'Tis . . . distracting, this."

"Oh, aye, 'tis indeed," he growled an answer, flexing his back to better serve her pleasure.

"Distracting from our objectives we've shared . . . forever. If . . . we are not to . . . if we are to keep our pact . . . we must not risk . . ."

"This is the . . . last lesson." Win set his hands at her waist to guide her maneuvers, then looked up at Kat. She nodded, her eyes hot tropic green, shaded by long lashes.

They moved together languidly this time, slowly, pausing to cool some just so they could commence again, to make the interchange last long, for once it was done, the love lessons indeed were really over for good and all. Their double deception, that neither loved the other, was working perfectly, appallingly well.

At the denouement of the final tutorial, which ended in bed hours later, there was no lingering. Kat removed herself swiftly from Win's bed and room. She set not a foot near either again until after he had ridden off to Bath three days later. Win remained at the inn that long only for the sake of Rooster Truckle, whose semiconscious rants and sighs included the names Chance and Beaumarais, along with the mystifying, oft-repeated cry of "shrimp."

Chapter 20

"Shrimp, shrimp, pink . . . boiled. And feather mongers!" shouted out Brewster Truckle from the depths of a nightmare, protecting his head from phantom assaulters with raised arms. "Feather mongers, sturdy beggars, and lazy loons!"

The monk had been given the finest room at the inn, one most often engaged by guests of wealth and rank. A Turkey-work tapestry hung upon one wall, and a silk arras on the opposite, both rare treasures brought to England on Win's ship *Conquest.* Fragrant nosegays and bundles of sweet herbs, placed on the mantel and upon the shelves of a tall cupboard, scented the chamber with feigned springtime. There was a burnished metal mirror and a pewter bowl and pitcher on a table near the bed, a massive object which had been built by a joiner, an artisan who did finer work than any carpenter. The tall bedposts were heavily carved, the bedspread, curtains, and tester expertly embroidered.

Upon the bedstead were not one but two deep down

mattresses and many fine feather pillows, atop which lay Friar Truckle looking very little in the large room amidst the outsized furnishings, sunk deep in feather and down. The most prominent, colorful feature of his weathered face, framed by thick white hair, was the red nose of the reformed drunkard.

"Feather mongers!" came another woeful yell.

"A feather in the hand is better than a bird in the air, eh, Brewster?" asked Win, standing perplexed at the old man's bedside, gauging how to help his friend. "Has there been any improvement, any change since he was found, Doctor?" he asked. A plump and handsome man, with soft features, richly dressed, cleared his throat with self-important dignity.

"He is receiving the finest care to be had in the land, sir. He is the beneficiary of the most current thinking, though he is but a humble creature, lacking any wealth of his own," said Dr. Turner. "No effort has been spared for the uncle of Lord Seton and Lord Seton's sister, Lady Montfort, herself wife to Lord Montfort, who is first cousin to Lord Seton's wife, my dear friend and loyal advocate."

"I know his pedigree. That isn't what I asked about. Has there been improvement in your patient's condition, Doctor?" Win demanded with irritable authority.

"I would have you know, Beaumarais, I am a member of the King's College of Physicians. I took my medical degree in Italy, where the most advanced medicine is practiced and the most expert herbals written. I am a master in the use of herbs and simples, and I have ministered to the old monk's abrasions and cuts. They are healing well and cleanly with no sign of putrefaction. His bruises, treated with mugwort and balm of Gilead, also termed balsam of Mecca, depending on the origin of the salve, have turned from purple to yellow, a sign they, too, are mending. But he has not recovered his wits. As you see and hear, he rants."

"Why?" Win asked. Rather than admit to not knowing why, the physician went off on another tack.

"I thought to relieve pressures inside the skull and elsewhere in that relic of a body, by releasing humors. He's been leached and bled, but to no avail."

"Dost thou or dost thou not know what ails him, man, and has stolen his sense and reason? Do you have even a conjecture?" Win had taken Brewster's hand and leaned close over his friend as if seeking clues in the battered old face. Jilly, Jenny, Jeannie, and Gwyn stood at the bedside. Kat looked on from across the chamber, the baby Roxelana on a blanket at her feet playing with a soft toy fashioned in the form of a mouse. Bessy and Dorsey were dealing Tarot cards, reading Truckle's fortune. Kat was keeping her distance from Win, even avoiding his eyes lest she blurt out her thoughts. It would be easier when he was actually gone, she thought. Then she'd be left in peace to her longings without the actual object of her heart's desire at arm's reach.

"Poor old man to be laid so low. 'Tis pitiful," said Harry de Morely, peering at Brewster. Coughing with ague and appearing frail, he had just entered Truckle's room leaning upon the arm of Horace, his courier, who was now recovered fully from his own ordeal in the snow.

"True, my lord, most pitiful," agreed Horace in a voice laden with commiseration even as he grinned across the bed at his pretty erstwhile nurses, all in a row.

"To allay headache, boil a lock of his hair in his own water, then throw it in the fire," Dorsey the Cunning Man suggested.

"I do not know for a certainty what has taken the man's reason," huffed the doctor. "Perhaps blows to his head rattled his brains. 'Tis more plausible that deep, lingering fear of his assailant has stolen his pluck, his fortitude, his will to be clearheaded. He speaks only in riddles."

"If you are proclaiming Brewster Truckle a coward,

you're wrong, Turner. What else may be afflicting him?" Win asked.

"See here, sir! I am never told I am wrong," bristled Turner, "but 'tis possible the cause for his lunacy is the intermittent fever by which the old fellow is also beset. It returns every fourth day, after a two-day lacuna."

"Lac-una? God's mercy, Doctor, that sounds near as terrible bad as the plague. What be that?" Gwyn asked.

"A lacuna is a lull, just a pause, is all," explained Win.

"Is that it?" exclaimed Gwyn with a snort of a derisive laugh. "We know he's been raving and fevered two days, and then tranquil two days, before it starts over again. Lacuna indeed! Why must doctors of physic speak so odd?"

"Brewster has the quartan fever," Win decided. "I've seen it do its worst in the wet heat of Italy during the summer months."

"Never has that blight been known in England, never!" protested Turner. "I'd sooner agree the man is possessed by the devil than that he has the quartan fever."

"Easier to cure, possession by the devil, than quartan," commented Bess. "Loose a bat in the room and out it will fly, taking Lucifer with it."

"I say Brewster's got a spell on him. I judge whoever waylaid 'im bewitched 'im," Dorsey suggested. "Take the spell off by placing a white duck's bill in his mouth and speaking a proper charm."

"Some sort of fever arises in the warm months from the damps of the Essex lowlands," de Morely said, glancing about for a chair, too weak all at once to stay longer upon his feet. "Lord Malebranche, my westerly neighbor, went hunting water foul at Osey Island and came home with the Essex ague. He laid ill for half a year before he departed this world."

"For quartan fever, in the warm climes, an elixir of chinchona bark is given," Win said, pounding his sound hand upon the table with determination. "Captain Bolling carries the nostrum in the *Conquest* for his crew. We shall try a dose, for whatever is plaguing Brewster."

"We shall try everything," Kat insisted, "to help Brewster."

"Bath. The sure cure for whatever ails one," interjected the doctor, feeling ignored. "If all else fail, he must be transported to Bath in Somersetshire. As I have writ in my volume, *a Book of the Bath of Bath*"—Turner paused for emphasis and admiration—"which I recommend to one and all, I tell of the pyrites and sulphur in waters so hot an invalid will, at first, suppose on seeing the sluice, that his flesh would be scalded from the bones, but the body accommodates and grows comfortable and eased by the warmth. For some, a gallon of hot water, stirred with a quart of cool worketh pleasantly. Prithee remember, no man or woman neither must undertake the bath cure without consulting a physician, forsooth, and learning what diet must be observed and which infirmities helped by which of the sundry different waters."

"Forsooth for sure, else how would physicians profit?" Gwyn heckled Turner merrily. He lacked any hint of humor in his nature, most especially about himself, and he scowled, composing a retort. In the momentary silence which followed, Brewster Truckle spoke again.

"Saved I was, by a Colchester hen from candy land and a bit of a chance," mumbled the old man. "I have et a fish named *gobius,* from a potter. I have tasted of other sea creatures, tailed and footed and shelled. Gurdgeons be best, though not a fish. Oh, and oysters, spake the hen, to be gobbled like candy from sugar land. A dainty circlet of coral stone and oyster shell mother-of-pearl, the shrimp thought to have of me, but I gave him naught. No!" Brewster shouted, throwing his hands before his face. The others in the chamber listening, puzzled and distressed, looked at each other helplessly.

"He's trying to tell something," said Kat, coming to the old man's side to soothe his brow with a cool cloth. "Will he ever be fully himself again, Dr. Turner?"

"Unlikely sith he's been so long insensible. But what cannot be cured must be endured," Turner pronounced.

"*Tempus fugit.* Time flies, time flies," moaned Brewster, agitated, rolling from side to side. "Stop them . . . them that's shipping sheeps and hunting hens."

"What day is it, in this bout of the fever?" Win wanted to know.

" 'Tis already near the end of the second. Methinks soon he will fall into a calm and this time he may come to his senses somewhat," answered Kat with typical optimism, a quality Win relied on and valued in her—one of many, he thought.

"I think you're right, Katesby, about Brewster having something to tell, and about his wits returning. I'll bide here a day or so longer with you . . . with Brewster. I may be able to help him some way, and I need to know what it is he has in mind to say, once he gets a hold of it."

He met Kat's inadvertent flash of a wide smile with a resigned shrug and a sheepish, one-sided smile of his own. They would not be parted quite as soon as expected. That was to be a reprieve, of sorts. That was good, and bad. They would be together longer, and that was good, but they would be an enticement to each other, and if they were going to keep to their pact, that was bad. As if their minds worked in unison, they each resumed the cool, resolute facade formerly worn.

"I will also leave here in a day or two," said Harry. "Charlie and I will be quitting London for home."

"Home? To Norland, my lord?" asked Kat. "Are you strong enough to make the journey? Is Charlie?"

"Damage to the viscount's back was minor," Dr. Turner interjected, "but my lord, you had best see to your ague," he said sternly, "or you will meet up with Lord Malebranche before you wish to. Keep to a warm bed. Better yet, take to the warm baths at Bath."

"Thank you, Doctor, for your advice," answered de Morely. "But I must go hence with all good speed. My courier, Horace, has brought me news of an amazing nature, word of the possible fate of my dear Lady Mary Wyat.

"Your young wife, milord, torn from your arms and lost to you long ago? She lives?" asked Kat softly.

"As I've told you, Katesby, I never saw her again after she was seized by her father from our carriage. The last I heard of Mary was she died in England of a broken heart, a year, perhaps two, after our forced separation. It was never proved. Now Horace has word of Mary from a tradesman at Caen, with whom I have other business. The man knew Mary's aunt, from whom the girl fled. This tradesman admits to having carried her back to England, where she was taken in by a humble family of fisherfolk. There, in the south, she fell ill, passed her last days, and was laid to rest. I must try to determine the truth of this report. My heart demands it."

"Why return now to Norland then?" Win inquired.

"I have there a perfect miniature likeness of my young and lovely, true lady wife, commissioned by me from the pencil of the Netherlander, Guillim Stretes. I have not looked upon it in many years for the pain of loss it gave, but now I will take the handsome picture of Mary into Essex to show about to the folk. When I have proved or disproved the truth of this clue to Mary's fate, only then will I take to my own bed, till spring if need be, to rid myself of this ague."

"He that is not handsome at twenty, nor strong at thirty, nor rich at forty, nor wise at fifty will never be handsome, strong, rich, or wise," said Brewster Truckle in a normal, almost pleasant voice. "Zounds, but I must have got awful deep into my cups to have ended here, wherever that may be, with no memory of how. It seems I left a bundle of marrow bones and turnips . . . somewheres. Well, and what am I doing in this huge, soft, warm featherbed when I should be out cadging and scavenging food for my waifs?" he asked wide-eyed, sitting up and gazing about.

"That is exactly what you must try to tell us, Brewster, my friend," said Baldwin, grasping the old man's hand. Kat clasped her hands beneath her chin in a silent prayer of thanks for Rooster's alertness and, smiling broadly, all with the same Goodkind family show of teeth, Jeannie, Jilly, and Jenny cheered.

"The lacuna!" Gwyn exclaimed. The baby participated in the happy excitement, cooing and laughing. Kat arose, beaming with relief.

"Welcome, *welcome* home to your friends, dear Brewster!" she sighed.

"Friends? Who be you, miss, and him there"—he pointed at Win—"to call me thus, might I ask? Who be all you fair and rosy folk?"

"Do you not know any one of us, Brewster?" asked Kat, crestfallen. "Have you truly forgot us all?" Brewster looked about the room from face to face, bemused.

"I am sorry, young lady, but I can't say I know a one of you, and if I should, why perhaps it's the spirits doing their worst."

"Ghosts, think you, good brother?" asked Bess brightly. "Dorsey said you was possessed."

"No, madam. It's another sort of spirits I blame. Too much drink has been known to confuse a fellow. Ah, will one of you kind folk, if you be me friends one and all, as you say, be so generous as to fetch a thirsty old man a nice tankard of brew and a jigger of brandy on the side? It's said that a nip of the hair of the dog that bit you may do wonders to jog the sluggish brain."

" 'Tis worth a try, I'd say," said Kat, hurrying off to comply with old man's request.

Hair of the dog, or something, did indeed work, partially at least. After a long draft of beer, Brewster Truckle knew his own name, and Baldwin's. "Last thing I remember was . . . was my favorite gargoyle at the gates of Graie Friars Poor House and you, Baldwin . . . ah, Beaumarais? Yes, Baldwin Beaumarais! You were slipping and sliding down Hog Lane on a snowy night. I was calling after you, to tell you something of great import."

"What?" asked Win.

"You said, 'Tell me tomorrow, brother.' I said, 'I'll forget again, by then.' I did."

"And?" encouraged Kat.

"And, nothin'," sighed Truckle. "By blanes, pox, blotch, and boils, I've not a clue, but attend . . ." He struck the heel of his hand to his brow. "Now I seem to be having a recollection of you, missy. Another sip of spirits will grease the wheels of my mind more, methinks."

"Brewster, try, *try* to call back my name, and when you do, *then* perchance I'll get you another drop to drink, but only one more, mind, for too many drops will have an effect opposite from the one we seek. You'll not remember nothing," cautioned Kat. "Aye, pretty girl, what irks thee?" she asked when the baby shrieked a complaint. "I see, little pretty! You have lost your mouse," Kat cooed, gathering up the child and the toy.

"I know that wee baby girl. K-K-Kat's her name!" crowed Brewster with a cackling laugh that shook his dangling chins.

"Oh, Brewster, how good that you recall a trifle of the past, but *she's* Roxelana. Do you not remember me?" Kat beseeched. The old man's toothless smile played at his lips and flashed over his face before it settled in his eyes.

"Kat is who *you* are! And I've known you since you wasn't much bigger than that baby you have. And the lad here, Baldwin, why I've known you and him near your whole lives. Is't so? Yes?" Kat nodded, happy and relieved.

"Brewster, you're on the mend, truly!" said Baldwin, shaking the monk's hand once more.

"Sith I recollected the pair of you, I'll have two nips now, if you please, one for each," Brewster said with an exultant smile. "The dear knows what more I might dredge from the depths of memory, given ample stimulant."

Chapter 21

After the others had gone off to bed, Kat and Win spent a long night with Brewster Truckle, prodding his memory with recollections of their own, with snatches of song and bits of verse, even some gossip, but chiefly helpful were certain facts and experiences only the three, in all the world, shared.

" 'The loss of wealth is loss of dirt, as sages in all times assert . . .' " Are you able to say the rest of the rhyme, Brewster? Try. See if you can," suggested Win. "When I asked you, long ago, why you gave away all your wealth and substance to serve the poor, you recited that verse to me."

"This verse," said Truckle, with spirit.

The loss of wealth is loss of dirt,
As sages in all times assert;
The happy man's without a shirt.

"Good, good, 'tis working, this game we play. Let us do more." He was resting on pillows in the huge bed, gnawing upon a lamb shank and drinking from a wineskin.

" 'St. Francis and St. Benedict, bless this house from wicked wight. . . .' " recited Kat. "You taught that to me."

"Yup. I know," Truckle nodded, gravy dripping down his chin to stain the sheets.

Bless this house from wicked wight.
Keep it from all evil spirits,
Fairies, weasels, bats, and ferrites.

"Right? Try me on another."

"Who was it caused alterations to be made to the old calendar?" Win queried.

"Julius Caesar, the pagan."

"Speak of the ides and calends of the months if you are able, in accord with the Roman mode," asked Kat.

"Ides—no, no, calends was the first day of a Roman month, nones the eighth, ides the fifteenth," Truckle responded proudly. "There was only ten months in the old Roman year, which had but three hundred and four days. So it was, to be right with sun, every two years another month, *Mercedomius,* was put in. There was ides on the fifteenth of March, May, July, and October, but on the thirteenth day of other months. Now, methinks, January eleventh was the third day before the ides, yet January fourteenth was the nineteenth day? Yes, the nineteenth day afore the calends of February."

"Hold, hold," protested Kat with mock dismay. "I'm all in a swithin of confusion."

" '*Junius, Aprilis, Semtemque, Novemque, tricenos* . . .' Can you render that in English?" fired off Win.

" 'Thirty days hath November, April, June, and September. . .' " Brewster shot back.

"Our days of the week Monday, Tuesday, and Wednesday were named how by the Saxons?"

"I'll tell you, Baldwin, me boy—Monendeg, Tuesdeg, Wodnesdeg is the Saxon. The Scots say Diu Luna, Diu Mart, and the like."

"Name out some of the principal fairs of the land in each month of the year," Kat suggested.

"St. Paul's Day at Bristol on the twenty-fifth day of January. The second day of February there's a fair at Bath, one at Saffron Walden on Midlent Sunday in April, the Hot Fair is on Salisbury Plain in summer, the. . . ."

In response to riddles and questions put to him by his young friends, Truckle was able to remember much of what was required of him and soon the three lapsed into talk of old times they had shared.

"Like when you were little, 'tain't it, us three playing at mind games and word puzzles?" the friar exclaimed happily. " 'Cept then it were me posing the questions and you pair racking your brains for answers. You was right quick children, and promising."

"That's not quite the way you described me then, Rooster," Win reminded him, laughing. "Then I was a runt of an urchin headed for Tyburn gaol, you said."

"You came close more'n once to meeting Old Bull, who was then Tyburn Hangman. A skin-and-bones runt you were, small for your age, called Carrots upon the streets, for the red that was in your hair." Kat, standing behind Win's chair, ruffled his now-bronze mane, then grabbed back her hand as if she'd touched fire. "You pair together like this makes me think back on how you were always united, a pair of resourceful, shrewd, alert young ones, bent on making your way in the world. And you did, both of you. It does me good to see it."

"Rooster, it was you taught us everything we needed to know to get by," said Kat.

" 'Tweren't me trained Carrots in the art of filching and

nipping," Truckle protested with a kindly nod. "That was old man Wottan who ran the school for cut-purses near Billingsgate. I think he saved near as many a starvling orphan as ever I did, over the years. Baldwin the Bastard Heir. You were dubbed that, too."

"My mother urged me up to London to seek my well-off sire. I never found him. No one believed he existed until Beaumarais's solicitor discovered me, after my father had passed on leaving his fortune to his only offspring—me." Baldwin stared into the hearth, firelight reflected in his eyes.

"I might at first have fretted over you, lad, fearing you'd not yet escaped the gallows, but I knew from the first Kat would turn out well. When I was putting away your ring for safekeeping, and the skin of rare old wine that come with you, I said to myself, 'She's something extraordinary.' "

"Hold, hold. You were putting away what? Where?" Win was on his feet.

"Old wine and a ring, mother-of-pearl it was. The man what brought her gave 'em over."

"What man brought me to you?" Kat asked. She and Win both looked intently at Truckle. He shrugged.

"I don't . . . recall. It was so long ago. A nip of claret, perhaps?" Truckle suggested hopefully.

"But you have proved how well and wonderful your mind is working. You are in command of it once more, mostly. Let us try to now talk of the night you were hurt, if you're feeling up to it. That was not long ago."

"Hurt, was I? You mean to say it wasn't drink laid me low?" Brewster shook his head as if to stir up thoughts within it. "What dastard villain would injure a poor old man who has got nothin' worth . . . nothin' . . . worth . . . taking," he whispered.

"It might be Dr. Turner is correct in saying 'tis fear keeping the attack from your recall," Win discreetly challenged. "But do not upset yourself, I prithee. When, if ever, you are ready to treat with this . . ."

"That quacksalver medicaster calls me coward, does he?" Brewster's eyes grew round with amazement. "Nothin' worth taking, I told the cad. By moldering gargoyles, I said that to him! That was after I asked, 'Are you here to rob me?' That's what I asked. 'I've nothing, nothing, naught. I long ago took vows of poverty.' "

"Go on, Brewster. Try to remember who was it you were talking to when you said all that," Win said, moving from the mantel where he had been leaning to pace the chamber. Truckle looked dazedly at him.

" 'If you would . . . rob for profit on the streets, you must . . . you must choose the better neighborhoods. Here we are all paupers.' I told him that, too."

"Who?" Win and Kat asked at once. She was wrapped in a comforter now, curled in a chair near the fire. Each time Win passed close by her in his striding, he inadvertently made some tactile gesture—a pat on her head, the press of his hand to her shoulder, a brush at her brow to set back an errant curl. She tried not to take particular notice. It was an innocent, easy habit of closeness between them, touching, from childhood. But they were no longer children, and their closeness was not innocent anymore.

"Who, you ask? Blessed fig! I'd tell you who if I knew who, now wouldn't I?" grumbled the friar. "What's it matter who, anyway? The scurvy knave got naught."

"It matters, for Win Chance has been accused of the nefarious deed," replied Kat, unable to tolerate more of Win's taps and grazes. She sprang from her place, and when their eyes met, they both blushed, her face going a pretty pink, his momentarily dark. She now also proceeded to pace, steering a wide swath past Win going in the opposite direction. He carefully looked not at her, but at Truckle.

"The king has taken personal offense at your drubbing,

Brother," he explained. "It is a threat to the security of the realm, he proclaims. The felon must pay. Every spy, snoop, busybody, government agent, and snitch, as well as the entire constabulary of the land, the horse guards and house guards, are on the watch and hunt for the outlaw. Hanging Jack Fletch is testing his rope and licking his lips," explained Win, watching Brewster closely for any sign of awareness.

"Aye?" said the friar. "Win a chance for the king? Hmm. That signifies nothing to me. Think you a sip of malmsey or alicante, perchance, would be useful now, to stir my sluggish brain?"

"It's worth the try. You are a right cunning bird, Rooster, to be wheedling drinks out'n us this way," chided Kat. "Sorry I do not have the shrimps you've been asking for, but I'll find you something to fill your belly," she added as she went off to fetch up what she'd promised.

"I'd prefer the claret, Kat!" he called after her with a wink at Win. "Last sip of claret I had, I was with the . . . oh, the king!" Truckle whooped with sudden recognition. "Our corpulent, petulant, close-fisted Henry, mean you, Baldwin? He who thinks himself the most excellent round person in the realm, in all his dominions, aye, in all of Christendom, *that* king? I spent the better part of three days waiting at court for a hearing with him, about feeding his poor. Finally I am summoned to the gold room to bow and beg, bow and beg, and the stingy monarch reminds me, not for the first time, that he was not Cynras, Croesus, Crasus, nor Midas."

" 'Tis a plaint the monarch often makes."

"He carped of the yeoman beggars on his roads—lazy, profligate masterless men he called them. 'Hunger setteth his first foot into the horse manger,' I told the king, for the poor eat the horse corn so their bairns will live to see the next dawn. Then they eat the starved horse. They take to the roads then. If they break into houses, I said to King

Henry, it is because they are too poor to buy britches. If they go about poaching by night with painted faces and stealing hawks' eggs, it is for the same cause, hunger." The old man's face was scarlet, and his chins shook with indignation.

"Calm yourself, Brewster," suggested Win. "Your dander is up and your choler rises. It mayn't be good for one in your condition to seethe so." Rooster Truckle's deafness, about which he'd forgotten, came to his mind and was put into service.

"Collar? What afflicts your eyes, boy? I wear no collar. I'm attired in a linsey nightgown, chafing like a hair shirt, meant to keep me old bones warmed some," blustered Brewster. "If you would hold your tongue, I would continue my tale of the king and I, if you are able to indulge a babbling old man."

"Rooster, any courteousness you may need or want, I willingly, happily offer you, my friend. Go on, then."

"I chided him, the king, for his long and stately sitting at meat. I hinted that he was a sleepy glutton and admonished him for pampering his belly."

"I heard tell it was more than a hint you gave the monarch." Win smiled.

"Well, perhaps so, for he was so downcast and blameworthy then, I was moved to guide him personally to evening prayers, for the good of his soul. I do not suppose he was redeemed or even much comforted for, alas, as soon as ever he could, Henry rid himself of me. The monarch delivered me over to his almsman, Algernon Willett, who is even stingier than himself. I got something out'n that one, not as much as I'd hoped, but better'n naught, praise be. Ah, Baldwin boy, I know I am no diplomat. I have failed in my life's work, disappointed my poor charges by causing the king to be ill at ease in my company and so plagued with guilt that he is eager to avoid me." Rooster's mouth turned down at the corners and his shoulders slumped.

"Do not flog yourself, good Rooster. You have done your best, my friend. The king, for all his bluster and roundaboutness, is no fool. He knows a noble cause, yours, and an honest man, you, when he sees one, and he heeds the voice of his people, by and by, if it ain't too loud and demanding.

"While we're awaiting Katesby, tell me what you can of the Colchester hens from sugar land you prated about at the same time you were demanding boiled shrimp. Hazard a guess if you don't know right off. Take a chance, eh?"

"Chances, chances, black-garbed Chances! They were all about, large and small—well, small and little's more like it—everywhere in the snow." Rooster sat up very tall in bed. "The littlest Chance ran this way and that after t'other one kicked me. I tried, I did, but I could not make it all the way home. When I fell again, I was helped by a girl, a big strong . . . Nan! *She's* the Colchester hen what helped me home. Except she wasn't no Colchester hen. She told me so. Told me what she *was,* but I can't recall it now, what she said."

"Do you know what the false Chances wanted of you, Rooster?"

"The littlest one wanted me to walk. The pink one, he wanted me to sing."

"Sing?"

"Sing, yes. I gave him some of 'Light O' Love.' He weren't pleased, as I recall, for it was then he clouted me the first blow. He's . . . he's coming back, at first cockcrow . . . " Rooster paled and fell back crouching on his pillows, pulling a quilt over his head.

"Whoever he is, he can't get at you here and now, my friend," said Win. "We're going to protect and care for you." Rooster peeped out from under the bedclothes. "Why was he coming back at cockcrow?"

"I don't rightly know, Baldwin. To hear me sing a song more to his liking, do you imagine?"

"I seriously doubt that, Brewster. Ah, here's Katesby with food and drink, which may stir more of your buried thoughts to the surface of your mind."

"A king's herald awaits you, Baldwin. Henry lays immediate claim to your lively company," Kat announced, moving to the side of Rooster's bed. "At once. The earl's squire, Warbeck, has come. Harry and Charles will set out in the morning for Norland and I shall be going with them."

Gwyn and the Goodkinds, mother and daughters, were left to run the establishment. They were guarded and watched over by a corps of Win's most trusted friends, who were also Chance's best brigands—Jeremy Edge, the gambler; pickpocket Perkin Thyn, Francis Wyggington, spy; Hugh Wyld, the theatrical highwayman who was hunted by the king's men with nearly as much diligence as Win Chance; and earless, olive-skinned Giles Hather, King of the Derbyshire gypsies.

Sooner than Dr. Turner willingly permitted and against the dire prognostications of Dorsey the Cunning Man, Win rode away from The Sign of the Kat, his wounded arm still bound. His face was ashen and his mouth was drawn in a tight line as he mounted Dart, sibling to Chance's horse, Dash. Win was feeling pain of various sorts, of the body and the heart. As he looked down from his mount at Kat, shivering in the inn yard without a wrap, he forced a smile into his green eyes that reflected the lantern light. The hollows beneath his cheekbones and the cleft of his chin were intensified in shadow when he flashed his rogue's wink. Which lacked, Kat saw, its usual twinkle.

"You should not be a-roving quite yet, you know," she said, gazing up. She was hopelessly in love and hoping it didn't show in her eyes. It did, shimmering there so bright and clear, Win felt a blow to his heart. What cavalier thoughtlessness had he shown, leading his best friend into heartache? "I *wish* you weren't going," she added with her brave little smile, and he so mightily wished the same that he had to consider he might not escape heartache entirely, either. He'd been reckless, and now they'd both pay a price, but blast and frogs, there was to be no future for them together, he avowed. She must have her earl. It was all settled and the only sensible thing to do. And he would have an elegant lady wife, blast it, no matter who the devil he loved! He'd told Kat a hundred times if he'd told her once, love was no part of marriage.

"Good-bye yet again, Kat," he said. "Marry Harry without delay."

"We leave before daybreak on the morrow, with Charlie and Squire Warbeck to play gooseberries . . . chaperones. The Montfort carriage and outriders will meet me at Norland to carry me the rest of the journey to Rockingham Castle. When I am made over into a lady, perchance you'll reconsider and accept my marriage proposal? If not, I might have to settle for Harry." As if jesting, she forced a laugh. So did Win.

"Kat, you're my best friend, but I'm not in love with you. He is."

"What if I did actually love you and not him?" She spoke in her foggy voice, virtually a sensual siren song to Win, and her eyes on his were the clear, inviting green of tropic waters. He held repressed his needful impulses and backed his horse a few steps.

"That would put us in a fine tragic love triangle—if you didn't resist, that is. A veritable briny barrel of fish that would be, wouldn't it? Luckily, you do *not* love me, so we're saved from playing in that melodrama, eh?" Kat nodded. His heart twisted.

"Aye, indeed," she said, then urgently called when he

began to turn Dart toward the inn yard gate, "Win! When . . . will we meet again, think you?"

"Your conjecture is as good as mine." He shrugged. "There are livestock, land, and marriage matters in the north for me to see to, the trap for Chance to be set, and withal I'm at the beck and call of our sportive king." The horse stamped and released two white plumes of steamy breath into the frigid air. "Katesby, remember what I've told you. If ever you have need of me, all you must do is blazon it, or whisper it, just think it hard as you can. I'll know. Word will reach me where'er I am. Never forget that."

She nodded, not trusting her voice to speak. Win hesitated a long moment before he pulled his great cape securely over his shoulders, and then he was gone into the dark and snowy night, leaving Kat with an aching heart, feeling lonely and helpless. She'd done all she could to make Win love her, to no avail. She'd lost him.

Take some cheer, Katesby, try to, she told herself. *You did at least endeavor to influence fate and shape your destiny.* "But I was a fool! I risked all on the vagaries of the heart, and I lost," she whispered. *So here I be,* she thought ruefully, *parted from him again, the pair of us tossed hither and thither by happenstance as leaves are strewn about by random autumn winds.*

"Blast and frogs, I could *not* cause Baldwin Beaumarais to love me!" she told a passing gray cat. The animal shied away and scurried on toward the inn's kitchen door. A sharp blast of winter wind urged Kat indoors also, but before she left the yard she looked up to see wind-shredded clouds blown from the face of the moon. In its ice-white light, Kat saw the Old Man wink at her and she laughed, her mood and her sprits beginning to lift

"Am I wrong, sire?" she asked the jolly, fanciful fellow. "Is that what you're telling me with a droll expression on your glimmering face? Is't your view from on high that I *did* make the man love me, only he doesn't know yet know that? Good enough, Old Man! I'll take your word for it. Why not? I've naught to lose now, have I? My heart's long gone. I *will* try again. Next time, if there is one, I'll behave in an altogether unlike way, show him another sort of bearing and conduct altogether. If spendthrift sensuality has failed, might not coquettish wiles and decorous restraint prevail?"

Might. Might not unless you look the part as well as play it. Become the sort of female he tumbles for—pretty, or prettified, leastways—dressed dainty, coifed fancy, sweetened with rose water or some such scent.

"Right!" she exclaimed, pleased with her plan, strengthened in purpose.

"Win's gone. Who you chattering at out there in the wind?" Gwynn asked, poking her head from the inn door.

"The Old Man in the Moon is who," answered Kat, skipping in through the open door to rush shivering to the hearth.

"You're daft, do you know?" said Gwynn, handing her a goblet of mulled hot cider.

"Oh, yes, I know," answered Kat, smiling happily.

Chapter 22

"Make me *beautiful*," said Kat. "And if you cannot, if I am irreparably plain, then teach me how to adorn, attire, and comport myself so that I seem so—beautiful." Brimming with enthusiasm for her new plan, these were the first words she spoke on being presented to her friends, Lady Monfort and Lady Seton—Cary and Addy, as she had come to know them—on her arrival at Rockingham Castle. She had been led through a majestic great hall that was adorned with terra-cotta busts of Roman emperors and of more recent forebears of the marquess, to the chamber room, the suite where the family passed its private time.

"Make you beautiful? Do not be disingenuous, Katesby. I've known you too long to let you get by with it. You are lovely. You *must* know it," Addy Seton answered with a hint of impatience, her shoulders squared and rigid, a posture she assumed when she felt strongly about a matter under consideration. "Else you're more of a dolt than I'd ever have supposed you to be." A tall, graceful woman with dark hair and dark blue eyes, Lady Seton's opinion of aristocratic society had become jaded during the considerable time she had spent at court. In particular, she harbored a special contempt for pretense and feigned naivete, and so her response to Kat was a trifle exaggerated.

"By my troth, Addy," twitted Lady Cary, "I know of no one more unaffected and straightforward than Kat Dalton. If she professes not to know if she be pretty or plain, why, she does not know." Cary, like her friend, who was also her cousin and sister by law, being the wife of Cary's brother and the cousin to Cary's husband, was an exquisite young noblewoman. Of complementarily opposite appearance, Cary was petite and delicate of form, where Addy was tall and had huge, dark, merry eyes and long golden hair, set off to perfection, as she rose to greet Kat with two hands extended, by her green velvet morning gown trimmed with cloth of silver.

"Of *course* she's lovely, beautiful actually, but not precisely in the way she wishes to be, and must be, when she is Countess of Norland, making calls at court. You are very pretty, Kat," Cary smiled warmly, patting the girl's hand. "If I say so, you may be assured 'tis true fact. But these"—she turned Kat's hands palms upward—"require attention. It will take countless rubs of rose glycerine and wraps in rich oils to soften this hard-working extremity."

"The nails are utterly dreadful," noted Addy, stepping forward to enfold Kat in a welcoming embrace and a splendid smile. "From this moment forth, Kat, you are to cease to do anything even resembling useful toil. You must not do so much as brush your own hair." Addy undid Kat's kerchief and let the girl's lush mane of curls tumble free. "Nor are you to do or undo the fastenings of your gowns—this one should be burnt forthwith, by the by," Addy declared of Kat's kitchen dress. "You must do naught but sit with your fingers folded in your lap—that is, when they are not encased in Cary's oily wraps, I mean to say. This will be apt rehearsal for ladyship. You know, I presume that a noble consort mayn't do anything at all that might be considered worthwhile or serviceable."

"Addy, you are irredeemable and well past praying for," Cary exclaimed. "Pay her no mind, Katesby. She mocks at silly twits of the aristocracy, of which there are a few. She knows full well how substantial and consequential is the enterprise of administering a great estate, or even a modest one."

"If managing a modest inn is an indication, Lady Cary, the running of an estate seems a prodigious enterprise," Kat remarked, disquieted.

"You are not to worry over that now. First things first. Sit." Lady Cary directed her to a chair at the table where she and Addy had been sitting over the last of breakfast "Tea?" she said, already pouring a cup for Kat, who was reaching across to a platter, helping herself to three or four peeled, hard-boiled quail eggs. She popped them two by two into her mouth, swallowed in loud gulps, then washed down the remnant with a slurp of tea.

"That little bite don't do much to quell your hunger, not like an ample goose egg. Well . . . what?" she asked the ladies, who were staring at her as much amused as aghast. They resumed their places at the table, one to each side of Kat, and proceeded to dine most delicately.

"Quail egg, cousin?" asked Addy, archly polite, passing the bowl.

"Indeed, thank you, my dear," replied Cary, helping herself and proceeding to daintily nibble with small teeth, making the minute egg last a wondrous long time, thought Kat, who grinned.

"Do indeed, if you please, pass the tasty morsels here, Lady Seton," she giggled, extracting an egg from the dish with the tips of two fingers only, arching her little finger when she brought it to her mouth to take a tiny nip. "Gratifying. Delectable, to be sure," she said in a perfect twang of upper-class enunciation.

"You've got it!" said Addy appreciatively "No haughty courtier will escape your discerning eye and dagger wit! You're a quick study, Kat."

"So I've been before apprised," Kat answered with a sigh. A blush spread from her throat to shade her cheeks intense pink, for it was Baldwin who had said the same to her, in very different circumstances.

Cary and Addy exchanged identical bemused, curious, discerning glances, both aware that a spark of memory had kindled a sweet heat in their charge. The ladies knew of only one emotion, love, and one variety of sensation, passionate, that worked thus in memory and moment. Was it Harry de Morely? wondered Cary doubtfully. Henry Tudor? thought Addy and nearly laughed aloud at the absurdity of the prospect. Baldwin Beaumarais! The name came to both Addy and Cary at the same instant and again their eyes met, though not in perfect understanding this time, for Addy dismissed that likelihood. Cary decidedly did not. Neither asked any question of Kat then. They both knew, without exchanging a word or even a look, that the exuberant, outgoing girl would unbosom herself, sooner rather than later, of her own volition. Addy offered her cool, patrician smile.

"There's much work to be done. You both heard King Henry's commands, as I did, that we are to cultivate you, Kat, glaze and polish and refine you till you shine and are indistinguishable from a highborn lady." Addy had risen from the table in a swish and rustle of her blue taffeta morning gown and petticoats, and gone to look out from the great bay windows, one of glories of Rockingham Castle, thrown out to give a view from the family rooms of a greensward rolling down to a distant lake shore. "We will now plan your transformation, Mistress Dalton, from erstwhile urchin to full-fledged countess. You must learn weaving, embroidery, music—the lute for your first instrument, I propose, for it is most easily mastered. And dancing, and of course riding. You will be soaked in baths, rubbed with creams, and anointed with oils until you are all over soft as rose petals. Perhaps we will choose to use saffron in your hair to lighten its shade, though after it is washed and brushed faithfully many times in a day for many days, it may be found to be glistening gold enough. There are languages to be learned, though in the short time we have I propose we settle upon Latin and leave Greek for some later time. Your portrait must done, your wardrobe created."

Addy swirled to face her companions again. Her back to the window, the light behind her, her face was in shadow. "Zounds, but we will have to scour the area for seamstresses. Do you think, Cary, that Lady Baldmuir will give us loan of her sewers? And Lady Carmathen at Cringle, what of her needlewomen? I don't know who else to—"

"Do not take on so, Addy," sweetly admonished Lady Cary. "You will terrify the girl. Kat has only just arrived after long travel. We know she's hungry. I suspect she has need of rest as well as food."

"Hungry indeed, not weary in the least, but ready and eager—aye, impatient rather, to be transformed!" answered Kat, clasping her hands beneath her chin.

"The earl will be most pleased and satisfied to know you are so inclined," Cary said, smiling. Kat dropped her eyes and turned away, then commandeered a whole loaf of bread before remembering her new manners. She set it in its place again and, with restraint, tore the loaf in half before proceeding to wolf it down.

"The time for breaking the fast is gone, and now 'tis close to dinnertime, but not quite that hour. I shall order up nuncheon for you, Kat, to bridge the gap and carry you through," said Cary, carefully observing the girl, who was still avoiding her eyes. At the pull of a bell cord, servants soon appeared to spread a clean table rug and then set before Kat an elegant silver salt cellar, a round wood trencher, pewter spoons, a broad carving knife with a silver gilt handle, a dish of buttered eggs, a new white loaf, fish, and other fine foods.

"It is odd to me to be served. I've always been the server," commented Kat. "What have we there beneath the brass lid?"

"Cod," answered Addy, wrinkling her nose with aversion. "I detest dried cod," she complained when the plank of fish was presented to Kat. "It is so stiff, it must beaten with a wood mallet for near an hour in the kitchen before it can be eaten. And then, 'tis not worth the bother. Try the pudding of suet sprinkled with dates and raisins, Katesby," she suggested. " 'Tis sweetened with *blaunch-poudre*—ginger ground with sugar."

"A costly spice be that," said Kat, dipping a finger into a silver bowl. "I never have purchased it for the inn, though Win brings from Mediterranean shores cinnamon, clove, mace, and goodly quantities of pepper, three-hundred-pound weight of it on his last voyage in the *Conquest*, along with ten pounds of raisins from Corinth. He also gifted me with oil of cinnamon, rose water, and olive oil, for my hands, he said, to make them soft and smooth. I never did take time to use it."

"We're here to acquaint you with the use of all the dainty womanly wiles and cosmetic artifices and strategies. We shan't have much to teach you of provisioning a great house. Surely a frugal victualer such as you be will, without being instructed, know to have broken wine, gone sour, made into vinegar," said Addy, "and serve servants black bread made with bran and the like."

"If you do not know, you should and now will, that the best, purest salt is gleaned from the sun-dried brine of the Bay of Bourgneuf on the coast of France," lectured Cary. "Pure or not, before use at a high table, bay salt must be wetted, poured through fine cloth and parched again."

The ladies walked to and fro while Kat dined, each offering her useful snippets of castle kitchen wisdom.

Addy: "I will gift you with a useful volume for a noble household, a courtesy book titled *For to Serve a Lord.* It has been put to great use by many stewards and serving men, and though you are to be served when you are countess, it will help you oversee cooks and stewards and table boys in the correct care and feeding of the earl."

Cary: "You will read there in the courtesy book that it is prudent always to offer his lordship his water in an agate cup, for agate will show a change of color should poison be infused."

Addy: "Unicorn horn may be used for the same purpose, for it too will be altered in color by taint or venom."

Cary: "Tooth of narwhal is designated unicorn horn, there being no such beast as the unicorn, eh, Kat? Now to wine. You are even now, Kat, drinking a fine and elegant white wine, one bought for my own particular use and pleasure. I prize its color and fragrance, its sparkling brilliance and delicacy, its velvety softness. . . ."

Addy: "Now *you* do go on, Cary. Wine is only a beverage got from mashing grapes, after all. More important for you to appreciate, Kat, is that you are munching upon the upper crust of a new-baked fine white loaf, a portion most usually reserved for the lord of the castle, in this instance my cousin, Lord Tom."

Cary: "At table with guests or alone with your lord, cups of ale and wine must always be kept full."

Addy: "The proper use of a trencher knife by the butler and his helper to scrape away scraps between courses, into the voider pail kept close to hand, is of utmost importance."

Cary: "A clean trencher and knife is brought for the fruit and cheese which . . ."

Addy: ". . . which is served with hippocras, either red or

white wine sweetened with sugar and spices and accompanied by wafers and biscuits."

"Cannot the wine be sweetened with honey?" Kat asked, dabbing at her lips with a napkin. "I supposed it could be."

"Then 'tis called clary, not hippocras," replied Addy firmly.

"Do you indeed say so, my *dear* Lady Seton?" Kat asked in her newly perfected noble twang. "And you, Lady Montfort? Am I to take it that you are in utter and complete agreement on this momentous point with Lady Seton? Hadn't we best consult with a higher authority?" Kat teased merrily. Addy and Cary, who had been absorbed in their own discourse, stood still, looking at their young guest quizzically, until she loosed peals of her irrepressible lilting laughter. At first the ladies, surprised, smiled hesitantly, then grinned abashedly before they finally entered fully into Kat's amusement.

"We *were* taking on like a pair of pompous, prating ninnies," Cary admitted.

"Speak for yourself," snapped Addy before joining the others in full-throated laughter herself. "You're a clever one, Katesby, putting us in our places so deft and kindly. You'll go far. I've always said so. Enough work for one day. You two be off to play at something now, while I retire to write a letter to my lord Arthur yet in London with Tom, serving at the king's pleasure. Oh, Kat, one more smidgeon of useful information: knights are called 'sir' and their wives, for courtesy, are addressed as 'my lady' or 'madam.' Be gone now." She smiled fondly.

Cary and Kat walked through Rockingham Castle, where numerous plaques, tablets and medallions embellished with the Monfort crest and coat of arms were hung in beautifully paneled chambers and along the gray stone walls of seemingly endless, twisting corridors and staircases connected by low, narrow doorways.

"They built the place like a Cretan maze, Kat, to make it easily defensible, in case the walls were breached," explained Cary, leading the way over tiled floors. Most were covered with reeds and rushes, though in the lord and lady's chamber, a Turkey carpet was spread upon the floor, a rare thing, for most such fine weavings were hung with tapestries and arrases above carved oak box chairs and oaken tables in the vast rooms.

Dutifully and sincerely Kat admired the oddities and graces of Falconbridge as her hostess presented them—the pink-hued sandstone of which it was constructed, its oddly shaped, irregularly placed little windows overlooking its several courtyards. The long court, the most spacious, ran along the south wall of the great hall, where the soaring, vaulted, timbered ceiling and a magnificently painted screen elicited a gasp of delight and wonder from the visitor.

"Customarily, when he is in residence, my lord husband keeps open table in our great hall. His forebears have done so for generations. Rockingham Castle has stood on this site, much as you see it now, Katesby, for more than four hundred years, though some of the outer boundary walls are more primitive. The walls of the place are wondrous thick, for defense, same as the narrow doors and such. It is written that kings of old, Offa for one, later Ethelred the Unready, ruled from this spot, though the ancient manor house is now vanished. My husband's kinsman, the first Duke of Durham, was granted the castle by his king for service rendered during the French Wars," Cary related. "Improvements were made, some by my father-in-law, most by my lord Tom, one specially by me." Cary smiled delightedly and gestured for Kat to follow her to the nursery apartments at Rockingham. The outer room, the day nursery, was hung all round with striking tapestries showing the twelve months of the year. There was a low bedstead, miniature throne chairs covered in cloth of gold and softened with gold-embroidered pillows which stood at a small table of light oak carved with the armored likenesses of the knights of King Arthur's court. In the inner nursery stood a rich cradle with down pillows and quilt, and a gilded bedstead hung with a scarlet taffeta tester and crimson curtains. At the center of the room was a chest overflowing with toys—drums, hobby horses, kites, and popguns. Strewn about the room were a dozen little lambs of gold-flecked, curly white wool. They had red cheeked faces of composition clay, black dot eyes, and tin horns and legs.

"A lamb alike to these was my favorite toy, as a child," explained Cary, fondling one of the sheep. "My little son adores them as well. I shall see to it all my children do!" She laughed softly, patting her belly which, Kat now realized, showed the first roundness of a new babe growing.

"When's it to be?" she asked Cary, feeling that familiar longing deep in her heart for a baby of her own. She had told Win of her craving, and he had given her one, pretty Roxelana with her black silky curls and oval, fawn-hued face, with almond eyes and little bowed mouth that rounded into the puckered O of a baby yawn.

"This baby will be born in late summer," Cary replied. "The cradle is for . . . her. A gypsy soothsayer prophesied a daughter. I wish her forecast to be unerring."

"How favored are the tykes whose haven this is," said Kat with a bittersweet smile, fingering a down pillow, then setting the cradle rocking and thinking of the street children she cared for at The Sign of the Kat. How grateful they were to be allowed to sleep, all curled together by the dozen, wrapped in blankets on the floor near the hearth with the old terrier, Deaf Jack, snoring in their midst. With Roxelana, they were being well looked after in her absence by Gwyn and the Goodkinds. But what of her favorite, Rob, Little Chance, just one small brave boy alone, hunted and hiding from the wickedest men in the kingdom—Wiltenham, Rattcliffe, and Blunt.

"You appear downcast all at once. What troubles you, my jolly little friend?" asked Lady Cary, setting a hand on the girl's shoulder.

"Naught, to be sure!" Kat hastily answered, trying to smile. "I was thinking of . . . London, 'tis all."

"Lord Tom has a grand town house on the Strand in London," Cary said, changing the subject, not the least fooled by Kat's protestations. "We have not visited since our son was born. My lord would protect his babes from epidemics and plagues and the dread sweating sickness that regularly descend upon the city. Here, there is good gravel soil and healthy air far from the fouled River Thames. Water for the household is brought to the castle through leaden ducts, from the spring that feeds yonder lake. Shall we walk to it, the lake? Better yet, shall we take to horse and ride there?" asked Cary in an effort to divert Kat from whatever rankled her so. The girl nodded. "Will it be your first time to mount up, Katesby?"

"Aye, on a fine horse, though I've sat a wagon nag, to guide him. Win had proposed to instruct me once in the ladylike way, with sidesaddle and all, but at the time it seemed unfitting for me, a striving busy innkeeper, and he was fast becoming a fine gentleman with wider-ranging interests, as you know, Lady Cary, who nurtured him so well, you and Lord Tom."

"Interests?"

"His classical education, the ways of commerce, travels abroad—and the ladies. He discovered *them,* and they have been his continuing diversion since. Win had better things to do than teach me to ride a horse in genteel and stylish fashion sith I'd not ever have had the time or leisure to put the knowledge to use, or so I thought then." Kat sighed.

"You miss him, don't you, Kat?"

"He has been my best friend forever, nearly. I miss him rather a lot, but we'll meet from time to time, and I shall get over it," Kat insisted, appearing enlivened. "It'll take a bit of time and distraction, like a gallop on a tall horse along a blue lake," she added, offering a genuine smile.

"Gallop, nothing, my fine girl! You must learn to walk afore you can run or risk breaking your pretty neck, albeit you are a quick study," Cary admonished gaily, setting off toward the stables, leading Kat by the hand after her.

That night, after vespers and the late sup, Kat's head was boiling with all she had learned from her mentors of aristocratic table manners, popper posture and gesture for a lady, and of horse sense. English mounts, she had been informed by the master of Lord Tom's stables, were mostly geldings and not overly tall compared to some of their race upon the continent, but were especially well colored and justly limbed and consequently of easy ambling pace not hurtful to riders sitting upon their backs. Kat, aching with saddle stiffness after two hours up, dismissed the truth of this last bit of information when she was at last alone in her chamber. Her hair had been brushed one hundred times, her hands oiled, and her face creamed by her own chambermaid, who left her with a good fire and a tankard of ale.

And so Kat sat in the window seat, listening uneasily to the country silence without, which was keeping her awake, and feeling homesick for all the sounds and sights and noises, even the unsavory smells, of London.

"What am I doing here," she asked her friend, the Man in the Moon hanging low in the dark sky, shining his light upon the dark lake, "so far from London, the only home I've known, my true place in the world that I love?" She missed the good work she did that occupied her days and much of the nights, and longed for the comings and goings and gossip and talk at home at the inn. But London and

The Sign of the Kat would be no home to her at all, she knew, without Baldwin Beaumarais.

"*That* is why I'm here, Old Man"—she winked at the moon dipping lower on the horizon—"to play my last, best whist card to win his love and have him beside me always."

With resolve, she willed herself then to shake off the bout of melancholy. She smiled with relief, strengthened in her resolve to become the soft and dainty, accomplished lady who would capture the heart of Baldwin Beaumarais. "He is going to love me! Tell him so for me, will you please, if you see him, sir, this night?" she implored the moon. She yawned and, feeling sleep stealing over her, slid into her bed.

Chapter 23

"Fornication ain't hard, Beaumarais. It comes quite naturally to most. If you're loath to love with your heart as well as your stave, so be it, but you'll be all the poorer in this life for disdaining love. Hiding from it's more the truth, I'd venture. You have got a problem, lad, if you ain't able to ratchet up your courage and become a veritable man."

"Andrew Danter, you strutting, burly-boned clown!" Win roared, his face dark with anger. "You've no call to speak to me thus, naming me a coward."

"He who would call himself man is able to love, sir. A coward cannot."

"From which theater piece is that line stolen?" Win asked his friend, the former actor, Andrew Danter, now a playmaker, who was also overseer of Win's inherited grazing lands and shepherd of Win's flocks. Danter, dignified, tall, and gray-eyed, with black hair graying at the temples, also looked after cattle owned by others that were grazed, for good fees, on Win's acres, and he negotiated sales of wool from the sheep and the butchering of animals sold for meat. Since Win had arrived from London the day before with his arm in a sling and grimness in his face, he'd talked only of business to Danter, the persistent loss of some their best animals—lambs, rams, and ewes as well as an excellent shepherd dog, raised and trained from a pup by the actor, who had taken the loss of his helper hard. Both men, churning in their emotions since Win arrived, were gruff and out of sorts and each had much kept to himself until Danter bridged the divide.

"You are not such good company as you are customarily. What's nagging at you, boy?" he asked Win.

"I'm young, strong, and prosperous. I am recovered from recent injury and wooing Gail Pebbles, a respectable lady of the neighborhood who will double my fortune and lands should I make her my wife. My future seems bright. Why should aught be ailing me?" replied Win brusquely, a hint of sarcasm in his tone. He took a a deep draught of ale and scowled darkly at the fire.

"I know not *why,* thou gravel-heart. That's what I asked of you, 'twas it not? Oh, I do regret our little Kat is not here, for she has the means to see through you and know what ails you and how to banish your foul tempers and moods."

"I rue her absence, same as you," Win grunted.

"Will anything hearten you, man?" demanded Andrew. "Though it is not a feast day, I would call up a troop of gypsy Morris dancers to cheer you, if you think it would help. The Egyptians will banquet with us and dance for us through a day and a night, them bedecked all in their suits of gay yellow and green, with calico scarves flying and all their forty bells jingling about their legs. It makes *me* gay, just thinking of them. I shall direct they have drums a-drumming and pipes a-piping. Ah, you do not reply, Baldwin, my fun-loving lad. I think it must be you are in love and despairing, and not over the Widow Pebbles, neither.

Nothing else so dampens the sprit of a normally mirthful, lighthearted man as pining for his love in vain. Who's taken your heart at long last? Who is it your thoughts dwell upon? Speak her name, you tongueless block!"

At this, Win, who had been slumped upon a fur rug at the hearth, rose to his feet like an arrow shot from a bow and took to walking the small chamber, the only room in the shepherd's hutch, which served Danter as kitchen, sleeping space, and shelter for birthing ewes and caring for young lambs left motherless. Win now scooped up one of the orphaned babies and proceeded to pace with it in his arms.

"It's not my heart she—the lady—has. 'Tis another part of me. I lust after her, is it?" Win said, to determine if stating his thought aloud would help him to believe it. He did not. Nor did Andrew.

"Whoever she be, the lady couples with you like a marten mink, eh? Your dilemma is easily solved. 'When all the candles be out, all cats be gray.' So it is written in Mr. Heywood's book of proverbs. There's a multitude of fair damsels will be only too glad to assuage your desires, Baldwin. The Widow Pebbles near ravished you earlier, friend. And you eluded her. 'A man has no better thing under the sun, than to eat and drink and have much fun.' "

"Only *she—my lady*—will do, you blathering prater."

" 'Tain't lust then. 'Tis love," proclaimed Danter. "And he who would call himself a man is able to love, sir. A coward cannot."

" 'It hurteth not the tongue to give fair words,' rude clod. Heywood's *Proverbs* says that, too," Baldwin replied. He set down the lamb and strode from the hut out into the moonlit night to ruminate on the time passed since he'd come away from London

* * *

Earlier that day, his second morning in the north country, he and Danter had paid a courtesy call upon their closest neighbor, the Widow Pebbles, whom they discovered, on rounding the last turn of her drive, standing out of doors as if expecting their visit. Their hostess waited before her house, a fine timber-framed country manor with two good brick chimneys, the centerpiece of a neat, prosperous-appearing farm. At some distance stood a cathedral-ceilinged barn and farther off still, ditched fields could be seen, brown and bare still in the first days of spring.

"Abundant expanse of land. Rich soil. Marry her," Danter muttered darkly.

"Can you never keep silence, Simple Simon?" answered Win. "Is she pretty?"

"I've set eyes upon the lady from a distance only, but what's it matter if she be pretty or homely? When all the candles be out, all cats be gray."

"Quiet, thou poisonous toad! She'll hear you," Win growled at Danter as he bowed from the saddle to the waiting woman.

"Mr. Beaumarais, I presume?" she called. " I heard you were visiting in these environs, sir. Welcome to Deepwells Manor."

"Yes, ma'am. Thank you, Mistress Pebbles. Baldwin Beaumarais at your service, " he answered as he dismounted and flashed his winning smile, a twitch of muscles only that did not touch his eyes. He kissed her proffered little hand, so pale and soft in his, it felt nearly boneless and lay clammy, like a limpet snail slug out of its shell. She was a small, slight, almost pretty woman, with tiny, sharp features—pointed little chin and nose and slanted pale blue eyes, a mite too narrow to be deemed beautiful but pleasing enough, Baldwin mused. Her hair, he saw, showing at the edge of a silk kerchief headdress, was of a light, unremarkable shade, neither red nor golden.

"Sir, fortunately you've come at the dinner hour. For the meat course today we are indulging in freshly slaughtered roast of young lamb, acquired only yesterday from Scoggin the Butcher. I would be most pleased if you would join me for the meal. Truly, I'd deem it a favor. I've had only country clods for company of late, and I crave clever talk and news of London from an urbane and cultured source." Win's boyish grin lit his face.

"You flatter me, ma'am. I shall be honored to accept your invitation and to attempt to amuse you in any way I am able," he answered.

"Good." Gail smiled. "Send your servant to the kitchen door and. . ."

"May I present Andrew Danter, ma'am? No servant he, but playmaker, thespian, and friend," Win replied, gesturing Danter to dismount. "He's a man of a trenchant wit, far more clever and amusing than I, I assure you."

"Your *friend*, Mr. Beaumarais, whom I took for a sheepherder, will of course join us at table," she answered, the look of arrogant distaste flitting over her face noted by both men.

"You've dealings with Alberic Scoggin, madam?" asked Danter in his rich and resonant thespian's voice as he dismounted.

"I do," Mistress Pebbles replied archly, her narrow eyes gone to slits with suspicion. "Why do you ask?"

"A slaughterer who dearly loves his work, is Alberic Scoggin," was Danter's reply.

"Indeed. He's good at what he does, and his talents do not end there. I have offered him the post of steward of Deepwells, a position that will allow him to continue as butcher of the region."

"What need have you of a steward when you've Esmond Quine, who has served your husband and your husband's father long and loyally on this property?" asked Win as the three proceeded to the house.

"I've turned him out, the doddering old fool, for filching my grain. A woman alone, a widow such as I be, needs a strong, honest man to look out for her best interests."

"That describes Scoggin—a strong man, sure, a very goliath," agreed Danter, declining to include 'honest' in his estimation of a lout he mistrusted in the extreme. "He sells his meat by candlelight to conceal the rancid parts. Where's Quine?"

"I know not, nor do I care, Mr. Danter," answered the widow. "I do know Scoggin's estimations of you are much the same as yours of him."

"It is widely held that players are of the same low criminal class with minstrels, Mr. Danter, with tellers of fortunes, bear-wards leading their dancing beasts hither and thither with chains, and other such rogues who gad about the country gathering illegal fees," spoke the widow. "What say you?" Ample food had been devoured and many flagons of wine drunk, all of which had loosened the hostess's tongue and freed her from any of the usual constraints of politeness. "Have you ever done a day's work in your life, player?"

"Madam, I would offer that manual work is the last forlorn hope of failures. My philosophy is this—keep your nose high and never do a day's work for any reason," Danter goaded with a wink at Win, who narrowed his eyes.

"What of hunger, Mr. Danter? Surely you'd work to quell hunger."

"No. Not even for food would I bend my back or soil my hands. There are other ways of enduring, eh?" For the first time, Gail Pebbles gazed with interest on the actor.

"I wouldn't know," she said, and almost smiled.

"I might have supposed otherwise," Danter answered with a nasty grin, and Gail Pebbles, showing an angry flush, turned her attention to Baldwin.

"I'm not one who has always dreamed of meads and orchards and primrose lanes, Mr. Beaumarais. Nor is animal husbandry my favored subject of conversation. My husband, Mr. Pebbles, and I resided in London, as do you, I'm told. Have you a house there?"

"Of a sorts, ma'am. I'm half owner of an inn, where I reside." Gail's nose wrinkled and lifted.

"Suitable bachelor quarters, sir. Not a fit dwelling for a *lady.*"

"I know some excellent ladies abiding at The Sign of the Kat, madam," said Danter with a loud theatrical yawn before resting his head upon his arms on the table and proceeding to snore with gusto.

"Down to business, Baldwin," the widow pronounced. "You seek a wife who can enlarge your fortune with a substantial dower. My husband bequeathed his soul to Almighty God and nearly all else to me—his fortune, his house with brass pots and pewter vessels, his lands, his ambling mares, heifers, hogs, poultry. As I have said, meads and orchards hold no charm for me. I am ambitious to move higher in society than Mr. Pebbles could ever have taken me, God rest his soul. Now I seek a husband of substance, style, grace, exceptional good looks, charm, and *connections.* Despite your humble origins, Mr. Beaumarais, you cavort with nobles and kings, it's said."

"Indeed," was Win's one-word answer. He went to stand at the mantel and in the firelight saw Katesby cavorting, her lush golden hair flowing, her big green eyes laughing at him. Danter snorted in his sleep, and Win turned to the widow again.

"Good," she stated. "We'll not quibble or beat the devil about the stump. We are not unworldly, Mr. Beaumarais. I have been wed and you, with your striking appearance . . ." She smiled suggestively and looked him over indecently, her eyes lingering on protrusions and swells beneath his fitted leggings. "You are unmistakably a man of—ah, parts, and experience."

"I thought animal husbandry was not of interest to you, madam," said Danter, raising his head and gazing bleary-eyed at the startled woman. "I'm for home, Win, my lad. You and the lady may continue this tender and sentimental dialogue—monologue rather—another time."

"Why not let this boor of a player amble on home alone, Baldwin? I would be delighted to have you pass the night here, with me, in talk and planning, of course, of how a union might serve us both." Gail poured out another goblet of claret and slipped off her headdress to reveal thin, lank locks. Danter hiccupped, stood, and stumbled, then clung wavering to the back of a chair.

"I'd best see this drunken fellow safe to his bed, ma'am," Baldwin replied, supporting Danter about the waist. The actor flung an arm over his shoulders. "The last time I led an inebriate to his door," added Win, remembering Rooster Truckle, "he came to dire harm."

"A loyal, true friend is Baldwin Beaumarais," said Andrew, his speech slurred as, lachrymose, with sentimental tears wetting his cheeks, he lurched from the chamber leaning heavily upon Win.

"Forget what I said before. Don't marry that scorpion no matter how many acres she owns, nor how fertile the soil be made by sheep dung," warned Danter, instantly sober on reaching the doorstep, and firm on his feet.

"You should go back upon the stage," Win said, grinning. "You're an actor of terrific talent."

"I know that well. I relied on my genius to save you, by a narrow squeak, from a near thing there—aye, lad? I kept you out of the widow's bed!" He laughed.

"That was no 'near thing,' man, but I appreciate your good intentions." Win shrugged, thumping Andrew on the back as the two friends mounted and set off across furrowed fields for home.

* * *

"The actor thinks you are a man of questionable honesty, Alberic. He calls you a slaughterer who loves his work over much," Gail Pebbles told the hulking person who entered her hall as the door was closing after her departing guests. Scoggin the Butcher bore some likeness to the king, for he was paunchy and huge, like Henry, but there the resemblance ended. Where traces of the king's youthful beauty still lingered, the big, broad-shouldered butcher was coarse of feature and slouched in bearing. With heavy red hands he pushed his hood back and shook a big head of tangled brown hair. His face was blemished and dented from the pox, and a long, thin mustache drooped beneath his bulbous nose. A patch covered one eye, while the other, small and black, bulged slightly and shifted unceasingly from side to side.

"He is exact on both particulars. I ain't honest as the day is long and I *do* like me work. The despised malt worm is always taunting me about the cruel way, he says, I do me butchering." Scoggin looked over the table. "Have you no marchpane or suckets, harridan?" he asked, coming behind the widow and setting his lips to her neck. "You know I desire a sweet after dinner."

"Not now, Alberic. After I've just missed out on bedding beautiful Beaumarais, with his green eyes and bronze curls, you don't appeal. It's the fault of Danter I'm thwarted, luring the boy off home."

"Ha! You didn't *just* miss out. You came not close. You bungled and botched the whole thing. You were not yet even near to spurring the comely fellow, though I agree that Danter was no help to you. I've a plan of vengeance afoot to play merry hell with that one, and cook his goose well. Danter shall learn what cruel is when I get to butchering him, the second-rate playactor."

"What mean you?" the widow asked, looking with revulsion and a measure of dread on Scoggin, who was sucking the last shreds of meat from a lamb shank.

"There's no wool, see, like that spun from the fleeces of English sheeps. A great price is charged abroad for the spun, woven wortseds of English sheeps. There's laws in the land forbidding our sheeps be sent out of the country. When Danter is found guilty of smuggling English rams and ewes, breeding pairs of sheep, out of the land to sell in Spain, he will suffer the penalty for the crime. A first offense brings forfeiture of all possessions, a year's imprisonment, and severance of the left hand, which is nailed up in the marketplace. Who do you conjecture, me harpy, is called upon to do the severing?"

"The local butcher, of course." The widow smiled, enlivened by her interest in this plot and pleased with the butcher. "What, prithee, is the penalty for a second offense?" she asked.

"Death," leered Scoggin, coming into her open arms. "We shall make haste now, madam, for I must be off to collect more sheeps from Beaumarais's flock to sell into Spain. A handsome price is paid to me, and Danter will get his comeuppings."

At the very moment Kat, at Rockingham, was prattling at the Man in the Moon, Win, with three young sheepdogs at his heels, was striding through his fields, which were washed in white moonlight, planning his next moves against Wiltenham and pondering over the whereabouts of Blaidd, for the boy had made no contact since fleeing the Tower. Most of all he was concerned for Kat, far from home for the first time in her life, and thinking of her set him to mulling over his contentious conversation with Andrew.

"Fornication ain't hard, Beaumarais . . . you're loath to love with your heart . . . ratchet up your courage . . . he who would call himself a man is able to love, sir. A coward cannot."

Win kicked a rock, cursed under his breath, and looked up chagrined. "What the devil are you laughing at?" he asked the moon. " 'Tis no laughing matter. Did you hear Andrew say all that? Did you hear him say, 'Oh, I do regret our little Kat is not here,' and me reply, 'I rue her absence, same as you,'? Hell, I more than rue it. I *need* her." Win shouted this last as if to keep the moon from disappearing behind the thick blanket of clouds enveloping it. But the moon went its way, leaving him in half darkness and without the shadow of a doubt that he was hopelessly in love with Katesby. No doubt of it and no arguing the matter. He had fallen in love with the imp! he marveled, turning back toward the hut to tell Andrew so. The dogs, ambling ahead and behind, kept pace with Win, striding fast through the misty rain that had begun, when his eye was caught by a large, shapeless form moving among the penned sheep. *Bear!* was his first thought when the dog closest to him bared its teeth, laid back its ears, and growled deep in its throat. The other barked excitedly as Win ran, roaring, at the intruder, but whatever it was—man, beast, or hellish fiend—quickly disappeared in the darkness.

"No bears about here, unless one escaped its warder, which is unlikely. It rarely happens," said Andrew when Win had reported the sighting. "What you saw, lad, is whoever it is been making off with our sheep two, three at a time. What say you? What see you in that fire you're always gazing at?"

"Visions of Katesby, my flower of brave and lovely womanhood. Do you know, Andrew, her eyes are immense, the clear color of tropic seas—blue green, aqua green, *lovely*."

"Aye?" said Andrew.

"You were right, my friend. I've been a coward, until now. Now I will tell you the honest truth, which I just told to myself—I love her." Danter's handsome face lit with a wide, bright smile.

"What you going to do about it?" he asked.

"Naught but leave England forever, soon as I see to a few important matters of business."

"Forever?"

"Hark unto me. She won't do better than to become a countess."

"Not if she loves you as you do her. Does she?"

"She does not. She said so."

"You believed her, did you?"

"Not altogether. But I don't believe in love, neither, for it is fleeting and makes fools of wise men while it lasts."

"For your own peace of heart and soul, wise man, you owe it to her and to yourself to determine for good and all if she loves you or no. Consider how much better you'll feel, knowing she don't love you a jot," the actor said with simulated concern, actually intending to prick Win's vanity.

"I could make her admit to love without over-much difficulty, you scolding crookback, but I'll not be the one to ruin her chances."

"Will you at least bid her good-bye and farewell?"

"I should not take the risk and tempt fate." Win shrugged. "But I will, though if aught should befall me before I reach her, you'll have to tell her for me, Andrew."

"Tell her what, good-bye," asked Danter sourly, "or that you loved her?"

"Both," answered Win. "Now, I need your help on another matter. I must call upon your skill as an actor once more afore I go. Will you help in a good and noble cause?"

"Have I ever said you nay, friend? What cause is that?"

"Freeing the friends of Win Chance—all of them—from Wiltenham's gaols."

"That's a good enough cause," said Danter. "When do we start?"

"Now's as good a time as any, eh?" Win answered, taking parchment, quill, and ink from the cupboard and settling at the table to inscribe a long list of names.

"Got other good works to do, while we're about it?"

"One or two, my friend. Even three." Win grinned. "You will begin by going into the horse markets at Ripon, Woolpit, Newport Pond to purchase twenty mounts of particular hue and height, which I will describe to you."

"And how will you proceed?"

"Win Chance will make haste to London Towne, to call upon Brother Truckle and search for a child known as Little Chance. He will also challenge certain of the king's agents and their knaves to a high-stakes game at the backgammon table, with a select group of contenders, to secure the future safety and prosperity of certain of his friends—you, sir, Rooster Truckle, and Blaidd Kyd among them, whom I intend to soon free from the Tower.

"Baldwin Beaumarais, meanwhile, will travel to Norland to pursue certain matters of import for the earl, who is too ill to travel on his own business. Harry has written to ask me to carry a likeness of his first wife to the Candy Isles, there to learn, perhaps, what fate befell his love. In turn I will ask de Morely to hand over to Wiltenham the list of the friends of Chance who are now in the king's gaols, folk I am suggesting be hanged within the fortnight."

Win held up the page he had covered in his clear strong script, waving it about to dry the ink. "Then Chance and Beaumarais will turn to investigating clues to the lineage of the future Duchess of Norland, our own Katesby Dalton. That done, Win Chance and Baldwin Beaumarais will disappear from England for good and all."

"Chance and Beaumarais are going to be very busy for a time, eh?" queried Danter, looking bemused. "How will you . . . they . . . them be in so many places all at once, pray?"

"By calling upon your talents to serve me further, Andrew, you and a troupe of your fellow players. Sit you down now and remove that look of amaze from your face while I relate all the particulars."

Chapter 24

"My lord husband, Viscount Seton, was fifteen years a prisoner of the infidel in the North of Africa," Addy Seton told Kat as they sat with Lady Montfort, embroidering near the fire in the great hall at Rockingham.

The hearth was so wide and the fireplace so tall, a mounted horse might have walked into it completely and his rider would not even have had to bend his neck. Many oaken logs burned brightly there, throwing off a great heat and lighting a portion of the hall at sunset on a very early spring afternoon in March, just after the celebration of the vernal equinox. Kat had been more than a fortnight, closer to a month, in the country with the ladies, now her dear friends, who had, with her excellent collaboration—they pronounced—worked a dramatic change not only in her appearance, but in her manner and mien and fluency of speaking the King's English. She was ready, they declared, to be presented again to the Henry, and preparations were under way for the journey back to London.

"My brother Arthur," said Cary, leaning to her work,

her little son playing at her feet with a golden lamb, "was named by my father for our greatest king. I think his name caused Arthur to become an overly romantic youth, consumed with the old tales of knights and ladies and dragons. Leastways, off he went at seventeen, on a crusade as he called it, though it was more a pilgrimage, to the Holy Lands. He was captured by corsairs and was not seen here again for years and years. Our father, a modest, comfortable nobleman, far from rich, ransomed him by selling off all the family had. He dispatched several great oaken chests filled with gold and jewels for his son's return, but neither son nor gold were found."

"Win had an adventure on his last voyage, along the northern shores of Afrique. He and his shipmates were seized by Hasan, a boy of seventeen, a grandson of ad-Din, the admiral of the fleets of the Ottoman Suleiman the Great."

"The Admiral ad-Din, who is designated by the Italians *Barbarossa* for his red beard? That ad-Din?" asked Addy. Kat nodded, her mouth engaged in biting a gold thread from the end of a row of neat cross-stitches on a fine linen handkerchief she was embroidering for Baldwin. "Prithee, do not mention this Barbarossa in the presence of Lord Seton. Until the infidels learned he was of noble birth, he passed years as a galley slave on a mammoth vessel among two hundred or more oarsmen, most delirious from lack of sleep, for they almost never were unshackled from their stations and dozed in place perhaps one hour in twelve for years upon end."

"For food we were given rotten biscuit, for drink seawater, or worse. I would have pawned my very soul for a drop of fresh water as others about me died for thirst." The women turned toward the sound of a voice both harsh and heartbreaking, to see Arthur Seton striding into the chamber, a small, rough-hewn, muscular man. There was a cold, bored expression on his scarred face, which revealed an arrogant shyness as he continued talking in his clipped, elegant speech.

" 'Twas my wife's cousin, my sister's husband, Thomas Montfort, found the culprit who stole the ransom. Tom made it right. Got me free. My wife, you know, had long been in love with her cousin Tom and . . . who be that, with the aspect of an angel and the carriage of a queen?" he asked, staring suddenly at Kat, who had been casting sweet herbs upon the fire and now turned to the room. At Seton's query, she stood still—tall, willowy, and slender in a green silk gown with gold slashes, the skirt shot with gold, a gold lace ruff framing her face. Under the man's fierce, blue-eyed scrutiny, a blush rose from her throat to the line of her honey-toned hair piled in curls atop her head.

" 'Tis Katesby Dalton, Arthur. She is abashed at your forwardness, sir," derided Addy.

"How now, brother?" wondered Cary. "What brings you here just as we are readying for a return to Court?"

"On the morrow we are all, by royal command, ordered to greet the king, who is making a progress to Bath with his court to take the waters for his cankered leg. Beaumarais this way comes also, with the de Morelys, father and son, and—"

"Lord Seton, Baldwin is to be at Bath, do you say?" asked Kat with a glow of delight on her face and joy in her voice.

"*And* Harry de Morely, Kat, your *suitor,*" Addy reminded her protégée.

"And is my Lord Tom here at Rockingham with you, Arthur?" asked Cary with a smile, gathering up the baby and moving toward the door.

"Indeed he is, at the stables," the viscount replied as Cary swept past him in a rush to see her husband. "My lady wife ne'er greets me with such delight," complained

Arthur. "In truth, Mistress Dalton, she does not even trouble to rise from her chair to welcome me and see after my comfort." Addy and Arthur exchanged bruising, cold glances before he turned upon his heel and left the hall.

"He is a passionate, angry, distant man. He was badly hurt and is stiff in his broken hands now. After his dungeon-shackled years, he has forgotten how to disclose his softer sentiments," stated Addy wearily. "If indeed he has any."

"Did you truly once love your cousin, Lord Tom?" Kat asked with great curiosity and a sadness.

"Yes, all my life. I made the mistake of telling my husband so. Though Arthur had captured my heart entire, he has never forgotten nor forgiven me for my earlier tenderness, though I knew *him* not. His jealousy has shadowed our life together, and now, though I love my lord in my own way, it is not *his* way, it seems." Lady Addy sighed. "We have been sundered since I was constrained to add to his scars by slashing his face with my riding crop when he sought to have me, in the stable loft, as if I were some trollop milkmaid. Wine turns him barbarous." Addy's hauteur and indignation were tinged with sadness.

"I am sorry, Addy," said Kat sorrowfully. "But . . . a stable loft mightn't be so awful a place . . ." She swallowed the rest of her thought under Addy's disapproving glare, which turned slowly to a look of alarm, then comprehension.

"Be off with you now," she scoffed, blushing, a rare thing for cool, worldly Lady Addy. "Ready yourself to leave for Bath on the morrow, to meet the king and Norland." *And Baldwin Beaumarais,* thought Kat with a wonderful, enfeebling rush of pleasure, imagining how lovely it would be to meet Win in a stable loft or barn fragrant with the scent of hay and dried herbs, and the warm smells and quiet sounds of animals below.

* * *

"The city of Bath is situated in the pleasant bottom land of the Avon Valley, the river of the same name flowing through the town to the Bristol Channel and the sea. It is surrounded by great hills out of which arise springs of health-giving waters which course so abundantly to the town by sundry winding pathways and runnels, that every house therein receives, by means of leaden pipes, its share of *Aquae Sulis*, hot water, as the old Romans named the place."

"Indeed, Lord Seton? Romans?" asked Kat, glancing from the viscount to his silent lady, with whom she rode toward Bath in their fine carriage. She sat, still and as careful as a child, so as not to abuse her unaccustomed, rich new clothes—a long, wine-colored velvet coat with gold buttons open at the throat to show a ruff sewn with pearls. Her head was held erect as the ladies had instructed, and also to keep from displacing a daintily cocked beaver-fur hat trimmed with the same sable fur as the muff in which her much-oiled, nearly soft, nearly white hands were sheltering. She was trying to imagine the look of all amazement Win would offer when he saw her thus, and the words he would speak, but she was distracted by Arthur Seton, who had not taken his fierce blue eyes from her nor ceased to talk since the start of the journey. It had begun some hours before and would continue several more.

"Indeed, Mistress Dalton. Bath is a place of great antiquity. You will see between the South and West Gates the antique head of a man with great locks of hair as Romans have upon old coins. Between the South and North Gates stands a Hercules holding a serpent in each hand and hard by a man afoot with raised sword and buckler. Farther on a greyhound is running past two naked images embracing. Oh, there are sundry antique heads with ruffled hair all bout the place, eh, Adelaide?" Arthur asked, not even glancing in his wife's direction. She made no reply, only wriggled in her seat as if to increase her distance from her husband, an impossible end to accomplish in the confines of the carriage.

"There are three large communal baths at Bath. One is called Cross Bath for the great cross atop a stone pagoda built at the center of its pool. It once served lepers and those suffering pocks and scabs and such, though such unfortunates are not seen in these modern days, for bathing has become as much a sport and diversion as a cure. The Common Bath, also called Hot Bath for the extreme temperature of its waters, is frequented by common folk, many suffering a variety of ills—palsy, dimness of sight, dullness of hearing, colic and ill digestion, the kidney stone, and so forth. These baths stand in St. John's Hospital Street, several hundred yards apart.

"The third, King's Bath, in the very middle of the town, is built with high stone walls concealing two-and-thirty private niches and arches within. These are reserved for the nobility—the king and his friends, both men and women—who are able to enjoy the deep blue spring waters separately from each other, thus preserving modesty within the recesses and alcoves, unmolested by the lascivious goings-on which occur at the Cross and Common baths."

"Indeed, Lord Arthur?" said Kat again, politely, though her eyelids were drooping with sleep induced by the rocking of the carriage and the drone of his voice. It continued still when she awoke much later to the sound of trumpets and drums proclaiming the arrival of the king's cortege at Bath, his outriders and wagons obstructing the road ahead of them. *Baldwin!* was the very first thought that came to Kat's mind, and she leaned eagerly to the carriage window, hoping to espy him also on his way to Bath.

* * *

"I have come hither," Henry announced at table that evening, "to strengthen my afeebled members, assist my lively forces, heal the green wound upon my leg, and disperse sundry bodily ills and griefs which no compound medicine more speedily cures than the waters of Bath, eh, Turner?"

"So I believe, Your Royal Highness. The springs draw their forces from sulphur and saltpeter," the physician replied to the king, who was ensconced upon the dais at the center of a groaning table in the Abbey of Bath. He was surrounded by some of his favorites and others less so. Henry looked about with pleasure to find Lord Tom, Viscount Seton, and their lady wives in attendance upon him. Harry de Morely, appearing wan and gray, Henry noted, and his son, Charles, in the pink of health, were there flanking a most beauteous young lady not known to him, the king observed with curiosity before his fond gaze passed over several of his most fearless and stalwart soldiers who were present as well—Lords Lovell, Randall, Pynings, Wyatt, Carew, Browne, Gray, and Greene. Less loved but equally indispensable were Francis Wiltenham; bespectacled, pink little agent Burgess Blunt; and the most unsavory but persuasive torturer, Rattcliffe.

"Where is Beaumarais?" roared Henry, pouting. "I asked for Beaumarais."

"He is delayed, Majesty," answered the earl, "attending to a matter of business for me, as I have been prevented by poor health from traveling far. He sends this list by my hand, to Mr. Wiltenham." Harry flourished a sheet of foolscap covered in script.

"What ails you, Harry?" asked the king.

"First 'twas ague, then catarrh, followed by a bout of gout and now a dull pain in the innards which robs me of appetite."

"You've come to the right place then, Harry. If you can't get cured of your ills here . . ." The king hesitated, but not long ". . . if not here, then nowhere. Where have you dispatched Beaumarais?"

"To Colchester and thereabouts, with a miniature portrait of a lady to . . . Methinks Baldwin is sure to be here forthwith, sire." Kat, who had been looking everywhere for Win in vain, was delighted and relieved to hear this news and showed her pleasure in her charming, crooked smile. The king smiled back at her.

"Who be you, lady fair, gracing my table with your youth and beauty?" he asked.

"Majesty, before you sits Katesby Dalton, commoner and innkeeper, transformed by myself and the Lady Montfort in accord with your directive," answered Lady Addy proudly.

"No! Indeed?" exclaimed the king. "The very same innkeeper you wish to wed, de Morely?"

"Indeed, yes, Majesty," the earl answered warily, not knowing what to expect from the obese, exasperating monarch sitting and staring, glittering in his gold-trimmed garb, his hands heavily spotted and speckled with jewels, his face an unhealthy suet yellow, his red beard sparse and straggly. Would he claim Kat for himself or grant permission for de Morely to wed her, or neither of those possibilities?

"I toast the lady's health and yours, de Morely. I toast all your healths"—he smiled, looking about the table—"for I am in a great sweetness of temper this day, my friends! Want to know why?"

"Oh, aye, sire!"

"Hear, hear, Majesty! Hear, hear!"

"Indeed, yes, my lord!" These cries of encouragement and others came simultaneously as Henry sat back grinning like a great cat, a lion, who had just swallowed a bird equal to him in size and station.

"It pleases me that my brother kings, my rivals Charles

of Spain and Francis of France, are going to war again—against each other! It gladdens me that Francis encourages the Turk to pursue the Spaniard. If I could contact Suleiman, I would turn him upon Francis *and* Charles. But, be that as it may, I'm delighted that far and wide, on land and sea, war seethes elsewhere, everywhere—in Germany, Bohemia, the Balkan lands, North Afrique, even in India and in the new Spanish lands of Peru and Mexico! It delights me that this fellow Calvin incites the Huguenots of France against the Pope, that the princelings of the north supported by Francis and Charles fight amongst themselves. And it pleases me, too, that Scotland is as good as in our grip!"

"Ach, Scotland. Who wants it? 'Tis a barren, wild, cold land with not a tree standing for firewood or house timber," grumbled Lord Randall. "There's no spoils to speak of neither, in war."

" 'Who that intendeth France to win, with Scotland let him begin,' " answered Montfort. "So said Thomas Cromwell twenty years ago, and it is still as true this day, for we do not want a French stronghold to our north. I have arranged a meeting with James Hamilton, Earl of Arran, whom we will help to become regent. I will broach the matter of betrothal of the infant queen of Scotland to Prince Edward, Majesty."

"Montfort, I am served by many fearless soldiers, but you can turn your hand to soldiering or negotiating, as need be. I value you specially for that and for your skill at the tables. We only await Beaumarais to begin the games. I will win all your fortunes from you, for Providence is with me. Know how I know? I'll tell you. I have found me a wife."

Oos and aahs and exclamations went round the table, goblets were raised, toasts made, and then an anticipatory silence descended, broken after a time by Kat.

'Majesty, you keep us in terrible suspense,'' she burbled. "Tell us, do, who the most fortunate bride is to be."

"Do, sire," added Harry de Morely, with a smile of relief.

"You will guess. He who first names the lady will win a prize of me of his or her desiring. Who will hazard a conjecture?" No one would, and Henry was in his glory, testing his friends.

"A clue. She is a widow and wealthy." There were no guesses. "She is young, twenty-eight, but not too young to be a good mother to my three motherless children." Harry de Morely whispered with his son. They nodded each to the other and waited. "She is a relation of the noble Throgmortons. She is rich, gracious, and noble," said Henry. His little eyes were mischievous. "Wait! Can none of you tell me her name? The lady, who is slim and dark-haired, has been twice married and widowed. . . ."

"Married for the first time at all of ten years of age to Lord Borough of Gainsborough, sire?" asked de Morely with a smile. "A man who was then near to sixty. And was the widow's second husband John Neville, Lord Latimer, himself twenty years her senior? Since you do not say me nay, Majesty, I say 'tis exemplary Catherine Parr you would make your next Queen of the Realm!"

"You've got it, de Morely, you've got it! I shall shine in comparison to the old men she had before. She will be skilled in the ways of pleasing and comforting a more mellowed spouse, eh? Well, make your request of me, Harry, so we may get on with the festivities."

"I ask your blessing, Henry, upon my taking this lovely lady in wedlock."

"By God's most precious soul, Norland, I grant you leave to wed your lady love. Music! Music of the flute and the recorder. Who will play? Who will sing? I know! I shall begin with a ditty from Wynkyn de Worde's song book:"

If idleness be the chief master of vices all,
Then who can say,
But mirth and play
Is best of all, nonny nonny!

"The king is in fine voice tonight, my dear." Harry smiled upon Kat, who stood beside him, shaken but determined, for the time had come, she knew, to speak the direct, absolute truth. "My dear?" he prompted under the cover of the noise and laughter about them. "Will you make me the gladdest man in this room by consenting to become my wife?"

"Harry, *dear* Harry, you do me very great honor, but I cannot wed you, ever." There were tears in Kat's eyes.

"Because you do not love me? I care not. Only take my love and I'll not ask for anything in return, merely to live in hope that you may come to love me someday, in some way. Think on this a fortnight longer, for you bring alive in me thoughts of my dear Mary. I grow more . . . more fond of you by the moment, Katesby." His narrow face was pained, eyes longing.

"You will have my answer then, again, my lord, if you wish, but it will be unchanged from that you have just had, for I must disclose to you that I love another. He loves me not, yet I will never love you." Kat set her soft hand along Harry's cheek; then she turned away and left the chamber.

Chapter 25

The night was mild for early April. The heavens were low, and to Kat it seemed the moon and stars were being tossed, glittering, about the sky by a warm wind. She had been told there was good civil order and little menace in the city, that proper courtesy was shown to visitors of all degrees, at all hours, and so she walked unescorted and at her ease to the Hospitaller's Inn at which she was lodged. The hospice was situated hard by the singing River Avon above Bath Bridge and she ambled slowly, listening to the song of the water and aching in her heart for Win, needing to know where in the world he was and what on earth kept him from her.

In her rooms she undressed with the unnecessary assistance of her "lady in waiting," the servant the earl had insisted attend her. The chambermaid counted out loud the last ten of the hundred firm brush strokes she applied to Kat's gleaming hair; then she made ready to quit the room.

"Will that be all, my lady?" asked the pleasant, competent, and quiet-spoken woman, some years older than her new mistress.

"Ellen, how does one go about entering into one of the baths?" Kat asked.

"A young lady is taken in a closed chair, clothed in her bathing dress—that is, a smock or shift—to Cross Bath. There soft music plays and serving women attend you with little floating basins of nosegays and snuff and the like. You must not take it ill, my lady, if a gentleman or two or three drift over from the men's side of the bath, to speak with their ladies and engage in lovemaking for the space of an hour or two, for the ease of the setting is conducive to such amusement. Also, ma'am, it is thought by many that the exceptional waters here procure conception. There are couples who go to sport at the baths for that reason alone."

"Oh? Oh, indeed!" replied Kat with a blush, startled. Instantly, Baldwin, never far from her thoughts, leapt into her mind's eye in all his gorgeous glory, grinning provocatively at her as he stood, waist deep, in blue pool water beneath a curved stone arch, the naked muscles of his chest and shoulders gleaming wet, his hand beckoning.

"I'll guide you thither in the morning, miss, and enlighten you to the ways here," added Ellen.

"I am not tired in the least. I may find sleep elusive," said Kat. "A hot soak, 'tis said, relaxes one in mind and body. Is it not possible to go into one of the lauded havens of ease and comfort in the night's small hours?"

" 'Tis possible, indeed. The baths are shut up only from half after ten in the forenoon until one of the clock after noon, and again at the strike of midnight for a brief time, for rinsing while the stone is buffed clean and burnished. Goers-in soon after the hot water sluices have overflowed will find the fresh water reeking of sulphur and bubbling as does a seething pot. Do you wish me to take you now, at once, milady?"

"Thank you, no, Ellen. Go now to your warm bed."

Kat smiled, understanding from her own experience how dearly a working woman, busy from before dawn until past dark, craved sleep. Moreover, unused as she was to having an attendant, or anyone, trailing after her, she favored venturing about on her own. No sooner had Ellen gratefully gone to her rest than Kat made ready to explore Bath and the baths. Loath to soil her superb new clothes in damp and dripping environs, she donned her old work dress and the worn cape she had managed to keep out of Addy's efficient hands, twisted her hair into a braid, and slipped out again into the deserted street. She looked left, then right before setting out toward the center of the city, where the King's Bath was to be found.

Kat, crossing Bath Bridge, paused for a time to watch the moonlit river slide beneath before she started on again, and had not gone far when she thought she heard the sound of footfalls behind her. She slowed, listened only to silence, moved on, and heard steps again. She was being followed! The once-homeless urchin who had survived upon London's infamous slum streets was unnerved to feel a cold runnel of fear rise along her spine. *I should have waited till the morrow,* she thought, that or kept poor Ellen awake to come with her this night.

Past experience and instinct prompted her to sidestep into an archway and press back against the stone, holding her breath. She waited for what felt an eternity, peered out, then skittered on tiptoe, keeping close to a wall, to the next cranny. And *knew* then, beyond doubt, she was the prey of some hunter after . . . what? She glanced about to assess her situation and found cupids and vines entwined about a gate that opened to the press of her shoulder. She darted through it and her senses were assaulted by the great sulphurous reek of Ellen's description accompanied by the sound of water a-bubble. She had fortuitously stumbled upon the King's Bath, and there was no one there but she.

The time, Kat reasoned, would be just past the midnight hour, for the place had recently been rinsed and polished. The air was yet steamy and hot, the stone benches, she found, warm to the touch. She sat well back upon one in a deep niche, getting her breath, praying she had eluded her tracker. Just as she commenced to compose herself, the sound of slow, steady, advancing footfalls close by wrenched a yelp of fright from her throat. Fright at once gave way to irritation, then panic, for she realized she had revealed her exact hiding place. The stalker was there, so close she heard the intake of his breath, then felt him reach for her in the dark. He found her, gripped her shoulders, and raised her from her place.

"Keep off if you be treacherous and full of guile, sir! Likewise if you are not!" she ordered, meaning to shout, though her voice came out in a birdlike peep. "I will not long be alone in this place. You will caught in the act of committing your nef-nef-nefarious deed," she went on in a more normal, though quavering tone. "My friend, who comes apace to join me here, will drop you direct with a dire blow into the rotten mouth of Hell, sir, if any harm has come to me, and . . . and furthermore, I've a dirk of me own under me cloak, which will plunge between the brow and eyelid of a man straight into his brain and kill him outright as happened to Will Wotan in front of the Maidenhead Inn by the Townditch. I . . . I would do it, I say! Keep back!"

Kat's pursuer, whom she could not see in the mist and the dark, released her shoulders and leapt sprightly backward. Kat, straining for a sound in the dark, waited for what seemed an unbearably long time before the sound of slow, deliberate applause echoed round and round the stone walls. Then she heard a deep, laughing voice rumble in the dark.

"Bravissima, lady, as the Italians say, brava positively on

that masterful performance! Finished with your monologue, are you?"

"I . . . wh . . . what . . . who . . . ?" she sputtered, starting to smile to herself.

"Oh, me, Kat! Oh, my! That was quite the speech, I must say!" exclaimed Baldwin jovially, coming so close to Kat, she could make out his smiling eyes in the dimness, but only his eyes for he was attired from nose to toe in the black garb of Win Chance.

"Where's Beau, you . . . trickster?" She sighed, too relieved and too angry that he had affrighted her, most of all too much in love, to say more at that moment.

"He's otherwise engaged. I'm here in his stead, to make certain you haven't forgot all he taught you." Win winked and Kat knew he was grinning behind his scarf, before the look in his eyes turned so deep and hot, it took her breath.

"Offering me a lesson, are you?" she asked, her voice quavering again, but not with fright. She undid his mask and, smiling, shaped his matchless, handsome face with her two hands.

"If you'd like one. I had in mind a refresher exercise, a bit of . . . review." She cherished the smile on his succulent lips and adored his eyes, as green as jade.

"Oh, aye, a lesson," she whispered, her intention to stay out of his arms, to be all unemotional and ladylike, forgotten, perhaps to be resurrected at some time, irrelevant now. Slowly, he leaned to set his lips to hers and kiss her, and she felt his heart beating fast. Her own was in her throat.

"Is not this is an interesting turn of affairs?" she said, low. He hardly heard, didn't reply, just yearned once more for her warm, strong, pillowy lips, and so took them again gently, then vigorous with possession, and he felt her melt into him, her body supple, shaping to his in a warm welcome of sweet homecoming

"Wait," he whispered, leading her to a warm stone

bench, spreading his cape upon it, then hers, his shirt, her shift, the layers of their clothing concealing their bodies peeling free and mounding to form into a soft nest upon which they sank, she below, he above just at the start, before the arrangement shifted, changing, as their bodies joined, parting only to recombine. "It becomes . . . unclear to me who is the master and who the disciple here," Win rasped as went into her and out, and she arched her body each time as if to hold him, to keep him from drawing away, but wanting, nearly as much as the pressure of the fullness within her, the thrust of his next drive.

They were side by side stretched upon the bench, then he above, and she below.

She perched upon his knees and he thrust up into her, holding her back against him with his arm about her waist, his other hand cupping her breast until she faced him. He tongued her nipples, took each one carefully between the abrading rows of his teeth, gnawed delicately, excruciatingly, bringing each to stand firmer than before. Then she sat over his thighs and sheathed him, scuffing the sensitized tips of her breasts against his chest, her mouth working upon his.

He was a ravenous lover, she bold, inventive with a need almost unquenchable. They held on to emotions too powerful to articulate, hoarded sensations, clung to these moments as if they were the last they would ever share, for that was what Win knew and Kat sensed but resisted to recognize.

In the first glow of the early spring dawn, they were still together, drifting in the warm waters of the bath, Kat pressing the round curve of her bottom to the firm ridges of his thighs and moving against the tight, hard muscles of his surging belly, taking him, holding him inside

"Practice surely does makes perfect, eh, Kitten?" he whispered against the nape of her neck seconds before he moaned and tensed, jolted by a spasm of release that was still rolling when hers had ended. He remained within her, holding on to to her in the warm water.

"When will we . . . ?" She curled back into him.

"Meet again? Tonight." His arms were hard, encircling.

"Here?"

"Not here. There's . . . things I must tell you, and if we come here . . ."

"Tell me now." She pressed her lips to his neck.

"Has the king given Harry an answer, about you?"

"Yes, but what's that have to do with . . ."

He released her, climbed from the bath, and extended his hand to lift her out.Win looked longingly at Kat in the brightening dawn light as they dressed. She coiled Chance's scarf about his neck; he fastened the hook at the top of her shift.

"You're different, Kat, changed since last I saw you, " he murmured.

"I thought you'd never notice," she answered, surprised he had taken so long to remark on it, until she recalled she had come in her old clothes with her hair down.

"I'm not changed . . . really." She smiled. "Some, but just the surface."

"Ah. You are altered *some*, on the surface, for him, de Morely."

"Not for you, Lord knows," she dissembled.

"Never change for me, Kat, " he insisted, thoughtful all at once.

"Now you tell me," she bantered in an effort to make light of what had become a solemn moment. Again, her instincts warned her that something was terribly amiss. She quelled them.

"I want to think of you always just the way you are now," he said. She caressed his face, distressed by these words, though she tried not to be, dreading what might come next, but he said nothing dire.

"Your hands have surely changed, and not a little, that's

certain," he said and forced a grin as he placed his larger hand over hers. "Fare thee well, until tomorrow . . . until later, for it is already tomorrow," he added before he wrapped Chance's scarf about his face and strode out into the morning light.

He thought about her all that day, as he tended to various strategic matters.

And she thought of him and could barely wait to be with him once more, even as she toured Bath in the company of the king.

"I sent the dastard collector of Peter's pence hence, packing back to Rome long since," Henry told her happily. "That was when I broke with the Pope and took over his lands in England. One of the better moves I have made in my reign, if I must say so myself." A chorus of affirmations arose from the courtiers who followed.

"Good move, Majesty."

"Fine stroke, sire."

"Most excellent decision, Your Noble Highness!"

"As are all your decisions, sire."

"Flatters and fawners, all," Henry said, playfully conspiratorial, to Kat.

"They had best be, sire, if they are fond of their heads. 'Tis said."

"Ha!" roared Henry, pleased. "A woman of spirit you are, and appearing most joyful, especially glowing and charmingly animated this day, my dear, in anticipation, I do not doubt, of your marriage to my old, ah . . . friend, de Morely. I'll come to your wedding."

"Thank you, Majesty. You do me great honor," she answered, a bit crestfallen about disappointing Harry and, it now appeared, Henry as well. The king took no notice of her momentary change of mood.

"Here we are at the Abbey Church of St. Peter and St.

Paul, with all the carved angels of Jacob's Ladder adorning it. 'Twas built in my father's day, on the spot an old Norman Church once stood, and Saxon antiquities before it, and earlier still Roman temples of Minerva, goddess of waters and such. Come, come along, for I would show to you now the great west window and fan vault ceiling of Bath Abbey, an architectural marvel. I have a special liking for fine and curious masonry, my dear. Thus, I have had built by the King's Works many excellent structures throughout the realm. My father started his reign with nine residences and added four. I began with thirteen and will have fifty before I've done. Come, come along quickly, child," commanded the king. "We must take our drink of the waters at Town Hall in High Street at once lest we be late for dinner, and if late for dinner, then late for the play and then for the evening ball, where there never fails to be a great deal of good company." Henry then scurried forward with alarming speed for one of his great bulk and sundry infirmities, his couriers stumbling after.

"What is it about this place," Kat said, giggling to Addy, beside whom she fell back into step, "which prompts all manner of men to lecture upon it?"

"Men." Addy shrugged, rolled her eyes heavenward, and slipped her arm through Kat's. "I heeded your counsel, Katesby, about . . . about love in a stable loft," she whispered.

"Oh, aye? And?"

"You were quite right. It is not at all a bad situation for an assignation," said the lady with a frank, contented smile, leaving Kat to wonder, because of the use of the word 'assignation', with whom Lady Addy had situated herself in the loft.

"I'm told the baths are . . . used for the same . . . thing," she answered.

"Indeed. I've heard the same," answered Addy with a thoughtful look.

* * *

Kat waited for Win on the bank of the River Avon, near the Bath Bridge, in the warmth of the evening that held the breath of spring in its breeze. Daffodils were showing on the sun-warmed hillsides even as patches of snow remained on the ground in north-facing shady corners.

Who is she, really? Kat wondered, looking at her own reflection in the moonlit mirror of the gently moving river. Her hair was pulled smoothly back, piled up under a fresh white cap and dancing dangles of gold and pearl shimmered at her ears. As she pondered, another reflection appeared beside her own, Win, leaning over her, a rainbow of ribbons in his hand.

With amazement, Win had espied Kat in the lane dressed in her new finery. It was the first time he had beheld her in a gown shaped to her tall form. She was marvelously slim and graceful in a rich maroon velveteen dress, with a deep white collar running down the bodice, drawing the eye to an amazing little waist. Unseen by her, he had followed as she crossed over the bridge and made her way to the riverside. Coming upon her, still unaware of his presence, he silently celebrated the fineness of her willowy neck, as elegant as any he ever had seen on any woman, of any rank, anywhere. The soft hollow cleft between the pair of columns supporting her pretty head was endearing, enticing, and he had been about to set his lips there when she saw his refection in the water and smiled at it.

"I brought these"—he fluttered the ribbons in the air—"for a girl who'd not ever had a frill her life, but just look at her now, a duchess to be, adorned." Kat set her hand in his, and when he had drawn her to her feet, he tossed the ribbons into the river.

Poised on the moon-flooded riverbank, they felt a

reserve unknown between them before, that of a man and woman, newly met, looking with interest into each other's eyes, hers the green of tropic seas, his jade.

" 'Tis a nice night," said Win.

"Spring is in the air," answered Kat.

"The Ides of March has passed," said Win.

"What was it you came to say?" asked Kat.

"I'm going away, Kat. I won't be back."

"How can you just . . . leave me?" She spoke reasonably while inside she reeled.

" 'Tis easy, sweetheart. You're well set up now, and those others I care for will soon be. New worlds call out to me and long have. I long to sail unpathed waters, step upon far, undreamed-of shores. You know that." He shrugged as if indifferent, needing her to hate him, doubting he'd be able to go otherwise. "I'll miss you, certes, but . . . when you are wed, and I as well . . ." His words trailed off. "Remember one thing, eh?"

"What? That you'll always be watching? That if ever I have need of you all I must do is blazon it, whisper it, utter it, just think of it, and you'll find me, where'er I be?"

"No. Remember this instead. You let me see the very best I could be."

Kat made no reply. This wasn't her footloose, flirty rogue talking, even if it was the role he was playing at the moment, or attempting to. This was a man in love who didn't know so and would not believe her if she told him. Perhaps he'd realize it himself one distant future day, in some faraway place, and then he'd come home to her, perchance. She'd wait.

"Aye, then, good-bye. Marry Harry. Forget me."

"Don't tell me what to do, Beaumarais! We're nothing to each other now," she replied, words that would soon ring tragically true and come back to torment her every waking thought and dreadful dream for a very long time.

Now she turned and flounced away to show her indifference and hide the tears welling in her eyes.

Later, after he'd gone, she would return to this place on the riverbank to claim his ribbon rainbow snagged not far from the shore on a protrusion of gray rocks.

Chapter 26

" 'Chances have been sighted hither and yon, from one end of the land to the other,' " read Thomas Montfort, perusing a dispatch just handed him by a messenger from London. The marquess was at table in his great hall at Rockingham with his wife, his cousin, her husband who was his friend, Arthur, and the increasingly frail-looking Harry de Morely.

"Chances?" asked the earl's son, Charlie, who spent all his time of late, Montfort noted, looking adoringly at his future stepmother, Kat Dalton. The boy, known as Stuttering Charlie, a card counter, poet, magus, a wizard at chesse-play, was now due a new epithet, Lord Tom decided, for the future earl's speech rarely stumbled of late.

"Chances. Outlaw Win Chances," Montfort clarified.

"Is there any news in your missive of Baldwin Beaumarais, Lord Tom?" Kat asked.

"No one has caught sight of him since he left the hanging list with the earl," answered Thomas. "But you know Baldwin, Katesby. We all do. He'll be along to join us when the time's right. I expect he'll make an appearance at the hanging, if not before."

"Prisoners are to be collected, orders Beaumarais, from the London gaols of Clink, Breadstreet, King's Bench, Bridewell, Newgate, and Ludgate," said Harry. "Gaols in other assizes all over the land will be relieved of certain lawbreakers. Even Bedlam is to yield up a pair of women, a mother and daughter thought by some to be mad and by others to be clever witches feigning madness."

"What did Wiltenham say to all this?" inquired Arthur.

"He growled," answered Charlie, who had actually delivered the list into the spymaster's hand. "He was a man bereft of words. But he did agree to all Beaumarais asked on advice from the fat, pink little agent, Blunt, and wretched Rattcliffe. They want Win Chance in the worst way." Charlie looked at Kat. "And if Rattcliffe ever does get him . . ."

"He will not. Chance is no fool," Kat interjected as much to reassure herself as her friends. "Where is this event—the hanging—to take place? St. Paul's Yard or Newgate Press Yard or . . ."

"Baldwin's instructions to Wiltenham instruct that scaffolds are to be built at Lizard Point on Cornwall, near Falmouth Town," said Charlie. "All the doomed are to be transported there, under heavy guard."

"Why Cornwall, of all places?" Addy wondered, not lifting her eyes from her embroidery, a very delicate work of linen and lawn on which she had for some days been working with especial care.

"Chance will be denied a route of escape if he attempts to free his friends from the hangman's hempen window, for Cornwall is a narrow peninsula, nowhere more narrow than at the promontory of Lizard Point, with cliffs on three sides above treacherous waters far below," Arthur Seton said as he sat comfortably beside his wife, a friendly hand lying upon her shoulder, an unusual occurrence noted by all. "An unbroken column of soldiers could line the land right across from Bristol Channel to the English Channel forming a solid impediment to escape. Will Win Chance take such a chance to save his friends?"

"We will have an opportunity to learn the answer to that question first hand," noted Thomas. "Enclosed with my news from town is a formal Invitation to a Hanging. The king orders us all to Cornwall, along with half of London, I don't doubt, for what promises to be one of the great outings of the decade if not the century. Not since the meeting on The Field of the Cloth of Gold years ago, of the young Kings Henry and Francis, has such excitement attended an assemblage. The Pilgrimage to Cornwall, as this business is being designated, is anticipated with the excitement of a universal holiday, a feast day and May Day combined. We had best make an early start. The road leading to the cliff at the western tip of Cornwall will be clogged and clotted with folk afoot, ahorse, in wagons and carriages and litter chairs, and with throngs of his majesty's soldiers and agents, all bent on one thing: seizing Win Chance."

"But if his likenesses, who have been seen all over the realm, also join the crowd at Lizard Point, how will the sheriffs and officers, or anyone for that matter, know which Chance is the real Chance?" mused Kat, certain Win was up to something very clever, wishing she knew exactly what it was.

Brother Truckle had declined the king's invitation, though it had bordered on a command, to take the waters at Bath and had instead returned to his priory to tend to his charges and await the more complete return of his encyclopedic, now erratic, memory. Full recall for his patient was unlikely, predicted Dr. Turner, for the old fellow had been notoriously absentminded even before his misadventure. The physician suggested, however, that familiar faces and surroundings might stimulate the friar's brain somewhat. He had been correct in this, for no sooner had Rooster set foot in own austere cell at the poorhouse than he recollected how useful his intermittent deafness could be—and the flagon of spirits he had packed into the pallet that served as his bed, which was rolled in a corner of the cell just as he'd left it. "More'n anything, *that'll* twit me brain," he told himself, making straight for it.

Baldwin Beaumarais arrived at Graie Friars a few days after Rooster had returned there, to find the old man relating to a cluster of children the story of St. Macarius of Alexandria and the Grateful Hyena. Rather than interrupt, he waited at the edge of the group and listened, thinking of his own childhood days when he and Kat had raptly listened to Brother Truckle relating this same or another tale of beasts and saints of ancient days.

"It happened one day as the saint was sitting praying in his cell that a hyena, weeping, came to him with a tiny whelp in her mouth, which she set down before the holy man. Macarius took the little creature up in his hands, turned it this way and that to see what ailed it, and saw that the baby was blind in its two eyes."

"Me brother is blind in his one eye," said a small boy, one of those in the circle at Rooster's feet.

"We know all about your brother, so hold your tongue. Let Friar Truckle tell the tale," complained another child, his suggestion seconded by a chorus of ayes from the others. "What did St. Macarius do about the blind hyena?"

"He observed it for a time. Then he spat upon its face and signed upon its eyes with his fingers, and lo, at once the creature opened its eyes to see and went straight to its mother's teat to suckle.

"The next day, the old saint heard a knock upon his door and opened it to again find the grateful hyena without, this time covered in a fleecy sheepskin, thick with wool. 'Where hast thou been and how come by this?' Macarius asked. 'If thou hast eaten a sheep, I will not accept this gift from you.' The hyena struck her head upon the ground and bent her knees as if praying so that the saint was moved and said, 'I will not take this unless thou makest me a promise, that thou wilt not vex the poor by eating their sheep.' The hyena moved her head up and down. 'That from this day forth you will not kill a creature alive but wilt eat thy prey only when thou find it dead.' Again she shook her head up and down, and the old man knew that he had done God's ordering and that it was God alone who had given understanding to the hyena as He had to the lion in its den with Daniel. From that day forth, the hyena became as a scavenger, useful in God's eyes, and the old holy man slept upon the hyena's gift, the wineskin—the sheepskin rather, for the rest of his days.

"Zounds! I remember," the friar suddenly exclaimed. "The wineskin! Katesby Dalton's wineskin. It is hid beneath this very room in the lower cellar of the abbey. Baldwin, I know the hiding place of the ring you sought of me, you and the False Chance who near killed me to get at it."

Each carrying a torch, Rooster and Win sent rats squeaking and scurrying before them as they followed damp spiral stone steps many levels below the abbey's basement to a dank chamber behind a heavy, studded door that opened with a terrible wrenching creak of rusted hinges only after Baldwin's strenuous exertions.

"They are worthless tokens, mostly," Rooster said of the scattering of bundles in the room. "They come with our lost or abandoned babes. We keep these little comforters and dresses, lockets, rings, for they are the only ties to the past these youngsters will ever have. After they go out from here, most of them never come looking for their lineage. Now, let me see . . . Here is a thing of interest, perhaps even of value, if the rats have not gnawed through the wineskin and leaked the contents." Rooster held up a tar-coated leather pouch. "I was told, methinks, though I'm not definite, that it held a rare old wine, pressed from Mediterranean grapes and carried to England in one of the last of the Roman ships to ply the seas between Gaeletha and Dover. And 'tis still full!" Rooster smacked his lips. "Are you for a taste, Baldwin, boy? I do not think Kat would begrudge us it. Do you?" Baldwin didn't and Rooster stuck his torch in a holder on the wall and set to work on the tar seal.

"Where is the ring?" Win asked. "And her ribbon?"

"I don't recall, not yet, leastways," grumbled Rooster, sitting on a stone ledge. "The little dress she wore is there in that parcel. Perchance I put the ring in a pocket. Ah, Baldwin"—Rooster smiled fondly—"I remember her clear as day in her little blue velvet dress, looking up at me with the greenest eyes I'd ever seen, eyes showing courage and fear both, and that pretty ring dangling on a ribbon about her neck. Well, is it there? An inscription could reveal a good deal, if there is one."

Baldwin was holding up the dress to his gaze, imagining the brave little Kat he had not known, his heart aching with desire for the woman she had become, the one he knew and loved better than anyone in the world. And would nevermore see or touch or hold again.

"There's no ring, Rooster," he replied with disappointment. "Pass that wine over here, if you please, if 'tis drinkable still."

"Blanes, pox, blotch, and biles, but this a clammy, cold room. Clammy . . . clams, barnacles, bivalves, and *oysters!*" Truckle's eyes opened wide. "A fishy man brought her to me to keep and how the tears did flow from the fellow's eyes, for he loved that baby as his own. Listen, Baldwin! Hear me," exclaimed Rooster with excitement. "Her mother was an uplander who came to Essex and succumbed to lowland swamp fever when her baby was about eighteen months old, giving her over to the fisherfolk to raise. They kept her until . . . the child's grandfather, I think it was, *Kat's* grandfather, discovered the girl and demanded she be delivered to the orphanage. Her name was never to be mentioned again by that fisherman, as long as he lived, not to anyone, on threat of pain of death."

"Who was the wicked grandsire, who the sire?" Win was fervent to know, pacing excitedly as he and Rooster handed the wineskin back and forth.

"That . . . I . . . cannot just now . . . say," groaned Rooster. "And Baldwin, lad, if I could recall, if the fisherman did tell me, I would not be permitted to break my vow of silence, if I took one."

"Never?"

"Never. Except only to prevent mortal sin."

"To whom would you have given your vow, if you gave it at all? Perchance *he* will tell me after all these years have fled, the secret of Kat's past. Think, man!" ordered Win before he set a finger to his lips to silence Rooster, strode swiftly to the door, pulled it wide, and got firm hold of the figure crouching there with an ear cocked to the keyhole. When he had pulled the eavesdropper, who didn't resist, into the light, he discovered he had caught a comely young woman, tall, solid, almost brawnily built.

"Why, 'tis my Colchester hen," gasped Truckle with surprise and pleasure. "What are you doing down here, me dear?"

"When you were beat up, sir, in Hog Lane, my son saw the man what done it. And the man what done it saw my Rob, and he's after the child. I've been hiding the boy down here, bringing him food and such, for they are lookin' for him everywhere and I have no means to get him out of London. Oh, and sir?" Nan smiled at Rooster. "A Winchester goose is what you mean to call me. I told you that the last time. I told you also that I'm not from neither Winchester nor Colchester. Do you recall?"

"Nan's your name, and you are not from Colchester, Winchester, nor Sugarland neither, but from Candy Island! Baldwin, Baldwin, 'twas Potter Shute, the oyster monger from Candy Island, who first brought Katesby to me!"

"He's always had a fondness for Kat, and Kat craves oysters as others do candy! It's all starting to fall into place," said Win, smacking his right fist into his left palm.

"I knew old Potter, when I growing up on the island, and I saw that baby child, some years younger than me, Potter and his wife had with 'em for a while," said Nan.

"I have a service to do in that vicinity, at Essex, for Harry de Morely, and I shall seek out Potter Shute as well, before I make my way up to Cornwall. I nearly forgot, Rooster. I bring you this Invitation to a Hanging. 'Tis from the king." Win handed the monk a sheet of foolscap.

"Best seek right quick, sir, if you would see Potter," suggested Nan, "for I came upon his nephew Cal not long ago, who told me that the old man was ailing bad."

"I thank you for that advice Nan." Win nodded. "I'm off, but before I go, I would get you and your boy safe away from London. Where is he, do you know? We leave at once," he said.

"Here I be!" announced Rob, stepping from behind a crate, Chance-garbed in black right up to his eyes. Win set his hands on his hips and broke into a great roll of laughter.

"How'd you get that suit of clothes, boy?"

"Katesby the innkeeper give me these hand-me-downs, to keep me warm, she said, one snowy winter night. I'm right used to 'em now, so perchance I'll grow up to be like Chance, eh?"

"I don't know if that's an altogether fitting ambition for a youngling, but there could be a worse one." Win grinned and riffled the child's dark head with a friendly hand. He squatted down on his haunches to be on more of a level with the child.

"I require information about the movement of the

moon and tides during the next several days. Jim Bolling's an expert on such matters. He's captain of my ship, anchored now in the Thames. I shall put you and your mother safe aboard the *Conquest*, Little Chance, which is readying to sail from England with a most remarkable cargo. What say you?"

"Ship's captain?" reflected Rob. "Might be near as good to be that as a outlaw. I say yes, if me ma is game to go."

"Being on the sea can nought but be an improvement upon hiding in a basement, eh, Robby? I'm for it!" declared Nan, taking the boy's hand and scurrying after Win, leaving Rooster alone with the wineskin which he happily proceeded to drain before he curled up for a nap, using the pouch as a pillow.

Chapter 27

The Pilgrimage to Cornwall, or The Chance Hangings, as the occasion was to become known, began many days before the scheduled event. The gallows builders were on the scene first. Crowds of ragged beggars with no call on their time were the next group to collect on the plateau at Lizard Point, soon to be followed by wandering minstrels and troops of mummers. They were all anticipating crowds of festive folk requiring amusement and who, all in a holiday spirit, would be free with coin. Harlots and bawds came with the same expectations and mingled with the poor of Ram Alley, Damnation Alley, Devil's Gap, and other London slums—men, women and children out for a rare respite in the countryside. Monks and friars arrived in twos and threes to save sinners sure to be found at such a happening, and to offer solace to the condemned, who were facing eternity.

The weather held fair, and country folk from surrounding areas, dressed in their Sunday best, set up encampments the day before the great public spectacle was to take place. Then came respectable kerchiefed women with their merchant and artisan husbands, lastly gentlefolk, lords and ladies, and the nobility gathered, dressed to the eyes.

" 'Tis better than a bear-baiting," commented Gail Pebbles to Scoggin the Butcher, who had a taste for gore and never missed a hanging if he could help it.

" 'Tis like a carnival," exclaimed pretty Gwyn Stark, holding to the arm of Horace, Norland's courier, and Cal Shute, the oyster monger's nephew, competitors for her favors. She was making straight for Charlie de Morely who was chatting with a fat little fellow near the lined carriages.

The wagons and carts of the prisoners, surrounded by a regiment of wary soldiers, were seen approaching, and the crowd surged closer to the long gallows on which the hangman and his helpers were securing a row of fifty noosed ropes.

"Hanging Jack Fletch will have the chief honors today," said Mean Mack Flick to Welsh Frank and Paul Penniless, pointing at a thick-necked, bullheaded man. "I have given the hangman a shilling for a piece of the rope that does for Giles Hather, King of the Derbyshire gypsies."

"I'd not had word he was to be one of those dancing on air this day," remarked Wadd.

"The Egyptian got caught doing his palmistry right out in the open at St. Paul's, as if he was eager to be gaoled," puzzled Mack Flick. "Look there! Norland's outriders approach in advance of his carriage and with him is sure to be our own Kat Dalton of Southwark who's to become a countess. There's to be nobles and aristocrats aplenty here today, including even the king himself, for 'tis said Win Chance will not stand idly by and allow his confederates to suffer and die."

"Do you see him? Do you see . . . Win?" whispered Kat to Lady Cary.

"Calm yourself, dear child. 'Tis harmful to the spleen

to be so wrought up as you are, Katesby. I see neither Chance nor Baldwin, but that does not mean that neither one nor the other or both are not here."

"The folk are behaving as though this were some sort of jubilee," complained Rooster Truckle. "This is a most sad and solemn occasion, or should be."

"I never have beheld so many soldiers and constables," worried Kat, " in uniforms so varied and splendid and . . . unusual." She stared about, particularly impressed by the guards posted immediately in front of the gallows, a squad of twenty mounted men astride dark chestnut mounts. They were garbed all in green silk, wearing feather-plumed deep helmets which cast their faces in partial shadow. Kat found the profile of one man, despite the helmet and feathers, especially striking and vaguely familiar with his strong jaw and fine nose and shoulders as broad as Hercules'. She regarded him, and as if drawn by her stare, the soldier turned fully toward her and boldly winked one jade green eye. Kat gripped Lady Cary's hand so hard, her friend squealed.

"Oh, sorry!" said Kat as she let her eyes travel from face to face of the men ranked in a row with Win and found she knew each and every one, actors and players all, whom Andrew Danter had brought to The Sign of the Kat. And there beside Baldwin was no other than Andrew himself, so fine an actor he made a perfect soldier, sitting ramrod straight beside his friend. *How will they ever perform in this perilous drama and live to tell the tale?* Kat anguished.

"Oh, weasels and moles!" she groaned. Too jittery to sit still, she rose from her place and climbed down from the carriage despite the earl's concern for her safety in the crushing crowd. Patting his hand and reassuring him with a fine smile, she went about to peruse the lay of the land and see whom she could see.

First she saw the king, who sat happily beneath the flags of his pavilion as though he were attending a joust in the tilt yard. With him was the animated Princess Elizabeth, who relentlessly waved to her father's subjects.

Kat found Rattcliffe and Wiltenham in the crowd, scanning their eyes this way and that. The fat, bespectacled little agent, Burgess Blunt, wriggling his piglike snout as if sniffing the air, was engaged in intense talk with Charlie de Morely. Kat froze at the thought that the viscount, who knew everything about Chance, might be in league somehow with Blunt, but then dismissed the possibility. Not *Charlie,* her own loyal, devoted knight, she decided, going on her way, lacking any idea of how much disturbed she would have been by their exchange.

"You commissioned me, Viscount, to do the innkeeper ill, if not precisely to do in the innkeeper altogether, though that was always a practical option, never an inconceivable possibility. In exchange for this service on my part, you were going to provide me with intelligence, details, facts, regarding spies for Rome and spies for Scotland and spies for Huguenots and for Quakers, student spies, clerical spies, *criminal* spies—most particularly the modern Robyn Hood of London, Win Chance, an instigator of outlawry and insurrection. Now, just because you have lost interest in defaming Katesby Dalton, you may not assume I've lost interest in destroying Win Chance. Serve *him* up to me, or I will serve *her* up to Rattcliffe."

Charlie swayed on his feet, suddenly weak with helpless rage as it came clear to him that he must sacrifice one of his dear friends if he was to save the other. But he knew not which to protect and which to throw to the lions, as his father was wont to say. Whichever, the other would despise him forever, and he could turn to neither now for advice without revealing his earlier try at treachery. In the end, the result for him would be the same whatever he did. He would earn the contempt and enmity of the two people he most admired in all the world. Charlie groaned aloud and looked with extreme hatred at little Blunt.

"If you do not catch Chance here this day, I'll see you get him tomorrow, Blunt," hissed Charlie. "Keep away from Katesby, do you hear, or I will get *you*. Understand?"

"I do indeed, my lord," tittered Blunt. "And may I say how pleased I am that we've reaffirmed our association?" he added, offering his hand. Charlie ignored the gesture and stalked away to overtake Kat. She was edging forward toward the gallows as the roll of drums set the pace for the condemned as they mounted the steps to meet their doom.

"Hangman, finish me tidily!" one weeping fellow implored and was instantly jeered by the crowd and pelted with old vegetables.

"Stand up and die game, like a man!" came a shout from the throng, and though it had no effect on the weeper, it appeared to enliven another condemned man, more a boy, one of several there dressed up in silk-and-satin peacock finery for the occasion. He bowed to the crowd before he strutted to his place beneath a noose, grinning as though he thought himself born to live forever.

"A hanged man's hand cures blights. I'll sell mine now for the best proffer!" he called.

"I paid five men ten shillings each to walk after me coffin, dressed up like mourners," said another of the about-to-be-hanged.

"Paid them louts in advance, did you?" asked the man to his left.

"They would not wait for their money till after."

"See 'em here? No, and you won't, neither!" joked the fellow to his right. Gradually, the jesting stopped, and as all stood in readiness, a hush settled upon the scene as one and all awaited a sign, a move, something, from Win Chance. The tension built. Kat had positioned herself directly in front of Baldwin, prepared to do anything to help save his life, if it came to that, though neither made any sign to the other until he leaned low over his mount's withers.

"You're too close. Move away, mistress. That's an order!" he roared and so startled was she, she took a few steps backward, treading upon Charlie's toe. The viscount looked from Kat to the soldier, took in matters at a glance, and gnashed his teeth in frustration until the solution to his dilemma presented itself and he melted back into the throng.

All was still again, with only an undertone of muttering to be heard, the atmosphere so strained, the air crackled when, in a great burst of activity, ten women, clearly bawds and harlots, all dressed in white, paraded up toward the gallows and the mood of the thing changed again.

"Keep away," bawled Danter from the center of the mounted row of false soldiers in green, most of whom seemed confounded at this new turn of affairs.

"Let the ladies pass," ordered the hangman, the official in charge, "for they've come to offer themselves as brides, and any man jack who will accept one to be his wife will be set free and escape the gallows! Any takers?" asked Jack Fletch walking along the line of the noosed.

"Oh, aye, if I can have me pick among 'em," announced the boy who had earlier offered his dead-man's hand to the highest bidder. Now he kicked at his ankle chains and squirmed like a hooked a fish until the hangman cut him loose and a priest was summoned to read the marriage vows on the spot. "I may be putting me head in a worse noose than the one I had," jested the boy, setting his very warm hand upon the shoulder of a pretty, dark-haired young thing of no more than fifteen years.

No sooner had the priest joined the pair and sanctified the union than shouts arose from several corners of the crowd that Win Chance had made his appearance at last, not once but tenfold, for armed mounted men swathed to the eyes in black were coming from everywhere at once, advancing upon the gallows where the hangman and his henchmen stood agog. The green-garbed actor-soldiers, swords drawn, waved other guard units away, claiming the right to stop the Chances on their own.

"Which one's the real one?" raged Hanging Jack Fletch.

"I am!" the men in black answered together, each exposing his face in turn. Kat recognized among them Win's favored inner circle—Jeremy Edge, Perkin Thyn, Francis Wyggington, Hugh Wyld, Tom Spratt, and Giles Hather. The hangman turned to the folk poised on the gallows.

"First one to pick out the real Chance goes free," he rumbled.

"Him!" called a man, pointing.

"No, 'tis the other lad, there!" came a contradiction.

"The one to the right is 'im . . ."

". . . to the left, you clod . . ."

The identifications came thick and fast and even included Burgess Blunt, who snorted and oinked in fear as pandemonium spread. London slum toughs rose to the occasion to show fidelity to their peers in nooses and to their hero Win Chance, even though not a soul among them knew at the moment which one of the passel was truly he. In the mayhem it came to pass that the street toughs, the Chances and the no longer about-to-be-hanged were slowly and steadily maneuvered by advancing soldiers, the green troop in the lead, until they were ranged along the cliff edge with their backs to the sea and turned to face their armed tormentors equipped with rocks and sticks they'd grabbed up from the ground.

"They're caught! They're caught!" croaked Wiltenham. "The king's men are ranked twenty deep across the land. There's no escape and among these scoundrels. I've netted Win Chance, I know. It only remains to learn, by every torture we have and new ones we will invent specially, if need be, to break just one of these curs and learn which of the rogues really be Chance!"

"Keep back! We have them now," shouted *the* Chance to the King's Guard as, one by one, his jail-sprung friends dove and jumped and hurled themselves every which way from the crest of Lizard Point into the sea below, soon to be followed by the men of the green guard until only Baldwin stood alone silhouetted against the blue sky.

"That's him . . . he! That one is Chance," croaked Wiltenham.

"How can you be so certain that *that* one is he?" squealed Burgess Blunt, hopping about at Wiltenham's side.

"Only Chance, a most noble and honorable rogue, loyal to his men beyond the call of duty, or even virtue, would have come here today to try and save this motley crew of riffraff. Failing at that as he has, only Chance would then expose himself to certain death at our hands on the unlikely hope that even a few of his men would survive in the wild, cruel sea off this coast."

"Francis Wiltenham, I do believe you have developed a soft spot for the cur," giggled Blunt.

"I *want him.* He is reputed to be a most charming, amusing fellow. I do look forward to sharing his company during his sessions with Rattcliffe and the rack, the iron maiden, the thumb screws, and such. Take him, take him!" Wiltenham shrieked, urging his men forward. "Get him before he . . . jumps!"

A puff of smoke obscured the figure of the last green guard on land, and with it there came an explosion, the roar of an arquebus firing. The scatter-shot balls hurtled forward, striking Win across the throat and hurling him from his horse, tumbling over the cliff into the water below. In the shocked silence, Kat wailed a long, heartrending cry of denial of what she had just witnessed, then led the crowd as it surged forward to peer over the cliff's edge. Below, men bobbed in white-foam waves as they were plucked from the sea by the fleet of small fishing boats which had been ready and waiting to ferry them out to a three-masted merchant vessel. The *Conquest* was riding close in to shore at a high tide, the only moment at which it could have navigated the treacherous rocks of the Cornwall shore.

"If the outlaw was not shot dead and the crash into the rocks didn't kill him and if he does not drown unconscious in the sea, he'll not live long with the wound he's got," smirked Wiltenham with satisfaction. "This, I'd say, has been a job well done, Blunt. Blunt?" he repeated, glancing down. The stunted agent, who had been standing beside him moments before, now lay blue in the face upon the ground, an unused hangman's noose about his throat, pulled tight, but not tight enough to do the job intended. Near to throttled but breathing still, the little agent opened his bulging eyes, sat up, and looked about myopically.

"I did not see who did it, but whoe'er it was cannot be far," Blunt squealed.

"You never see much anyway, with your poor sight," said Charlie, helping the little man to his feet while considering how next time to succeed at his objective, for this time he had failed by not pulling the noose quite tight enough about Blunt's throat.

"Arrest every man, woman, and child within the square league! One of 'em is bound to be the dastard who near to choked me," ordered Blunt, rubbing the rolls of fat at his bruised neck.

"Do be quiet, little man," Wiltenham answered impatiently. "I'll not ruin the high mood of the day on which we killed off Chance at last by making arrests on the site of our triumph. And besides, the men, women, and children within a league of you include the king, his daughter, his guards, and Hanging Jack." Blunt looked distrustfully from the hangman, standing nearby, to the man's signature knot on the noose just loosed from his neck.

"I know who here wishes me ill and near killed me," he said, "and you may be sure his days are numbered."

Wiltenham and Charlie exchanged glances over the little man's head. The spymaster rolled his eyes; the viscount shrugged.

"If the days of all those who wish you ill are numbered, Blunt, England will be near to empty, eh?" Rattcliffe laughed, slapping Blunt upon the back and provoking the spy to append the torturer's name to his lengthening enemies list.

Chapter 28

More dead than alive, Win was pulled into one of *Conquest's* longboats, the only casualty of the day's triumphant rescue other than one of the Beldam witches, who had skinned her knee. All the friends of Chance were out of his majesty's prisons, snatched from the cruel hands of agents and torturers and saved from the hangman's hempen window.

The *Conquest,* which flew no flag and was further disguised by a recent change of hull color from white to black, unfurled full sail to get under way and evade pursuit, as well as a more imminent and likely danger—breaking up on hidden rocks as the tide and wind shifted. The vessel headed due south with her contraband cargo of somber souls who eschewed the freedom celebration Win had planned for them, with feasting and wine, to hold vigil at his bedside and on the decks near the captain's cabin where he lay.

"He won't likely live," the ship's barber-surgeon prognosticated. "I'll do what I can, but don't expect much."

At that Win's eyes opened. He tried to speak, but due to the wound at his throat the words came in a rasp.

"What . . . ?"

"You were hit by a mosquet shot. Do not try to speak," advised Captain Bolling.

"Kat," Win whispered. "Blaidd! Must help them."

"Rest easy, lad," said Danter, still in his guard uniform, the soaked feathers of his helm trailing across his face like long green hair. "I'm going ashore at Guernsey Island and sailing home. I'll see Kat, tell her you're . . . alive."

"No!" Win coughed. " Do . . . not. If she thinks me . . . dead . . . she will marry . . ." Win closed his eyes, exhausted by the effort of speech.

"Marry Harry. Yes, I know," said Danter, troubled. "But what if . . ." He went no further, for Win was unconscious again, his breathing shallow.

"If he is able to fight off the fever, there's a prayer for him," said Andrew.

"We will do turn and turn about sitting with him, cooling his brow, and cleansing his wound," said Nan, who stood holding little Rob by the hand, a mad witch of Bedlam to either side of them.

"Sure, and it takes a woman's touch at such a time," said Emma Toule, the younger lunatic, sounding neither mad nor witchy.

"Aye. When he swallows his first sip of broth, we will have cause for cautious cheerfulness," said Emma's mother Madge, a white-haired old hag, bizarre in appearance, with the gentle, kind voice of an angel. "Barber, take your implements away."

When Danter went ashore at Guernsey a week later, Nan and Rob went with him, their plan to go all together to Win's lands at Bath and remain there until the fuss and furor blew over and little Rob was no longer the object of a manhunt.

"Boyhunt," the child corrected Danter. Win, awake though weak, smiled.

"Did you fancy your jaunt at sea, Rob?" he asked.

"Oh, aye! I learned there's three kind of ships in the King's Navy—some for war, some for burden, some for getting fish. Captain Bolling promises that in a year, when I am seven, or near to it, he will take me on as his cabin boy."

"There's a future for a likely lad at sea," said Bolling. "*If* he works hard."

"Rob has got yet another hero now," said Nan with a smile first at the captain, then at Win as she pressed his hand. "Thank you both, thank you all"—she looked about the cabin to include the Bedlam witches, the barber, and several of the ship's officers—"for being so kind and good to us, getting us safe out of London. If ever we may return such kindness . . ."

"I've a service or two to ask of you, Andrew," said Win. "Look in on Rooster Truckle as you pass through London, for whoever it was hurt him before may come back for whatever it was he was after in the first instance."

"Aye," said Andrew in a tight voice, sad at the parting, perhaps forever, from his friend.

"Buy Blaidd Kyd out of gaol. Sell all I have, if need be, borrow from one and all, enlist the aid of Montfort, Seton, the blasted Devil himself if need be to help that boy."

"Aye, Baldwin," sniffled Danter, near tears with emotion.

"Andrew will watch out for you now, Nan," said Win. "Keep you off the streets. You cook for him in return. Rob can help him look after the sheep. That's a good life's work for man, Rob."

"Apprentice shepherd, sure, it's okay," said Danter.

"But apprentice actor and playmaker, there's another likely possibility."

"You must be gone, while the tide is right," said Bolling. Andrew gripped Win's hand.

"Fare thee well, good old friend. May all your endeavors prosper," said Danter.

"And yours, my good Andrew. One thing more I will ask of you. Take this, please, to Harry de Morely. It's a portrait of his wife. I never did get so far south as Essex, to show it about."

"Aye," the actor nodded. "And when I see Kat, what do I . . ."

"I told you. You are to say naught of me. I'm dead to her."

"I know what it was you told me. I was hoping you'd forgot, is all."

"Andrew, go to her soon as you can, to see how she does and to make her . . . laugh."

"Go to her, make her laugh, and say not a word of you? Assuredly I'll be able to do that, sir, assuredly." Andrew shrugged and tipped an imaginary cap to Win, then left the cabin with Rob and Nan at his heels.

"Won't be easy to make her laugh, or to keep your promise not to tell her nothing of him," worried Nan, climbing into the longboat and reaching up for Rob.

"Easy? I'd say not! In truth, it will be well nigh impossible," answered Danter with certitude and conviction. "Know you this, Nan, there's some promises maybe shouldn't be kept, if they were bad promises to start with."

"Oh?" answered Nan thoughtfully.

"What will you do," Harry de Morely asked Kat, "if you will not be wed to me?"

"I will go back to my true life in London, at the inn. I miss it something fierce."

The pair walked along the lake at the Montforts' north-country estate where Kat, in a swoon, had been taken after Win was shot at Cornwall and disappeared into the sea. She spoke not a word for many days, not until she had made up her mind to go back to London and her actual calling. Now, in the company of the earl, Kat looked off up the greensward at the high-pitched gables and gracious chimneys of Rockingham, where she had been for the past fortnight, and she sighed.

"What will you do there?"

"Live quiet."

"And Baldwin? What will he say if you refuse me? He's ambitious for you, you know."

"Baldwin will say naught. Now it can be told, my lord, that . . . that Win Beaumarais and Win Chance were . . ." Her voice broke but she quickly regained command of it, if not her true feelings. "Beaumarais and Chance were one and the same, both lost to me now."

"You will not live quietly in London. You will live lonely. That is closer to the truth, Katesby, my dear, for it's not your old life you miss. 'Tis Baldwin, and you'll miss him all the more, there at the inn, where he is absent from every place he used to be." Kat looked up at the earl with surprise. "I lost a love of my own and I understand, my dear. I know how you feel . . . felt about Beaumarais. He loved you, too, I believe. But now he's gone, my dear," said the earl firmly. "Now you are free to love me, or will be when your heart has mended, in time, when you have done grieving for Baldwin. Leastways, you are now unfettered to be wed to me, if not love me, sith there's no hope of you ever becoming wife to the man you . . . loved." He stumbled on the word.

"And if I always do love him?" Kat asked.

"I will endure that, for the comfort and ease I find in your proximity. If it will console your mind, we will enact an agreement prior to our nuptials, a written one if you like, a compact between us before we take vows. I promise you all the time you need, even if that be forever, to love me. I will not bring any but the most gentle persuasion to bear upon you. Never ever will I force myself upon you, if you do not want me in your bed, though I am quite hopeful, optimistic, you will one day," Harry added with a wistful look. "I wish you to wed me now, Kat, so that I may care for you, and soothe you, and keep you safe. What say you?"

The wedding date was set then and there, with plans made for Kat to arrive at Norland Castle in the week before. His lordship would see to all the arrangements for the grand celebration, which the king was expected to attend.

The banns were to be read from Norland chapel on the feast day of St. Blaise and again on the Sunday after. The marriage would take place a month later near to St. Dunstan's Day after the Ides of May.

"Beaumarais, your preposterous alchemical formula was not the cause of my freeing you and the others of your crew on the occasion of our previous meeting," proclaimed the corsair Hasan, grandson of Barbarossa.

The *Conquest* had encountered the pirate's small, swift, usually lethal fleet along the north coast of Spain off Cape Finisterre. As Hasan had told Win he intended doing, he had ventured past Gibraltar to sail from the Mediterranean Sea into the Atlantic Ocean. The Algerians, Hasan, and his colleague, the infamous Moor, Dragut, had been successfully raiding the western, low-lying, unprotected coasts of Spain and Portugal for captives to hold for ransom. They had also been prowling after slaves and gold on the high seas, all the while beating a leisurely northern course to keep a rendezvous with Win at Malden in England near the time of St. Swithin's Day, some months hence. When the slower *Conquest,* flagless and disguised to elude English pursuers was sighted, the corsairs gave chase and easily overtook her. It was not until the pirates, howling their shrill, pulsing war cry, made ready to board, knives clenched in their teeth, that Hasan sighted his friend on the upper deck. Win brandished a sword in one hand and a parchment in the other, the document Hasan himself had furnished, with the Sultan's seal, to guarantee his English chum safe passage through Barbary-infested waters anywhere in the world.

There was a cheerful reunion, and then a most unusual gathering was convened aboard the *Conquest.* Turbaned Moorish sailors and dark-eyed Algerian corsairs in colorful full pantaloons mingled with their English counterparts wearing plain canvas breeches, and with the friends of Chance, highwaymen, pickpockets, poachers, and Bedlam witches, newly freed from English gaols and rescued from the hangman. These disparate segments of humanity, in many ways more alike than different, outsiders all, shared food and grog and, lacking a common language, talked with their hands to mime sea tales, acts of piracy, kidnaps, gaol tales, purse-cutting, and dice play, with much sword slashing, rolling about, leaping into the riggings, and laughter.

In the captain's quarters, a more verbal form of communication was made possible by the merging of several tongues—French, Spanish, Arabic, Latin, English—and with the help of a charming linguist and translator. Among the recently-absconded-with-by-pirates was the willing conscript, Julia Gonzaga, who was reputed, Win recalled, to be the most beautiful noblewoman in all Europe. Upon being presented to her by her young lover, Hasan, Win did indeed find her exquisite, with raven black hair and dark eyes, though he did not grant her the title of "most beautiful woman in all of Europe." The ideal of beauty which, he knew from experience, varied from place to place, from person to person, from one episode of the heart to another, was in the eye of the perceiver. The diadem of supreme resplendence was unfailingly set by a man upon the head of his own lady love. In Win's heart and to his eye, no woman matched Katesby for comeliness, no smile equaled her wonderful crooked beam of happiness, no eyes were as deep or true green, no . . . no!

No, Beaumarias, this will not do, he admonished himself. *You will never see her again, not ever. 'Tis for the best, so forget her, fool, try to or . . . suffer,* he told himself. *Can't. Won't. Not ever,* he answered, and would have argued with himself further if his inner dialogue had not been interrupted by Dragut, a tall, black-skinned Moor, a lieutenant in Barbarossa's service, friend and mentor of Hasan and former galley slave who harbored no love for his cruel captors, the Spaniards. He was also, Baldwin knew, a man who had seen the fabled *Isle of Española* in the New World.

"We performed all the twelve steps of your alchemical formula for turning lead into gold, all the way to the final stage," said Dragut. "We acquired a red philosopher's stone from a Cadiz merchant. We acquired the Cadiz merchant as well. He is now pulling an oar for the sultan, but we did not transform dross to gold."

"Ah. So you say, gentlemen, that Cunning Man Dorsey Dibdin's twelve-step alchemical formula for turning lead into gold did not work? I *am* dismayed to hear it," jested Win, as a cabin boy filled the goblets of his guests with rare red wine from the Rioja region of Spain. "Did you remember to invoke the black crow symbol and the dragon symbol?"

"Neither did the trick, my friend," said Hasan with a grin and a shrug, turning his hands palms upward in a helpless gesture. "But 'tis not a surprise. We of North Afrique are well in advance of you northern Europeans in many sciences. And of course, you have taken from us your system of numbers called Arabic."

"We had numbers before we took to using yours,

Hasan," Win retorted. "Rome gave us numbers before you."

"Oh, so cumbersome, Roman numerals," answered Hasan dismissively. "No, no, we are far more civilized than you. Persians go only once each day to meat, and that after dark. Only our sultan dines when the sun is high."

"Oh, very civilized indeed," answered Win with friendly, bemused sarcasm, "eating meat in the dark."

"Your alchemy failed us, jester, but we care not. We care not, for you it was who taught us to play the card game of piquet, which has taken the sultanate by storm, my man. It is being played by all, from the highest to the lowest members of Suleiman's court, in the sultan's bedrooms, in the queen mother's pavilion, in the quarters of the princes, and in the baths of the harem by the girls and their eunuchs. So we have been well rewarded by the padishah and have much to thank you for. Thus, we will share our next adventure with you, a raid upon the rich Spanish Isle of Española. Dragut knows the way there."

"And back?" asked Win. "Assuming we wish to come back, that is."

"With your large, fine cargo ship to carry off spoils, and our armed fleet of marauders to fight off Spanish galleons, we will gain wealth enough so that every man in the expedition will be able to live like a sultan for the rest of his days, here—there—anywhere he chooses. What say you, Baldwin, to joining forces with us?" Dragut said in a low, rumbling, persuasive voice.

"Yes, yes, Beaumarais, what say you?" asked Hasan with bright-eyed enthusiasm, leaping from his chair.

"I think this Englishman has some reluctance to commit himself just yet. I think you must not vex him so," said Julia Gonzaga, Dutchess of Traietto, an aristocratic beauty of perception and feeling, Baldwin recognized. "My vivacious boy-corsair with his dark and flashing eyes, Mr. Beaumarais, is often carried away by his zeal." she smiled.

"And glad you are of it, my love," declared Hasan, "for since I seized you from the shores of Italy as you walked along the beach below your castle, we have often been carried away together by a shared . . . zeal."

"Hasan swore to take me and run with the wind the next time he found me in residence at my Fondi castle. And he did. I have been freed by him from one form of bondage—wife to a husband I loved not—and made a willing slave of another sort!" The 'abducted' duchess beamed her smile upon the handsome corsair, and Win recognized love in her eyes. His heart twisted, for he had seen the same look in Katesby's glance time and time again and refused to fathom it.

"It is held in England," proposed Win, "that love and marriage have but little to do with one other. Marriage is a transaction to enhance wealth and power, and love is an ephemeral malady."

"I have heard troubadours sing the English ballad of the Lady and the Wraggle-Taggle Gypsy, who sang beneath her castle window and melted her heart as the sun does snow," answered Julia. "It tells how she laid aside her silken gowns, her shoes of Spanish leather, her rings of gold, and took to the street in her 'bare bare feet, all in the wind and the weather.' Do you know this ballad, Baldwin?"

"Indeed, Duchess," he replied. "When the runaway lady's new-wed lord came after her asking how she could put aside her treasures and lands and her soft feather bed, he was told she had rather sleep upon the cold, cold ground with her gypsy than with him upon goose feathers."

"*My* runaway Duchess of Traietto had agreed to signal me with a torch and await me at the edge of the sea," said Hasan.

"And I did not have to wait long, once the flames flared, to become my handsome pirate's spoil of war," said Julia with a charming trill of laughter. "Hasan saved me doubly from slavery, one time by taking me from a loveless marriage, another time by keeping me from being sequestered and enslaved in the seraglio of Suleiman and . . ."

"My dear duchess, you would have undone the harem of Suleiman," said Dragut. "A thousand women, following your lead, would have rioted for freedom behind those thick marble walls." The Moor rose to his full impressive height, a slash of sunlight illuminating the onyx darkness of his face. "Win Beaumarais, I have heard tell, is alike to you in that way, madam, a man who would not long be enslaved. His vigor and valor, his stamina and largeness of heart, his shrewdness and pride guarantee that he would lead an uprising against the padishah's authority, not unlike the fabled English outlaw Chance, who defied the sultan of that land."

"The outlaw Chance! Now he must be as wild and romantic a lover as is my corsair Hasan," agreed Julia. Win abruptly stood and left the cabin, and moments later, Lady Julia found him in the bow, staring out to sea.

"True love must never be denied," she told him softly. "Go get her for whom you pine with such obvious deep yearning."

"She is likely wed to an earl," was all Win could say.

"I also was wed to a nobleman, sir. Does she love you? Does she know you love her?"

"I'd not ever told her so, nor asked, but . . ."

". . . but she may?"

"I think now, in retrospect, and on consideration at a distance of time and place, she does. She thinks me dead, howsomever."

"Go get her!" exclaimed Julia indignantly. "At the least let her know you live and love her and allow her to decide her own fate, as did I. You owe her that, to give her heart's ease, if for no other reason at all."

Chapter 29

"I have been corresponding with de Morely, planning your wedding feast, Katesby. For this rare occasion, the earl will unlock his rice cabinet."

"It's a rare costly commodity, is rice," answered Kat. She smiled a little, looking out across the greensward at Rockingham Castle toward the lake, which was lost now in mist as a steady rain streamed down the windowpane.

"Costly indeed, particularly when colored with saffron and spiced with pepper and ginger. 'Twill be one only of many dishes, of course. Harry has ordered the catching and slaughtering of three hundred red and fallow deer, and of game birds and rabbits and pigs and boars in countless numbers. Sixty-thousand salted herrings are on his list, five-hundred conger eels, swans served whole . . . Katesby, have you no interest?" carped Addy. "Harry is beside himself with delight and spares no expense."

"Harry is a dear, kind man. My affection for him is true, and I will try to bring him happiness and contentment always," said Kat. "If that requires my enthusiasm for the wedding feast, I will of course be most enthusiastic. Aha, here now arrived is one of my most favorite knights, the future Marquess of Montfort. How be you, young sire, James Roland?" she sang out as the four-year-old, followed by his mother, doting Cary, came into the hall. The child flung himself into Kat's embrace when she went down on her knees to greet him, and the two went to sit near the fire and build a block castle. "I have a little girl called Roxelana, who would dearly love to play with us," said Kat, straightening the boy's lace collar.

"Where is your Roxelana, milady?" asked the child. "Bring her hither," he said in a tone of polite but confident command befitting his rank and upbringing.

"What a grand idea, Jamie." Kat grinned with unfeigned delight. "I will send to have her brought from London at once—that is, if I may," Kat added glancing up at Cary and Addy.

"My dear, every wish and whim of the soon-to-be Countess of Norland is to be fulfilled, that on orders from her future husband, the earl. If it would please you, a carriage with outriders in force will depart at once to collect the child."

"And her nursemaid, Gwyn Stark?" Kat queried.

"Of course. Now, as for your gown, Katesby . . ."

"Mean you the green moire silk I am to wear to be wedded in?" she asked distractedly.

"Of course! What other gown would I be prating of? The ball gown, the traveling dress, the riding costumes, the morning outfits, the fine linen undergarments, the bedclothes, the cloth-of-silver slippers and cloth-of-gold wraps are all ready. But the wedding gown will require another fitting this day so the needlewomen may sew apace and finish in time. They are to begin joining the gathered sleeves to the bodice of the gown and securing the waistbelt at the lower edge of the bodice. I have seen the belt, Katesby, encrusted with pearls. You are to have a jeweled, starched lace ruff, pearls as big as hens' eggs in your hair, and gold sequins . . ."

Lady Addy was ecstatic on Kat's behalf and wished the bride was somewhat more excited by the wealth being showered upon her. A natural sorter and arranger of details, Addy was seeing to the adornment of the bride's lovely person and supervising her continuing dancing lessons, riding instruction, and tutoring in matters of English history and protocol. For the hundredth time, Kat thought, she had been informed that only the king created barons and bestowed titles of higher degrees, that knights of all ranks were called sir and their wives by the courtesy title, my lady or madam.

"I cannot help but think how many orphans could be fed on a mere fraction of what I will wear upon my person on the day I become Countess of Norland," said Kat uncomfortably.

"Is there nothing in all of this you can accept with a clear conscience and true pleasure?" asked Cary.

"I have been given a truly luxurious rarity that is also useful—stockings knitted of silk, not cloth," Kat replied with a reluctant smile.

"Oh, my *dear,* unaffected, charming child, of all the riches lavished on you by the earl, I am pleased you've found one object truly pleasing to you. Oh, I know, little Kat, how sensible you are, and practical, and how many orphans you might feed and clothe with a fraction of what you have been given. I know, too, there is much chafing and fretting during the fittings, Katesby, but the earl wishes perfection for you. Once you are wed to him, you may become the munificent, charitable, generous countess and care for many more needy tykes than you did before." Kat brightened and nodded and stood.

"I thought the rain would keep me from my outing this day with the mare and hawk, but the downpour has slackened and turned all to mist. If you will excuse me, ladies, and my little lordship Jamie, I'll be off." She curtsied to the delighted child, and then her smile vanished. There was about Kat then, in the set of her shoulders and the tilt of her head, an aloof elegance. "Unless I am needed further?" she added.

"Only this: So that your skin will be as white as snow, I have acquired powder of ground alabaster and a lotion of beeswax, one of asses' milk, and another of the ground jawbones of hogs." Lady Addy recited a list of the cosmetic preparations she had on hand. "Further, if you are not rendered pallid enough by those, we will have to turn to applications of white lead and vinegar. To make your lips very red, we will use crimson ochre. For spots and freckles there is ground brimstone. At the last moment before the beautiful bride appears before her lord, we will apply a glaze of egg white to her face to give her—*you,* Katesby—the cast of polished marble. The nobles will be struck breathless by your beauty, and their ladies will be green with envy."

"And if green, they must resort to ground hog jawbones for remedy," replied Kat with a little shrug and an indulgent smile for Addy, whom she loved and would not offend no matter how nonsensical her concerns.

"If the sun appears, let it shine upon your hair!" called Addy as Kat withdrew. "But never must it shine on your face, do you hear? Do you have your mask I gave you?"

"The one I am to hold in place with the little knob between my teeth?" asked Kat, stepping back into the great hall.

"Yes," replied Addy.

"No!" Kat laughed, suddenly struck by the silliness of the conversation "Oh, please don't worry so, Addy. The aristocracy must accept me as I am, spots and all, or not, as they choose. I suspect they will choose not, and I will care not."

"But you have no spots," Addy answered, bemused.

* * *

"Katesby Dalton is to be wed to Harry de Morely soon after the May Ides," Andrew Danter told Nan, reading from a scroll. "We are invited to Norland for the festivities."

"What will you do, Danter?" asked Nan, scrubbing a pan just emptied of bread pudding. "About Beaumarais, I mean?"

"Don't know. I need guidance, and 'tis time I went to see the old Rooster anyways, like Win asked me to. Nan, Rob, we are bound for London without a moment to waste," said the actor, setting out to saddle his horse and the one he'd acquired for his newest lady love, whom he had been calling Nervous Nan but who would have been better suited by the appellation Tranquil Nan since she had come to the country and under his loving care.

"Best take that likeness with you of the earl's first countess, Danter, so's you can give it back to 'im, that or go on to Essex with it after the wedding festivities, to delve into the mystery of that poor woman's fate."

"Hey, hey! Here we are all called to Norland for a grand gathering!" Rooster Truckle announced with a cackle of a laugh to the dozen waifs waiting to accompany him on his daily scavenger walk about the London streets. "There's a wagon coming on the morrow to take us thither, so gather what goods you got, tykes, and make ready to eat till you come near to bursting! Think you we should do a play, a little morality play for the amusement of the gentlefolk? And for their enlightenment, too, of course, for if a morality play is meant to do anything, 'tis to encourage moral behavior through enlightenment, eh?" he mused, stroking his dangling chins.

"Aye, aye!" came a chorus of responses from the youngsters following him down Hog Lane, where they discovered the first prize of the day for their stew kettle—a cache of rotting marrow bones not too far gone.

"We are to shut up the inn and put a sign upon the door saying, 'Gone to a Wedding,' " said Jilly to her daughters, Jeannie and Jenny. "Go get your best church dresses, girls, 'fore the wagon comes to get us!"

"We will see Gwyn, then, and Roxelana," giggled Jenny with pleasure. "I miss 'em."

"We shall meet men and boys there, in countless numbers—the grooms of the chambers and of the horse, the outriders, cooks, bakers, and *all* their apprentices—even Yeomen of the Guard I don't doubt. I can hardly contain meself," marveled Jeannie.

"Containing yourself's one thing. Behavin' yourself's another," cautioned her mother. "I don't want to spend all me time digging you out of hayricks and stables and stubble fields with one lad or the next, hear?"

"Sure I hear, Mam," answered Jeannie with a big wink at Jenny, who giggled.

"Elizabeth!" bellowed King Henry, pounding his breakfast table. "Where's Elizabeth? We will make a progress to Norland, to see the earl wed to his young lady. Elizabeth must bring her ladies and her fool. I will, of course, have Clarence Kite along. My fool is sometimes rollicking on a merrymaking occasion. Even if he is feeling glum, he is a source of the best gossip. Zounds, but I'd not miss this for the world!" roared the monarch, gulping wine.

And so it went all over England that spring, from north to south and east to west, in places of high estate and low, couriers delivered scribed parchments of invitation to the revelries of Harry de Morely and his lady, Katesby Dalton, on the occasion of their nuptials on the second day after the Ides of May in the year of the Lord numbering 1542.

Dr. Turner of the College of Physicians would attend. So would Jack Brundage, the Lord Mayor of London; the Bishops of Bath, York, and Tilbury; Sir Robert Southwell, Master of the King's Rolls, and John Russell, Keeper of the Privy Seal; as well as Lords Lovell, Randall, Pynings, Wyatt, Carew, Browne, Gray, and Greene, England's crusty old soldiers. Edward Seymour, Earl of Hertford, Henry's Lord Admiral of the Navy, would not have missed the event for anything short of war abroad, for several noble Throgmortons of his acquaintance were expected, as was a collection of ambassadors of the German princes and a few German princes themselves.

On the night before the first day after the Ides of May, Kat stood upon her balcony at Norland Castle, wistfully gazing at the flat, full moon. "Old Man, have you anything to say to me this night?" she whispered, looking up. A pair of night birds, hunting hawks calling one to the other, flew across the bland face of the moon. Glancing down, Kat watched a pair of rabbits gamboling in the moonlight, a stable boy and a girl—could it be Jeannie?—holding hands, slipping off toward the woodland.

"Old Man, 'tis spring, the season of young love, but my young lover is lost forever and my heart *aches.* What am I to do?"

But this night, the moon was unresponsive and left Kat, sighing, to her own thoughts.

The *Conquest,* restored to her former paint color and flying her pendant flag from her masthead, came up the Thames upon the late tide under a near-full moon only two days waned. In its clear light, a longboat was hurriedly lowered over the side of the *Conquest,* and her captain and owner were rowed ashore to alight at Southwark across the river from the Tower palace and prison.

With long strides, Win, Jim Bolling beside him, made his way through familiar London streets, not slowing his pace until he came to the inn door under The Sign of The Kat.

"The landlady has locked it for once," Win said to Jim, rattling the latch.

"All is dark within," said the captain, who had stepped back from the door to look at the overhang of the upper stories of the inn. "Hallo!" he called, hurling a handful of pebbles at an upper window. "Little Gwyn's a light sleeper. She'll arise to give us entry," he said. "Hallo?" he called again, puzzled that there was no response.

"Here is something, Jim, a note. Frogs and newts!" exclaimed Baldwin, crumpling the paper in his fist. "They've closed the inn for the first time ever and all have gone off to the country for . . . a *wedding.* Perchance I can yet be in time to claim my Kat, if I ride like the very wind to Norland, for my lady's heart!"

"There's few mounts in all the land that go like the wind, Baldwin," said Bolling. "If the wind and tides are with us, we can make Scarborough in two days' time in *Conquest* and you can ride from there across the North York Moors to—"

"Rather than risk a chance upon the wind, at such a time as this, I'd trust to horses who go like wind. I have a pair that do," said Win, running for the stable at the rear of the inn. The grooms, though sleepy-eyed, greeted Win with shouts of joy and welcome.

"Man, we thought you lost at sea or sumat, you not making it home to England in time for Katesby's wedding to the earl," said the younger lad. His fellow groom, a confidant of Win Chance and of Baldwin Beaumarais, elbowed his assistant into silence and with tear-flooded eyes clasped his friend to his breast.

"We thought you long gone in a watery grave, Win, for we heard how Chance was blasted by an arquebus and thrown into the sea at Lizard Point. But here you are, here you are, and what service may we do you, eh?"

"We'll take the pair, Dash and Dart, if you please, Gregory," replied Win, thumping the man upon the back. "Hurry! Every moment may count!"

"I have kept 'em both in prime shape, Win, like always," snuffled the groom, smearing happy tears over his face, "but do Captain Jim there know—"

"Know that Beaumarais and Chance are one and the same man? He will, soon as he sets an eye upon the most renowned mount in the realm, and the fastest, Chance's Dart."

"I thought the fine steed went down with his master," said Jim Bolling with awe.

"His master went over the cliff pretending to be one of the king's yeomen. He was astride a tall chestnut gelding such as all the guardsmen ride. I'll say I bought Dash from the gypsy who cared for the animal for Chance."

"Exactly! There's further confirmation, if any were needed, of Chance's death," agreed Jim.

"And we'll just let the outlaw lie, eh?" Baldwin grinned. "So Win Beaumarais may live out his days quiet and peaceful, with his loving lady."

"*If* she has not wed another before he speaks his love. Let us go, man!" insisted Jim, mounting Dart. Dash reared in high spirits and danced about the inn yard, eager for a run and was held back only a moment more by Win.

"I see, Greg, the inn's closed so all the ladies could attend Kat's wedding. When's it to be, exactly?"

"The date's come and it's gone, Win, but I heard—"

"Come . . . and gone?" Win repeated, stunned. "No! It cannot be!" he roared, setting his heels to Dash, who leapt into a full gallop. "I believe it is not so that Katesby is another man's wife, but if it is so," he whispered, leaning low over the animal's withers, "I'll pour out my heart to her and then go far away from England, this time forever, for as the Lady Julia said, 'True love must not be denied.' "

Chapter 30

When Baldwin first saw Kat, the view took away his breath. She was riding at high speed upon a pure white mare of Andalusian descent. In striking contrast, Kat wore a black velvet riding dress with pink slashes and a black hat spangled with gold and trimmed down one side with curling, pure white feathers. Her back was straight, her shoulders squared, and upon her outstretched, guantleted wrist sat a gyrfalcon of yellow-eyed beauty. Following were a pair of greyhounds in gold-trimmed collars, and peeking from the bosom of Kat's dress was a diminutive and dainty white canine of the sort Win had seen on Malta, a pet and playfellow purely, for a grand lady.

"She is alike to the goddess Diana, so revered by the ancients for her beauty, and skill at the chase," Win whispered, enthralled by Kat's patrician grace and high beauty, for her face was flushed and her eyes sparkling with pleasure as she rode.

Dash nickered at the mare. Kat heard the sound and reined in to look about. Unwilling so soon to address her,

Win drew back into the mist, out of her sight beneath the overhang of a great oak, to admire Kat as she listened; then, hearing nothing more, she rode on her way.

"A beautiful sight, is she not, Beaumarais?" Someone spoke at his shoulder and Win turned to find the earl approaching on foot, walking slowly, leaning upon a silver-handled cane. "Where have you been, man? Have you just returned from a voyage?"

"Yes to all your questions, milord," answered Baldwin, dismounting. "I was called away of a sudden. Andrew Danter has the likeness of your first countess, and he will pursue the investigation on my behalf. Yours, really."

"So he has told me," said the earl as he and Win, who walked Dash, headed toward the stable yard. "Danter is here with his lady, a fine-looking woman."

"Nan!" exclaimed Baldwin with pleasure. "Fine she truly is, Harry, and a godsend for Andrew. Speaking of fine women, I looked upon the portrait of your first countess and I congratulate you upon the exceptional beauty of your wives, Harry."

"My . . . wives?" said Harry with a raised brow. "Ah, yes. Of course. You have just arrived, have you, Baldwin?"

"Yes. I see that you have many guests still in residence, the king among them."

"Indeed. There is to be a ball this night. I trust you will attend, Baldwin."

"To dance with your bride, Harry? I think not." Win shrugged. "After the festivities have come to an end, before I quit the country, I'll return here to bid her—and you—a final farewell. I intend to sail for the New World within the fortnight. I'll take my leave of you for now. Please do not speak of me to Kat, not just yet, until—"

"Beaumarais, hold, please," wheezed Harry, leaning heavily on his cane, his face gone pale. Always slim and austere-looking, Harry now appeared gaunt and dwindled in his doublet of dark wool. The man's cheeks, Win realized, were more hollowed than ever before. The gray eyes, though as calculating as ever, showed an unhealthy blaze of fever and a look of desperation.

"What ails you?" asked Win.

"Stomach."

"Bessy Mortlock, the Wise Woman, has a recipe to treat the stomach. She cuts a frog through the back with a knife, takes the liver, folds it in a coldwort leaf, and burns it in a new earthen pot. The ashes are then given the sufferer, mixed with a good wine, to drink."

"I'll try anything now, but if this cure fails as others have, I believe I'm not long for this world, man. I intend to leave Kat with my estates and jewels and riches beyond measure. I had hoped to leave her with my child, as well, but . . ."

"But only time will tell on that count, eh, Harry? But do you do all this for Kat at the expense of Charles, your son and heir?" asked Win, offering a supporting arm to the earl as they resumed walking.

"Charles needs little. He is a poet, a magus. He will be generously enough endowed with titles and riches to pursue his interests, but my line will end with him unless . . . well, I've no hope he will ever take a wife."

"Kat may bear a child and—"

"I ask you to guide and comfort her always. Her soft heart will grieve for me when I'm gone."

"Aye."

"I recommend her to your guidance, more so to your care and affection," said the earl, sounding snappish. Win glanced at him skeptically.

"Kat is wise and resourceful. Your countess will not need me, Harry, to help her make the most of her inheritance, assuming you are not long for this world as you say, and I do not accept."

"Blast you, Beaumarais, will you force me to state it in so many words? She will need a lover and a friend. A husband. There, I've spoken. And there's more I must say. She and I have been close, 'tis so, but know you she is not a countess, for she had no wish to become one. She is Katesby Dalton, Innkeeper, no more nor less, exactly who she always had wanted to be."

"Pardon?"

"I thought you were quick-witted, man! Listen well. She let our wedding plans go so far as they did only because she knew not how to extricate herself without bringing pain and dishonor to me."

"Aye? Mean you that she . . . that Katesby and you . . ."

"We are not man and wife. Now stop stammering, Beaumarais. You put me in mind of Charlie as he used to be, until Kat cured him of his stutter with her gentle kindness and solicitude. Going to escort her to dinner, I came upon her unexpected. She was talking to the moon, would you believe? There were tears in her eyes. To render a long tale brief, I freed her. You have won her and the bet, Beaumarais."

"Bet?" Win asked blankly, for he could think of one thing only—getting Kat into his arms.

"Have you lost all your wits? Do you not recall you offered to bet your life that I would not succeed in making her my wife? That not being practical, you wagered the *Conquest.*"

"And you? What did you put up?" Win asked, starting to smile.

"My acreage on Cottswold Hill. You would rather have played for naught but—"

"For my lady's heart!" Win whooped, grinning. "But . . . but why the ball this night?"

"We had to do something to entertain a castle full of guests. Ah, look now. Here is the good Squire Warbeck with my fur mantle," commented the earl. "Salutations, Will."

"My lord, you will catch your death," a dour Warbeck

grumbled, draping the cloak over Harry's shoulders, so thin the blades were like vestigial wings beneath his black clothing.

"I've caught it already, my death, Will. You needn't worry over me further. Yes, yes, Beaumarais, what's on your mind now?" Harry asked Win, who had begun pacing about him in circles.

"Where is she?" Baldwin inquired, making an only partially successful effort to sound collected.

"There, murmuring at the heavens for a change," replied Harry, indicating a balcony on which a slim figure was to be seen. "I for one am jealous of the damn Man in the Moon, Baldwin. Are you?"

Wrapped in a shawl woven of the earl's livery colors, red and blue, Kat stood peering upward, washed in moonlight.

"*Tonight* you smile upon me, Old Man? What am I to make of that?" she sighed, studying the heavenly orb. "And you wink, you old tease! Have you anything to say to me, such as where my love can be, for I know now in my heart he lives and breathes and walks, and if he does not come back to me, I will set out to find him in Malaga or Barbary or the Canary Isles, even *Española* in the New World. And I will find him, if it takes forever! What have you to say to that, you old wheel of green cheese?"

A narrow cloud passing across the moon gave the face the appearance of a frown, then a grin as the shreds of cloud blew off. Kat laughed. "That's better, sir. Keep smiling on me, for I meant no insult, eh? I'll dress for the ball now, Old Man. No doubt I shall see you later when you've dropped down the sky to make way for the rising sun." The first sounds of music arose from the great hall below, and Kat turned on her heel to step directly into the circle of Baldwin's arms.

"May I have this dance?" he asked.

"I'm not attired in a ball gown," she answered, clasping

her hands beneath her chin, her shining face filled with joy.

"Dance with me nevertheless, here . . . now." Baldwin's dark bronze mane gleamed in the moonlight as he stood before her, tall and slender, a well-made, manly man with a heart-stopping smile and a boyish manner. Kat was compelled to brush an errant curl from his brow.

"I'm not much good at it," she sighed.

"At what?"

"Dancing."

"I don't give a tinker's damn," he growled fiercely, drawing her closer.

"I've a few natural inclinations, but they do not include a proclivity to music and dancing. I must concentrate. I must labor at it, if I am not to trip you up and tread upon your feet."

She was incredibly beautiful, Win decided, with her narrow waist and her honey hair piled atop her head, adding to her graceful height. Her eyes were huge, turquoise tinted this night, or perhaps tourmaline would be the more apt description. They stepped together, moved together to distant strains of music, parted and pranced side by side, twirled, foot crossing foot, eyes meeting.

"You do well enough at dancing, though not as well as you do other things, such as riding and . . . but what troubles you so?" Win asked with sudden consternation, seeing the gleam of tears in the corners of her eyes.

"I'm happy, is all, to see you," Kat said. There was silence, for the music stopped. "You must love me."

"I do. Always have," Win replied

"Not *that* way, not only as a friend The *other* way."

"I do. Always have," he repeated. The music began again. She offered a hand, bent daintily at the wrist. He moved as easily as a breeze leading her, and she followed his lead perfectly, not needing to count out the measures or notes.

"You have always?" she asked, smiling through happy tears.

"You knew, of course," he replied.

"Of course, but you did not," she answered. They whirled together, needing no music.

"Marry me," Win said.

"I'm with child," Kat replied.

"Ah, so you *must* marry me." He smiled before he kissed the top of her head.

"Is that the best you can do, Beaumarais?" Kat asked, falling back upon her old habit of teasing banter with Win.

"You know better than that!" he roared with mock ferocity before he took her in his arms and kissed her well and long and deep—before he took her to bed and loved her the very same way.

"You kept secrets from me, Kitten," Win said, holding Kat close as she curled back against him, warm and easy in the aftermath of love.

"The one secret I ever even tried to keep from you, Beau, was that I loved you," Kat answered, turning in his arms to face him and look into his jade eyes, still very dark and soft with passion. "But you kept secrets from yourself as well as from me. When did you concede you loved me?"

"I began to suspect it during the first love lesson you beguiled me into, wench. Not until after the last lesson did I concede as much to Andrew Danter. He said I must tell you so or else be marked a coward in his book. I declined to hinder your rise to high title and great estate for so fleeting and foolish a thing as love," Win said, sheepishly grinning.

"Ah, 'tis such a silly business, love," Kat tenderly mocked, "is it not?"

"It was Julia of Traietto, who had fled from a duke to be with her corsair, who helped to turn me round and send me back to you. She reminded me of the lady who put aside her gowns and gold and soft featherbed for love of her wraggle-taggle gypsy. Love is worth more than gold is the message of that ballad."

"More than gold, yes, and cannot be bought, my love," agreed Kat. "I understand now what you said to me long ago, that even a most independent woman may *want* to be in a way enslaved by . . . what was it you told me, exactly?"

Baldwin grinned and rolled her in his arms so that he loomed over her and she possessively traced the broad outlines of his shoulders and the ridged muscles of his arms. His laughing eyes reflected glints of candlelight, while the hollows and clefts of his face were exaggerated by dancing shadows. He gave Kat his famed rogue's twinkling wink.

". . . by a powerful, adept man, with wealth beyond measure, I said. That 'tain'ts me, miss, except for the powerful, adept part."

"I care not for great wealth, my sweet fool. As a matter of fact, I don't want it. I want my own life back. I want to go *home.* With you."

"Might as well get it over and done with now, as there's such a goodly number of guests already assembled for a wedding. They'll not care about a little detail like a last-minute change of groom," Harry de Morely said with more than a slight touch of irony while shaking Win's hand cordially.

Kat and Win were joined in matrimony that very evening during the ball at Norland Castle. In a cloistered yard open to the moonlit May sky, Princess Elizabeth was a flower girl when King Henry gave Katesby Dalton, the bride, to Baldwin Beaumarais, her groom. Then dancing began in earnest.

"Look up!" Addy Seton was in the midst of a reel when

a flock of doves—aroused by night hawks, conjectured Lady Cary—soared over the cloister, cooing.

"A good omen, that. If you see a flight of birds on your wedding day, it means a long family," commented Lady Cary. "I know 'tis true, for on my own wedding day a flock of London pigeons flew through St. Paul's Cathedral, and look at me now!" she added, patting her swelling belly.

"Where *is* the new husband? I've something to say to him," Rooster Truckle smiled, tapping his toe at the edge of the dance pavilion. He had happily joined the new couple in matrimony and was now peering about looking for Win.

"What be the cause of your distress, Uncle? Art thou taken ill?" asked Arthur Seton when the old friar, standing beside him, gasped as if for breath.

"No, no, Arthur. I'm right well, thank you. 'Tis only that I have just seen a face in this crowd, one I was told never to forget by the man leaning over me, buffeting me about the head at the time."

"The dastard who came near to killing you is here? Where?" demanded Arthur, drawing his dagger.

"The little one," Rooster said, "with the pink face."

"By God, 'tis that skiving little agent of Wiltenham's! Methinks there is some conspiracy here, Uncle," Arthur said. "What did he want with you?"

"Katesby's ring is what he was after. I'd no idea then where it was, but I found it unexpectedly in the dregs of an old wineskin Win and me had emptied. Mostly me. I had the ring here with me today, safe in my purse. It was the one Win slipped upon Kat's finger when I joined 'em."

Arthur sheathed his dagger again. "I'll avenge you in a more private setting when I've discovered what's afoot. Now look! There's the young groom dancing with his beautiful bride. They make a handsome, happy couple, eh, me love?" Arthur asked his wife, who had come to stand beside him with an unmistakable invitation in her eyes.

"I would dearly love to take a stroll, husband, down to the stables perhaps," said Addy. "Would you care to join me?"

"Arthur Seton and Addy are off to the stable loft again," Kat told Win. During a pause in the dancing, they turned to watch their friends slipping away.

"Stable loft?" asked Win with a humorous look. "What . . . for?"

"Remember, love, what you told me during one of those first love lessons, when I asked a silly question about why I could not just . . . touch you as I was inclined to? You said you'd think me a twit if I could not answer myself the question I had just posed to you. Now I'm saying the same to you." Kat sparkled with happy mischief.

"Harken to me, imp," he graveled, drawing Kat closer. "I remember right well what you were doing and fingering when I said that to you. And why I said it. If you had gone on pleasuring me in that most delicious manner, I'd not have been able to return the kindness, not for a time. What say we go off and do each other some kindnesses right now, eh?"

"In a stable loft, husband?" Kat laughed prettily.

"No, in a bed—our own, wife. I'm taking you home now, for good and always, so's we can begin to live together happily ever after under The Sign of the Kat."

Chapter 31

And they might have done just so, had not fate still held in store for them another momentous surprise or two, the first delivered by Harry de Morely's courier, who mistakenly switched the messages he was delivering on the day baby Beau Paul Harry was born. He handed Win one intended for a London solicitor and, contrariwise, gave Win's missive to the lawyer.

But before that mixup occurred, during the months leading up to the birth, Kat glowed with happiness and, Win said, increasing beauty as she grew great with an active, kicking child. All went auspiciously for them at the inn among their dogs and urchins and paying guests. Outside their immediate, happy little world, certain events occurred further afield which affected their futures, directly and indirectly, clemently and tempestuously.

Soon after their wedding, Baldwin arranged an audience for the Moor, Dragut, and Hasan, grandson of Barbarossa, with King Henry. The infidels anchored one galley in the Thames, while the rest of their fleet stood waiting out to sea in case of treachery, and came ashore to the Tower palace. When the two corsairs and their retinues departed, they bore gifts and warm greetings from the English King Henry for their sultan, Suleiman the Great, and a document specifying the points of a secret alliance between the monarchs to collude against King Charles of Spain. For his part in helping to arrange this historic meeting, Baldwin Beaumarais was greatly enriched by his appreciative king with gold and, though a commmoner, a coveted apointment to the Privy Chamber.

Making immediate use of his new position, Win arranged another meeting of sorts, this a very high-stakes card game with an unusual assortment of participants—Charlie de Morely, gamesman and card-counter; his father the earl; Lords Montfort and Seton; Dorsey Dibdin the Cunning Man; Agent Blunt and his masters, Wiltenham and Rattcliffe; and Baldwin himself. On getting wind of this exciting game, Henry insisted upon being included, and so the monarch sat down at the gaming table with, among others, a Welsh prisoner brought directly from the Tower dungeon. Blaidd Kyd, his blond hair grown long and looking somewhat the worse for wear, was there through Win's machinations, to play for his life against his torturer. Also present, and not happy about it, was the pair of touts and foul spies, Francis Flud and his cousin Paul Wadd, who had perpetrated the lute-string chicanery on Kyd's father, causing the man's demise.

"Them two dastards got me poor dad's bond for a loan of twenty pounds, Majesty," Blaidd told the king, who required an explanation for the presence of the the lowlifes. "They gave me dad but five pounds in coin of the realm and the rest in lute strings to sell. There being not much market for lute string, me dad hanged himself with 'em. The lute strings."

Viscount Charlie de Morely dominated the play and won, by fair and, as necessary, underhanded means, over everyone every time, except Blaidd and his majesty, who took it ill to be beaten at anything, particularly if riches were changing hands. At the end of play, which lasted a night, a day, and another night, Blaidd was a free man with a royal pardon and a goodly sum of gold in his purse. Wiltenham had lost an estate, Rattcliffe a merchant ship, Blunt a small cottage in Clareford, which was all he owned, and Wadd and Flud their shirts and their freedom. In gaol for swindling, they made the acquaintance of the Butcher of Bath, Alberic Scoggan, who, with Gail Pebbles, his mistress in more than one sense of the word, had been discovered sheep-shipping and awaited the attention of the axman, who would carry out the penalty for his crime.

Soon after the card game, Burgess Blunt was found murdered. There was speculation in certain circles about the possible identity of the perpetrator. Some leaned toward Arthur Seton, taking vengeance for Rooster; others named Rattcliffe and Wiltenham, for whom Blunt had outlived his usefulness. Actually, mild-mannered Charlie de Morely, whom no one suspected, did the deed when Blunt tried again to menace him with threats to Kat and Win and demanded money. The viscount set out for Italy soon after to study mathematics and philosophy, which his now fond, indulgent, and almost proud father called "magik." Harry had recovered his health and strength with the use of Bessy Mortlock's frog-liver cure, and sent his son off with his blessings.

Lady Addy, after years of marrriage, conceived, and Lady Cary's confinement produced the daughter she expected.

Danter and Nan were wed on July 12, 1542, and Henry the King, by pure coincidence, set his wedding day to Catherine Parr for a year later to the day.

Some Graie Friars orphans were taken out of London to the country, to Win's sheep farm, to be taught the skills of shepherding and also playmaking and stage acting by the great, admired Andrew Danter.

Graie Friars Poor House was endowed by the king and the Earl of Norland as a school, under Rooster Truckle's direction, for the education of promising poor boys, who became known as the Blue Coats for the color of their school uniform jackets.

On January 25, in the new year of 1543, a son was born to Kat and Win. He was named Beau for his father, Paul for the saint's day of his birth, and Harry for his godfather. Descending the stairs at the inn after visiting with his adored wife, before he was shooed from the birthing room by her women, Win found a courier waiting at the bottom of the steps, draped in de Morely's red-and-blue livery.

"You look winded. Have a drink, man," Baldwin offered the rider.

"His lordship sends for word of your lady wife, sir," the man said, "and of the child."

"They both thrive and are beautiful," Baldwin replied, grinning happily.

"Glad to know it, as his lordship will also be," said the messenger. "Is it a boy or girl, sir?"

"We've a son! Beau Paul Harry."

"Ah. In that event, I'm to hand you this missive, sir, the one for a boy. I was given another in the event of a girl child." The man put forward one of three letters he drew from beneath his cloak, all sealed with red wax imprinted with the earl's crest. "I am to be on my way at once. I've another message to deliver in London, to his lordship's solicitor, and then I'm to take the good news, sir, to the earl at Norland with all possible speed."

The courier was gone by the time Win, with Andrew and Blaidd reading over his shoulder, broke the wax seal of his letter and realized the document in his hand, which he'd scanned without intending to, was meant for Harry's lawyer, Lord Hilaric Fitzregan, Esquire. It read in part:

> "*. . . and to my new offspring, who must not know for some time the source of this endowment, I now give one thousand pounds gold to be invested by you, sir, with my broker in the Netherlands, there to produce for my child an annual income of . . .* "

"Old woman!" Baldwin roared at Bessy Mortlock when he strode into the tavern, sending a chill of silence through the noise and merry chaos of the room. "Deal those cards for . . . for the boy." Win stradded a chair opposite the Wise Woman and waited. She began to deal and speak.

". . . The Lion tells the child will have strength . . . The Emperor card predicts greatness. The Sun . . . the Sun is the power of the universe." Bess hesitated. "The child born this day, who will grow to be strong, great, and powerful, is of noble blood."

"No!" Baldwin rasped, leaping to his feet and hurling the chair aside. "Read the cards again, old woman."

"I'll read them all night as I have been doing all day." Bessy shrugged. "But nothing will change. The cards don't lie. You know that, Beaumarais."

"There's always a first time," he insisted, shuffling the deck and placing it on the table in front of her. She dealt all of the night until, at the stroke of noon next day, Brother Truckle, breathless, accompanied by Cal Shute, the oysterman's lad, bustled into the inn.

"Baldwin, hear me," crowed Truckle. "On his deathbed, Potter Shute told this boy here, his nephew, the truth about Kat's mother. The woman cared for by fishermen before she died of lowland fever, was Mary, Norland's first wife, though of course he was not Norland then, for his father still lived and held that title. Well, be that as it may, Old Potter cared for and loved that woman's little girl-child for three years until Harry's father—Kat's grandfather—discovered her and told him to deliver her to the orphanage and not speak her name as long as he lived, not to anyone, on threat of pain of death." Truckle gulped and went on. "See, that's what Potter told me—all that—but I could not recall a word he said until now, but even if I had—"

"I know, I know, you could not have broken your vow and told me," Win said. "And Harry—he never knew he had a daughter. It was hidden from him by his own father. I have just dispatched a messenger with a letter to the earl." Baldwin, doubly distraught, turned to Danter.

"My God, Norland might be the child's godfather *and* grandfather," he said, devastated. "If only I had told her sooner that I loved her, if I'd wed her before . . . all this might have been prevented."

"Forget the ifs and might-haves, boy," Danter growled. "The truth of Kat's paternity is out, but the mystery of this child's is not absolutely known and perhaps never should be. Try to recall, Baldwin, that true love thinketh no evil and seek to find yourself in him."

With a roar of pain, Win rushed out, taking the stairs two at a time to reach his wife's side.

"Kat, I must ask you this. Tell me the God's truth," he said softly, his expression one of chagrin and misery. "Who fathered this boy?"

Kat's countenance showed surprise, then pain, sadness, finally anger, all in the space of seconds before a blankness settled over her features.

"First you must tell me, *please,* what has occurred, what seed of foreboding is taking root in your heart?" Kat asked.

"You're my best friend, you know. I love you, Kat. And I *will* rear the boy as my own," he replied. "But the baby was born a little early or a little late, hinging upon who fathered him." Win took up the sleeping baby and gazed into the tiny face.

"Early or late for what?" Kat whispered.

"I've learned a . . . truth which makes it . . . necessary for me to know for a certainty who sired the boy. Speak now and I will never mention or even think on this again, no matter what your answer."

"I'll answer that . . . that desolating question only if you order me to, husband, but be warned. I'll never again speak another word to you in all our lives, together or apart, if you do."

She spoke coolly, trying for the veneer of indifferent bravado which she had invoked in the past for self-protection. Now the ploy didn't work, and Win saw the sorrow in her eyes. He hesitated.

"Oh, Win! How have things come to such a pass between us?" Kat asked with a stricken look. Baldwin, cursing himself, set the infant in her arms and moved away to lean at the mantel and stare into the fire.

"It began that winter day you asked a 'small favor' of me, as you termed it, that I relieve you of the impediment of your virginity to save your intended husband the bother. I did. And I've no regrets. I never have and never will I *order* you to do anything, nor will I ask again about . . ." He shrugged.

"Why won't you ask? Are you fearful of knowing?"

"No. I fear naught but losing you. It's just that I've no wish to live without the whisper of your love words in my ear, nor without seeing your crooked little smile every day of my life. When I left you and went to sea, I took to feeling like the homeless, ragamuffin stray I'd once been. You're home to me. I could not bear it, losing you, Kat. I won't query you again, but if you wish to tell me one day, do." His back was to her as he went on staring into the fire.

"I wish to tell you about baby Beau's father *this day*. He is a man of honor, strength, and courage, noble qualities all. He is fierce and proud and gentle also, and generous and kind, and his accomplishments are many and . . . and I could go on, but suffice it to say, I love him."

Win turned quickly to see on Kat's lips the beautiful, crooked smile he'd been hearing in her voice.

"I'll always love the boy he was, but more, I love the man he is. You're him."

"Him . . . who? Say, *please!*"

"You, Baldwin Beaumarais, and no other, are the father of our son. We made him during our tryst in the King's Bath, a place known to have that effect upon lovers. There! Now what say you, sir?"

Win went down on one knee at the side of the bed, a quiet smile on his mouth, jubilation in his loving eyes. "Harry always favored me with his esteem and devotion," Kat continued. "He kept a seemly distance from me, though. I prize the friendship which flowered between us. Friendship was all that flowered, naught else."

"I'm sorry," Win said in a low, choked voice. "Can you forgive me for doubting you? Will you love me as you did before?" Her fingers stroked through his copper curls.

"What do you think, Beau?" she sighed.

"Say it in words, please." His voice was rough with hot smoke and gravel.

"I love you, now and always. There. Look at your son." The baby had awakened and was instinctively searching for the breast. He found his mother's nipple, and with her help took suck. "I have not yet got milk to give him and won't for a day or so, but he pulls hard."

"Ha!" Win barked his exuberant laugh, leaping to his feet. "He's like you and me, Kat. We're strong and we know what we want and what's good for us, eh? Before you knew the truth of who Harry de Morely was, you gave up the noble Earl of Norland and all he could offer you because you loved a mere, insignificant commoner, me! You're not near as smart as I thought you to be, but certes, Kat, I'm glad of it!"

"A commoner you be, yes, but not insignificant, you dear fool," Kat protested. "And I still do not know what truth it is you talk of," she reminded him, laughing, "or why it was so momentous. Who the devil *is* Harry de Morely, really, then?"

Before Win replied, there was heard a commotion from below, and almost at once Harry himself stood in the doorway.

"I could not just wait about at Norland for news to be brought of this babe, so I've come to London, *daughter*, and I demand to see my grandson this instant! I met Rooster Truckle's rider on the road and he gave me the news!"

"Zounds, Bess Mortlock's cards told true again! There is noble blood in Beau Paul's veins—Beau Paul *Harry's* veins, that is!" Win laughed as he and the earl peered down on their heir, curled safe and happy in his mother's arms.

There were tears and smiles and then some explanations, but mostly there was pure joy that day and for many days after, under The Sign of the Kat.

ABOUT THE AUTHOR

Jane Howard lives with her family in New York. She is the author of two Zebra historical romances. She loves to hear from readers and you may write to her c/o Zebra Books. Please include a self-addressed stamped envelope if you wish a response.